Th

MW00774265

"Ryan Rapier's new book, *The Reluctant Blogger*, is a refreshing addition to the growing LDS fiction market. Unabashedly, Rapier embraces the vernacular and culture familiar to LDS readers, but he does so in a way that seems honest and unobtrusive. Using language that is very much natural to contemporary Mormon 'hipsters' and the college-aged LDS crowd, the novel comfortably and naturally approaches topics and relationships that are authentic, germane, and engaging. It's easy for me to recommend the book."

—Kurt Bestor, Emmy-award-winning
and Grammy-nominated composer

"This is a powerful story told by a superb storyteller. From the very beginning, *The Reluctant Blogger* introduced me to a wide range of emotions that had me laughing, crying, and connecting with each character in such a way that I felt as if I were saying good-bye to old friends as I finished the last page. Rapier has done an incredible job of writing a story that I believe every member of the LDS faith ought to experience."

–Brad Hull, songwriter and vocalist with The Nashville
Tribute Band and Nashville recording group, Due West

"Man, I liked this book. Warm and human and real. A novel about growth and loss and pain, about Mormonism and judgment and forgiveness, about recovery and redemption. I read it in one afternoon—just couldn't put it down. A winner."

—Eric Samuelsen, playwright and former president of
The Association of Mormon Letters

THE Reluctant
BLOGGER

RYAN RAPIER

Bonneville Books
An Imprint of Cedar Fort
Springville, Utah

8/13

©2013

This is a work of fiction. The characters, names, incidents, places, and dialogue are products of the author's imagination and are not to be construed as real. The views expressed within this work are the sole responsibility of the author and do not necessarily reflect the position of Cedar Fort, Inc., or any other entity.

ISBN 13: 978-1-4621-1254-8

Published by Bonneville Books, an imprint of Cedar Fort, Inc.
2373 W. 700 S., Springville, UT, 84663
Distributed by Cedar Fort, Inc., www.cedarfort.com

LIBRARY OF CONGRESS CATALOGING-IN-PUBLICATION DATA

Rapier, Ryan, 1973-
 The reluctant blogger / by Ryan Rapier.
   pages cm
  ISBN 978-1-4621-1254-8 (mass market : alk. paper)
 1. Widowers--Fiction. 2. Single fathers--Fiction. 3. Spouses--Death--Psychological aspects--Fiction. 4. Mormon men--Fiction. 5. Psychotherapist and patient--Fiction. 6. Psychological fiction. I. Title.
  PS3618.A726R45 2013
  813'.6--dc23
                                         2013017472

Front cover design by Shawnda T. Craig
Back cover design by Kelsey Webb
Cover design © 2013 by Lyle Mortimer
Edited and typeset by Melissa J. Caldwell

Printed in the United States of America

10 9 8 7 6 5 4 3 2 1

This book is dedicated to my mother,

Alberta Lee Rapien

We miss you.

Prologue

DR. MELVIN SCHENK peered over his reading glasses at the younger man slouched on the couch in front of him. The question he had posed minutes earlier continued to hang in the air as his patient stared off into a world he had thus far chosen to keep private. He considered clearing his throat to elicit a response, but since the same approach hadn't worked ninety seconds earlier, he grudgingly decided against it.

Despite the doctor's best efforts, a combination of the enveloping quiet and a warmth hovering just above comfortable was causing his mind to drift. For the third time since his patient's arrival, he allowed himself to ponder a furniture upgrade. The idea of a psychiatrist's couch had become quite clichéd, and most of his contemporaries were moving to a matching chair set for both doctor and patient.

Another minute passed in silence as the doctor

mentally remodeled his office. What started as an exercise in furniture replacement grew quickly to include new earth tones for his walls and a laborious decision regarding where to display his soon-to-be-acquired Maynard Dixon. Before long, he had committed himself to contact an interior designer the second this appointment concluded.

Recognition that his current appointment was, in fact, not over startled Dr. Schenk back to reality. Blinking several times in rapid succession, he forced himself to refocus on the individual in front of him. The patient hadn't moved an inch. Dr. Schenk's mental diversion had gone unnoticed.

Deciding to clear his throat anyway, Dr. Schenk waited a moment before gently prodding, "Todd, we've been sitting in silence for five minutes."

His patient looked up in surprise. "Hmm?"

"The two of us. You and I. We've been sitting here in absolute quiet for the past"—Dr. Schenk consulted his watch—". . . make it six minutes."

Bewildered, Todd blurted, "I'm sorry. What was it you asked me?"

Dr. Schenk sighed in frustration. "Todd, you haven't listened to a question I've asked you in three months. Tell me, why are we doing this?"

Todd shifted in his seat. "Doing what?"

"Come now, I believe the time for game playing has passed. You know what I'm referring to. Why do you come and sit here week after week, refusing to engage in anything other than monosyllabic conversation?"

His inquiry was met with more silence.

"During your first few visits, I tried to be patient and give you time. When it became apparent you had no interest in actually speaking to me, I employed other methods to try and help you. Finally, when all else had failed, I asked you to write down your thoughts and feelings in hopes that you could express in the written word that which you have been unable to verbally. I explained several times that this option might be our last, did I not?"

Todd's eyes filled with panic. It was the same expression that had led Dr. Schenk to continue his efforts with Todd several weeks beyond what his professional experience dictated. However, if things did not change today, he knew that his visits with this patient had come to an end.

Adopting a stern tone, Dr. Schenk continued, "I asked you to blog—nightly if possible—about what you're thinking, what you're experiencing, how you feel . . . how you feel about how you feel . . . anything! Thus far, I must admit to being less than impressed with your results. I know you are probably aware of your paltry writings, but strictly for my benefit, may I recap for the both of us?"

Todd bowed his head, appearing to fixate on the light prism reflecting off the beveled glass table in front of him.

"The first week, you made one entry and one entry only. And I quote, 'Blogging is Stupid!!!' That was *quite* helpful. The following week, when I suggested that I would need much more from you, your one and only entry that week read, 'Blogging is Really Really Really Stupid!!!' While it pains me, I am forced to admit you did increase your word production by 100 percent over the previous week's labors. However, it was still not helpful."

Dr. Schenk glanced over in time to see a tear escape the eye of his patient before being hastily wiped away.

Knowing how difficult it was for this young man to even be here, Dr. Schenk couldn't help but feel for him. He had liked Todd from the moment they'd met. However, the doctor knew if tough love wasn't exerted now, all efforts moving forward were guaranteed to end in failure.

"Two weeks ago, I explained that in order for us to continue, I would need at least a thousand words. Again, I take responsibility for the lack of clarity in my instructions. Your discourse on the lethargic state of Arizona State football was well thought out and, in my opinion, entirely correct. But again, the essay failed to help us with your emotional well-being."

Without looking up, Todd replied, "It was my first attempt at writing on a blog. I was just trying to get my feet wet."

"I would say that is understandable, but once again, it was your only entry for the week. And you provided me nothing to work with. Last week, I explained we would give this one more chance and then I would be finished. So what did you do?"

Todd's defeated gaze shifted to the window opposite Dr. Schenk. "Doc, come on. I'm paying you. Why do you need more than that?"

Dr. Schenk stiffened in his chair. "Because, as

shocking as this may be, I don't practice psychiatry strictly for the money. I do what I do to help people, and you are making that impossible. Your latest entry explaining why you won't get your kids a dog—while very convincing—doesn't help me. I've given this my best effort, Todd, but I'm finished. I cannot help someone who will not help himself."

Todd's head swung around to face the doctor, his eyes rimmed in red. "Doctor Schenk, please . . ."

Refusing to be emotionally hijacked, Dr. Schenk pressed on over his patient's pleading. "I have no qualms admitting I may be the problem. It's not uncommon for a therapist and a patient to be incompatible. It's likely someone else out there will be able to find a solution I could not."

Todd kept his pleading gaze fixed on the doctor. "You know if I leave here, I'll never go to another therapist. I've had to swallow every ounce of pride I have to come here. I know everything's my fault and you have every right to say what you're saying, but please, I can't do this again."

The seasoned doctor regarded Todd silently, stroking his goatee. Finally, he removed his glasses and delivered his verdict.

"Against my better judgment, I'm giving you one more chance. But believe me, this is it. I want multiple entries. And these entries had better deal with what I've asked for. I know it's hard, but find a way. As I've explained before, this is a private blog accessible to only you and me. You do not need to worry about prying eyes. I'll be checking the blog nightly in preparation for our visit next week. Understand that if nothing appears on that blog before next Wednesday, I will instruct my secretary not to allow you in and not to schedule you for any future appointments. Am I clear?"

Todd's eyes drifted downward as he nodded his understanding.

"Do not write something and then erase it. If you type it, leave it. Some of the most helpful things show up in writings people wish they could take back. Do we understand each other?"

Without looking up, the patient responded, "We do. I really am sorry."

"Don't be sorry anymore. Just do it." Dr. Schenk relaxed, and his tone softened. "Todd, you are not the first Mormon to come in here struggling with inner conflicts over seeking therapy. It's actually common for people of your faith."

This comment was met with a glare of puzzled defiance. "What's that supposed to mean?"

Dr. Schenk shifted his middle-aged frame and chuckled. "Oh, Todd. Mormons like to think they are the most emotionally stable people on earth. In your case, I think it caused you physical pain to seek out my help. What you, and most members of your church, don't realize is that Utah leads the nation in antidepressant prescriptions per capita."

Todd's eyes narrowed. "So?"

"So, nothing. It's just an observation. Maybe one you could think on and blog about should the desire strike you."

"Very funny."

Without offering any form of farewell, Todd

stood and angrily stalked out of the psychiatrist's office. Studying his patient as he departed, Dr. Schenk perceived defiance in Todd for the first time. Reaching for his notepad, he jotted down this unexpected observation.

"Is it possible," he murmured to himself, "that we actually made some progress today?" Despite his intense desire to believe it, years of experience suggested otherwise.

Closing his notepad, he stared at his office door for a second or two longer. Then, as quickly as an electric light being turned off, Dr. Melvin Schenk removed all thoughts of Todd Landry from his mind and reached for his Rolodex. Stuffed somewhere inside was the business card of Russo and Russo— the finest interior design firm in the greater Phoenix area.

I've Fallen and I Can't Get Up
Wednesday, March 19

"WHY DO YOU seem so hesitant to seek help from your family?"

I know Dr. Schenk thought I wasn't listening, but I heard his question. My problem was the answer. I have countless reasons why I don't seek help from my family. First and foremost, I'm Todd Landry, son of Adrian Landry, and for generations dating back to our pioneer forebears, Landrys have set the gold standard when it comes to pulling ourselves up by our own bootstraps. We can provide service, but we never receive it. I think it's in the family bylaws.

Out of the corner of my eye, I observed Dr. Schenk sitting comfortably in his wingback chair, legs crossed, studying me over the top of his hexagonal-shaped reading glasses. His impatience was obvious.

Several minutes had passed when suddenly Dr. Schenk jerked awkwardly and then shook his head as if startled. That was odd. The grandfather clock in the corner had been the only source of sound or movement for some time. Glancing at his watch, he grimaced and then looked in my direction before obnoxiously clearing his throat.

"Todd, we've been sitting in silence for five minutes."

I knew that. I was the one with the perfect view of the clock. However, I'm sure he wasn't making a general observation about the passage of time. I decided to play dumb.

"Hmm?"

"The two of us. You and I. We've been sitting here in absolute quiet for the past . . ." Once again, Dr. Schenk glanced at his watch. ". . . make it six minutes."

It could have been half an hour, and I still wouldn't have wanted to answer his question. I decided to feign a memory lapse.

"I'm sorry. What was it you asked me?"

Dr. Schenk sighed deeply. I hate it when he sighs deeply. It usually means I'm about to get lectured.

"Todd, you haven't listened to a question I've asked you in three months. Why are we doing this?"

Mentally, I groaned. His question signaled the beginning of the same tired discussion we'd had countless times before. I know it's frustrating for him when I don't talk, but sadly, there's so much I don't want to say.

For instance, I don't want to talk about what a disappointment I am to myself and my family. I don't want to talk about my abject failure as a parent. And as ironic as this may sound, I really don't want to talk about the reason I'm seeing him in the first place. I know that's irrational, but if I was thinking rationally,

I probably wouldn't need a psychiatrist in the first place, now would I?

So when I don't want to do something, I find it much easier to play passive-aggressive games and evade questions. I shifted my weight on the sofa. "Doing what?"

"I believe the time for game playing has passed. You know what I'm referring to. Why do you come and sit here week after week refusing to engage in anything other than monosyllabic conversation?"

The answer to that question is simple. Because coming to Dr. Schenk's office means I have to get up, put on clothes, and try to make myself presentable. Thanks to telecommuting and the flexibility provided by life insurance payouts, I can just as easily stay home. But if I do, I'll remain in my pajamas, binge on unhealthy food, and sink into a black pit of despair. I've actually tried that approach already, and it doesn't work very well. I'd much rather spend $200 an hour to sit on a comfortable sofa and frustrate a fifty-some-thing-year-old doctor who has one of the most symmetrical goatees I've ever seen.

Nevertheless, none of those reasons could be stated out loud, so I continued to stare at the floor without speaking.

Unable to elicit a reaction, Dr. Schenk elected to recap my less-than-stellar attempts at following his counsel. Bless him, but when he drifts into ser-monizing, his mellow baritone voice can become hyp-notic, making it easy for me to tune him out. I know he means well, but he's wasting his time. I know the blame for our communication problems is all mine.

But then he said something that gained my undivided attention. He stated he was on the cusp of cutting me off completely, and this time he sounded serious. Panic quickly spread through my chest, and I worriedly glanced in his direction.

I know I'm a lousy patient. I know I don't put in the effort that I should. But I need this man. Deep down, I know he's vital to my escaping this depression that enveloped me nine months ago.

Dr. Schenk acknowledged my concern with a pause. However, when I added nothing further and returned my attention to the table in front of me, he resumed summarizing my attempts, or rather non-attempts, at blogging. As I listened to him, I was surprised to realize how fortunate I'd been that he'd kept me around as long as he had.

Without warning, the colors reflecting off his coffee table's beveled glass formed a vision of my wife's angelic face. My reaction was immediate. Tears filled my eyes and my entire body felt numb. The grief was so overwhelming that my only desire was to pass out in order to make it go away.

To pull myself out of this unexpected emotional tar pit, I exerted all of my efforts into listening to Dr. Schenk. I wish I hadn't. He'd gotten around to describing my essay on the sad state of ASU football. I do happen to believe that is some of my best writing in years. But his point that it was entirely unhelpful was admittedly valid.

Still, it only seemed right that I offer up some sort of feeble defense. "It was my first attempt at writing on a blog. I was just trying to get my feet wet."

The withering glare with which he delivered his response spoke volumes. "Understandable. However, once again it was your only entry for the week. And you provided me nothing to work with. Last week, I explained we would give this one more chance and then I would be finished. So what did you do?"

Lifting my eyes to meet his gaze was impossible. He was right. I'd been given more than my fair share of opportunities, and I'd wasted them completely.

In my defense, I did sit down at my computer last week with full intentions of chronicling my children's struggles as they've dealt with the loss of their mother. I wanted to put into words how my thirteen-year-old daughter, Alex, has changed from a vivacious free spirit to a worried child struggling under the weight of adult problems that should not be hers to bear. I can't remember the last time I saw the crooked smirk that passes for her smile come across her face.

My other two children have also been affected, but not as noticeably. Samantha (Sam) has been quiet and studious her entire nine years of existence. Still, I'd have to say she's become even more withdrawn than I remember. Meanwhile, my son, Drake, is still a typical four-year-old boy, but there are times when he craves his mother's comforting touch that I'm powerless to replace.

My head had been full of a thousand thoughts and examples, but as I faced my blank computer screen, I was intimidated. I didn't know how to begin. So I chickened out and blathered on for several paragraphs about why my family isn't ready for a pet. At the time it seemed clever. Under the light of Dr.

Schenk's scrutiny this morning, it felt much closer to idiotic.

Knowing I'd wasted every chance I'd been given, I grasped at one of the few dwindling options left to me. "Doc, come on. I'm paying you. Why do you need more than that?"

For the record, that was the wrong move. His incensed response made that clear immediately. "Because, as shocking as this may be, I don't practice psychiatry strictly for the money. I do what I do to help people, and you are making that impossible. Your latest entry explaining why you won't get your kids a dog—while very convincing—doesn't help me. I've given this my best effort, Todd, but I'm finished. I cannot help someone who will not help himself."

It had finally come down to this. I needed to beg. "Doctor Schenk, please . . ." But he quickly cut me off.

"I have no qualms admitting I may be the problem. It's not uncommon for a therapist and a patient to be incompatible. It's likely someone else out there will be able to find a solution I could not."

There's a saying that when all else fails, try the truth. It has merit, apparently. It's not that I was trying to be calculating; the truth was simply my only option left. Had I left his office today without the ability to return, I would never have gone to another therapist again. It had cost me every lingering bit of pride I had left to come and see him. I wasn't sure Dr. Schenk fully understood that. If I was going to get help, it had to be in his office. And so that's what I told him.

I can't describe the relief that flooded through me when he elected to give me one more shot, and I hope as I write this recap of our visit that he sees his ultimatum has been received and acknowledged.

But as I was preparing to leave, he said something I found puzzling. He shared a factoid regarding Utah leading the nation in taking antidepressants. Was that a shot at me? He's offered to write a prescription for Prozac several times, and each time I've declined. I can't remember if I've ever told him why.

Right or wrong, I believe that if I need medication to function day to day, then I'm really in trouble. Besides, if my father discovered he had a son on "happy pills," it would likely kill him.

In hindsight, I don't think Dr. Schenk meant anything by it, and I feel a little guilty about walking out so rudely. But once outside, I felt as if my head were going to explode. I knew this week had to be different, but still I faced the uphill battle of putting my feelings into words. I needed a moment to stop and figure things out.

Located in the middle of Dr. Schenk's building is a quiet little atrium. I don't recall how I ended up seated on one of its benches, but that's where my epiphany occurred. Over and over I asked myself—*why won't you talk to this man?* That's when it hit me. I don't talk to anybody.

Glancing into a nearby window, I was troubled by what I saw. My reflection revealed hints of gray streaking throughout my sandy-blond hair. My blue eyes appeared dull with age and the lines in my face appeared deeper than I could ever remember. And that's when my mind became clear. I finally understood my problem.

I'm mad at God.

I think it's really that simple. I'm thirty-eight years old, and God took my life away.

I don't want to talk about it because no one I know would understand. My friends and my family would try to empathize while working to help me see "the big picture," but they would never really understand. I did what God told me to. I kept all the rules, and the payoff was supposed to be Marci and me enjoying a long life together. Instead, I haven't yet reached my fortieth birthday, and I'm alone . . . and it's God's fault.

Dr. Schenk, I don't know if what I've written amounts to a breakthrough or not, but I hope you know how difficult this was for me. I also hope this proves how serious I am.

What surprised me, though, was realizing that expressing myself with the aid of a keyboard isn't so bad. Now that I know, I promise to do better. I swear there will be more entries before we meet again. And who knows, if you're lucky, I might even try speaking in complete sentences during our next session.

TODD'S LANDRY LIST

Welcome to the Jungle
Friday, March 21

FOR WEEKS NOW my dreams have been haunted by a faceless menace. It's always there, like a lion silently watching a defenseless zebra, and I know it stalks me. Day after day I run, and night after night I hide, but from the beginning I've known: I will eventually fail, and when I do—I will become one of them. I'm frightened. Truly frightened.

Okay, describing the LDS single adult organization that way could be construed as negative and cynical. I get that. But after having just attended my first single adult activity, negativity and cynicism seem perfectly reasonable.

The only reason I went was to appease my father. Originally I'd planned to blow it off and take my kids out for ice cream. That's what I've done every other time he's tried to corner me into one of these things. But tonight he decided to play hardball. He enlisted my best friend and long-time bachelor, Kevin Brockbank, to pick me up—thereby guaranteeing my attendance.

Now I realize I could have told him to mind his

own business. I certainly was tempted. However, when it comes to my father, that approach has been proven to have a low success rate.

The sound of my doorbell echoing down the hallway announced Kevin's arrival. He was early. I was still getting dressed and had yet to decide whether my two days' worth of stubble was worth shaving or not. As usual, he promptly made himself at home with my kids and my refrigerator. Finding our leftover grilled chicken, he made a sandwich and then pulled up a chair next to Alex to help her with her homework. Clearly, Kevin feels comfortable in our home.

Early on in our relationship, Marci discovered Kevin and I came as part of a package deal. Thankfully, she never had an issue.

Nevertheless, tonight I was a tad annoyed with my closest friend. Whether it was fair or not, I considered him at least partially responsible for my current dilemma. Down the hall, I could hear him laughing with my children as I stood in front of my closet debating which shirt to wear. That only irritated me more. How dare he enjoy himself while I was stuck in front of my closet experiencing flashbacks from high school.

As I mentioned, before tonight I had never attended a single adult activity in my life. Kevin, on the other hand, has been to hundreds. In reality, most of my reservations about these events have been based on his endless supply of horror stories. And now he had the nerve to sit in my kitchen acting as if he wasn't Brutus to my Caesar. He, of all people, should've known better than to do this to me. He'd been there that night.

Marci's death was unbelievably sudden. One minute we were arguing about whether or not to have spaghetti for dinner, and the next she could no longer talk to me.

Five days later, I stood across from her open casket as a stream of well-wishers filed past, offering condolences. I'd never felt so alone. I spent the entire two hours in a daze.

That is, until I shook the hand of John Marstow. I didn't know John well, but I remember him clearly that night because his disposition seemed so oddly out of place. Everyone else present had been exhibiting a natural level of sorrow. By contrast, John seemed almost jovial. In the moment, I was quite taken aback, but since then I've come to understand that for John this was pretty typical. He never seems able to gauge the proper emotion for a given situation. Shockingly, John is divorced.

As I stood there shaking his hand, I vaguely remember him going on and on about how pretty Marci had been, which, again not surprisingly, seemed odd given the surroundings. After a while, I began to tune him out and nodded only when it seemed appropriate. I'd just started to count the number of birds on my Aunt Vivian's dress when his voice, already three decibels too loud, cut through my thoughts and smacked me upside the head. "Well, as the single adult rep, I guess you're my responsibility now."

I literally felt like he'd punched me in the gut. I think I opened my mouth to respond, but nothing came out. I was just too stunned to react.

The room went completely silent as every eye

stared in astonishment at my unwitting tormentor. Reacting instantly, my mother grabbed him by the hand and politely whisked him away. It took several minutes for me to recover and regain my bearings. Slowly, the noise level in the room returned to normal, like a 45-speed vinyl record starting up with the needle already in place.

In the moments following that encounter, I made a solemn vow. John Marstow was never going to be responsible for me. Even under threat of excommunication, I would not allow myself to be associated with anything that man had a part in. I suppose I may have been overreacting, but shock, trauma, and five days of no sleep can have that kind of effect on a person.

I still don't particularly care for John, but I've come to accept he wasn't trying to be malicious. In his mind, he was merely doing his duty. But therein lay my problem.

Any organization represented by someone as obtuse as John Marstow couldn't possibly be beneficial to me. Factoring in Kevin's experiences over the years and my feelings on the matter could not have been more concrete. I needed no part of the single adult crowd. Kevin was well aware of my feelings. So in my mind, he had some serious explaining to do as to why he was involved in my going tonight.

Staring at myself in the mirror for the fifteenth time, I sighed and recognized it wasn't going to get any better.

I entered the kitchen and spent two full minutes stomping, muttering, and slamming at every opportunity. Sensing an ugly showdown ahead, Alex stood and whispered to Kevin just loud enough for me to hear, "Good luck tonight. If he kills you, will you leave me your car?"

Kevin laughed, but it was the nervous laugh of someone trying to joke with their dentist prior to a root canal. Reaching for his jacket, his voice cracked as he tried to sound cheery and nonchalant. "You ready to go?"

I didn't respond immediately. Emotional torture is best administered slowly. After a full routine of opening the cupboard, retrieving a glass, letting it fill at a glacial pace by only opening the tap to 25 percent, we were getting close. I drained the contents of my glass and then turned to glare at him.

At six foot one, I've always had a three-inch advantage over Kevin. However, when I point this out to him, he's quick to respond that his full head of thick black hair and olive complexion are far greater assets than a miniscule height difference. Add in that he still looks as thin as the day he arrived home from his mission, and he generally wins that argument. Tonight, though, I used every bit of my superior stature to my advantage. Finally, when he'd suffered enough, I broke the silence with just one word. "Why?"

Exhaling nervously, he said, "Look, you need a change of scenery. I'm not saying this would've been my first choice, but when your dad pressed me on the subject, I didn't have any better suggestions. And, frankly, you know he scares me to death."

As if sensing a shot at the moral high ground, Kevin squared his shoulders and continued. "Besides, I did you a favor. Once he had it in his mind you were going tonight, you were going. By agreeing to take you, I'm providing you a lifeline. You owe me."

Up until then, I'd been enjoying my platform of righteous indignation. Then he had to go and ruin it with something as ridiculous as the truth.

Alex and Sam wished me luck as I kissed them good night. I don't think they understood exactly what was going on, but I appreciated their support nonetheless.

Walking out to Kevin's car, I glanced quickly at my van. Secretly, I was grateful to Kevin for driving. I know it's shallow, but no way would I have been able to drive myself to a dance in a minivan—especially one with a booster seat visible just behind the driver's seat.

Our entrance into the church gymnasium produced my first real experience with déjà vu. The lowered lights and the refreshment table in the corner appeared just as they had when I'd come for youth dances years earlier.

On the other hand, one major difference instantly noticeable was the activity level on the dance floor. No one here was content to waste time standing against a wall. Actual movement appeared to have a direct correlation to age, but everybody seemed to be having a great time.

Yet I still wanted to run. No matter how much I tried, I didn't want to accept that I was staring at my new life.

Glancing over at Kevin, I suddenly saw him in a whole new light. I'd left this scene far behind years ago. He never had.

I've never understood why Kevin isn't married. His kind and considerate nature is exactly what women are always claiming to be looking for. The world is crawling with men much less personable and not nearly as good-looking who have managed to find a wife. So why couldn't my best friend?

Kevin and I met the summer before kindergarten when his family moved into our neighborhood. Since then, our friendship has managed to endure grade school, puberty, crushes on the same girl, different interests in college, and a two-year separation during our missions. Even more astounding is how close we remained once I was married.

I have three younger siblings, and I can easily say that I'm closer to Kevin than all three combined. Naturally, I love my brothers and sister, but the age difference between us has never lent itself to a close bond. Kevin is an only child.

All of our lives, Kevin has been more comfortable around girls than me. In high school, he was on girlfriend number four by the time I got a second consecutive date with the same person.

Tonight, it didn't take long to see nothing had changed. We hadn't been in the room for three minutes before he was introducing himself to a woman he'd never met. Grunting my displeasure at his abandonment, I turned away and began plotting my escape to the nearest dark corner.

However, before I could move, Kevin grabbed my arm and introduced me to . . . Karen . . . Carrie . . . something. I managed a non-frown as I shook her hand. She smiled back kindly, but I could tell my first impression was lacking as her attention reverted quickly back to my friend. They decided to dance, and I made a beeline for the chair farthest from the dance floor.

When I was in high school, there was a code. If a guy chose to sit alone at a dance, you left him alone and worried about yourself. It was an unwritten rule accepted by all. Unfortunately, no one at this dance seemed to be aware of the code at all. Before I could sit down, a woman, who I believe was old enough to be my mother, was asking me to dance. Since my actual mother raised me right, I said yes. And thus began my descent into the inferno.

The next hour and a half consisted of enthralling conversations covering such topics as ex-husbands, delinquent children, upcoming surgeries (three gall bladders and a knee replacement), business opportunities (I need to verify that I didn't commit to hosting a vinyl lettering party), and, in one surreal exchange, how much I looked like a young Cesar Romero. Not having any idea who that is, I'm choosing to believe it was a compliment.

When I finally caught a glimpse of Kevin heading for the refreshment table, I pried myself loose from an extremely short woman who was in the middle of extolling the virtues of guacamole as a skin care supplement and followed him. It's a small miracle he didn't spill red Kool-Aid all over himself as I approached him from behind and slipped my arm around his shoulders in a less than genial embrace.

"Where have you been? I thought you were my— what did you call it again? Oh yeah, lifeline!"

Turning to face me with a broad grin, he responded. "From my vantage point, it looks like you've been doing just fine for yourself."

"Really? I hope you aren't my only hope for survival if I'm ever attacked by a ravenous wolf pack or Girl Scouts on the last day of cookie sales. You're useless."

Looking out onto the dance floor, Kevin dismissively replied, "Lighten up. You're meeting new people. I'll grant you, there are a few wing nuts out there, but everybody you've talked to tonight is in the same situation you are. They're single and they came to have a good time."

"Yeah? Well, I'm not having a good time, and I want to go home. I didn't think this could be worse than I imagined, but amazingly, it's exceeding my expectations in every way. When can we leave?"

"Give me twenty minutes. I'm really liking this Caralee."

He said this name as if I should know who he was talking about. Dumbfounded, I replied, "Who's Caralee?"

Turning back to me with an expression of bewilderment, he answered, "The woman we met when we first got here."

"That's her name? Really? Whatever. I'll give you ten minutes."

Kevin rolled his eyes. "Twenty. My gosh, what a wimp you've turned into."

Inching half a step closer, I leaned forward and whispered with all the venom I could muster, "Fine. I will be at that door in twenty minutes. Do *not* be late!"

He brushed me off with a raise of his glass as he walked away. Staring after him, I couldn't help but wish he had spilled Kool-Aid all over himself.

Suddenly, like a hunted animal in the wild, my survival instincts alerted me to danger lurking nearby. Glancing to both sides, I caught sight of the "guacamole lady" closing in fast. I can endure just about anything for twenty minutes, but I was not going to spend one more second discussing the healing qualities of a dish made from avocados.

Spinning quickly in the opposite direction, I collided directly with an oncoming glass of punch. Now *I* was wearing red Kool-Aid. I despise karma! I looked down at my shirt and then back up into the striking blue eyes of my redheaded assailant. She was frozen in place with a horrified expression.

In retrospect, I find it amazing I held my composure at all. I was standing in the middle of a crowded cultural hall with my shirt stained and my pride shattered. Several people began moving toward me to offer help when the redhead suddenly grabbed me and escorted me toward the nearest exit.

I'm positive that as we rushed down the hallway toward the kitchen, this woman's focus was on protecting my feelings and not on the close proximity of our bodies. The same cannot be said for me. Her touch was intoxicating. I'm not saying I'd fallen in love or anything—I just wasn't prepared to be held this closely by another woman and enjoy it.

My initial reaction was to find Marci and confess. Unfortunately, thoughts of Marci tend to produce an avalanche of emotion, and by the time we reached the kitchen, I was crying. It wasn't much, but it was enough.

I can't imagine how I must have looked to this woman. She already felt terrible about spilling punch on me, and now here I was weeping like a little girl. A note of apprehension entered her voice as her apologies continued.

"I am so sorry. I was taking that glass to an older gentleman and I was rushing too fast. I should have seen you coming. Please don't cry. I feel absolutely horrible that I've done this to you and if there is anything I can do to make things better—please don't cry."

"Look," I said, trying desperately to regain control of myself and the situation. "I'm not always this emotional over fabric. You have absolutely nothing to apologize for. I walked into you. Thank you for your help, but please don't feel bad. This is totally my fault."

I wiped away the remaining tears from my cheeks and then began searching for a cloth to clean the red stain covering a good portion of my chest. It was pointless, but it gave me something to do and kept me from having to look at her.

"Are you okay?"

Keeping my eyes fixed firmly downward, I laughed nervously. "Yeah, um—no worries. I always take it hard when cherry-flavored Kool-Aid is needlessly wasted. It's my favorite."

"I have a feeling this has nothing to do with punch."

I looked up and suddenly there they were again. Two of the bluest eyes I've ever seen. Their brilliance made it seem as if they were radiating their own light. I couldn't look at them and think straight, so I returned my attention to my shirt. After a few moments, she tried again to fill the awkward silence.

"I really am sorry, I didn't mean to—"

"No. Again, this is all me," I replied, cutting her off. "I, uh—I've never been to anything like this before. The truth is, I didn't want to come tonight. This is probably getting way too personal, but my wife passed away about nine months ago, and I'm still dealing with that."

I took a deep breath to avoid another round of tears before continuing. "I'm usually pretty good at keeping things bottled up, but I haven't had the best night. I could try, but I don't really know how to explain what just happened. Let's just say these outbursts occur when I least expect them and usually at the worst moment possible. I'm really sorry you stumbled into this, but if you go now, you can probably save yourself. I'll be fine. I just need to, you know, clean up and . . ."

Unable to stop myself, I raised my eyes and glanced nervously in her direction. A tear was running down her cheek. Before I could stammer out additional assurances regarding my well-being, a slender silver-haired woman with an empty cookie platter walked into the kitchen.

"Emily, do we have any more chocolate chip—" Finally taking notice of the scene playing out in front of her, the poor woman froze on the spot. I can't say I blame her. Stumbling upon a real-life episode of Dr. Phil can be unnerving.

Without taking her eyes off me, the redhead addressed our new visitor. "Maureen, could you give us a minute?"

Backing slowly toward the door through which she'd come, Maureen stuttered, "No problem. I'm so sorry. I . . ." Without completing her sentence, she turned and disappeared.

Nothing could make my humiliation more complete. My shirt was stained, I'd now cried in front of not just one, but two women, and I was the cause of a chocolate chip cookie shortage. I was out of things to say. Utterly defeated, I cast my eyes toward the window and sighed.

The redhead took a tentative step toward me. I made no effort to stop her. I didn't do anything. As she took hold of my hand, I braced for the familiar words of comfort I'd been hearing for months. I didn't want to hear them, but I'd come to accept that saying them made others feel better. But to my surprise, she never uttered a word.

Instead, gently grasping my wrist, she lifted my arm and began to write on my upturned palm. That captured my attention. Where did she even get a pen? When she finished, she removed her hand to reveal a phone number.

"My name's Emily. Emily Stewart. I won't pretend to understand what you're going through, but I'm a good listener. If you want to talk about . . . things, or talk about nothing, I'm available. That's obviously my phone number, but if this is too weird, it will easily wash off later. You can use that door over there to escape without having to face the crowds that have probably heard about us in here from Maureen. Trust me, she's quick."

With that, she walked out of the kitchen, leaving me alone.

Not wanting to face Maureen again, I slipped outside and waited by Kevin's car until he arrived. He was fifteen minutes late.

I'm pretty sure I'll never call Emily. In fact, I'm positive. But later, as I stood in front of my bathroom sink preparing to wash away all traces of this horrible night, I stopped. My eyes would not pull away from the ink on my skin. Reaching into my pocket, I pulled out my cell phone. Without stopping to think, I dialed the number and put the phone to my ear. Following a single ring, I pressed the disconnect button and placed the phone on the counter.

I smiled thoughtfully as I allowed the mixture of warm water and scented hand soap to cascade through my fingers. The soap had been Marci's favorite, and ironically it was proving very effective at removing all evidence of Emily Stewart's involvement in my life. All evidence that is, except for the number now stored in the recent calls file of my cell phone just ten inches away.

The Sun Devil's in the Details

Saturday, March 22

I HATE WALMART.

All right, that might be a little strong, but then again . . . no, it's not. I really hate Walmart. If I have to go shopping, I definitely prefer Target. Unfortunately, the closest Target to my house is over five miles away, while a brand-new Walmart sits exactly 528 yards from my front door. And on a day like today, when time is of the essence, proximity wins out every time.

My reason for being under the gun this morning revolved around my annual March Madness college basketball party. Each year, a few of my closest friends come over, and we grill, watch basketball, and play board games until sometime after midnight. By party standards the world over, it's probably pretty lame. For those of us involved, it's the blowout event of the year.

As the first rays of dawn broke through my window, I realized I wasn't ready for my own party. My yard resembled a South American rain forest.

And my grill? Oh, my poor grill. It needed some serious TLC to make up for months of neglect.

As if those concerns weren't enough, I'd forgotten all about the shopping until driving home from the dance last night. Kevin had volunteered to stop, but with my shirt stained red and my mind wildly preoccupied with the phone number scrawled on my palm, I determined shopping could wait. Besides, why would I ever have wanted to interrupt Kevin's recap of his hugely successful evening? (Sarcasm intended.)

All the way home he'd practically crackled with excitement describing the date he'd lined up with this Caralee woman. Of course, he hinted here and there that this one could get serious. I let it go because we've been down this road before. *Let's give it a month,* I thought to myself, *and then we'll see.*

Eventually, he got around to asking about my evening. I told him everything. As I finished, he displayed no reaction other than tightening his grip on the steering wheel. Finally, his curiosity won out. "So . . . what're you gonna do?"

"Nothing, I guess."

"Why?"

I sighed. "Come on. It's too soon. You know that."

Shooting me a quick glance, he nervously disagreed in a tone suggesting he feared my reaction. "Actually, I don't know that. And if I'm honest, I really don't think you believe it either."

Choosing to ignore him, I replied, "Whatever. What time are you coming over tomorrow?"

It was an easy question, but Kevin remained silent. Glancing toward the driver's side of the car, I discovered Kevin nervously biting his lip as if fighting the urge to say something.

"What's the matter with you?"

"Todd, Marci's gone."

I felt as if he'd shoved a hot poker into my stomach. Defensively, I retorted, "Well, that's one of the dumbest things you've ever said. I think I understand that better than anyone."

After surveying the traffic for a few moments, he quietly asserted, "I know you tell yourself you understand, but what you say and what you do don't match. You act like she's on vacation or something and that eventually she's gonna come back. I don't know if that makes sense . . ." He let his voice trail off.

I didn't want to admit it, but I understood exactly what he was saying, and his portrayal of me was far too accurate for comfort. A bigger man would've admitted this to him right then and there. But in that moment, I discovered I am not a bigger man.

Refusing to look in Kevin's direction, I turned my focus to the passing scenery and said, "Your point is duly noted, and I will take it under advisement. Now I believe I asked when you were showing up tomorrow." Conversation over! The topic shifted to food and basketball, and within ten minutes I was home.

Nevertheless, Kevin's assessment had struck a nerve. When I finally made it to bed, my overactive mind refused sleep as I fantasized through a hundred different scenarios. Still, no matter what justifications I came up with, calling Emily felt like cheating on my wife. Finally, sometime after 1:30 in the morning, I drifted off.

Before I knew it, the sun was up, and the clock was cruising past 8:00 a.m. The shopping still needed to be done, and time was no longer my friend. Leaving Alex and Sam in charge of housecleaning, I put Drake in his booster seat and checked my watch for the fifth time. I was dreadfully behind.

Buying into the fallacy of "closer means quicker," I pulled into the overflowing Walmart parking lot and joined the closest tributary feeding into the river of defeated souls streaming toward retail's version of Darwinism.

After finagling a cart and muscling my way through the front door, I spent an additional ten minutes navigating through a human tidal wave to the potato chip aisle. How could I have forgotten the state of Walmart on a Saturday?

Pulling my cart out of the flow of traffic, I grabbed three bags of Ruffles and began breathing deeply in preparation for round two of this gauntlet of insanity. However, before I could insert myself back into the swirling masses, I was distracted by an argument picking up steam next to me.

A quick peek sideways revealed a young couple in their early twenties. A baby carrier was perched in the child seat section of their cart, but I didn't dare look long enough to verify an actual baby. I just assumed.

Apparently, the young man had been caught allowing his eyes to wander. Pretending to have a newfound interest in the nutritional value of Ruffles, I listened as this poor kid received a verbal thrashing complete with multiple expletives. I don't consider myself an eavesdropper, but in this situation I wasn't given a choice. The aisle had become congested with dozens of carts, and the wife was making no effort toward discretion.

Several uncomfortable minutes later, the cart chaos resolved itself, and the couple's voices faded as they continued past me down the aisle. During their entire exchange, I'd been watching Drake carefully. I was sincerely worried my son would latch onto a new word he'd never heard before and put it in a secret place until he could try it out tomorrow during church. Luckily, he seemed fully entranced with the flat screen television above us showing clips of Bugs Bunny.

Wedging my cart into a small opening, I forced my way back into the rushing tide of humanity. As I did so, I grinned. For some odd reason, what I'd just witnessed reminded me of the day I met Marci—and that memory always brings a smile to my face.

Right after I returned home from my mission, I enrolled for the fall semester at Arizona State University. The night before classes were to begin, I participated in a yearly rite of passage for young single Latter-day Saints everywhere. In China, it's referred to as the matchmaking ceremony. In Tempe, Arizona, we call it the LDS Institute opening social.

The night was hot and sticky. August nights in Tempe always are. Despite waiting until dusk, the temperature was still above 100 degrees as hundreds of Mormon students between the ages of eighteen and twenty-nine descended on Riverview Park three miles from ASU campus. Officially, we'd all assembled for hamburgers and ice cream, but everyone there knew the food was the undercard. This was the first opportunity to scope out the year's new models of the opposite sex. I've always thought this annual convergence of hormones and hair spray would make for a perfect Discovery Channel documentary.

Commentator (British accent of course): The freshman boy is by far the most aggressive. You can see how he fearlessly attempts to flirt with the females of the herd. However, his inability to gain attention is mystifying to him. Slick lines and smooth moves that achieved great levels of success just months ago in his adolescent nesting ground no longer seem to have any effect here in the harsh, real-world environs. What he does not now understand is that he lacks the designation of having served as a missionary. Not holding this "returned missionary" status removes all interest on the part of the females in the herd. Occasionally, a female not ready for the commitment of courtship will take pity on the young male. Yet this token interest never lasts long. Cutting off affection serves to enforce the herd's underlying message that the returned missionary designation is required for mating.

Kevin, our friend Jason, and I arrived in time to get a fresh hamburger before migrating to an area where we could observe a group of particularly attractive freshmen. None of us had any real interest in talking to the giggly eighteen-year-olds in question, but we certainly weren't above "window shopping."

As a mature adult, this admission embarrasses me, but as we sat together taking in the sights, I became fully engrossed in one particular girl's relationship with her Calvin Klein jeans. I'd only been staring for a few seconds when suddenly a cascade of freezing water hit the top of my head and poured down my neck, drenching my back. I gasped in shock. Had my mother followed me here? In a mixture of humiliation and confusion, I spun around and came face-to-face with my future wife.

The look in Marci's emerald-green eyes was one of absolute terror. She managed to utter a panicked, "I . . . oh my gosh . . . I thought you were someone else. I'm so sorry."

Unable to articulate further, she turned and ran. Her two friends in the distance couldn't have been less supportive. One had already sprinted twenty yards in the opposite direction while the other was laughing so hard she required the assistance of a nearby tree for support.

As the night wore on, I kept picturing her horrified expression and couldn't help but feel pity for her. I wanted her to know there were no hard feelings, but I had no idea who she was. When I finally saw her again, I happened to be next to Louis Derkin, Latterday Saint Student Association (LDSSA) president. I knew him from before our missions, so I tapped him on the shoulder and asked if he knew the cute girl in the peach T-shirt. He wasn't sure who I was talking about, so I pointed her out. Big mistake!

Seeing my outstretched finger aimed in her direction caused her face to go deathly pale, and before I could catch her, she'd rounded up her friends and was moving quickly across the parking lot.

Recalling that night and the memory of Marci in a dead run caused me to laugh out loud, which prompted some strange looks from the shoppers around me. Sheepishly, I ducked my head and moved on before continuing my stroll down memory lane.

Once Marci and I were married, I was forbidden to speak of that night again. Ever! When we would discuss how we met, Marci would avoid mentioning our initial encounter and proceed directly to the account officially recorded in our family's history.

This edited version had us meeting while working together on the Latter-Day Saint sorority/fraternity float for Homecoming. In hindsight, I understand how civically minded that makes me sound, but the truth is, I never would've volunteered for float duty had she not been on the committee. I desperately wanted to meet her, so once I discovered the name Marci Johnson on the sign-up sheet, I knew I'd found my best opportunity.

On the day of float construction, I arrived at the prearranged parking lot a few minutes late. Okay, it was thirty-five minutes late, and I actually arrived a little earlier than I'd meant to. Regardless, I found her struggling to attach maroon and gold bunting to the trailer's side. Approaching from behind, I grabbed the fabric and held it in place, allowing her to staple it more easily. With the bunting fastened securely, she whirled around prepared to thank her rescuer. Once she recognized me, though, her broad smile regressed in an instant to the crazed look of a cornered animal.

Sensing I had a small window of opportunity, I launched into my explanation before she could bolt. I made it clear that I held no ill feelings toward her, and to prove my sincerity, I offered to take her to dinner. She thanked me but said her boyfriend probably wouldn't approve.

Working hard to mask my disappointment, I offered instead to help with the rest of the stapling. After all, it was what I had signed up to do. Tentatively, she agreed.

Over the next three hours, the float committee's vision took shape as we talked, worked, and laughed before eventually parting ways as friends.

At least that's how she viewed our relationship. I, on the other hand, knew I had met the girl of my dreams. Dismissing the fact that she had a boyfriend, I spent the next three weeks memorizing her daily routine. Once I had the schedule down, I created opportunities to "randomly" run into her. Each day brought a new quest to engage Marci in as much idle chitchat as possible.

Today my quest was much simpler, at least in theory. All I wanted was to check out of Walmart with my few paltry items and be home before sunset. Sadly, as I approached the bank of registers, I could see my goal would not be easily met.

Drawing near to the first checkout line, I began to assess which express lane had the best odds of moving quickly. Regardless of a person's ability to predict or prophesy, choosing an express lane is always tricky business. Nothing's worse than making your final selection only to see the cashier you rejected begin to move through shoppers at a pace just short of magic.

Crossing my fingers, I inhaled sharply and ventured forward. At first, things looked positive as my cart made steady progress toward the cashier. Then suddenly, things came to a grinding halt. The individual two spots in front of me began to raise her voice regarding which brands should be included in the price-match guarantee for whipped cream.

Seriously? I looked at my watch. My quick in-and-out trip was now approaching three quarters of an hour.

Ten minutes and a manager's visit later, the line moved forward once more. Believing we might actually escape, I started to unload my items when I felt a tugging on my shirt. I looked down into the anxious face of my son.

"Dad, I gotta go."

My chest began to tighten in despair. I closed my eyes, took a deep breath, and asked, "Is there any way you can hold it?"

His pained expression deepened, and I knew that holding it was not an option. Taking note of the wild-eyed glee in the eyes of those in line behind me, I replaced my items in the cart and set off to find the restrooms.

For whatever reason, Drake's visits to the little boys' room are always marathons rather than sprints. I don't know why, but it's just another one of life's cruel twists I've had to accept. Trying to rush the process only makes it longer.

Leaning against the men's room wall, I began

to think about the number of hours, and even days, I'd spent in my life waiting on another person. With Marci, it ended up being five months.

As fall and winter gave way to spring, I'd begun to lose hope regarding any chance with Marci. The holidays had broken my rhythm, and her new spring semester schedule required a second surveillance period. When I was finally able to stage an encounter, her reaction to me was cooler than I'd hoped. She was friendly, but the familiarity from before had all but evaporated.

However, I'm nothing if not persistent. I kept putting myself in her path and eventually got the chance I'd been hoping for.

On the Wednesday before spring break, I was walking into the LDS student center on campus when I passed two girls discussing Marci's boyfriend and his sudden availability in the marketplace. Instinctively, I spun around and followed them at what I considered a safe distance that would still allow me to listen in on their conversation.

I learned two valuable things that afternoon. One, Marci and her boyfriend had broken up the week before; two, ASU coeds are very aware of their surroundings and very adept at noticing strange men who might be stalking them. After ninety uncomfortable minutes in the campus security office, I emerged ready to step up my efforts in the pursuit of Marci Johnson.

The next morning, I made sure to be in front of the social sciences building ten minutes before her history class. I was in the middle of checking my breath when I caught sight of her trademark blonde ponytail and baseball cap coming around the corner. I'd already moved to intercept her when I realized she wasn't alone. I sighed mournfully.

"Hey, how's it goin'?" I asked, not breaking stride, as if my intention had always been to continue without stopping.

I startled her, but instantly she recognized me, and I was greeted with a warm smile. I was feeling pretty good about myself as I passed her when suddenly things took a dramatic turn.

Out of the blue, I felt someone grab my arm. Twisting awkwardly due to my sudden shift in momentum, I found Marci staring up at me suspiciously. Without releasing me from her skeptical gaze, she instructed her friends to go on without her. Exchanging confused glances, they moved on leaving us alone. Once they were out of earshot, she asked, "What's up?"

Her question terrified me. Something in her eyes told me I was in trouble. "Nothing much. Just heading to class . . . you know. How about you?"

A sinister smile crept into her eyes. "We both know you don't have a class here right now, don't we?"

My stomach tightened. I wanted to slink away and immediately begin the process of dropping out of school. But before my jelly-filled legs could move, another thought occurred to me. This girl knew something about my schedule.

Mustering what little dignity I had left, I decided to lay my cards on the table. Standing up straight and looking her directly in the eye, I said, "You're right. I don't."

My honesty seemed to catch her off guard. Her eyes widened for a split second before her grin expanded to a snicker. "Several months ago, you asked me out to dinner. If I accept that invitation, can we drop these silly charades that have us bumping into each other at all hours of the day?"

I felt nauseous. Had I really been so transparent? Clearly she'd been on to me for a while. On the other hand, wasn't this what I'd been after all along? In the heat of the moment, I decided to press my luck.

"I'm sorry, but it will take at least three dinners to guarantee that."

She laughed again, only this time more genuinely. It was the most beautiful sound I'd ever heard. Taking a couple of steps backward in the direction of her next class, she cocked her head and said, "Well then, I guess you better start planning . . . and when you're ready, you seem to know where to find me." She waved flirtatiously before turning and walking away.

"Dad, I need you!"

There's nothing like having your daydreams interrupted by the words every parent loves to hear from beyond the door of a bathroom stall.

Minutes later, we reemerged into the store only to find someone had taken off with our cart. Breathing deeply to avoid committing an act of violence, I headed outside, grabbed another one, and started again.

One hour and eighteen minutes from the time we'd arrived, Drake and I finally returned to the warmth of the late-morning sun. On the way to our car, my cell phone rang. I glanced at the number and sighed.

"Hey, Dad," I said.

"Todd, this is your father."

Every time! He's been calling my cell phone for two years and not once has he listened to my greeting.

"Yes, Dad. What can I do for you?"

"I was calling for a full report on last night."

"Well, not much to tell. I went, did a little dancing, and came home."

"That's not what I've gathered from other sources."

This was unreal. Had he already been burning up the phone lines with Kevin this morning? And why was Kevin divulging anything to him anyway? He and I had specifically covered this on our ride home last night.

"Other sources?"

"Maureen Littleton said she saw you talking with an attractive young woman . . . what was her name? . . . Emily. She said you were off together alone in a separate room, both clearly emotional. I would describe that as more than a little dancing."

His revelation brought me to a standstill in the middle of the parking lot. "Oh my gosh, Dad! Are you serious? How do you possibly know the cookie lady?" Instantly, another thought struck me.

"By the way, I've never met that woman. How would she know who I was, anyway?"

"I gave her a thorough description and asked her to be on the lookout for you. After she happened upon your little clandestine meeting, she inquired around and verified it was you."

I was not prepared for this. Not now. "Dad, like

I've said before, my personal life is none of your business. Please stop spying on me. I've given you my full report, and I'm going to hang up now."

"Nonsense. I insist you come by for dinner tomorrow and tell us all about this Emily."

In frustration, I closed my eyes and exhaled slowly. "First of all, there's nothing to tell. Second, we're going to Marci's parents' for dinner tomorrow."

"Right. Well, how about Tuesday?"

The writing was on the wall. "Make it Wednesday and you've got a deal."

"Great. We'll see you then."

Hanging up, I stood unmoving for several seconds, staring at my phone as if it might somehow explain the previous conversation to me.

Driving home, my frustration with my father continued to rise until it reached the boiling point. I practiced several different monologues designed to really put him in his place, but as I pulled into the driveway, I groaned in defeat. At sixty-four, there's no changing him. So I will go to dinner, and I will survive the three longest hours of my life. At least I know if things get too bad, I can always count on my mother to protect me.

A Good Cart Ride Spoiled

Tuesday, March 25

MY NAME'S TODD LANDRY, and I'm a golf addict. I say this with no shame; it's simply a fact. I'm addicted to golf. Unfortunately, addiction doesn't guarantee results, and, as such, I'm not very good. Not that I care. If being good was a requirement for me, I'd have given it up years ago. But I've never even considered anything so drastic—until today.

The thought was extremely fleeting, but it was there. And it was there because of Jason Stowell—an exceptional golfer, one of my best friends since grade school, and, on occasion, the biggest jerk I've ever met.

Now, most of the time, Jason is adept at hiding this personality flaw. But when it surfaces, like it did this morning, he rarely disappoints in revealing himself capable of being a true horse's rear end.

The day started out innocently enough as just another golf outing with the guys. Generally our foursome consists of me, Jason, Kevin, and our married friend, Grant. However, when Grant can't make it, we usually invite a nice but somewhat socially awkward acquaintance named Frank to fill our foursome.

Today was a Frank day.

In hindsight, we never should've paired Jason in a cart with Frank. I wouldn't say Jason dislikes Frank, but Jason is the type of person who considers himself a little bit better than everyone else. As such, he wants to be surrounded by people he finds ... acceptable. Frank struggles on several fronts to reach that bar.

Our first Jason the Hun sighting happened right after Frank's first shot. The second the ball left his club, it began heading in the wrong direction. I was preparing to say something supportive about it being early and that there was plenty of golf left to play, when his ball hit a tree and careened an additional one hundred yards farther off course. I can't say for sure, but I think Frank's second shot actually wound up being farther from the hole than his first one had been.

And suddenly there it was. Jason looked at Kevin and me, put his hand to his temple in the shape of a gun, and "fired." It would've been bad enough had he done it behind Frank's back, but instead he waited just long enough to allow Frank a perfect view. I glanced at Kevin with a slight shake of my head, and he nodded in return. Neither of us had to say what we were thinking.

Being Jason Stowell's friend has never been easy. He's a gifted athlete, highly intellectual, and was once described by a female admirer as *dreamy*. Then again, he could just as easily be described as arrogant, argumentative, and just a tad calculating.

Jason's favorite story to tell to anyone who'll listen

is about the day he walked away from a college basketball scholarship to Arizona State University. He'll set the scene by conjuring up a look of great introspection and then regale his listener with the tale of his tough personal decision to serve a mission. Hearing him describe the struggle he went through almost brings a tear to the eye. But thankfully, he made the right choice in the end. He knew a mission was where he was supposed to be.

He's told that story so many times, I've often wondered if he really remembers it that way. Because if Jason has managed to forget the actual events, then Kevin and I are probably the only individuals alive who remember what really happened.

As our group approached the fourth hole and the heat of the day was beginning to set in, my feelings were conflicted. For me, the morning was beginning to feel magical. I was playing some of my best golf ever. On the other hand, my heart was going out to Frank. Jason was struggling, and while that might seem like an additional positive for me, it wasn't. Jason has never lost to any of us. Ever! So trailing me by two strokes after playing three holes was simply unacceptable. And when things become unacceptable for Jason, someone's going to pay. Today, that person was Frank.

As I watched Jason belittle Frank's swing on the fourth tee box, I couldn't help but recall the number of times Jason's temper had messed up his life—beginning our freshman year at ASU.

Despite being a heavily recruited high school basketball star, Jason received almost no playing time his freshman year of college. At the end of the season, the coach called Jason into his office and explained his desire to have him redshirt the following year, a process where Jason would retain his scholarship and practice with the team but not be eligible to play in any games.

That was more than Jason's ego could take. He threw a tantrum and demanded to know why, without actually giving the coach an opportunity to explain. When he did finally calm down enough to shut his mouth, he was told the coaching staff felt he hadn't made the progress during the season they'd been hoping for. They felt the additional year of practice at the college level was needed before he could be effective in actual game situations.

Jason fired back that the reason he wasn't improving was because he wasn't playing, and if the coach had any sense at all, he'd put him in the starting lineup rather than redshirt him.

The coach just laughed. He then informed Jason he could either redshirt or lose his scholarship. Jason used some colorful language to explain he had no intention of redshirting and walked out. He was officially released from his scholarship and the team the next day.

At first, Jason believed he had nothing to worry about. He'd been recruited by other schools and was sure he could easily transfer to another program. But as he reached out to different coaches, he discovered the interest level in Jason Stowell had declined severely.

Kevin and I are the only ones who know this

part of the story. Right after that meeting with his coach, Jason had come to our apartment and vented for three hours. He angrily recounted every detail and told us repeatedly what a fool everyone associated with ASU basketball really was. As the night wore on, the list of schools he could be starting for got longer and longer, but over the next few days, reality told a different story.

Neither Kevin nor I have ever mentioned that week of his life to him again. To this day we've allowed him to live in denial regarding his ASU basketball career. But I always wonder if he resents us. The whole episode is a chink in his armor, and Jason Stowell doesn't like having people aware of his weaknesses.

Frank may not realize it, but he owes me a Dr Pepper. Had my tee shot on the fourth hole not landed in a lake, I believe the authorities might have found Frank's body at the bottom of that lake with Jason's putter wrapped firmly around his neck. But thanks to my hideous shot, Jason was able to erase the two strokes he'd been down, and all tension surrounding our foursome disappeared.

For the next three holes, Jason started to do what he normally does. He pulled further and further ahead until he was leading me by three strokes and Kevin by five. Because I'm a religious man and believe in the concept of mercy, from this point forward, we will never speak of Frank's score again.

But then on hole eight, the unthinkable happened. I hit my first ever hole in one. That changed everything. Once again, I was back to playing golf at a level I'd only dreamed of. In fact, even in my dreams I'd never done quite this well. Either way, my miracle shot brought me back to within one shot of Jason.

From Frank's point of view, I can only assume he was as thrilled by my hole in one as I was. Jason's temper was flaring again, but by playing this far above my pay grade, all pretenses were being shoved to the side. There would be no more sacrificial lambs to absorb his wrath. I was now the sole focus.

However, since my friendship actually matters to him, Jason seemed to be channeling his anger differently to avoid causing a permanent rift. This is an area Jason excels at. If I hadn't known him better, I'd have thought everything was fine as we celebrated my pinnacle achievement in golf. But I do know him, and I know when the charm starts to get a little thick, things are not always what they appear to be.

Never was this behavior more evident than when Jason finally had to accept that his basketball career was over. He was desperate to find a story that would allow him to save face with his family and friends. Quickly he realized that even though he'd rejected the idea of a mission since he was fourteen, serving would provide the easiest path to minimal humiliation. And so he went.

Today, Jason is exactly what I'd expect him to be. He's a salesman. In fact, he's a really good salesman, although sales is not where he started out. Initially, he used his business degree to land a solid corporate job, but it didn't take long for his issues with authority to surface yet again. Following a particularly nasty exchange with his boss, Jason walked out. In that moment, he realized that what he needed was a job where results trumped bad behavior every time. And there's no better industry for that than insurance sales.

Jason was just recently promoted to regional manager and oversees agents throughout the greater Phoenix area. With this new title and salary, he's now more financially secure than everyone else within his social circle, including me. On the other hand, when it comes to his personal life, he hasn't fared nearly as well.

With each successive hole, it was becoming harder and harder for Jason to suppress his rage. But what was I supposed to do? For whatever reason, my ability to royally screw up a golf round had gone AWOL. I just kept making shot after shot. Meanwhile, Jason was still struggling to perform at his typical level of greatness.

As we stood on the tee box of the fourteenth hole, I had a brief premonition that today might not end well. But I was playing so well, I couldn't help but brush it off. I knew if I somehow managed to win, Jason might throw the mother of all tantrums, but I figured that in the end, it could be good for him—and for our relationship. I know that sounds weird, but despite how much Jason hates to lose, he actually hates not being challenged even more. His marriage had definitely taught us that.

Jason met and married Tiffany Fulton within a year of returning home from his mission. Sadly, their relationship would have been great material for a Shakespearean tragedy. In all my life, I've never met two people more suited and yet completely destructive for one another.

As a wife, Tiffany turned out to be exactly what she advertised herself as when they were dating. Hot! Nothing more, nothing less.

Within two months of their wedding, the first signs of trouble surfaced. Jason would constantly describe his wife as an airhead or complain about being saddled with his new "ball and chain."

Though he was the first of my friends to get married, he acted more "single" than any of us. He was always organizing the next party or guys' night out. At the time, Kevin, Grant, and I thought nothing of it. Now, with over a decade's worth of hindsight, I can see we never should've allowed him to use us as his escape. By the time I met Marci and began the transition to adulthood, Jason and Tiffany were already entrenched in destructive patterns that were all but unalterable.

After ten years and two kids, everything fell apart. To hear Jason tell it, Tiffany went crazy and there was nothing he could do. But I don't believe it. I've been around him enough to know that regardless of who called it quits, Jason's level of culpability starts at 50 percent and likely goes up from there.

I've wondered many times why I continue to have anything to do with Jason. He hasn't always been the greatest influence. In fact, once I started dating Marci, he and I began to drift apart.

But following Marci's death, Jason's greatest talent suddenly coincided with my greatest need—there's no one alive more fun than Jason Stowell.

When we get together, we create more memories in an hour than I can make by myself in a week. It's his ability to pull me out of the doldrums that has sparked this revival in our friendship.

Deep down I think there's a good person inside of Jason. For example, he now believes it's his calling in life to get me through this period of mourning. He's constantly planning some kind of get-together designed to emotionally keep my head above water.

On the other hand, sometimes Jason's ultra-competitive nature will cause him to lose focus on his newfound purpose in life. By the time we were finished with hole sixteen, today had become one of those occasions.

Over the previous two holes, I'd retaken the lead by one. Stalking off the green, Jason abandoned all efforts at civility and helicoptered his putter thirty feet past the cart. He followed that up by bellowing a swear word that shifted the rating for our friendly golf round from PG to PG-13.

As Kevin and I climbed into the cart, he subtly gave me a fist bump. We immediately checked to make sure Jason hadn't seen. Luckily, he was too busy retrieving his putter and roughing up his golf clubs like a petulant five-year-old. I really did feel bad for Frank at this point. He was staring out from the passenger seat of his cart like a puppy on its way to be euthanized.

Because I had the best score from the previous hole, I was rewarded with the honor of hitting first on seventeen. Stealing a glance back as I put my tee in the ground, I saw Frank and Kevin standing together while Jason pouted six feet away. Returning my focus to the ball, I uttered a quick and silent prayer that I'd somehow survive these last two holes.

While beating Jason would've been extremely gratifying, I was mostly concerned with my individual score. The way I was playing, I was on track to post my best round ever and then some.

As I started my swing, Jason broke the most important unwritten rule of golf. He talked. In a voice barely loud enough to be heard, he mumbled, "Don't go right." Of course, that's exactly what my ball did. It went right . . . into someone's backyard.

Whirling around, I unloaded, "It's really that important to you, isn't it?"

"What?" he asked incredulously. "I was just talking to myself. I didn't think you could hear me." His look of mock indignation only made it worse.

"Bull! It's so important you win . . . no wait, I take that back. It's so important you don't lose to *me* that you'll do whatever it takes to guarantee victory. In all the years we've played together, it's been tradition to cheer on anyone who's about to score their personal best. But since you run the risk of losing to me, someone far beneath your vaunted superiority"—I use big words when I get mad—"you're willing to throw tradition right out the window."

He started to retreat with a look of wounded offense. "Hold on! That's ridiculous."

"Shut up! I'm done talking to you!" I yelled.

Storming off the tee box, I began walking toward the area where I'd be forced to take my next shot. I was so furious I didn't stop to consider that I didn't have a ball.

As we gathered on the tee box of the final hole, Jason gave a halfhearted attempt at an apology, but I refused to acknowledge him. I might have thawed a little bit had he not achieved exactly what he wanted. My score on seventeen was so bad he was guaranteed to win and my opportunity to record my best score ever would eventually come up short by one stroke.

Jason will never know how close I came to punching him in the face today. However, I've been through things like this with him before, so by the time we parked our carts at the clubhouse, I was already on my way to calming down. What would yelling at him further accomplish, anyway? Instead, I chose to pop the balloon of hostility hanging over us and accepted his handshake. I muttered something about wanting to shove my putter directly into his eye socket, but I said it with a slight smirk. He laughed, and Kevin and Frank quickly joined in with obvious expressions of relief.

I smiled, but I didn't laugh. I was too busy evaluating. If this was how it would always be with Jason, I had to seriously ask myself if continuing to play this stupid game was worth it.

Now that I've had some time to think about it, I've decided my answer is yes. It's totally worth it. So later tonight I'll call Jason and apologize for getting so upset. He'll say words that sound like an apology, but when I analyze them later I'll realize he's only sorry that I was wrong. We'll laugh and chat for a few minutes, and all will be forgotten. We've done it before and we'll do it again.

In the end, I guess I was struck by a startling realization this morning. Jason and golf are really one and the same in my life. Both have caused me bucketloads of heartache and both have come dangerously close to forcing me into court-ordered anger management. But, just like golf, I could never walk away from Jason. I've invested way too much time and effort in both.

TODD'S LANDRY LIST

Would You Like a Salad with Your Inquisition?
Wednesday, March 26

"WHY DO YOU hate talking to me so much?"

Staring suspiciously at Dr. Schenk, I waited several seconds before answering. "That seems like a loaded question."

Dr. Schenk sighed. "It is not a loaded question; it is a legitimate question. Over the last week, you've blossomed in your blog posts, but today we are back where we started when it comes to conversing with one another. What is the difficulty about being here and having an open discussion with me?"

"Didn't you read about my issues with psychoanalysis and counseling?"

"Of course I read about them, but I want to hear you talk about them. I want you to engage me in conversation so that we might eventually work through some of your issues that are manifesting themselves quite clearly in your writing."

"Writing and talking are two different things."

"I am acutely aware."

Our eyes remained locked together as the clock

ticked in the background. Finally, I looked toward the bookshelf behind him. "When I'm writing, if my subject matter gets too difficult, I can walk away and come back later. But with talking, walking away really isn't an option."

"You want to avoid exhibiting emotion like you did in front of this girl . . . Emily."

I chuckled humorlessly. "I don't consider that my shining moment."

Dr. Schenk leaned forward, his eyes gaining intensity. "You do realize in order for us to make real progress, you will eventually need to let go of these emotions you are holding in. Consequently, there is a real probability you will experience an emotional outburst in my office more than once. In fact, your well-being likely depends on it."

"I've cried in front of you."

Dr. Schenk shook his head. "The wipe-away tear does not count. You need to weep. And you need to weep in the presence of someone who can offer you hope. Right now, you prefer to do your weeping alone. Am I correct?"

My pride would not allow me to answer. Instead, I continued gazing at his literary collection and let my silence speak for me.

"Your mature response communicates volumes."

Dr. Schenk removed his glasses and continued, "Your vow of silence comes at a perfect time as our hour is up. Please continue with the blog posts. They are extremely helpful. I've learned more over the last seven days than in the three months prior. I look forward to visiting with you next week."

Leaving Dr. Schenk's office, I was disappointed to realize I didn't feel much better than when I'd arrived. I wanted to blame the good doctor for this, but I knew better. The problem was the dinner I had scheduled that evening with my parents. The dinner that would inevitably lead to confrontation with my father.

My dad's full name is Adrian James Landry. He's neither tall nor impressively well-built, but that doesn't matter. In my world, he remains the most imposing man I've ever met.

A great source of pride for my father is being descended from the first Mormon settlers to establish what is now known as Mesa, Arizona. As his son, I haven't found it so much a source of pride as a source of pressure.

While I was growing up, my father volunteered our family for every service project or Church assignment available. We were legendary. And every time a new service project arose, my siblings and I would be summoned to the living room so my dad could deliver his "Brother Brigham" speech.

It always started the same way. He'd begin by relating the story of how his great-great-grandfather had been one of those to receive a direct call from Brigham Young to come to Arizona and establish a settlement. For fifteen minutes he'd regale us with the story we all knew by heart and then finish by saying, "When Brigham Young issued the call, the Landrys were there to accept. That is who we are."

Then we'd grab our tools and be off.

It wasn't a bad way to grow up. I learned the value

of work and the blessings of helping those in need. Nevertheless, as a teenager, I started to notice our family was receiving a whole lot more "blessings" than everyone else.

Yet no one could ever claim my father was a hypocrite. As busy as he liked to keep us, his expectations of himself were even higher. When my dad wasn't fulfilling his Church calling, he was offering his assistance wherever he could find a need. And while that may have been a noble pursuit, it also meant he was never home.

By the time I was sixteen, I'd really grown to hate the "Brother Brigham" speech. I still respected my dad, but I was tired of being the only boy my age hauled out every other Saturday morning for another "opportunity" to serve. My dissatisfaction reached a boiling point during spring break of my junior year.

We'd never been on a family vacation in my life. Between Dad's construction business and his Church callings, there was never any time. At least that was his excuse. In hindsight, I've realized he's a homebody and traveling just isn't his thing.

So it was completely unexpected when one January evening over dinner, Dad surprised us with the news that we would be heading to San Diego for spring break. I was beyond ecstatic. Several of my friends had captivated me with tales of a mystical place known as *The Beach*. And now, the time had finally come to experience it for myself.

Two weeks before we were scheduled to leave, the family was summoned to the kitchen for a family council. Sitting down at the table, I felt a knot forming in my stomach. My mom seemed really upset. Her eyes were downcast, and she refused to look at anyone, especially my father.

He, on the other hand, was sitting ramrod straight and greeted each of us with a stern look of determination. Once everyone was seated, the infamous speech began.

By the time he finished with, "When Brigham Young issued the call, the Landrys were there to accept. That is who we are," I was praying I was wrong.

With resentment flooding my eyes, I inquired, "What's the job, Dad?"

"The stake president has asked us to go and help with repairs for our girls' camp."

"When?" I asked.

His pause told me everything.

"Tuesday through Friday of spring break."

The reaction around the table was bedlam. My siblings began to howl in protest. My mother, who usually ran interference, continued staring at the floor and offered no support whatsoever. My father began calling for order, but it was my standing without permission to be excused that caused an immediate silence.

My first intention was to leave without saying a word. I was so frustrated I could feel the tears stinging the corners of my eyes. I knew our stake president well enough to know he wouldn't have asked us to cancel our vacation for this. Dad had never told him about our plans. In that moment, I wasn't sure I could ever forgive him.

But as I turned to go, a nasty retort sprang to

mind. I spun back around and looked straight into his eyes. "Two years ago, grandpa told me the real reason the Landrys were asked to come to Arizona, and according to him, being obedient had nothing to do with it."

That stopped my father cold. Before he could recover, I continued. "And I swear if I hear that story used to justify one more pile of garbage being dumped on me, I'm done helping anyone ever again. This trip was important to me."

As I turned to leave, I spied a tear rolling down my mother's cheek. That was devastating. To an inexperienced teenager, that tear meant I'd disappointed her. It would be years before I understood that her tear had been shed *for* me, not because of me.

Two weeks later we went to girls' camp, but to this day I've never heard the "Brother Brigham" speech again.

Arriving at my parents' house is always a production. My mother answers the door and is immediately engulfed by her adoring grandchildren. Tonight, as I smiled at the commotion, I was struck, as I always am, by my mother's youthful appearance. Remove the barely perceptible crow's-feet from her eyes and she doesn't look a day over forty. In fact, with her trim physique and raven-black hair, some days I'm convinced she's younger than me.

Drawn by the raucous greetings, my dad joined us from his study and received a round of hugs as well. As my kids moved on to the kitchen, he turned to me with an expectant look in his piercing gray eyes.

In a voice barely loud enough for my parents to

hear, I whispered, "My children know nothing about what you want to discuss. I wish to keep it that way. I will not talk about last Friday night until after dinner and only when we are alone. So please do not ask."

His disappointment was evident, and I could see him forming a rebuttal, but a hard stare from my mother was the final word on the subject.

Watching my dad throughout dinner reminded me why I respect him so much, even if it is grudging at times. He truly loves his family. Each of my children received individual attention and the opportunity to tell him about anything they wanted. It was definitely the most enjoyable part of my evening.

As soon as dinner was cleared away and a gallon of ice cream had been consumed, Dad gathered my kids and whisked them off to the living room to watch the movie of their choice. Minutes later, he returned to the table where my mother and I sat waiting. Sitting down, he cut right to the chase. "Well? I told you I want details."

Before I could say a word, my mother turned to me and asked, "How did your appointment with Dr. Schenk go today, dear?"

To this day, my father refuses to acknowledge Dr. Schenk at all. Through her question, my mother was subtly communicating her intention to shield me from comments or questions she deemed over the top. The fact that she might derive joy from my father's discomfort was simply an added benefit.

"It was all right. He still believes I'm progressing too slowly, but . . ."

My father couldn't resist such an obvious

opening. "Of course you're moving too slowly. I don't know why you feel the need to pay someone to tell you exactly what I've been saying all along. Which brings us to Friday night. Will you please tell us about this girl?"

I breathed deeply and reminded myself to proceed carefully. Taking my father's bait on comments like those regarding therapy never ended well.

"Dad, there isn't anything to tell. I went like you asked me to, and bottom line, nothing's changed."

"But Maureen—"

"Dad, with all due respect, I've never met Maureen. I don't know her. I'm a little concerned that you're discussing my private life with her, but, regardless, she knows nothing about me."

Paying no attention to my irritation, he continued, "She said you were talking with this Emily girl. She said you both looked like you were crying. I want to know what happened."

I closed my eyes and exhaled slowly. "Again, I wish to emphasize how much I don't appreciate you talking about me with someone I don't know, but to answer your question—Emily is a nice person who happened to spill punch on me. That's it."

"You cried over having punch spill on you?"

"I'm not discussing this."

"Then why was she crying?"

That was it. In rapid fire, I responded, "Fine, she spilled punch on me. She felt guilty about it and grabbed my arm to take me to the kitchen and help me clean up. She didn't mean to, but she invaded my personal space and it kind of freaked me out. Without going into specifics, I had a small breakdown. No big deal, but enough that I felt like I needed to explain myself to her. When I finished, she was a little misty. Those are the details. Are we done?"

As if I'd said nothing at all, he pressed on. "I've done a little checking, and this Emily sounds like an ideal young woman. I know her father from the Highland Stake. I could call him and get her number for you. She sounds exactly like what you need."

Before I could stop myself, I muttered, "She already gave me her number."

How I wish I'd kept that to myself. The light at the end of the tunnel had been in sight before I blasted it into oblivion with that little nugget.

My father nearly leapt from his seat. "Are you serious? So you've called her, right?"

This was not going the way I'd hoped at all. Even my mother was looking at me with an optimistic glint in her eye.

"No, I haven't called her. I don't intend to call her. Can we please pretend this conversation somehow resolved itself thirty seconds ago and move on to another topic?"

His reaction was stunned disbelief. "You're not going to call her? How can you so easily dismiss such a clear blessing from the Lord?"

I lowered my gaze to the table and whispered, "Dad, please don't do this."

Ignoring my request, he continued, "Why do you have to make everything so much harder than it needs to be? It's just like this therapist thing. You don't need someone to tell you what to do. You just need to trust in the Lord and accept His help when He offers it to you."

Looking up with daggers in my eyes, I shot back, "This would be the same God that took Marci nine months ago, right? It may seem easy to you and Him, but I'm still struggling with my wife dying. I apologize, but I haven't gotten around to seeing that as some great opportunity for growth like you have."

As I spoke, I knew a line was being crossed. My mother tried to jump in before it got any worse. "Adrian, Todd, let's just relax. We don't need to talk about this any further."

Dad's face flushed as he struggled to contain his anger. "No, your son has decided blasphemy is the best way to win an argument. I can't let that stand."

Armed with a full dose of righteous indignation, he turned his focus back to me. "I realize what you've had to endure is tough. But, frankly, your trials are nothing compared to what our pioneer ancestors went through. If you'd give half as much effort to seeking for answers through prayer, fasting, and temple attendance as you do through psychological mumbo jumbo, you'd understand that and be working on what your real goal should be—getting remarried."

Now it was my turn. I spoke quietly but with a steely edge to my voice. "First of all, I told you a long time ago not to throw the pioneers in my face. Second, you have no idea what I do or don't do when it comes to spiritual things. I may not make it to the temple once a week like you do, but then I'm a single parent trying to raise my kids alone. Now, for the record, I'm still in love with Marci, and that means something to me. The suggestion that I should turn around and marry the first woman that comes along is offensive, and if it's mentioned again, I'll just leave."

His tone softened as he retreated, "I'm not saying you should forget about Marci. I miss her too. But, son, a man needs a wife. Your children need a mother. You're getting caught up in emotion and refusing to look at the practical realities you're facing. God gives us trials to make us stronger, but He always provides opportunities to deal with them. I'm worried you're turning your back on the very solutions He's trying to provide."

Shaking my head, I tried to answer him without letting my irritation boil over. "I've always had trouble seeing things as black and white as you do. You see Marci's death as a trial, something to learn from and move on. To me, marriage is about committing yourself fully to another human being. I'm still committed to Marci, and I'm not ready to think about plugging someone else into that role.

"You also like to talk about God giving us everything we need to deal with trials, but right now, I don't know if I believe that. Case in point: Alex started her first period yesterday. I don't know what to do. Praying about it isn't going to fix anything because that was Marci's job. Alex is humiliated, and honestly, she needs her mom. She doesn't need some random woman; she needs *her mom*! So far, God hasn't given me an answer for that. And to be honest, I don't expect one. It's just life."

"Son, I—"

"Adrian, shush." My mother grabbed my arm

with a look of serious concern. "Is she okay? What do I need to do?"

Bless my mom. She might be willing to let us act like two cock roosters all night long, but if one of her precious grandchildren is in trouble—cockfight over.

"I just think she needs a woman to talk to."

She let go of my arm and suddenly, without warning, flicked me on the knuckle like she'd done when I was a child. "What's the matter with you? Why didn't you call me? I'll be by tomorrow and we'll take care of this." She stood and pointed at my father while still addressing me. "You may think you're nothing alike, but you're just as prideful and stubborn in your own ways as he is. Something like this better not happen again."

"Yes, Mom."

Seeing his opportunity slipping away, my father resigned himself to one final plea. "Son, just consider calling this woman."

I looked into his eyes and said, "I threw her number away, and I don't want you to get it for me. Please just give me space and let me work this out on my own."

His expression made it clear that giving me space was the last thing he wanted to do, but, grudgingly, he conceded.

A few minutes later, my family and I prepared to leave. Drake had fallen asleep, so I picked him up and began herding my daughters to the door.

Both of my parents spent several minutes saying good-bye. When my dad came to kiss Drake on the forehead, I reached around and hugged him with my one free arm. Speaking softly so only he and I could hear, I said, "I do understand that you're only trying to help, and I appreciate it. I love you, Dad."

He hugged me back and softly murmured, "I love you too. Don't be a stranger."

Dad returned to his study while my mother followed us outside. Once I'd loaded the kids in the car, I returned to the porch to wish her good night.

Placing her hand on my cheek, she commented, "All he wants is for you to be happy. I know he doesn't express himself very well, but that doesn't mean everything he says should be discounted."

I dropped my eyes to the ground and chuckled.

"I know, Mom. I really do. Please don't tell him, but I actually called Emily this afternoon. I don't want there to be any expectations, but we're meeting this Saturday for what I guess you would call a date."

A hint of a smile crossed her lips as she pulled me in and kissed me on my forehead. Then she turned and walked back into the house without another word.

TODD'S LANDRY LIST

Different Perspectives of Midnight
Thursday, March 27

THIS MORNING, WHILE driving my girls to school, I was surprised to hear my cell phone ring. Seeing Kevin's name on the digital display, I pressed my hands-free speaker button without a second thought.

Simultaneous to this, my subconscious began doing everything within its power to get my attention. Just as the connection was completed, I remembered the message I'd left him last night. I groaned inwardly as I braced for the collision of worlds I'd hoped to avoid.

"Hello?"

"Good morning! I just got your message, and I had to call to say I'm impressed. Our little boy's all grown up and got himself a date." He chuckled at his own joke. "So when's the big day?"

From the corner of my eye, I saw Alex's body stiffen. Leaving my kids in the dark regarding my social life suddenly felt like a bad decision.

70

"Um . . . Saturday," I responded tentatively.

"You don't sound excited. You're not backing out are you?"

Alex's expression was shifting from warily curious to downright hostile quickly. I needed to get off the phone and begin damage control ASAP. "It's possible. I can't seem to remember what made me think calling her was a good idea."

"Because you're a man."

With another sideways glance at my daughter, I replied, "I'm in the car with my kids. Just so you know."

"Fair enough. All I'm saying is spending an evening with a woman wouldn't be the worst thing that could happen to you."

"I'm not sure that's true."

"Whatever. I know you're sticking with this denial thing, but you and I both know why you called her. Just go. Have a good time. No one's saying you have to marry this woman."

"Are you kidding? My dad did last night."

"No *sane* person is saying you have to marry this woman. Look, as your friend, I'm telling you not to cancel. You'll regret it if you do. And call me the minute it's over."

"Fine." I sighed as I reached over to press the disconnect button. Checking the rearview mirror, I quickly assessed the mood of the car. Samantha was reading and apparently hadn't heard a word I'd said. Drake was . . . Drake's four. The clear problem was seated in the front seat next to me.

Alex's toffee-brown hair was pulled back into a

ponytail, allowing me a perfect view of her growing resentment. The furious scowl on her face was clearly reflected on the glass. After several minutes of silence, I couldn't take it anymore.

"So what's on the agenda for school today?"

No reply.

"Alex, would you please talk to—"

In a tone filled with accusation, she cut me off. "Am I really doing that bad of a job?"

"Job? What are you talking about?"

She continued to stare out the window. "Nothing. Forget it. Can we go home? I don't want to go to school today."

It felt like a conversation with a hummingbird. "Honey, I'm confused. I don't understand what you meant."

"Forget it!" The finality in her voice returned the car to a tense silence.

Suddenly aware of the hostility, Sam put her book away and stared at the floor until we pulled up in front of her school. As she opened the door, she first looked at me and then at her sister. "Alex, are you okay?" she asked timidly.

Alex didn't answer, so I did. "She's fine, honey. Go ahead and go."

Stepping out of the car, Sam nervously glanced back before leaving. To reassure her, I smiled and said, "Everything's fine, sweetie. Have a good day and know that I love you."

My younger daughter smiled back and waved one final time to her sister slouched angrily in the passenger seat.

Making a snap decision, I pulled back into traffic and drove two blocks to a nearby park. Drake, who hadn't been fully awake when we left, had fallen asleep in his booster seat. I found a parking spot, turned off the ignition and removed the keys, letting Alex know I was ready for the long haul.

"Alex, please talk to me. What did you mean about not doing a good job?"

Tears escaped down both sides of her face as she continued to hesitate. My heart was breaking for her, and I didn't even know what was wrong. Finally, she took a deep breath and found her voice.

"Do you remember the night you came home from the hospital and told us about Mom?"

"To be honest, not very well."

She nodded. "You were really out of it. You kept trying to tell us what had happened but you weren't making any sense. I was kinda glad when you gave up. Grandma Landry said you were in shock."

"That was not a good night for our family," I murmured.

As if I hadn't spoken, she continued, "Later, when I couldn't sleep, I came into your room and you were crying. That freaked me out. I didn't know what to do, so I hugged you. I was really scared." She paused before adding, "I held on to you because I was afraid to let go."

The father in me couldn't resist, and I reached over to brush away a tear. Once again, there was no acknowledgement.

"Things got better when you finally stopped crying. I wasn't as scared anymore. Grandma had told

73

me you would need my help, so I asked you what I needed to do."

I remembered the question and the sheer hopelessness it had left inside of me.

"You said we were partners, Dad. You told me we'd get through this together. And I've tried to do the best I can. But now I don't know what else to do."

"Oh, honey." I sighed. "You're doing great."

"No, I'm not. Kevin just said you need somebody else." She leaned her head against the window as more tears cascaded down her cheeks. "I'm sorry I'm not good enough. I promise I'll try harder, it's just . . . I'm not sure how."

The anguish in my child's voice made me realize how little I understood her suffering. My chest tightened as guilt swept through me, unlocking a flood of memories from that horrible night—the night my world fell apart.

For weeks Marci had been complaining of headaches. When she almost collapsed one afternoon, I'd seen enough. Despite her fervent protests, I insisted we go to the emergency room.

We'd finished checking in and had just taken our seats in the waiting area, when suddenly, it happened. Marci's eyes rolled back in her head, and she started to convulse.

I remember screaming as I reached out to grab her. Within seconds, hospital staff surrounded us and I was pushed back. I realize now someone had to be holding me because I remember trying to get to her but I couldn't move. I watched from ten feet away as they did some of the most awful things to my wife. I don't know what I was doing or saying but it wasn't long before a doctor insisted someone take me out of the room.

That was the last time I saw Marci alive.

The next hour felt like an eternity. Eventually, a man dressed in regular street clothes approached me and introduced himself as Stan. He told me that as the hospital's social worker, it was his job to explain what had happened with my wife.

He told me that the preliminary results suggested Marci had experienced a brain aneurysm. With a great deal of hesitation, Stan began describing how the doctors had done all they could. It was then that I started to pray. I begged God to stop him from saying the words I knew were coming. But my prayers went unanswered.

The second he verified my worst fears, I went into survival mode. With no outward sign of emotion, I asked what would happen next. He gently explained what was required, but assured me there was no rush. Little did he know all I could focus on was getting out of that hospital as quickly as possible.

Hours later, as the van from the mortuary pulled away, I stood outside the ER doors feeling completely alone. In a surreal moment, I realized my feelings were similar to the day I'd first taken Alex home from the hospital. I needed someone to tell me what to do.

Knowing the time had come, I forced myself to place the call I'd been dreading. My mother's voice sent a chill through my body, and I began to shake. In a trembling voice, I barely managed a hushed, "Hey, Mom."

In the same breath, my mother sounded both panicked and relieved. "Todd, I'm so glad you called. We were starting to get worried. How's Marci? Were they able to find anything?"

Forcing myself to speak, I stammered, "Uh, Mom? Marci's gone."

And suddenly, my memory goes blank. I don't even remember how I got back into the waiting room, but that's where my father found me when he arrived. Rushing to my side, he held me as I finally let go and sobbed uncontrollably on his shoulder. I can still recall the feeling of sanctuary his arms provided. At the time, I felt they were my only anchor to sanity.

Once I'd composed myself, Dad volunteered to drive me back to his place where my children were waiting. Out of respect for me, no one had told them what had happened.

Alex and Sam were sitting together on my parents' couch, looking completely disoriented and scared. Drake had fallen asleep earlier.

As I sat down in front of them, Samantha began to cry. Alex, on the other hand, resembled a wounded animal. Her eyes darted from person to person until they came to rest, unblinking, on me. Her unwavering stare did not make my task any easier.

I've long since forgotten how I told my children of their mother's death. It seems Alex's recollection is much more lucid than mine. I do remember Sam scrambling frantically onto my lap and burying her face in my shoulder.

Alex, meanwhile, sat rigidly still without

shedding a tear. She wore a terrified expression and her lip quivered slightly, but she refused to cry.

Much later that night, after I'd brought my children home and put them to bed, I sat alone in my living room listening to Samantha cry herself to sleep. I couldn't imagine a worse sound—until I heard the silence that followed.

The thought of sleep was terrifying. So as weird as this may sound, I turned on the television. I didn't want to watch anything. I just needed to do something normal. Unfortunately, normal didn't help, so a few minutes later I gave up and headed toward my bedroom.

Seeing my perfectly made bed triggered another breakdown. Marci had always had an irrational fear of leaving our bed unmade. She worried about friends or family having to enter our home and finding our bed in shambles. It was just her thing. As we'd been preparing to leave for the hospital, making our bed was the last thing she did.

I fell to my knees and began to weep. Some time later, I felt Alex's arms around me. Her strong hold on me never broke as my body shook uncontrollably.

As my tears began to subside, I gently pushed her back and took in her grief-stricken face. Her eyes were swimming, but no tears had yet managed to escape. Once again, I hugged her tightly with an embrace of gratitude I'd never shared before with one of my children. Long gone was the innocent child I'd known as her muffled voice asked, "What do I need to do, Dad?"

When Alex was little, she possessed an

exaggerated independent streak. The only way I could ever get her to accept my help was to offer myself as her partner. I might have exerted all the effort, but she was granted the illusion of being invaluable. As we knelt on the floor of my bedroom, her question awaiting my answer, those partnerships were all that would enter my mind.

So I said it. I told her we could do this together as partners, not once taking into account she wasn't a little girl anymore.

Over the next month, it became clear I was in over my head. Thankfully, the money we'd received from Marci's life insurance was enough to provide options. I approached the owner of the small marketing firm where I work about the possibility of going part time. It's a family-run business, and he couldn't have been more supportive. Now, I go into the office twice a week but handle the rest of my responsibilities from home. The plan is that I'll eventually return to full time once Drake is in school.

Nevertheless, even without the stresses of a full-time job, my new day-to-day obligations were overwhelming. It was incredibly tough for a while, but we eventually found our rhythm. I even reached the point when I would occasionally congratulate myself for transitioning to a single dad so successfully.

Now I realize I may have been the most unaware human being on the planet. As we sat there, my mind opened up to all Alex had been doing to ease our family's burdens—things I hadn't noticed but should have.

I hadn't given Drake a bath in weeks, yet he

was a clean and presentable little boy. Sam doesn't ask for my help with homework. To be truthful, I don't even know if Sam needs help with her homework, but there have been plenty of nights when my daughters have been huddled around the kitchen table, feverishly engaged in something. Dishes have been done, carpets have been vacuumed, and never once could I remember this sweet girl complaining. Now she sat suffering next to me, believing her efforts had fallen short—all because I'd been scared to tell her about Emily.

I opened my mouth to try and console her, but nothing came out. I had no idea where to begin. Slowly, I reached over and gently pulled her toward me. Because we were in bucket seats in a minivan with an armrest between us, it was possibly the world's most awkward hug, but we hardly noticed. After a minute or two, I worked up the nerve to say something.

"Alex, without you, I wouldn't have survived. The only reason our family is functional is because of you. You're not only doing enough, but because of my failings, you're doing too much. I appreciate you with all my heart, and I'm sorry I haven't told you sooner.

"But, honey, Saturday night isn't about that."

I paused, struggling with how to help her understand. "Let me ask you a question. Who do you talk to about . . . things?"

"Things?"

"Yeah, you know. Things like missing your mom or . . . not even problems necessarily." I closed my eyes in frustration before trying a different tack. "Who do you talk to about what's going on in your life that you don't want me to know about?"

"Nobody, I guess."

"Are you sure? You don't talk to anyone about personal stuff?"

"Well, sometimes I'll talk to Grandma." She hesitated before adding, "I guess I talk to Jennifer too, about music and school."

"Exactly. You have different people for different stuff. For me, your mom was the person I talked to about most everything. Not golf or basketball, but almost everything else. Now that she's not here anymore, it's left a big hole for me."

Alex's expression remained puzzled. I sighed and pressed on. "These days, I rely on some people more than I used to. I call Grandma or Kevin several times a week. But a lot of people think that's not enough."

"Like who?"

"Dr. Schenk, Grandpa, Kevin . . . basically every other adult we know."

"What do you think?"

Her question was a good one. I stared out the windshield as I contemplated my answer. "I don't know. Sometimes I feel pretty alone. I guess that's why I'm giving Saturday night a try. I have no idea if it'll be a good thing or not, but it feels like I have to at least try."

"Are you gonna get married again?"

"Oh, honey . . ." I turned back and looked deeply into her light green eyes—eyes so much like her mother's. "I'm not even thinking about marriage."

My declaration seemed to be what she needed to hear. She didn't respond, but her body relaxed noticeably.

"Are you okay?" I asked.

"Yeah, I'm fine."

"You know you have to go to school, right?"

"I know. I have a test today, anyway."

Minutes later, I dropped her off just as the bell rang. After school, I tried to be accessible in case she wanted to talk more, but she seemed content to pretend our morning heart-to-heart had never happened. Maybe if I was a better parent, I'd have forced the issue, but something inside told me to let this one go. So I did.

It's Actually Nothing like Riding a Bike

Saturday, March 29

AS I SHUT the passenger door to my minivan, my eyes closed. What could I have possibly been thinking? I was not ready for this.

But be that as it may, here I was—out on a date, with no other options available to me but to continue. Slowly, I trudged around to the driver's side door and climbed in.

Things had started out well enough. Emily, dressed in an emerald-green blouse and contemporary black skirt that highlighted her long, cascading red hair, had warmly greeted me. Her outfit, which perfectly complemented her striking figure, stood in stark contrast to mine, which consisted of my best blue jeans, penny loafers, and a button-front shirt that might have been stylish sometime between 1986 and 1991.

But as I turned to escort her to my vehicle, things immediately started heading south. Staring down her walkway, I realized it was too narrow to be navigated comfortably by two people side by side. Scrambling quickly, I constructed a pro and con list as to whether

I should walk in front of her or behind her. The deciding factor was her gate. With a gate, I clearly needed to walk in front so I could be a gentleman and open it for her.

Unfortunately, as soon as I took the lead, I wanted to kick myself. My internal devil's advocate started suggesting that I'd just exhibited a dismissive male-chauvinistic attitude likely to cripple our date before it had a chance to begin. AHHHHH!!!! The whole night was ruined already because of my indecisiveness and her stupid, skinny sidewalk.

To add insult to injury, our single file line provided no opportunity for small talk. Since I was sure I'd botched everything already, I didn't want to compound it by trying to hold a conversation with someone I couldn't look at, so I said nothing.

Glancing nervously in her direction as I positioned myself behind the steering wheel, I reached to shut my car door. Its closing sounded like a mausoleum sealing shut. I wanted to die.

I knew I needed to say something. The problem was—what? Finally, I reached for the stereo and asked the only question my nerve-addled mind could generate. "So what kind of music do you like?"

"Do you have any Mormon Tabernacle Choir?"

My heart froze. I consider myself a well-rounded person, and I love music of all kinds. But seriously— the Mormon Tabernacle Choir?

"Uhhh, no."

The nervous tension, which had been hovering at dangerous levels already, became so thick it threatened to crush us.

Then suddenly, Emily began to snicker. "I'm sorry. I'm just teasing you."

I cocked my head to the side in confusion. "Teasing me?"

Taking a deep breath to compose herself, she explained, "That was one of the best MoTab reactions I've ever seen. I apologize. That probably wasn't very nice of me, but the look on your face was priceless."

Still feeling three steps behind, I hesitantly volunteered, "So . . . you don't like the Mormon Tabernacle Choir?"

"Not really. I just wanted to see what you'd say."

"Why?"

Emily seemed to study me a little more closely. "You really haven't been around the LDS singles' scene much, have you?"

"Not since I was twenty-two."

Emily's face took on a look of grave concern. "Oh, you've got a lot to learn then." Shifting in her seat to face me directly, she asked, "Before you got married, did you know guys who tried to impress girls with their massive levels of spirituality?"

"I suppose," I answered warily.

"Well, a lot of those guys either never got married or, more likely, got divorced. I'm not saying every guy I've gone out with is insincere or fake, but I've met plenty. And you generally can spot them right away."

Hearing her describe these things with such frankness made me nauseated. I felt like I was a greenie in the mission field again. "Really?"

"Oh, yeah. They'll usually have a set of scriptures in the car or your first date will be to the temple grounds. But another big giveaway is the Mormon Tabernacle Choir ready and waiting in the car stereo."

I leaned back against the headrest and sighed. "This is too much."

A tenor of apprehension entered her voice as she asked, "Is this your first date since . . ." She let the question hang in the air.

"Yes, it is," I acknowledged.

"Are you sure you want to do this? My feelings won't be hurt if you say no."

I turned and stared at her as I seriously pondered her offer. "Well, I need to stop at the temple and cancel the catered picnic I had planned. But after that, I should be okay."

She burst out laughing, and, as if by magic, the nerves raging in my stomach eased considerably.

After so many years, I'd forgotten how exciting it can be to learn new things about someone you've just met. For instance, Emily does not share my love for country music. She's more of a Jack Johnson or Michael Bublé kind of person. Also, I discovered she grew up in the small town of Springerville, Arizona, before moving to Gilbert during her eighth-grade year. By the time we arrived at the restaurant, the uncomfortable silence from earlier had long been forgotten.

All of my life, my mother has stressed the importance of good manners. During my teenage years, she may have felt her efforts were in vain. Truth be told, I not only listened, but I also took her instruction seriously.

The second I placed my gearshift in park, I

practically sprang from my van as I rushed to open Emily's door for her. In my mind, I was thinking, *Never let it be said that Todd Landry made a lady wait one second longer than necessary to be escorted from her chariot.* Unfortunately, my speedy attempt at chivalry coincided perfectly with Emily dropping her purse onto the passenger side floorboard of my van.

The one item that managed to escape her handbag was a tube of ChapStick that rolled into a crevice where no human hand could reach without opening the door. At the precise moment I arrived, she, unaware of my record-breaking time in circling a stationary vehicle, opened the door herself to recover the wayward lip balm. I'm not sure which was louder—the crack of metal on my knee or my shriek from intense pain that followed half a second later.

Rushing to my side, Emily appeared on the verge of tears. "Oh, my gosh! I'm so sorry. Are you okay? I can't believe I didn't see you."

Unable to speak, I bit my lower lip and shook my head vigorously. I was trying to assure her that everything was fine, but I think my pitiful whimpering conveyed something else entirely.

For at least five minutes, I leaned against the side of my vehicle as the pain subsided. I have to admit, I felt really bad for Emily. Insisting that the damage was minimal, I refused to let her see my leg. So in her desperation to provide comfort of some sort, she gently rubbed my shoulder and neck.

As it had during our first encounter, her touch sent an electric current coursing through my body.

My initial instinct was to beg her to stop before I broke out in tears again, but as her soft, thin fingers worked their magic, I elected to tell my initial instinct to get lost.

When the pain finally subsided, I stood up straight and found myself staring directly into Emily's eyes. I was instantly mesmerized. For a week those eyes had refused to leave my brain. I could have stood in that parking lot for the rest of the night studying them, but her anxious concern broke through my concentration.

"Look, are you sure you don't want to go home? I can't imagine what you think of me."

And that was true. No way she could imagine what I was thinking of her right then. She was making me feel alive. Her face was filled with concern and embarrassment, but that only made her more attractive. My leg would have to actually fall off before I'd consider going home.

Inside the restaurant, it didn't take us long to be seated. Ignoring her menu completely, Emily leaned forward, perching her chin delicately on her clasped hands. "Tell me about her."

I'd known it was coming, but that didn't make it any easier. Closing my menu, I inquired, "What would you like to know?"

"Whatever you want to tell me."

"Well," I began tentatively, "her name was Marci, and we were married for fifteen years."

I couldn't look at her anymore. I dropped my gaze to the silverware in front of me. "I was lucky, really. Our time together was amazing. She knew everything about me and still somehow wanted to spend time with me. The older I get, the more I realize how rare that is." Not sure of what else to say, I looked up with my eyebrows raised, signaling I was done.

"How did she . . . ?" Emily stopped midsentence, suddenly self-conscious. "What happened to her?"

"Brain aneurysm."

She said nothing more but continued to search deeply within my eyes as if they were sharing more about my past than I'd chosen to convey. Unsure of what to do, I stared back. Eventually, the moment passed and she transferred her attention to the unopened menu in front of her.

Soon after, our waiter arrived and we placed our orders. As he made some final notes about our drink selections, Emily reached out and grabbed his hand.

"This is gonna sound awfully strange, but has anyone ever told you what great teeth you have?"

I couldn't speak for our waiter, but if some crazy woman had grabbed me in a public place and commented on my teeth, I'd have been a little concerned.

But to my amazement, the server broke out in a wide, appreciative grin that illuminated his previously well-hidden personality.

"Thank you so much," he stammered. "They took a lot of work, so it's nice of you to notice."

"Well, they look great. They brighten your whole face."

Beaming, our server practically danced from our table with our food selections in tow.

"What was that about?" I asked suspiciously.

"What do you mean?"

"With our waiter. What was with the whole *teeth* thing?"

"He had nice teeth," Emily declared innocently.

"Yeah?"

"Didn't you notice? They'd obviously been whitened."

Somewhat sheepishly, I admitted, "No, not really."

"Well, they had. And judging by the way he hardly opened his lips when he spoke, I'd assume he just recently had some braces removed."

I was speechless. How on earth had she noticed all that? With my mouth slightly open, I blinked several times trying to piece together what I'd just witnessed. "So you just make random comments to people about any noticeable characteristics they have?"

Exasperated, Emily corrected me. "Well, of course not. That poor boy had one of the biggest noses I've ever seen. I had no intention of pointing that out to him."

I shrugged and nodded my head in acceptance. "Fair enough. So let me rephrase—you just like to hand out random compliments to complete strangers?"

Emily stared at me for several long seconds, as if she were surprised that I was failing to understand. "You make it sound like it's a bad thing. But no, I don't go looking for things to compliment people on. The way he moved his mouth reminded me of when I had braces as a kid. I hated them. I really didn't think about it beyond that—I just said something. And it seemed to make him feel better. That's it. No big deal."

Oh, but it was. I'd never done anything like that for a stranger. Suddenly my attraction to this woman was expanding beyond her hypnotic eyes and electrifying touch. I was starting to discover something deeper. But in the back of my mind, a nagging thought took root.

"So is that all you were trying to do for me the other night? Make me feel better?"

Emily blushed. "Not exactly."

"Then what? I mean, why would you go and give your number to some crazy person who clearly has emotional problems that cause him to weep uncontrollably?"

Lowering her gaze, she admitted, "When I first noticed you were crying, it did weird me out a little bit. But once you explained, it was the tears that convinced me to take a chance and write my number on your hand."

"I'm sorry, but *what?*"

Raising her eyes back to mine, she explained, "It kinda goes back to the compliment thing. I mean, the first time I saw you, I knew you were attractive."

My eyebrows shot up at her revelation. "Really?"

Emily rolled her eyes at my interruption. "Stop. You have to know that you're certainly not ugly. But that's just it. What I learned in the kitchen last week is that superficial things like appearance aren't what you're about.

"I mean, I've met a ton of guys who are just as good-looking as you, or even better. No offense."

"None taken—I think."

"But that's all they are. Beneath their chiseled

chin or perfect hair, they're empty. Your emotions when you talked about your wife told me right away that you were a man who had substance. How could I not want to know that guy?"

Narrowing my eyes, I asked, "Then why the Mormon Tabernacle Choir thing in the car?"

Emily's face flushed again. "Well, a girl can never be too careful."

Her honesty caused me to laugh. "I'm sorry, I'm not sure I've ever met anyone like you. How on earth are you not married?"

As soon as the words escaped my lips, I'd have done anything to take them back.

"I'm so sorry. That was incredibly insensitive of me."

Emily shook her head as she quieted my apologies. "Don't worry about it. Trust me, at thirty-one, it's a question that comes up a lot."

"Well, that doesn't excuse the way I asked it. However, I'm not going to lie. I am curious."

She sighed. "Trust me, it's not that interesting."

"I highly doubt that."

Emily leaned back and let her gaze drift off to the bar in the corner. I assumed she was deciding what to share and what she intended to hold back.

"It's not that I haven't had the chance."

I almost said, "Duh!" But, thankfully, I held my tongue.

"There've been several times when I could've gotten married—if I'd wanted to. But honestly? There's only one guy I regret letting slip away."

I sat without moving a muscle. For some reason,

I was worried if I made any sudden movements, she'd think twice about what she was saying and her story would go untold.

"His name was Scott, and he was my high school boyfriend. I know I'm probably viewing this through rose-colored glasses, but even now it's hard not to feel like we were made for each other.

"Right after our graduation, we made a pact. I'd wait for him while he served a mission, and then he would do the same for me. I'd dreamed about going on a mission since I was a little girl, and, at eighteen, the idea of waiting for each other sounded so romantic to the both of us."

All of a sudden, Emily broke from her trancelike state and returned her focus to me. "You can probably guess what happened. He went on his mission and I waited, but when he came home, he didn't want to wait anymore. He begged me not to go, but I was young and headstrong and didn't listen to what he was actually saying.

"About a week before I was supposed to leave, he went for broke and proposed. I turned him down. I told him I'd waited for him and now it was his turn to wait for me. I left on my mission . . . and he married somebody else."

"What a jerk," I injected, trying to sound supportive.

Emily smiled wistfully. "No, Scott was never a jerk. He was a really great guy. I was the jerk."

Despite my desire to say something encouraging, I maintained the wherewithal to keep my mouth shut. Emily sat silently for a moment before abruptly coming back to herself. "Enough about me. We came here to talk about you."

But any discussion of me would have to wait as our supremely cheerful server arrived with our food. I'd been so preoccupied with our conversation that I'd forgotten how hungry I was. The heavenly aroma of my entrée reminded me with a vengeance.

Nonetheless, my reprieve from the spotlight was short-lived. Midway through my third bite, Emily asked, "Do you have kids?"

Taking time to swallow before I answered, I eventually acknowledged, "I do. I have three children—my daughter, Alex, is thirteen; Samantha, nine; and Drake, who recently turned four."

Realizing I didn't intend to say more, Emily raised her eyebrows and inclined her head slightly. "And?"

And so I began to talk about my kids. I didn't intend to go on very long, but with every detail I shared, her eyes seemed to gain excitement. Occasionally, she'd interject with questions, but mostly she seemed content to learn about my children.

Finally, I realized I'd been talking nonstop for over ten minutes. I felt instantly self-conscious. "I'm so sorry. I'm sitting here droning on and am probably boring you to death."

"Not at all. I love kids. That's why I'm a teacher. And yours sound absolutely amazing. How are they handling . . . everything?"

The innocent question reminded me of my conversation with Alex. "Let's just say some days are better than others."

I'm fairly certain that Emily was about to ask a follow-up question, but whatever it was going to be, I will never know.

As we'd been talking, our server reappeared and had been reaching to fill our empty water glasses. Emily, trying to be helpful, picked up her glass and began moving it toward the already tipping pitcher despite leaving most of her attention on me. Right as I had finished speaking, her glass hit the pitcher with enough force to swing it in my direction, spilling its contents all over my half of the table—and beyond.

An unexpected shot of ice-cold water is a shocking experience every time it happens. No exceptions. So as the freezing liquid splashed somewhere around my navel, I attempted jumping to my feet as a reaction to the stunning jolt.

And I would've made it had I not been seated in a booth that prohibited me from moving backward. Consequently, my upper thighs hit the table at a relatively high rate of speed.

For the second time in less than an hour, sections of my lower body were experiencing excruciating pain. Only this time, the pain was accompanied by an element of sloshiness. Mumbling an unintelligible excuse, I flailed my way out of this previously unrecognized deathtrap and hobbled away to the restroom.

When I returned, I was mostly dry and again able to walk without a visible limp. I found Emily seated at our freshly cleaned table with her head buried in her hands.

Sliding back into my side of the booth, I gently asked, "Are you okay?"

"Take me home . . . before I accidently kill you."

A genuine laugh escaped my lips. Reaching across the table, I gently removed one of her hands from her face and held it until I had her full attention.

"I'm not taking you anywhere. This place has the most amazing fried ice cream, and I'll be darned if I'm leaving here without any."

Her relieved smile melted my heart.

We got the server's attention, and before long we had a delicious bowl of chocolate-covered fried ice cream sitting between us. Armed with a spoon apiece, we enjoyed the decadent dessert while chatting about all kinds of nonsensitive topics.

Finally, sensing that our time was drawing short, I began laying the foundation for the question I'd been dying to ask all evening.

"Look, I don't want to get all serious again, but I have a question."

Emily's eyes widened. "Yes?"

"How do you deal with being alone?"

Hesitantly, she replied, "I don't think I'm qualified to answer that."

Her reply startled me. I realized it was a personal question, but I thought it was a logical thing to talk about since it was something we had in common.

"I'm sorry. I wasn't trying to dampen the mood, but you told me when we met that if there was anything you could do to help, I should call. Well, I called."

Slowly and deliberately, she placed her spoon on the table. When she spoke, her voice was filled with compassion but left no doubt as to the sincerity of her statement. "I can appreciate what you're asking, but when it comes to advice, you need to understand our situations are not the same."

"Okay. I mean, I realize we got to the destination by different paths, but lonely is lonely, isn't it?"

I wanted to take the words back as soon as I said them. Bracing for the incensed response I certainly deserved, I closed my eyes. But her soft tone conveyed no animosity.

"Please don't take this the wrong way, but you have no idea what you're talking about."

I started to acknowledge how right she was, but she continued on without giving me the chance.

"I can't even begin to imagine what you're going through, but there's one big difference between us. You're alone because life doesn't always play fair. But you had fifteen years with someone who wanted to spend her life with you. I haven't had that. I'm not going to pretend I know which is worse, because I don't. But what I do know is that you have fifteen years of memories I'd kill for and children who need you. You have a purpose. I'm still looking for mine."

I felt incredibly small. I wanted to say something conciliatory, but I knew how hollow my words would be. So I barely managed a whispered, "I'm sorry."

"Please don't say that. You've lost your wife. You have nothing to be sorry about. I'm sorry for offering to help and then not being able to."

Reaching over and taking her hand once more, I countered, "I hope you know that's not true. You've helped me tonight more than I would've ever thought possible."

Her eyes narrowed suspiciously, "Really?"

"Really. I may be confined to a wheelchair by the time we're done, but every minute spent with you tonight has been worth it."

She jerked her hand from mine and playfully slapped me on the arm. "I told you I was sorry."

"I'm just kidding."

"I know—and thank you. This has been good for me too."

Sitting up straight, I declared, "Wait a minute. Who said it has to be over? Surely there's something else we can do tonight. You want to go walk the mall?"

Emily giggled. "Boy, when it comes to dating, you really are out of practice. What would we do at the mall?"

"Keep a date going I don't want to see end."

For the third time, her cheeks flushed a brilliant pink. "All right, then. Let's go walk the mall."

The next hour and a half was amazing. We both adhered to an unspoken agreement and avoided all topics of substance. I've never enjoyed mindless chatter so much in my life.

As we arrived back at her house, I played it smart and allowed her to take the lead on the skinny sidewalk of doom. Unlike me, Emily had no qualms about keeping a conversation going despite our inability to talk face-to-face. Regrettably, I was no longer hearing a word she said.

We were quickly approaching the one moment I'd been dreading for days—the end of the date. Reaching her front door, she playfully spun around to face me, wearing an expectant grin on her face. I responded with my best head-scratching Neanderthal impression. I have no excuse; I simply froze.

Luckily, Emily took pity on me. Rising to her toes, she kissed me lightly on the cheek. Shocked, I could do nothing more than gawk at her as she stepped away and winked mischievously.

"Good night, Todd. I had a great time. You're under no obligation, but you still have my number. Use it if you want to."

Giving me no opportunity to react, she turned and disappeared through her front door. I managed to stutter a "good night" before it closed, but just barely. I was still reeling from the kiss on my cheek. I knew to her it probably meant nothing, but to me it was huge. I'd survived a date—and enjoyed it. That kiss meant hope. Hope I hadn't felt in a long time.

I pray she wasn't looking out her peephole as I walked away. I did a fist pump. Immature? Probably. But regardless, I would definitely be using her phone number again.

TODD'S LANDRY LIST

It's a Small LDS World After All

Sunday, March 30

ALL MY LIFE I've been told there must be opposition in all things. Well, I have a question. Why? I could totally get behind opposition in some things. I could even see in a majority of things. But why all things?

For instance, take my date with Emily. I had a great time. As I left her doorstep last night, the air around me suddenly felt lighter than it had for months. I dared to think that maybe, just maybe, my life was starting on an upswing.

But then that night in my dreams, I was haunted by visions of Marci. I can't recall the context in which I saw her, but the one thing I remember with vivid clarity is Marci's face filled with disappointment. Apparently my subconscious didn't have nearly as good of a time last night as I did.

Around four thirty this morning, my dreams intensified to the point of waking me. As reality slowly came into focus, I tried desperately to hold on to Marci's image in my mind.

There are a dozen pictures of Marci throughout our house, but each day I find it harder to recall the little things photos don't capture. Her mannerisms, her expressions—all the things that made her the woman I love. I miss those things. So when a dream allows me to see her again, I want to keep her alive as long as possible.

At some point I must've fallen back asleep because at 7:00 a.m., my alarm ripped through the morning's calm like a shotgun blast.

Normally I don't stress about getting to church on time, but as I stumbled to the shower, I realized I was way behind. My Saturday night routine had been preempted, so now my Sunday morning would require a more finely tuned execution.

Sadly, we didn't do so well.

Sacrament meeting was well under way by the time my family slid into a pew in the back of the chapel. I'd hoped once we were seated, I'd be able to relax and enjoy the Sabbath tranquility. My desires turned out to be somewhat delusional.

As the sacrament was being passed, Drake bent down to retrieve a hymnbook off the floor. Suddenly, he jerked his head up and made direct contact with the water tray Samantha was holding in front of me. For the second time in twenty-four hours, I was covered in water—and Drake was screaming.

Grabbing Drake, I made a beeline for the bathroom. Once I'd managed to staunch the flow of tears, I proceeded to try and minimize the water damage inflicted on my clothing. When I was done, I still appeared to have been sprayed in the gut with a garden hose, but at least I was no longer dripping.

Back at our bench, I slid in next to my daughters in time to witness Alex end an argument with Sam by flicking her in the forehead. As a seasoned parent, I know it was my responsibility to restore peace in a calm and loving manner. Instead, I opted for threatening them both with instantaneous death if they didn't knock it off.

With an uneasy truce in place, I returned my attention to the front of the chapel and groaned.

Sister Hughes, a formidable octogenarian in our ward, was mid-lecture on the topic of family history. How had this happened? Every member of our ward knew she was not to be allowed within ten feet of a speaking assignment.

Horrified, I shot my attention to the second counselor in our bishopric. My friend Grant stared back at me with a Cheshire-cat grin that confirmed my suspicions. He'd organized today's sacrament meeting program. Suddenly everything made sense.

Like the rest of us, he may have known better, but Grant happens to be the kind of individual who finds watching a congregation squirm, under a monotonous verbal assault, entertaining. I narrowed my eyes and mouthed, "I hate you." His grin grew even wider as he returned his focus to Sister Hughes and adopted an expression of rapt attention.

Grant Barney and I met during our sophomore year at ASU. While on my mission, I'd developed a love for the game of racquetball. Sadly, I returned home to discover none of my friends had done the same. Wanting to keep my newly acquired skills fresh, I started hanging around the Student Activity Center after classes in hopes of finding friendless gladiators like myself.

One evening, while trolling along the massive complex's upper level, I noticed a tall, gangly guy about my age standing nonchalantly against the metal rails overlooking the courts below. In his right hand he held a battle-scarred racquet. I began to study him more closely. From his awkward appearance, he certainly looked beatable enough, so I approached him confidently and issued a challenge.

We ended up playing for two and a half hours. If I were to do that today, I'd wake up in traction. Nevertheless, by the time we parted ways, I'd not only found a new racquetball partner, but I'd discovered a pretty good friend as well.

Of all my friends from college, Kevin was Marci's favorite. But if pressed, she would admit Grant placed a close second. She liked him so much she practically forced him on a date with her best friend, Stacy. She just knew they were perfect for each other.

Apparently, she was right. Four months later, Grant and Stacy announced their engagement.

To Marci and me, Grant and Stacy were family. Since Marci's death, it's been humbling to learn how much they felt the same.

My recollections were interrupted as the clamor around me began to rise ever so slightly. A sense of relief was drifting through the congregation as Sister Hughes appeared ready to relinquish her stranglehold on the podium, signaling a possible conclusion to our sacrament meeting.

Following the benediction, the congregation stood and began filtering off to their separate destinations. I watched the migration shuttle past me with a sense of relief. I'd survived one more Sunday without familial bloodshed. My reprieve was cut short by the arrival of an obnoxious friend.

"I didn't realize one sacrament tray could get a shirt that wet."

Choosing to ignore Grant's observation, I attacked with a hearty dose of righteous indignation. "What's the matter with you? Asking Sister Hughes to speak on family history just so you can watch everyone go to sleep is kind of sick. You realize that, don't you?"

Feigning innocence, Grant replied, "I didn't ask her to speak on family history. I specifically assigned her the topic of gratitude."

I scoffed. "Don't give me that. You knew she'd ignore the assigned topic when you asked her. This lack of concern for your ward members' welfare should get you released immediately."

Grant laughed again as he provided his signature slap on the back. "I couldn't agree more. If you could take that up with Bishop, I'd appreciate it. By the way, you guys still coming over tonight?"

"Hmm, let's see. My pathetic cheese quesadillas or Stacy's famous pot roast—it's so hard to decide."

Grant shook his head mischievously. "You, my friend, are behind the times. Forget pot roast. I splurged and bought T-bones for the adults and hot dogs for the kids. I have the grill primed, and the seasonings are already on the counter."

Sighing, I looked at my watch. "You should stop talking right now. Are we still shooting for six?"

"Unless you wanna come before. I've got the DVR recording basketball as we speak."

"Four thirty it is, then. Thanks."

Grant slapped me on the back once more before walking away.

By this time, all three of my children had deserted me, and it appeared I was completely alone. However, as I reached down to pick up my scriptures, I sensed a presence lurking nearby.

Instantly, I was on alert. Rarely do people hover in church unless they want you to do something, like substitute Primary or fill in last minute for a Sunday School class. Fearing the worst, I slowly raised my head.

In the space of a heartbeat, I wished I were subbing Primary. Standing rigid at the end of my pew was Sister O'Donnell. Sister O'Donnell is a unique and intimidating soul who was able to look beyond the tragedy and pain of my wife's passing in order to find opportunity.

This good woman has a daughter, Jerlene, who is rapidly approaching forty and has never been married. Now, I don't personally believe Jerlene wants to be married. In fact, I'm fairly certain Jerlene hates the whole concept of marriage, as well as men in general.

Nevertheless, Jerlene's lack of interest has never once tempered her mother's dreams of a wedding. For over a decade, Sister O'Donnell has served as the chief marketing specialist in the "Get Jerlene Married" campaign.

Two weeks after Marci's funeral, I was surprised by a knock on my front door in the middle of the day. Curiosity quickly turned to dismay when I found both Sister O'Donnell and Jerlene waiting on my porch with a plate of beef jerky.

It quickly became obvious that one of my two visitors was hoping to be invited in for a lengthy stay, but I'd been around long enough to know where this visit was headed.

Sure enough, when it became clear that no invitation was forthcoming, Sister O'Donnell plowed ahead with her prepared introduction of Jerlene and asked when I might be available for dinner and a movie. Meanwhile, Jerlene never uttered a word. She just gripped that beef jerky plate tightly in her hands and attempted to melt my head with a stare of contempt and scorn.

I did my best to remain cordial, but I recognized any weakness on my part would be exploited immediately. I had to be firm. Explaining in no uncertain terms that I was not ready to begin dating, I graciously thanked them for their offer but stated I would have to decline. I thought I expressed myself quite clearly. Evidently, I was wrong.

Cornering me at a ward activity several days later, Sister O'Donnell once again laid out her sales pitch/hostage demands. This time, I flirted with being downright offensive.

I told her I wasn't sure if I would ever date again and that having people bug me about it caused such a rage in me, I wasn't sure if I could be trusted not to hurt someone. I may have even cursed. I don't remember. What I do remember is how much I wanted to curse when I saw how effectively she had me trapped this morning.

Rising to my full height, I met my tormentor head on. "Good morning, Sister O'Donnell."

"It's afternoon, Todd."

With a slight nod, I acknowledged my gross oversight. "You're right. I'm sorry. Good afternoon, Sister O'Donnell."

Taking one step closer, further blocking my exit, Sister O'Donnell began, "Todd, when last we spoke, you told me you had no plans to date for the foreseeable future. It has come to my attention that you have recently changed your stance and have, in fact, been seeing women socially."

Dumbstruck, I stammered, "Excuse me?"

"Larry Arnold, from the Mesquite Ward, informed me this morning that he witnessed you out on a date last evening."

She could've told me of her recent acceptance into the space program and I wouldn't have been more surprised. I immediately racked my brain, trying to figure out just who Larry Arnold was. Then it clicked. "Brother Arnold from the high council?"

"Of course Larry Arnold from the high council." Sister O'Donnell doesn't believe in using the titles *brother* or *sister* to refer to anyone younger than herself. She's been known to ask a person's age solely to verify if they are worthy of the designation or not.

Meanwhile, clearly frustrated at having to confirm something off topic, she speedily returned the conversation to her intended course. "We were having our stake missionary training meeting this morning, and he mentioned seeing you last night with a red-headed woman."

Suddenly nauseated, I began to stammer, "*What?* H-how does my name possibly get mentioned in a meeting this morning by a man whose first name I didn't even know until just now?"

Further annoyed that she was once again being taken off topic, Sister O'Donnell grudgingly admitted, "I wasn't actually part of the original conversation. He was speaking with some lady named Maureen and was saying that he saw you last night at a local eating establishment."

"Maureen Littleton?" I asked cautiously.

"Yes, I do believe that's her name."

Unbelievable! I meet this woman for fifteen seconds in a stake center kitchen and suddenly she's become the bane of my existence.

Sister O'Donnell continued, "Anyhow, Maureen was asking if your companion had red hair. When he confirmed that she did, they began discussing this woman and her family. Since I have no interest in the redhead whatsoever, I interjected myself, for only a moment, to verify that it was indeed you who had been out on a date. Larry Arnold stated emphatically, almost rudely one might say, that yes, you, Todd Landry, were most definitely on a date last evening. As such, I would like to revisit the topic of your availability to take out my daughter, Jerlene."

Inhaling deeply, I responded with barely restrained fury. "Umm . . . never. I will never be taking out your daughter. I apologize if I'm being rude, but I'm certain Jerlene hates me, and frankly, I'm not interested either. Have I been direct enough to ensure this conversation never happens again?"

Sister O'Donnell retreated, looking seriously affronted. "Todd Landry, you are the most impertinent young man. I'm beginning to think you might not be worthy of my Jerlene." (That won the award for best unintentional joke of the day. I know for a fact that if Genghis Khan were to rise out of the grave and produce a temple recommend, he would've made the list of people worthy of Jerlene.) "But as you are a Landry, I'm willing to give you the benefit of the doubt and broach this subject with you later when you are demonstrating a better temperament."

I sighed. "Whatever."

Sister O'Donnell stalked away while I remained frozen in place. The fact that my dinner with Emily had been the lead story in at least one church meeting this morning was bothering me significantly. What had I done to justify such intense awareness of my personal life? Grabbing my scriptures, I distractedly ambled out of the chapel.

Entering the hallway, my preoccupation nearly caused me to collide with a slender blonde woman sporting four-inch heels. I started to offer my apologies when I realized she wasn't alone.

"Jason?" Seeing my friend for the first time since our run-in at the golf course only added to my bewilderment. "What're you doing here?"

Also startled, Jason replied defensively, "Going to church, same as you."

"Well, duh! But what are you doing in this building?"

With his eyes darting suspiciously toward an unconcerned father comforting his baby, Jason replied, "They changed my ward boundaries two months ago. Remember? Ever since then my new ward meets in this building right before yours."

With a puzzled shake of my head, I acknowledged, "Okay, I'm sorry. I guess I never put two and two together. I'm just surprised I haven't run into you before."

"Well," Jason's expression of discomfort deepened, "that's because I really haven't been attending here most weeks. By the way, this is Kimberly."

He gestured to the blonde woman I'd nearly leveled earlier. We shook hands as Jason continued, "I've been attending Kimberly's ward for a while now, but the reality is," he said, shrugging awkwardly, "I own a home. And since Kimberly's renting, we decided my ward makes more sense."

Between his explanation and my recent run-in with Sister O'Donnell, I was seriously starting to wonder if I'd woken up in an alternate universe. "Am I supposed to know what you're talking about? Because if I am, I'm really sorry—I have no clue."

Jason laughed nervously. "No, no, it's not you. Um . . . Kimberly and I have been dating for a while and we kind of got engaged this weekend."

My confusion quickly gave way to annoyance. I may have been out of commission lately, but I knew I hadn't been told about *this*. My eyes flicked over to Kimberly. She was staring uneasily toward the front door as if contemplating a sudden break for freedom.

Returning my attention to Jason, I spoke slowly, with a hint of accusation in my tone. "Just to be clear, we've been hanging out on a regular basis for several months, right? And somehow this never came up?"

Shifting uneasily, Jason explained. "Todd, don't be upset. Kimberly and I have known each other for a couple of years. We're good friends who have similar problems. I mean, you know all about my troubles with Tiffany. Well, Kimberly's marriage wasn't any better. She's been someone I could talk to about my divorce, and when she finally decided to leave her husband . . ."

I tuned Jason out and once again observed Kimberly. From the dismayed look on her face, it was obvious she was mentally begging him to stop talking. Of the three of us, only Jason seemed unaware of how inappropriate his explanation sounded.

Forcing my attention back to Jason, I managed to catch the end of his commentary. "That was six months or so ago. We were going to wait until her divorce was final to start dating, but it didn't exactly work out that way. But we both felt it was best to keep things under wraps until her situation was a little more . . . official."

"Uh-huh," I grunted disdainfully.

Like a drowning man unaware he's in water, Jason kept going. "So Thursday, her divorce was finalized, and since we'd been talking about it for months, I asked her to marry me last night."

As he concluded, Jason's tone took on a note of pleading. "I'm really sorry. I didn't want you to find out this way. I was going to call and tell you tonight as a way to invite you to our engagement party this Friday. Obviously I don't need to call now, but I still hope you'll come."

I stole another fleeting look at Kimberly. She looked perfectly humiliated. I attempted a weak smile in her direction before answering.

"Well, first of all, congratulations. I'm happy for you. Completely stunned, but happy. I'm sure I have nothing planned for Friday, but even if I do, I'll find a way to cancel it. Have you told your parents?"

Jason's guilty expression answered before he did. "Not really. We told Kimberly's parents last night, but it was so late we didn't get a chance to tell mine." He hesitated and glanced quickly in his fiancée's direction. "Kimberly hasn't actually met them yet, and we wanted that to be special, so . . . if you could keep this quiet, we'd really appreciate it."

My mind flooded with questions I would never be able to ask. How was he going to break the news to his parents that he was getting married to a woman they'd never even heard of before? I couldn't even begin to imagine their reaction when they found out she'd been divorced a grand total of five days. I wanted to choke him to death right on the spot. Instead, I hugged him, shook Kimberly's hand once more, and then strode down the hall toward Sunday School.

Did You Book That Guilt Trip through Expedia?
Wednesday, April 2

"MY, WHAT A difference a week makes."

Eyeing Dr. Schenk suspiciously, I asked, "What is that supposed to mean?"

Dr. Schenk laughed as he removed his glasses. "I'm simply observing that with one date under your belt, you have become a veritable chatterbox compared to our previous meetings."

Suddenly I felt extremely self-conscious. "I thought you'd want to talk about my first official date in almost a year."

"I do. Please do not misunderstand me. I'm simply struck by how exuberantly you are willing to discuss it."

"I could easily go back to being the strong, silent type."

Chuckling, Dr. Schenk shook his head. "No, no. I much prefer your talkative side. But as you are suddenly willing to verbalize your feelings, I have a few other items I wish to discuss." Returning his glasses to the edge of his nose, he asked, "Why did you seem so disappointed by the news of your friend's engagement?"

"Jason?" I stammered.

"Yes, Jason. Why did you react so negatively? Do you disapprove of his engagement?"

The change in topic left me reeling. Struggling to form an answer, I managed, "Well, yeah."

"Why?"

"I guess because there's so much to disapprove of." My mind was finally beginning to catch up, and I felt stirrings of the same anger I'd experienced the previous Sunday.

Moving to the edge of my seat, I added, "Here's what really bugs me—if we're such good friends, how come I'd never heard of this girl before? I think he's ashamed of himself."

"So you would have preferred he tell you about her sooner?"

"Of course."

With a verbal nudge bordering on goading, Dr. Schenk coaxed, "And what would your reaction have been if he'd told you, say, three months ago?"

I wanted to avoid the obvious trap, but my heightened sense of righteous indignation demanded I continue. "I probably would've discouraged him from getting involved with her."

"Why?"

Irritated by his questioning, I snapped, "Because she was still a married woman. For that matter, he was still a married man when they started their so-called *friendship*."

"So I take it you consider their entire relationship inappropriate."

"Uhh . . . Yeah!"

"And why is that?"

"You know."

"No, I don't know." Dr. Schenk reclined in his chair, placing his fingertips together, as if calling my bluff. "And I'm willing to bet you don't either."

"Come on. Both of them practically screamed 'I'm guilty' the whole time we were talking. They'd crossed lines and they knew it."

"What lines are those?"

This was maddening. "Okay, I don't know the specifics, but it was obvious things weren't right."

Dr. Schenk inhaled deeply and turned his attention to the window behind me. I could sense he was working to craft his next question perfectly. "Is it possible he didn't tell you about his relationship for fear of being judged in exactly the way you've ended up judging him?"

Startled by his query, I warily admitted, "It's a possibility."

Cocking his head to one side, Dr. Schenk continued, "Now, for the sake of argument, let us assume nothing physical has occurred in their relationship. Is it possible there are facts currently unknown to you that might alter your opinion of their behavior?"

"I suppose."

"Have you even thought of asking about those possibilities, or are you content to be disappointed in him?"

I didn't answer. He took my silence as permission to continue.

"Why won't you take Prozac?"

Dr. Schenk let the question hang in the air. For the second time in our session, he'd changed gears so abruptly that I found myself struggling to keep up.

"We've been over this. It would feel like I'm admitting defeat."

"Defeat to whom? The drug companies? They don't know who you are. So tell me, to whom would you be admitting defeat?"

"Myself," I replied guardedly.

Dr. Schenk leaned forward in his chair. "I'm sorry, Todd, but that's a lie. Your refusal to try medication is tied to a deeper issue. An issue that prompts me to ask, why do you feel guilty for seeing me in the first place?"

Defensively, I folded my arms and retreated as far back into my chair as possible. "Are you going to turn this into an Oedipus thing and tell me all of my issues are related to an unexplored hatred of my father?"

Dr. Schenk scoffed. "You need to brush up on your Greek literature. Unless you're planning on gouging your eyes out, this doesn't resemble Oedipus at all. I'm trying to help you understand something. Guilt often leads people to make irrational decisions. Conversely, irrational expectations can often lead people to experience unhealthy guilt."

"So, you're saying that my refusal to take antidepressants and Jason hiding his married girlfriend from everyone are really the same thing?"

Dr. Schenk sighed and relaxed his posture. "Todd, do you know how long I've been treating members of the LDS faith? Twenty years. Now, that doesn't make me an authority on your doctrine, but

I've come to learn several things about Mormons. You tend to see life as black and white."

Feeling the need to defend my religion, I huffed, "There's nothing wrong with standing for something. God deals in black and white. It's the world that invents shades of gray."

"For the most part, I would agree with you. And I happen to believe that what the LDS Church stands for is admirable. Nevertheless, some of the pressures you place upon yourselves are concerning.

"For instance, I completely agree with the idea of promoting abstinence before marriage. On the other hand, I am not in favor of the *Scarlet Letter*–type shame a number of your members feel when they fall short. During the course of my practice, I've treated a significant number of LDS women who suffer from feelings of inadequacy. Often, the root of their problem is an unresolved sense of shame for a moral indiscretion years in their past. Almost unanimously, the women in question have resolved the issue through your form of spiritual cleansing but years later are still struggling emotionally over something they cannot change. Do you know why?"

Suddenly finding my cuticles to be of the utmost interest, I responded, "No."

"Christianity teaches that sexual misconduct is second only to murder in the rankings of sin. Actually, in your faith, I believe it comes in third after denial of the Holy Spirit, but regardless, sex outside of marriage is one of the ultimate misdeeds. Am I correct?"

"You are."

"Then answer this question for me, Todd. Would you rather your daughter Alex be guilty of a moral indiscretion in her youth that is resolved before she marries a fine young man, resulting in her living happily ever after; or would you rather she live a chaste life but marry an emotionally abusive man who, over time, breaks her? In each case, a sin is committed. Which one is worse?"

Feeling trapped, I lashed out aggressively, "That's not a fair question!"

Dr. Schenk shot forward to the edge of his seat. "Oh, it most certainly is a fair question. It's one members of your faith ought to be asking themselves. You've done a grand job in creating high expectations of chastity, but what about your expectations of respect and equality?"

Pointing my finger at him and stabbing the air as I spoke, I retorted, "I was taught respect for women from the day I was born."

His softly spoken comeback was edged with steel. "I'm sure you were, but I've visited with dozens of LDS women over the years. In that time, would you care to guess how many LDS men I've counseled for being emotionally abusive and controlling?"

I looked away without answering.

"None!" he seethed. "Not one in the twenty years I've been in practice."

Dr. Schenk inhaled deeply to collect himself before posing his final question on the subject. "If the expectations are the same, how does this discrepancy occur?"

I hated this conversation. All I wanted to do was to change the subject as quickly as possible.

"What does this have to do with me?" I asked in exasperation.

"It has everything to do with you. Tell me why you feel guilt for being here. Tell me why taking Prozac would make you feel like a failure. Tell me why a need for help in coping with the death of your wife is so abhorrent to your natural instincts."

"I don't know!" I yelled.

"Yes, you do!" he roared back. "You wrote about it one week ago. You may despise the expectations your father places on you with the aid of a well-placed pioneer story, but that doesn't stop you from trying to live up to them at every opportunity. It's time to let those expectations go. They aren't realistic."

I was so angry that I wanted to stand up and throw his table across the room. I let out a primal scream in frustration and then, without any warning, I began to weep.

For several minutes I sat with my hands covering my face as I sobbed. No matter how much I wanted to, I couldn't gain any semblance of control. Finally, as my tears began to subside, Dr. Schenk continued.

"Todd, it's important you understand. Everything we've discussed is focused on you and you alone. Personally, I think highly of your church and its efforts to strengthen the moral bedrock of society. I also believe your judgments of Jason are well founded. But I need you to see that you are part of your own problem."

He gave me a minute or two more to finish

composing myself before he added, "Our hour is up. Think about what I've said. Accepting the loss of your wife is not your largest hurdle. It's simply part of the greater issue—accepting yourself."

Throughout the afternoon, my session with Dr. Schenk weighed on me. Based on his premise, my path to eventual healing suddenly appeared a lot longer.

Thankfully, as evening approached, I was forced to put Dr. Schenk and his analysis aside. Two days earlier, Kevin had called and suggested a double date. I was leery about asking Emily for a second date so soon, but to my surprise, she agreed enthusiastically.

With dusk fading into darkness, I found myself knocking on Emily Stewart's door for the second time in less than a week. She greeted me with a radiant smile so infectious I couldn't help but grin stupidly in return.

As I turned to lead the way back to my car, she grabbed my elbow and stopped me. Some stray blossoms from a nearby tree had wafted onto my collar in the spring winds that were gently blowing all around us. With a light affectionate gesture, she brushed them off for me and, in the same stroke, drove all remaining thoughts of Dr. Schenk from my mind.

Kevin and Caralee were waiting for us at his apartment, and the four of us spent the next three hours cooking, talking, laughing, and eating. It was the perfect second date.

After preparing and devouring a fantastic dinner, supervised by Caralee, we set about making chocolate chip cookies for dessert. Emily was in charge of mixing, and I was assigned to scoop the dough out onto the cookie sheet.

Before long, a good-natured argument arose over which was better—raw cookie dough or a properly baked cookie. To taunt me, Emily scooped a wad of dough with her finger and then placed it in her mouth with a look of sheer ecstasy.

"That's disgusting," I groaned.

"Oh, really?"

The next thing I knew, a large chunk of dough was shoved directly into my mouth. The flavor was divine. However, I was distracted by a far more pressing issue. Emily's finger was in my mouth.

My eyes widened in panic. Staring at Emily, I saw my alarm reflected back at me tenfold. We both seemed to recognize that if she pulled her finger out before I removed the dough, the result would be completely revolting. But if I used my tongue to . . . well, that just seemed obscene. Fortunately, an idea struck me and I puckered my lips around her finger as she drew it out.

Emily's face flushed to a shade darker than her hair. "I'm so sorry."

"Don't be," I countered through my own embarrassment. "You were right: cookie dough is amazing."

She rewarded me with a smile that landed somewhere between gratitude and humiliation.

Later, as we resumed our familiar positions on her front porch, I realized I was no better prepared to say good night than I'd been the week before. Sensing she had no intention of bailing me out this time, I said the first thing I could think of. "Look, I want you to know I had a great time tonight."

Leaning her head back, Emily closed her eyes regretfully and apologized. "I'm sorry I burned your finger on the cookie sheet. I promise I'm not trying to cause permanent damage every time we go out."

"Not a problem. I still have nine fingers left with no visible scar tissue, so—no worries."

Bending down, I kissed her gently on the cheek and whispered, "Good night, Emily."

As I moved away, I saw a dreamy realism reflected in her eyes. Their message seemed to mirror my concerns exactly—*I hope I know what I'm doing.*

"Good night, Todd," she murmured in return before slipping silently through her front door.

Back in Kevin's car, I endured more than my fair share of friendly ribbing. Caralee couldn't stop gushing over how cute a couple we made, and Kevin kept staring at me with the stupidest grin I've ever seen. Within minutes, I was ignoring them completely. Instead, I let my thoughts drift back to the faint hint of Emily's perfume as my lips were brushing her cheek.

However, by the time we dropped off Caralee, my euphoria had devolved into an all-too-familiar sense of shame. I hadn't intended to say anything, but as Kevin returned to the driver's seat, his declaration left me little choice.

"Well, I like her. I mean, I really like her. I haven't seen you this happy since..." Embarrassed at his obvious faux pas, he struggled to recover. "You know, for a long time. What about you? What do you think?"

Staring ahead glumly, I replied, "I feel guilty."

Kevin's head fell to the steering wheel. "Oh, for heaven's sake. Are you serious?"

Annoyed at his callous reaction, I turned and answered indignantly, "Of course I'm serious. I don't know why this is such a hard concept for everyone, but dating again feels like I'm being unfaithful."

"You honestly think Marci wouldn't want you to have a meaningful relationship with another woman now that she's gone?"

"I don't have to think about it because I know it. We're talking about a woman who hated to share french fries, let alone her husband."

He sighed and looked out the driver's side window. "So what're you gonna do?"

"What do you mean?"

Kevin's face had lost all traces of humor as he turned back and repeated, "What are you going to do? It's a pretty straight-forward question. Whether you want to accept it or not, she is big-time into you. If you don't have any intention of taking this seriously, you need to end it, and soon. Otherwise, you're being completely unfair to Emily."

Sighing, I acknowledged, "I know. The last thing I want to do is hurt her. She deserves better."

"No, she deserves you, and you deserve her. You just have to decide if you're gonna get out of your own way or not."

Placing his hand on my shoulder, he added, "Either way, I sure enjoyed seeing the old you tonight. I've really missed that guy. And I know the only reason he showed up is because of that pretty redhead you just kissed on the cheek."

I narrowed my eyes and glared at him.

"What?" he countered defensively, "You thought we wouldn't be watching you? Then you really are stupid. Caralee's already got the four of us playing bridge together in our eighties."

I arched my eyebrows. "She's that serious, huh?"

Kevin withdrew his hand and looked away. "Yeah, I think so."

"What about you?"

He began rubbing his eyes as if he were trying to force rational thought in through his tear ducts. "I've been here so many times. I'm trying not to get my hopes up, but I feel like she could be different."

I started to chuckle and shake my head. In a voice filled with annoyance, he challenged, "See, I know what you're thinking. Yes, I've said that before. That's why I keep telling myself not to get excited."

Despite my skepticism, it was not my intention to bring him down. In an effort to repair any damage I'd done, I said, "Look, if you feel good about this, then run with it."

Searching my eyes for any hint of deception, he asked, "Tell me honestly. Do you think I'm gonna blow this one too?"

I hesitated because I knew how much this question meant to him. Treading carefully, I replied, "Kevin, don't worry about what I think. Don't worry about what anybody thinks. If Caralee's the one, great! If she's not, don't settle because of the pressure from others."

Kevin has always been an emotional guy. Tears had begun to form in his eyes as I spoke, so we sat in silence until he felt comfortable to continue.

"I appreciate that. I really do. A number of people in my life see it differently."

Carefully watching my friend's expression, I could sense a head of steam building just under the surface. He breathed deeply as if he were going to let it pass when suddenly he changed his mind.

"I'm so sick and tired of people I barely know lecturing me on the importance of marriage! My dad told me a couple of months ago that maybe it was time I stopped looking for the perfect woman and just settle for the closest one. I know he was trying to be funny, but it hurt.

"Where is it written that because I'm over thirty I don't get to have my 'Wow!' moment? I don't care what Brigham Young supposedly said a hundred and whatever years ago about being a menace to society. I shouldn't have to treat getting married like a business arrangement devoid of emotion."

I waited a few moments to see if he was done. He was. Once I could see that he was starting to cool off, I proceeded cautiously.

"Kevin, you know you're like a brother to me. So when I ask this, I'm asking because I care. Do you really believe Caralee can provide that moment you're looking for, or does she satisfy enough of everyone else's criteria that you're forcing the issue?"

His tears returned. "I honestly don't know. And that's what scares me."

Feeling a need to lighten the mood, I reached

over and slapped him on the shoulder. "Well, when you figure it out, make the right choice and don't ever look back. And as your best friend, I'll be there to support you either way."

TODD'S LANDRY LIST

San Diego Rerun
Saturday, April 5

TWICE A YEAR, on the first Saturday evening in April and October, the men in my family gather for a raucous night on the town. By raucous, I mean attending a religious broadcast from Salt Lake for two hours followed by a subdued dinner together in white shirts and ties. Conversation consists of sports, politics, and religion. Now tell me, how does it get any crazier than that?

For a family with an overabundance of traditions, this is one I enjoy more than most. It started when I was twelve and had just attended my first priesthood session broadcast with my dad. Driving home from the church, he leaned over conspiratorially and asked if I wanted to go out to dinner, just the two of us. As any boy of twelve would, I jumped at the idea. The best part was getting to choose the restaurant. At the time, I was obsessed with Joe's Barbeque in old town Gilbert, so that's where we ate. Later that night, when my brothers found out (because I told them), their jealousy was an ideal cap to a perfect evening.

My fascination with Joe's lasted another two years, and by then, the restaurant had become part of the ritual. There was something slightly rebellious about wearing our Sunday clothes to a barbecue joint. Each time my mother had to buy new shirts, she would suggest a venue change, but her proposals have always gone unheeded.

When my brothers and I were teenagers, Dad would try and direct our conversation toward the conference we'd just listened to. He had little success. On the other hand, if he was willing to talk sports, specifically the ones we were involved in, he got a much higher level of interaction.

As years went by, my brothers, Mike and Brock, joined the family construction business while I embarked on a career in marketing. Our twice-a-year dinners continued, but soon, the conversation turned from sports to the latest project on the table for Landry Construction. Those were some long and boring nights for me. Then my brother-in-law, Scott, joined our family, and, in deference to him, Dad decreed that business would no longer be discussed at Joe's. Politics quickly took its place.

Tonight, though, as Mike, Brock, Scott, and I sat conversing enthusiastically, my father was not acting like himself. Whether it was talk of the Diamondbacks or the national debate du jour, his distracted responses, devoid of passion, were highly uncharacteristic. Since he and I hadn't spoken since our dinner last week, logic suggested I was the source for his behavior.

Sure enough, within minutes my suspicions

were confirmed when Mike broached a new subject and unwittingly provided my father the opening he'd been looking for.

"Hey, Todd, did I hear Jason Stowell is getting married again?"

Nodding slowly, I replied, "Apparently so."

Mike whistled softly in amazement. "After Tiffany, I thought he'd never go down that road again."

From across the table, Brock asked, "Have you met her?"

Taking note of my father's heightened interest, I warily answered, "Yeah, Kevin and I went to Jason's house last night for their engagement party."

Before Brock could follow up, my father's cool tone cut across the table. "Did Emily go with you?"

A dull headache began to form at the base of my neck. If obscure members of my ward were aware of my personal life, why had I dared to hope my father would remain blissfully ignorant?

Lowering my eyes, I acknowledged, "Yeah, she did."

Glancing upward, I noticed confused looks on the faces of both Mike and Scott. Meanwhile, my father was watching me closely, his face unreadable. I attempted a repentant smile in his direction as a sign of surrender. He looked away quickly, wounded disappointment flashing briefly across his features.

In typical fashion, Brock remained oblivious to all subtleties occurring around him. Still focused on Jason's engagement, he asked, "So what's she like? I mean, this new girl would have to be quite a catch to compare to Tiffany."

Thankful for the reprieve, I turned my attention to my youngest brother. "Oh, she's beautiful. What surprised me, though, is how smart she is. I talked to her for about twenty minutes last night, and, in my opinion, Jason seems to have found himself a winner."

Brock just shook his head and laughed. "Well, I wish him luck. At least better luck than last time."

I chuckled. "Yeah, me too."

Sadly, the diversion of Jason's engagement reached its end as Mike asked, "I'm sorry, but who is Emily?"

Instantly, all eyes were on me.

Shifting nervously in my seat, I replied, "She's a girl I met a couple of weeks ago. I took her out to dinner and . . ."

The rest of my words were lost in the resulting verbal explosion. I was peppered on all sides by eager questions mixed with exuberant congratulations. Every word was unintelligible until my father restored order with his soft but firm voice.

"So allow me to clarify. Jason met Emily before anyone in your family was informed you'd been on a date. Pardon me, make that *multiple* dates."

An uncomfortable silence settled over the table.

"Yes, sir."

"Has Kevin met her yet?"

"He has."

"When did he meet her?"

I almost choked on my answer. "This past Wednesday, when he and his new girlfriend invited us over for dinner."

The edge in my father's voice hardened even further. "That makes three dates."

"Yes, sir."

After a short eternity, my father sighed heavily. "I'm sorry, Todd. I just can't understand why you would keep something like this from your family. This is wonderful news, yet you seem almost afraid to share it with us. Why?"

Meeting his gaze, I responded truthfully. "Dad, please understand—I was worried that if I told you about her, you'd want to meet her. Meeting someone's family is a big deal. I . . . just wasn't ready for that."

Little by little, a smile of understanding spread across my father's face. "I suppose I can see the logic in that. But I hope you know all of us, including your mother, love and support you."

"Of course I know that, Dad." I nodded to everyone around the table to ensure they knew I meant them as well. "I'm sorry. I know I should've been more open about this. It won't happen again, I promise."

As if by magic, my apology defused the tension. My father's smile broadened and the barrage of questions began.

It turned out Brock had known Emily in high school. She'd been a year behind him and two years ahead of my sister, Katie. From the beginning, I'd been aware of our age difference. But having my siblings revel in the fact that Emily had been a sixth-grader during my senior year of high school made me feel depressingly old.

Finally, after I'd been properly interrogated, my father resumed control of our gathering.

"Well, son, she sounds wonderful, and I look forward to meeting her soon. As it turns out, your timing couldn't be better. I've recently—with Mike and Brock's help—reorganized responsibilities within the business. I'm getting older, and it's time for them to take over the day-to-day operations. They've proven themselves to be up to the challenge, so I've scheduled an appointment with our bishop. Your mother and I are going on a mission."

His announcement was met with stunned silence.

Mike and Brock had clearly not been expecting this decision, and their shocked faces conveyed a thousand questions. I was speechless.

Scott, on the other hand, was quick to recover and offer his congratulations. As Dad shook his son-in-law's hand, he did a poor job masking his annoyance with his sons. It bordered on inexcusable that an in-law had beaten them to the punch.

Visibly irritated, he groused, "I didn't realize the news of our serving a mission would be so paralyzing."

His statement managed to elicit the reaction he'd expected. Both of my brothers stood, hugged my dad, and assured him of their excitement. Dad welcomed their newfound enthusiasm and then turned his attention to me.

Through everything, I hadn't moved.

My father's joyous expression faltered as I remained motionless, staring at him with disbelief bordering on anger.

"Todd, you don't seem very happy."

In a quiet, but steady voice, I asked, "How does Mom *really* feel about this?"

His intake of breath, the straightening of his posture, and the disappearance of his jubilant smile told me everything before he uttered a word.

"She's a little apprehensive, but now that I can confirm your situation is under control, I think she'll be fine."

I laughed derisively. "My situation is under control? That's priceless." I directed my attention to my brother. "Brock, Dad rode with you tonight, correct?"

Like a deer in the headlights, Brock glanced quickly between my father and me. "Yeah," he replied cautiously.

"Would you mind if I took him home?"

A layer of ice enveloped our table. I knew I was responsible, but I didn't care.

Waiting for my father's barely perceptible nod, Brock answered, "Nope, that would be fine with me."

"Wonderful." I'd already stood and was in the process of removing my wallet. Throwing a twenty on the table, I said, "It's been great. Can't wait until October. Dad, I'll be in the car." Without waiting for an answer, I marched out of the restaurant.

Almost forty-five minutes later, my father climbed into my van and immediately took the offensive. "That was the rudest display I have ever seen."

Undaunted, I leaned toward him. "Well, I figured screaming a curse word at you might be even less appropriate, but we can go back inside and give that a try if you'd prefer."

"What on earth is prompting this level of boorish behavior?"

I didn't answer. Letting the tension build, I backed out of the parking lot and made my way onto Gilbert Road. Once we were in the flow of traffic, I continued, "It's one thing to put me through the ringer, but now your bullheaded attitude is threatening my children. So if this is what it takes to get your attention, so be it."

Dad laughed. "That's insane. I've never put you through any ringer, and now I'm threatening your children? I have no idea what you're talking about."

I slammed my palm against the steering wheel. "Taking Mom away, Dad. That's what I'm talking about. She's the only mother figure they have right now. They need her. If you want to go on a mission, great! But would it kill you to wait a year?"

He turned and looked out his window, clearly perturbed. "If it's you we're waiting on, it'll be a decade."

"Nice, Dad. And maybe by the end of that decade you'll have figured out what it means to put family first. But then again, probably not."

Indignantly, he whipped back toward me. "Now hold on. I have always put family first."

"That's bull! I'm not even sure we crack your top five."

Lowering his voice, my dad said, "You know what? We need some separation. Pull over, and I'll walk home."

My father's newly softened tone was costing me the high ground. Feigning remorse, I pleaded, "Look, I'm sorry. I shouldn't have said that. But we need to deal with this right now. I can't understand how you suddenly feel this is the perfect time to leave for a year and a half."

"We're not getting any younger, son. Right now our health is good, the finances are in order, and the Lord continues to open up avenues for this to happen."

Inhaling deeply, I asked, "Not to rain on your inspiration, but again, what about my kids? Mom is hugely important to them right now."

"That's what I'm talking about. Your family situation is just one more thing the Lord is taking care of."

It took every ounce of restraint to keep my teeth from clenching. "And how is that?"

"Well, Emily, of course."

I gritted my teeth. "What does Emily have to do with this?"

His patronizing smile seemed to suggest he saw me as a stubborn child refusing to learn a valuable lesson. "Well, obviously you've found someone to take over the role your mother has been filling."

I laughed out loud to keep from screaming. "Three dates, Dad. Three!"

"Your mother and I were engaged after two weeks."

"AAGGHHH!!!" The sound of my rage filled the car. This whole conversation was starting to take on a surreal quality.

"That was remarkably mature, son."

We rode in brooding silence for several minutes. Finally, as we exited the freeway, I accused, "You do realize this is why I wasn't in a hurry to tell you about her?"

"Why? Because as your father, I might encourage you to recognize the Lord's hand?"

"Dang it, Dad! You don't get to do this. I barely know this girl. She's nice and I intend to keep seeing her, but any inspiration I receive regarding her, or anyone else, is between me and God."

Indignantly, my father faced me, thumping the console in between us as he spoke. "As your father and patriarch of this family, I'm entitled to guidance from our Heavenly Father regarding each of my children."

There was absolutely no point in arguing. As exasperating as it was, I wasn't going to win.

"Fine, I've heard your counsel. But, understand, I have no intention of rushing into marriage. My children are still coming to grips with the loss of their mother. They don't need the additional stress of having a new mom shoved down their throats. I can already tell you, Alex isn't thrilled with me seeing anyone."

My father shrugged his shoulders dismissively. "Alex will adjust in time. Children always do. They're much more resilient than we give them credit for."

Glancing away out my window, I muttered, "What a load."

"Todd!"

I shrugged as I returned my attention to the road. "I'm sorry, but it is. Any decision I make will affect each of my kids forever. If I don't pick the right woman, it could be devastating."

"But that's just it. Obviously you need someone who's grounded in the gospel. From what I've heard, Emily is."

Bewildered, I chose to remain silent. It was obvious he was refusing to understand my point.

As we pulled off the main road and into my parent's subdivision, my father decided to switch gears. "Do you really believe I care so little about you and our family?"

"Dad, I shouldn't have said what I said. It wasn't fair and . . . I didn't mean it."

"I think you meant some of it."

"Look, I know you care about me. I really do."

"But do you honestly believe I care about other things more?"

I didn't answer until we'd pulled into his driveway and I'd placed the van in park. Turning to face him directly, I declared, "You missed seniors' night at my last football game in high school."

My pointed recollection startled him. He thought for a moment and then slowly shook his head. "No, I didn't. I arrived just after kickoff."

Nodding, I admitted, "That's true, but all the parents escorted their sons onto the field before the game. Mom walked with me by herself."

"Well, yes. But I had—"

"I know—an assignment at the cannery. You were supposed to get away earlier, but they asked if anybody could stay and help unload a truck. You felt obligated. I remember."

His eyes filled with regret. "Todd, I . . . I'm sorry. I didn't realize it had mattered that much to you. I was just trying to do what was right."

"Trust me, Dad, I know. That's why it's so difficult to be your son sometimes. How am I supposed to compete with *what's right?*"

I waited for an answer, but one never came. Finally, I said, "Look, I'm not trying to make you feel guilty about a football game twenty years ago. Like I said, it was a comment I shouldn't have made. You've been a great father and I love you. I'm just asking if you'll consider postponing the mission for a while longer. Please? I really need Mom here."

He stared down at his hands as he considered my request. "I suppose we can put it off for a couple of months."

Two months fell far short of what I'd hoped for, but then again, a concession of any kind felt like the ultimate victory.

"Thanks, Dad. I really do appreciate it."

Looking up, he added, "Don't ever create a scene like that again. It represented us badly."

"I won't, and I apologize."

"Accepted. Good night, son."

As he stepped out of the car, he turned back as if he wanted to say something more. His eyes remained fixed on my floorboard for a moment before he shook his head and shut the door.

My heart ached as I watched him walk away. For a second or two, I considered getting out of the car and calling him back for a hug. I really could've used it. Instead, I put the car in gear and drove away.

TODD'S LANDRY LIST

Kids Say the Darnedest Things
Sunday, April 6

I HESITATE POSTING tonight. My fear is that I'll say something I don't actually mean, but having said that, I need to vent.

Today, I gave serious thought to killing my daughter. Wow, there it is already—something in writing I wish I hadn't said. I mean, I didn't *really* think about killing her. But I did daydream long and hard about making her life miserable, just like she did to me today.

I knew the time had come for Emily to meet my children. It wasn't something I was looking forward to, but I'd run out of valid reasons to avoid it any longer. So I invited her over to watch the Sunday broadcasts of general conference with my kids and me. I figured it would be relatively safe. Not so.

As the harsh tone of my doorbell echoed throughout the house, Alex jumped from the living room floor as if several volts of electricity had suddenly coursed through her body. With the speed and agility of a world-class hurdler, she cleared the couch and darted to the entryway, far outpacing the rest of us. To the unbiased observer, one might have assumed she was excited to meet our visitor, but that would be wrong. Alex was merely drawing lines for the territorial war she was about to declare.

As I approached from the kitchen, I was just in time to see Alex open the door. From my vantage point, it was apparent that Emily's nerves were on edge just beneath her exaggerated smile.

In a faintly quivering voice, she exclaimed, "Good morning! You must be Alex. Wow! You're just as beautiful as your dad described."

"I look like my mom," Alex replied, her voice cold and emotionless.

With no further comment, she turned and walked out of the room without extending an invitation to enter our home. I was so proud.

Emily's wounded astonishment was obvious. As I approached the door and invited her in, her pleading eyes begged for understanding as to what she had done wrong. Reaching down to give her a hug, all I could offer was a shrug of my shoulders and a heartfelt apology.

Mercifully, Alex's insolence was immediately cushioned by my other two children. Samantha was shy at first and hid quite effectively behind her tumbling blonde locks during introductions. But that all changed once Emily saw the book she was holding and commented on her love for the main character. Within seconds, Samantha had opened up, and soon they were chatting happily on the couch about a wide selection of shared literary favorites.

Subtly, as Emily and Samantha were discussing

worlds of fantasy and romance, Drake sidled his way into the room and hovered nearby, waiting patiently for his opportunity to pounce. When it arrived, he wasted no time seizing control of Emily's attention by introducing his favorite stuffed alligator, Spike.

Thirty minutes later, the conference started.

For the first time in his life, Drake sat quietly for at least half of the two-hour broadcast. I'd love to believe he was listening, but even I am not that naive. Emily had allowed him to remain in her lap, and occasionally she would absentmindedly stroke his hair. I'm not sure what it says about me, but several times, I caught myself fighting back feelings of jealousy.

Eventually, Samantha managed to sneak her way into the four-inch space that existed between Emily and me on the couch. I'm sure we were quite the sight—four people huddled so closely together we resembled a small group of explorers lost in the Arctic without jackets.

Alex, on the other hand, sat as far from our little group as humanly possible. She refused to make eye contact with any of us and said only two things all morning. Both of them referenced her mother. It was lovely.

When the meeting ended, Emily and I moved to the kitchen to prepare lunch. Alex refused to eat Emily's homemade fried chicken, citing some vague stomach ailment. Instead, she chose to make a sandwich and spent all of two minutes with us before stalking off to her bedroom.

After two solid hours of teenage attitude, I was livid. I'm not big on making scenes, but Alex's behavior demanded a response. But before I could move, I felt the gentle touch of Emily's hand on my shoulder. In my adrenaline-fueled anger, I whirled to face her.

Calm down, her eyes told me, and my fury was instantly replaced by shame. Emily was the one being wronged here, yet she was the first to react with compassion. I was horrified to think what message my anger was sending to this sweet and caring woman and what second thoughts about me might be brewing in her mind.

Emily had originally planned to spend the full day with my family. But with a pressure cooker–like atmosphere building throughout my home, she excused herself gracefully and decided to leave after lunch.

As we walked to her vehicle, I tried to express to Emily my frustration and embarrassment over Alex's treatment of her. I also desperately wanted to know where we stood now that my kids were part of the equation. I'm certain I failed to coherently address either.

"I can't . . . I'm so sorry. I knew Alex wasn't crazy about me dating again, but I had no idea she would act like *that*."

We'd arrived at her car, and it was then that Emily paused. "You know, Todd, it's not a big deal. I have a mom, and she means the world to me. If I ever felt like she was being threatened, I would do or say anything to protect her. I'm pretty sure that's what just happened. Please keep that in mind before you go back in there and rake her over the coals."

I nodded halfheartedly and reached forward to

grasp the door handle on her Honda Civic. As I did so, I fought through my nerves to ask the next question that concerned me even more than my daughter's behavior.

"So where does this put us?"

Emily stifled a laugh. Her lustrous blue eyes danced as she gently grasped my elbow and reassured, "I once dated a man for two months who talked non-stop about the towing capacity of his monster truck. If I'm willing to put up with that, I don't think you need to worry about a couple of hours with a mildly rude teenager. Besides, I think I've fallen in love."

My shocked reaction must've been brilliant because Emily immediately burst into laughter before clarifying, "That adorable little boy of yours has stolen my heart."

I could feel the color in my face rising as I awkwardly replied, "Oh . . . yeah, he's a real cutie." (I'm totally ashamed that I let myself use the word *cutie*.)

Capitalizing on her momentary advantage, Emily removed her hand from my elbow and eased several inches toward me. I watched, petrified, as her forefinger rose to caress my cheek as she added, "His dad's not bad either."

My suave response was to grin stupidly since my vocal cords had entirely collapsed within my throat.

Stepping back, she lowered herself into the driver's seat before adding, "Remember, go easy on her. For me?"

My grin melted away at the reference to my daughter. Nevertheless, I nodded in agreement.

Once her taillights disappeared from sight, I turned back toward my house and contemplated my next move.

The door to Alex's bedroom was shut. I hesitated briefly as I calculated whether this was a battle I wanted to pick. Deciding I had no other option, I closed my eyes and knocked.

Her muffled response was barely discernible through the door. "Yeah?"

"May I come in?"

"I guess." I could almost feel her eyes rolling backward.

I opened the door but chose not to move beyond the threshold. Her defiant face had reignited my blood to boiling as she stared at me from across the room. Instantly, I was ready to unload. On the other hand, I had promised Emily not to overreact. So I took a deep breath and calmly asked, "Are you proud of yourself today?"

Her self-righteous façade cracked and she lowered her head to stare blankly at the stuffed otter she held in her lap. There was no reply.

"More important, do you think Mom would be proud of you today?"

I didn't wait for an answer. Shutting the door, I returned to the family room where the afternoon broadcast was already underway. A short time later, Alex joined Sam, Drake, and me without looking in our direction. It was obvious she'd been crying.

Tonight, after her siblings were in bed, she came to my room and apologized. It wasn't a long conversation, but it accomplished what it needed to. In the end, we hugged and parted on good terms. My future involvement with Emily was not discussed.

TODD'S LANDRY LIST

I'm a Gentleman out of Spite
Wednesday, April 9

"I'M CURIOUS, WHY do you blog about our visits?"

Dr. Schenk posed his question with a bemused smirk, as if such a development would never have occurred to him.

"Well, for one, it's my only opportunity to vent any underlying hostility I'm feeling toward you."

His smirk disappeared behind an exasperated eye roll. "You are such a profound comedian. Really, you should look into appearing on the Johnny Carson Show."

I glanced in the direction of a desk calendar several feet away. "Uh . . . Doc? Johnny Carson's been off the air for almost two decades. Plus, I think he's dead."

"I was being sarcastic. I'm surprised you didn't recognize it."

"Touché," I granted. Clearly neither sarcasm nor pop culture references are his strong points.

Returning to his original question, I considered my answer carefully. "I guess the reason I blog about

144

our visits is to clear my head. When I leave here, my mind is usually jumbled. If I let some time pass and then write everything down, I seem to process it a little better."

Dr. Schenk broke out in a wide grin. "That's a good exercise. I'm impressed. You have got to be one of the most brilliant patients I have ever had the pleasure of working with." (Okay, he didn't really say the last sentence, but I'm sure he was thinking it.)

Back in reality, Dr. Schenk consulted his notes. "How are things between you and your father?"

I winced at the memory of our last encounter. "We haven't spoken since last Saturday, so not great."

Dr. Schenk nodded and then asked, "How many times have you seen Emily since our last visit?"

"Four."

"Four? That's a fairly significant number for one week. On a scale of one to ten, how would you rate your enjoyment of these interactions, other than on Sunday, of course, when Alex elected to be a typical adolescent?"

I almost said seven before I stopped myself. Seven would be a lie. "I guess, ten."

"No continued feelings of guilt to bring it down a point or two?"

I smiled to myself. Just last night I'd been asking myself a similar question. "I don't think so. I mean . . ." Unsure of how my sentence was meant to end, I cut myself off. "I don't know."

"How decisive. It's not complicated. Either you are still struggling with guilt or you are not. Which would you say it is?"

Sighing, I admitted, "I love being with Emily. Whatever problems I may have, guilt over time spent with her isn't one of them."

"So problems still exist?"

Several moments passed before I confessed out loud what had been plaguing me for weeks. "I had plans. I had expectations for my life, and now," I exhaled audibly, "it's starting to hit me how many of those things are gone."

Dr. Schenk's expression softened. "I wondered when we would reach this point. With regards to your wife, I believe you have come to a level of acceptance that is healthy. However, Marci represented so much more to you than simply a life partner. Large portions of how you see yourself are tied directly to her. You may have accepted her passing, but now you have the unenviable task of rediscovering yourself."

His words were helpful, but one nagging thought remained. Deep down I knew it was silly, but I couldn't let it go.

"I'm a one-woman man, Doc. That's all I've ever been, and I don't know how to see myself differently. I know it's acceptable to date again, and I know how much I enjoy being around Emily, but this relationship is threatening things I like about myself."

In a voice filled with empathy, Dr. Schenk responded, "Todd, this is normal. But eventually you will accept that you are creating a new reality. All the things you see as being lost now are making way for new things to come. It just takes time."

Dejectedly, I slouched down in my chair. "Yeah, I suppose."

Glancing down at his notepad once again, Dr. Schenk changed course. "I would like to return to the topic of your father. When he suggested that Emily could fill the motherly role for your children, your reaction was remarkably negative. Yet all signs indicate that you are having similar thoughts. Why did his observation warrant such a violent response?"

Slumping even further at the mention of my father, I muttered, "I don't know. Habit?"

"Oh, very good, Todd. Were I not a highly trained psychiatrist with more than twenty years of experience, I might have been deflected by that deep-sounding, yet nonsensical, one-word answer. Try again."

I would like to take back a previous observation. He may stink at pop culture references, but sarcasm he handles pretty well.

Sitting up straight, I replied, "It's not that he's wrong; it's just that it isn't any of his business. Whether or not I move forward with Emily should be my decision, not his. But he never sees it that way. He prefers to proclaim his will as law and then expects me to follow, no questions asked."

Memories of Saturday night's dinner flooded my mind, and I could feel the anger returning. With the intensity in my voice rising, I continued, "When he announced his mission plans the other night, I knew what he was going to say long before he ever got there. I knew it because I'd lived it a thousand times. I really wanted to be wrong, but I knew I wasn't."

Counteracting my agitation, Dr. Schenk calmly interjected, "So the fact that his observations were accurate meant little to you."

"I don't care if they're accurate or not. I don't care if he's right, wrong, or indifferent. He should let me make the decision. But that *never* happens! He just pushes forward with what he assumes is right for every member of his family. Heaven forbid he check with us to see what we think about our own lives."

Without speaking, Dr. Schenk removed his glasses and began cleaning them with his handkerchief. The resulting silence was deafening. Finally, he held them up to the light, and while studying each lens for any additional spots, casually remarked, "Clearly this is a deeply personal issue for you. Were you aware of your voice's decibel level during that diatribe?"

My face flushed. Adopting a more rational tone, I made one more attempt to explain my irritation.

"When he does things like this that affect everyone, we're never consulted; we're just told. It was one thing when we were kids, but as adults, it's insulting. I don't believe my dad cares what I think about anything."

Dr. Schenk replaced his glasses on the bridge of his nose and then asked thoughtfully, "And if he doesn't care about what you think, does that lead you to believe he doesn't care about you?"

"No. I know my dad cares about me. I just don't think he *knows* much about me, nor cares to."

"That's interesting. Have you ever considered that your problems with your father might be of your own making?"

My brow furrowed. "Come again?"

"With the exception of your planned trip to San Diego, has anyone in your family ever seriously opposed your father prior to Marci dying?"

I pretended to think long and hard about his question despite knowing the answer instantly. "No, not really."

"So for all of your childhood years, your father was able to make decisions in a somewhat dictatorial fashion without any obstruction. Is that description accurate?"

Shifting uncomfortably, I responded, "Yeah, I suppose so."

"Why didn't that change when you were adults?"

In the back of my mind, a vision of me on the witness stand at my own trial emerged. "Well, because I guess you could say he was never wrong."

Dr. Schenk inched forward in his seat. "I notice you didn't say he was right."

That was true; I hadn't. Cautiously, I began speaking as if I were afraid my words might explode back in my face. "My dad has a very rigid view of right and wrong. Every decision he makes is based on that view. Therefore, it's difficult to argue that anything he's ever required of our family has been wrong. It's just, at times, I might have chosen a different version of *right* had I been given the chance."

"But you never asked for the chance, did you?"

I shook my head in response.

"So in your father's world, who has upset the apple cart—him or you?"

Indignantly, I declared, "That doesn't justify what he's doing."

"I never said it did, but by your own definition, it doesn't make it wrong either."

That was it. My irritation was melting into pure anger. How could *my* therapist be defending my father?

"What is your point?" I asked curtly. "And when did you become my father's chief apologist?"

Ignoring my insolence, Dr. Schenk replied, "I'm not apologizing for your father. I'm simply trying to help you see your reality more clearly."

"And what's that gonna help me do?"

"Avoid ruining a perfectly wonderful relationship simply because your father approves."

Feeling majorly chagrined, I retreated to the safety of the couch's back cushion. Timidly, I asked, "Do you believe he's ruining my relationship with Emily?"

"He's not doing anything. But let me ask you something. Have you kissed her?"

"No."

"Why? Don't you want to kiss her?"

I rolled my eyes. "That's a stupid question."

"Is it?"

"Of course I want to kiss her."

"Are you afraid she doesn't want to kiss you?"

I smiled wryly, remembering my final moments with Emily when we had been together two nights ago. "I don't think that's a problem."

"I know it isn't guilt that's stopping you. So why haven't you kissed her?"

Apprehensively, I offered, "We're taking things slow?"

Dr. Schenk laughed. "That would be commendable if it were true, but it's not. If you were taking things slowly, you would not have been together four times this last week. I'm also confident in assuming the four times you mentioned don't include telephone calls or text messages. If we did include those, how high would our number be?"

My answer was unintelligible due to extreme mumbling.

"I'm sorry, I didn't quite hear you."

"A lot higher," I confirmed.

"So you are, in fact, not taking things slowly. You are just refusing to do the one thing you know will take your relationship to the proverbial 'next level.' Why?"

I stared at him, dumbfounded. Admittedly, there was logic to his argument, but his explanation felt overly simplified. Fortunately, I was not expected to respond.

"Don't answer me, Todd. In actuality, I have no interest in rushing the physical relationship between you and Emily. If you'd been given time to formulate a proper argument, it would probably include issues with Alex; your mentioned desire to be faithful to one woman; and quite possibly the fact that you're a gentleman; and you're frightened. All of these things are perfectly normal and understandable."

At this point, I was too confused to get frustrated. Shaking my head in bewilderment, I asked, "Then why did we just go through all of this?"

"Because I need to ensure that the idea of winning a stalemate with your father doesn't creep onto the list I just enumerated."

My eyes narrowed as an indication that he should continue.

"Your wife's passing has created problems with your father that didn't exist before. The man you now see as some kind of tyrant is the same man you used to admire."

I looked away in disgust. Dr. Schenk continued on, ignoring me.

"Todd, your father hasn't changed. You have.

"And it's imperative you understand this so you don't make life-altering decisions based on a perceived misunderstanding that's not real. He's doing the same things he's always done. You're the one who's now reacting differently."

Overwhelmed by this new perspective, I sincerely asked, "So what are you afraid I'll do?"

"I don't know. Maybe nothing. I'm simply trying to make certain that you don't jeopardize the one thing proving successful in your battle against depression."

The finality in his statement was powerful. There was nothing more to say. Finally, Dr. Schenk stood, signaling our session had come to an end. We exchanged good-byes, and I left his office still mulling over the implications of everything he'd said.

There's a good chance I'd have spent the rest of my day obsessing over my father issues had it not been for my son. Following my session, I picked him up from my mom's and took him out to lunch at McDonald's.

After devouring a couple of hamburgers and a large amount of fries, we both sat contentedly in our booth, licking ice cream cones. Without warning, Drake casually stated, "I miss Mom."

Having no idea what prompted this declaration, I cautiously agreed, "Me too, buddy. I miss her too."

Drake looked up at me, his face scrunched in consternation. "I saw a picture of her at Grandma's house and it made me think of her. Why do you miss her?"

Grinning sorrowfully, I reached over and tousled his hair. "Because she was pretty cool."

Drake looked stoically ahead while nodding. Returning to his ice cream, he added, "Yeah . . . but Emily's pretty cool too."

Once more I regarded him in surprise. "Really? What makes you say that?"

Without losing focus on his dessert, he stated, "I like her hair." Then, without missing a beat, he added, "Dad, how do they make these ice creams swirly with brown and white?"

That quickly, we were off to other subjects, never to return. I don't know what prompted his outburst, but unexpected validation from a four-year-old can feel pretty good. And for the record, I like her hair too.

An Inconvenient Truth Not Associated with Al Gore

Thursday, April 10

TINY CHICKEN WINGS combined with large-screen televisions are key building blocks in my personal version of heaven. So, when Kevin asked where I wanted to go to lunch with him, Jason, and Grant today, it made perfect sense to me that we convene at the local Buffalo Wild Wings.

Once the location was set, we decided to arrive early so we could see golfer Phil Mickelson tee off in the first round of the Masters Tournament. Since Phil is a fellow Arizona State graduate, my friends and I feel a certain kinship. Phil, on the other hand, has no idea we exist.

From the outset, I'd hoped that today would be all about golf, or at least sports in general. But as usual, Jason had other plans.

We hadn't been seated two minutes before he launched into a tirade about some book he'd just read, detailing the loneliness of Joseph Smith's plural wives. For some reason, he felt blaring music and greasy food provided the perfect setting for a discussion about a long-dead practice of the Church.

My Dr Pepper arrived, and as I inserted the straw into my mouth, I began switching my attention between golf and various baseball games on display all around us. My interest in their conversation was below nil, but despite my best efforts I couldn't shut it entirely out. Then all of a sudden, it happened.

Who said it? I don't know. What exactly did they say? No idea. But something sparked a thought in my mind that I was stunned had not occurred to me before.

Early on in our relationship, I learned that Marci had no patience for frivolous doctrinal debates. She considered arguments about LDS theology a waste of time. If God wanted to provide clarification about anything, He would tell the prophet. And that was good enough for her.

Except when it came to plural marriage. That was a doctrine she was definitely not okay with.

Whenever the topic would arise, she and I would spend hours trying to produce a scenario we could live with. But try as we might, the whole idea of sharing me with another woman remained unacceptable to her. (FYI, I was never a big fan either.)

Exacerbating Marci's issues with plural marriage was her passionate interest in family history. She'd researched her ancestors stretching back hundreds of years. As her inner conflict with plural marriage grew, so did her fascination with one particular forebear—Mary Childress. Mary had been the third wife in a polygamous relationship, and Marci longed to know how this woman had remained devoted to her faith.

Several times, Marci tried to learn more about Mary from her mother. But in each instance, she was stonewalled. Finally, she decided to approach her grandmother. In hindsight, she should've heeded the warning about curiosity and the cat.

Marci's grandmother had a copy of Mary Childress's diary. She lent it to Marci with a warning—what those pages contained was not for the faint of heart.

The diary's account described a life of misery. Although it would not have been diagnosed back then, it seemed obvious to me that Mary suffered from depression. She also had severe self-confidence issues that could be easily attributed to her abuse suffered at the hands of her husband's first wife. As far as the relationship between her and her husband, there was no mention of love at all. In fact, he hardly seemed present.

But perhaps the most devastating thing for Marci was that Mary's testimony was weak when she entered the marriage. Halfway through the diary, there was nothing left. She didn't stay because of her belief in the gospel. She stayed because she had no other options. The account was unbelievably brutal.

There was a time when I wondered if Marci was going to make it. She despised the diary but couldn't leave it alone. In the end, my wife's mental well-being demanded we confront the issue head on.

One evening, I came home to discover Marci curled up on our bed, clutching that cursed book, crying. We spent the next several hours trying desperately to find a compromise between our faith and a practice we found abhorrent.

By the end of the night, we both acknowledged that our belief in the Church was undeniable. But we also agreed that neither of us was comfortable with the concept of plural marriage as we currently understood it. We returned the diary to her grandmother the next day and vowed never to think about it again.

It's been years since I thought about that conversation. So much of what we discussed is gone from my memory. But today, I remembered vividly one of Marci's last pronouncements on the subject. She stated emphatically that she had no intention of sharing me. Ever!

At the time, I blew it off. Why would we ever have to worry about anything like that? But today, in the middle of a crowded restaurant, it struck me how that conversation suddenly had real implications.

Emily's never been married. That means Emily is not sealed to anyone. I felt sick.

Kevin was the only one to notice my sudden change in appearance. Staring at me with a great deal of concern, he leaned over and quietly asked if I was okay.

Barely acknowledging his question, I nodded and made an excuse about needing to use the men's room. I don't think he was convinced, but at that moment, I didn't care.

To my relief, the men's room was deserted. Walking to the sink, I leaned against the counter and stared at myself in the mirror. In my eyes' reflection, I saw all of the insecurities about dating again returning with a vengeance.

In that moment, I did something I never thought I'd do while standing in front of a bathroom mirror in a public restroom.

I prayed.

I prayed like I hadn't prayed in a while. I begged for understanding. I pleaded to know if my wife was supportive of my current relationship. I asked for any kind of comfort and reassurance that I would not have to walk away from the best thing that had happened to me in months.

Eventually, I ran out of things to say. No answer-filled visions had come, but at least I felt calmer. I splashed some water on my face, dried off, and returned to our table.

As I approached, I noticed Kevin watching me closely. I gave him the "please don't draw attention to me, we'll talk about it later" smile. He nodded slightly in acknowledgement but continued to look concerned.

Grant, obviously sick of Jason's pot-stirring, noticed my return and gave me a chance to weigh in on their discussion. "I'm surprised we haven't heard from Todd. Please tell me you have an opinion that will help me out with this moron."

For no logical reason, I was suddenly livid with Jason. Why had he brought this up? I'd have been fine if not for him. I decided to retaliate by firing a verbal fastball right between his eyes.

"To be honest, I don't get why Jason is worried about plural marriage in the first place. He's already found a way to get the only benefit polygamy offers without having to worry about the responsibility. He'd make Henry the Eighth proud."

Jason's pained expression triggered instant remorse. I hadn't meant to be quite that cruel. Quickly, I went to work on damage control.

"Sorry, man. That was below the belt. Let's just drop this subject and talk about whether you and Kimberly have decided on a date."

Jason visibly relaxed. "We're looking at the twelfth of July."

Grant snorted with disgust. "Why is it people in Arizona continue to schedule weddings in the middle of the summer? Do you hate your family and friends, or what?"

"Look, if it was up to me, we'd be married this weekend," Jason protested. "But I'm not getting a lot of say in the matter." His words implied frustration, but his tone revealed the truth. He was smitten.

"What about you two?" Grant asked, looking pointedly at Kevin and me.

I didn't say a word. There was no way Grant could've known how bad his timing was. Kevin, on the other hand, surprised everyone.

"We're talking about it."

"*What?*" Jason and I demanded in unison.

Insulted, Kevin laced his retort with a shot of bitterness. "Don't act so shocked. We've been seeing each other for a while now. I think it's a natural conversation for us, given our ages."

I knew it wasn't the time or the place to get too personal, but I couldn't help myself. "Are you sure? I mean, just the other night . . ." I wasn't sure how to finish my sentence.

"I know. I said I didn't want to settle. But I've thought about it, and I don't feel like I'm settling. Besides, we're not engaged yet. We're just batting it around a little . . ." He paused to allow a slight grin. "And it feels good."

Men are wonderful creatures. In this exact scenario, a group of women would've had a three-hour discussion dissecting Kevin's feelings. They'd have rehashed every moment Kevin and Caralee had ever spent together and cried. A lot. My reaction was to reach over and slap him on the shoulder twice while speaking for everyone at the table. "Well, good. I'm happy for you." And with that, we finished our chicken wings and debated Mickelson's chances of winning over the weekend.

A mother's intuition is an amazing thing. After my panic attack at the restaurant, I'd managed to put on a good face and fake my way through an entire hour with my three best friends. Yet, when I stopped at my parents' house afterward to pick up Drake, my mother immediately asked, "What's the matter?"

I was shocked at her level of perception, but I still tried to pretend like nothing was wrong. "I'm fine, Mom. Is Drake ready to go?"

"Son, I'm your mother, and I can tell that you are not fine. You may not want to talk about it, but something is definitely bothering you."

I love my mom. Her no-nonsense approach reminded me that, regardless of age, sometimes a man just needs his mother.

Not knowing where to start, I just blurted out, "Emily's not sealed to anyone."

"Yes?" Her expectant grin indicated she was waiting for more. When nothing else came, her smile faded as the realization of my statement hit home. "Oh, Todd. Come here."

Her embrace was exactly what I needed. I managed to keep my emotions under control, but I held onto her as tightly as the first day she'd dropped me off at kindergarten decades earlier.

Eventually we separated, and she ushered me into the house. Drake was engrossed in a movie, so we sat down at the kitchen table, and I shared everything.

When I finished, she shifted her gaze to the window and sighed. "Todd, I'm so sorry. As your mother, you know I'd do anything to help, but I don't have any answers on this one."

I groaned. "That's disappointing. I just wish I knew what Marci really felt about this. Well-meaning people tell me all the time how sure they are that she would want me to get remarried. If that's true, how come I'm not sure?"

Placing her hand gently on my knee, she soothed, "Son, lots of times people profess to know things when they really don't. I guarantee that no one truly knows what Marci thinks. They can tell you what they want to believe, but no one actually knows. And we likely never will in this lifetime."

Defeated, I closed my eyes and slumped back in my chair. "So what do I do?"

"The simple answer is to stop worrying about it. But I understand how easy that is for me to say. The truth is, I don't know how I'd feel if your father were in the same situation. I do know I don't want to share him with anyone. But I have no idea if that will change once I have the added insight of the afterlife. The one thing I can say with certainty is that I wouldn't want him to be miserable."

I chuckled humorlessly. "I love you, Mom, but that didn't help at all."

She laughed quietly in return. "I'm sure it didn't. Look, if it's advice you want, all I can suggest is living the life you have in front of you. I respect your concern for Marci's feelings, but she isn't here. Emily is.

"Now, I know you bristle when your father says things like this, but trust that God will provide some help along the way as well. He's effective at that if we allow Him to be."

Hearing my mother's rational thoughts provided the peace I was looking for. She squeezed my knee in her reassuring way and then reclined in her chair as well. Together we sat in silence as I allowed the peace of the moment to settle my soul. In due course, I recognized it was time to go, but a final thought had occurred to me.

"Should I discuss this with Emily?"

My mother bolted upright in her chair. "Oh, my heavens, no! What on earth would cause you to think that's a good idea?"

Stunned at her reaction, I stammered, "I . . . I don't know. I just want to be honest with her."

Mom shook her head at my naivety. "Son, there's honesty and there's idiocy. Talking to Emily about this would definitely fall under the latter."

She stood and I quickly followed suit, but before I could move to retrieve Drake, she gently grabbed me by my shoulders. Staring deeply into my eyes, she said, "Relax, sweetheart. Take time to get to know this girl and see where life leads you. Most things in life work themselves out in the end if you'll just have the patience to let them."

My lips turned upward in a half-smile my heart didn't feel. "I'll try."

"You do that. And remember, every time you're tempted to open your big mouth and mess things up, think back on what I've told you. Then remind yourself your mother always knows best."

I smiled fully and kissed her on the cheek. "That's true, Mom. You always do."

TODD'S LANDRY LIST

The Best Laid Plans
Saturday, April 12

I'VE OFTEN WONDERED how kissing, as a concept of showing affection, came to be universally accepted. Don't get me wrong—it sure beats any alternative I can come up with, but still.

Nevertheless, since the practice has been around for a while, those of us in today's world face an intimidating level of pressure to be "good" at this mating ritual. Everyone knows it's true—few things are worse than having a first kiss go badly.

As vividly as if it were yesterday, I remember how nervous I felt before my first kiss with Marci. More than anything, I wanted it to be special. So when I felt I was ready to make my move, I tried to prepare for it by creating the perfect evening.

However, as one might expect, everything that could go wrong that night did, and I found myself driving her home, frustrated and kiss-less.

In Marci's defense, I never fully explained my intentions ahead of time. And to make matters worse, she ended up having a major confrontation with one of her professors just hours before I picked her up. For the entire evening, she fumed about male chauvinistic instructors and the injustices of the American educational system. It wasn't until we were driving home in silence that I think she realized more was at play than just a random subpar date.

When we arrived on her doorstep, I told her I was tired and was just going to head home. She kept asking me what was wrong, but my bruised ego wouldn't allow me to acknowledge any problem at all.

I wish I could say I didn't mean to hurt her feelings—but I did. After all, it was only fair. Her obliviousness to all of my planning and hard work was crushing. The only weapon I had at my disposal was to be a uninterested jerk, and I chose to exploit it to the hilt.

As I turned to go, I began congratulating myself on what a fantastic snot I'd been when suddenly I was stopped cold. Marci had started to cry. Whirling around, my first inclination was to rush to her side and offer comfort. But with my pride still smarting, I hung back.

Tentatively, I offered, "Are you okay?"

Amid many tears, her apology burst forth like a tidal wave. "I'm so sorry. I've been absolutely horrible tonight. You did all these nice things for me, and all I could think about was school. I ruined everything."

I really wanted to scream at her, "Uh . . . YEAH!" But instead I gently placed my arm around her shoulder. "Don't worry about it. You had a rough day. I should've been more sensitive and not forced this on you in the first place."

Now had I resorted to nasty sarcasm, who knows

how things might've ended up? Instead, my kind (although admittedly insincere) response turned out to be exactly what she needed to hear. Slipping her arms around my waist, she gazed up into my eyes longingly and waited.

As it turns out, understanding subtle feminine nuance is not my strongest quality. I continued to stand there, gaping stupidly back at her until finally, she softly, but firmly, grabbed the back of my neck. The next thing I knew, she'd pulled me in for what is still the most passionate kiss I've ever been a part of.

If I concentrate hard enough, I can still feel the exact pressure of her lips on mine. I'd never experienced anything quite as magical. I knew right then that this was the girl I had to marry.

When we eventually separated, with a shy, self-conscious smile, she warned, "You better be careful, Mr. Landry. It's possible I'm falling for you."

My initial reaction was to giggle like a concussed caveman. Instead, I managed to blurt out, "Well, Miss Johnson, considering I fell for you weeks ago, I suppose I'm willing to take my chances." That line earned me the second best kiss I'd ever had. And I've never kissed another woman since.

Until tonight.

My day started out miles away from any thoughts of romance. Alex and Sam had left mid morning for an all-day shopping extravaganza with Marci's mom. When it comes to shopping, I rarely allow my girls the amount of mall time they truly desire. On the other hand, Grandma Johnson is a deal-finding, card-swiping, shop-all-day dynamo. The woman is amazing.

Mid afternoon, the phone rang. It was Alex calling to see if Drake and I wanted to meet up with them for frozen yogurt. Not wanting to intrude on their grandmother's time, I declined.

Before hanging up she asked, "So what are we doing tonight?"

Drawing a deep breath, I answered, "Well, Drake and I weren't sure what time you'd be home, so we invited Emily over for movies and pizza. Is that all right?"

The silence on the other end of the line spoke volumes.

Desperate to find safer ground, I changed subjects and asked how their day was going so far. Her attitude brightened instantly as she described her two-hour quest to find the perfect handbag.

My first impulse as a father was to inform my thirteen-year-old that she needed a purse like I need a matching beret and scarf set. Nevertheless, I was thankful for the tension break, so I said nothing. Following a lengthy description of her newfound leather masterpiece, we said our goodbyes and hung up.

Almost immediately my phone rang again. This time it was Marci's mom asking if she could keep the girls overnight. Alex's manipulation of her grandmother was incredibly transparent. Even so, I agreed.

When my girls arrived home to pack their overnight bags, it was quickly discovered that Alex hadn't mentioned anything about Emily to Samantha. Once that news was on the table, Sam tossed her small duffle bag back into her closet and declared she wasn't going anywhere.

Alex, on the other hand, remained undeterred. So, together, she and I walked out to her grandmother's car so I could say good-bye and explain Sam's sudden change of heart.

Marci's mother understood completely. In fact, when Alex was buckling her seat belt, Grandma Johnson grabbed my hand and squeezed it in a way that expressed, "I'm sorry Alex is acting this way, but please know that I'm so happy for you." It was quite impressive. I've never been able to make pressure from my hand say so much.

In response, I half smiled and then walked around the car to the passenger window. I gave Alex a quick peck on her cheek, which she instantly wiped away with the back of her hand.

Glaring at me, she huffed, "Dad, I'm thirteen."

I raised my eyebrows. "And your point is?"

"I'm too old for kisses from my father."

I leaned my head through the open window and moved within an inch of her ear. "Someday you'll be thirty, and I'm still going to kiss you on the cheek. You can accept it now or you can fight it. I really don't care which."

Backing away from the car, I shrugged my shoulders and presented my warmest, loving smile. Her vicious stare would've frightened me had it not been the exact reaction I'd been hoping for.

As I stood waiting for their vehicle to disappear from sight, a sense of disappointment enveloped me. Just as Alex could do nothing about my fatherly displays of affection, neither could I force her to give Emily a chance. The irony was not lost on me.

My regret over Alex's departure dissolved quickly as I returned to my living room. Drake and Sam were arguing over who got to sit by Emily when she arrived, and their excitement warmed my heart.

Injecting myself in their dispute, I suggested neither one of them would get to sit by her because I planned on taking both sides. I should've paid closer attention to their conversation. Up until then, they hadn't figured out that two spaces would be available. Suddenly everything was fine. Sam would take her right side while Drake would take her left. I was to be left on the floor.

An hour later, Emily knocked on the door.

I have to hand it to her. While she may not be making any headway with Alex, in the eyes of my younger two children, she's a rock star. She brought an entire pizza each for Drake and Samantha, covered in their favorite toppings. When she announced that they each had their own carton of ice cream as well, both seemed ready to request her immediate deification.

Before we were even done eating, the debate over which movie to watch began. We eventually settled on *The Sound of Music*. It wasn't my first choice—or even my 183rd—but I lost fair and square in a democratically held election. So not only did I get to sit on the floor, but I would do so while being subjected to the dulcet tones of Miss Julie Andrews.

Less than twenty minutes into the movie, the nuns had kicked Maria out of the abbey, and Sam had succumbed to the effects of pizza, ice cream, and an overly scheduled day.

My daughter looked almost angelic as she lay with her head resting on Emily's lap. Meanwhile, Emily's focus had drifted away from the television and was fixed intently on the face of my sleeping daughter. I couldn't help but notice the affection in her eyes as she ran her fingers through Samantha's hair.

After an additional half hour of von Trapp family exploits, my attention was drawn to the steady breathing of my son. I stole a glimpse behind me and found Drake nestled tightly against Emily, snoring softly as only a little child can.

Despite being buried by my offspring, Emily politely declined when I suggested carrying them off to bed. Disgruntled, I resumed my position on the floor.

Finally, feeling far too much in common with the lonely goat herder, my patience could take no more. I stood, stretched my back, and reached for my daughter.

Sam's breathing never broke rhythm as I carried her to her room. I was hoping for the same with Drake, but as I extracted him from his little corner of Nirvana, his foot caught on something and he was instantly awake.

Glancing around like a startled animal, he quickly surmised his time with Emily was coming to an end. It was then that negotiations for a reprieve began in earnest. Once it was apparent none would be granted, he played his last bargaining chip and demanded Emily be the one to tuck him in.

I smiled as I watched Emily lay him in his bed. Kneeling by his side, she whispered softly in his ear and smiled lovingly as she stroked his face. His dreamlike grin was priceless. As she moved to go, he grabbed her hand and coerced one final hug. Squeezing her tightly, he stage-whispered in her ear, "I love you, Emily."

"I love you too, Drake. Sleep well."

His smiled broadened even further as he released her and closed his eyes.

As she backed out of his room, Emily closed the door silently and turned to face me.

Leaning against the wall, I said, "You're amazing. Other than his grandmothers, my son has shown no interest in a female for almost a year. It drives my daughters crazy, not to mention my baby-hungry sister, but he doesn't care. Then you come along and suddenly he's snuggling up and confessing his love."

She smiled and looked back as if she were able to see him through the closed door. "He is one of the sweetest little boys I've ever met."

Unsure of what to say or do, I bulldozed the tender moment by blustering, "Thank you for telling him you love him. I know he seemed out of it, but trust me—he'll remember. And he'll brag about it for days."

Through the shadows of my darkened hallway, I could just make out the faint blushing of her cheeks as she turned back to face me. "Now you're just trying to make me feel good."

"No, really. If a beautiful woman says she loves

you, you're required to get as much mileage out of that as possible. He may be four, but he's no dummy."

Subtly moving several inches toward me, she murmured in a voice betraying uncertainty, "Do you really think that?"

"Think what?"

She dropped her gaze as if ashamed. "That I'm beautiful."

Now it was my turn to blush. "Well . . . yeah. I told you that the first time we went out."

"I assumed you were just being nice."

Her vulnerability was both heartbreaking and intoxicating. Unconsciously, I further closed the gap between us.

"I *was* being nice. That doesn't mean I wasn't being truthful."

As she raised her eyes to mine, pooling tears reflected some inner struggle that I assumed had little to do with me.

"Todd, what are we . . ."

I'll never know the rest of that question as I tenderly pulled her toward me and kissed her.

The touch of her soft lips was even better than I had imagined it could be. As she warmed to my impulsive advance, I could feel her initial tension melt away as her body pressed closer to mine.

I don't know how much time we spent standing in my hallway locked in each other's arms. What I do know is how quickly we separated when the bedroom door behind us opened.

Drake was standing in his doorway staring blankly in our direction. I'm fairly certain he had no idea what he'd just interrupted, but as a parent, I was still mortified. For a brief eternity, the three of us stood frozen in place, staring at each other. Finally, I decided to prompt him.

"Drake, buddy? You okay?"

He looked at me with a frown before turning to Emily. "I need a drink."

Emily smiled warmly as she bent down to pick him up. "Well, then let's get you a drink."

Together, they disappeared into the kitchen. I stayed behind.

Running my fingers through my hair, I exhaled slowly as I tried to make sense of what had happened. I couldn't come up with a concrete answer, but I knew I liked it.

A short time later, Drake was fully hydrated and back in bed—and the moment between Emily and me had ended.

At no point did we try to talk about what had happened. I'm sure that will come eventually. Instead, Emily suggested it was time for her to go, and despite how much I wanted her to stay, I reluctantly agreed.

The walk to her car passed in silence, but as I opened her door, I felt like I should try and say *something*. The best I could come up with was, "Sorry that Drake kinda . . . interrupted . . ."

She placed her index finger on my lips as she interjected, "Look, I know we aren't sure where this is ultimately headed. But please don't ever apologize for your children being a part of it. Everything about tonight was perfect. And I mean everything. To be completely honest, it felt like a wonderful dream."

She paused, as if unsure whether she should continue. "But then I guess that's how I know it's real. If it were a dream, your son's hair would've been red."

Her timid expression hinted that she'd just revealed a small portion of her soul. I knew the next few moments were critical. Uttering a quick prayer, I bent down and kissed her gently one more time.

"You're right. Everything about tonight was perfect. I can't wait to do it again. Good night, beautiful."

TODD'S LANDRY LIST

There's a New Sheriff in Town
Sunday, April 13

BEING A BISHOP in the LDS Church has got to be one of the toughest religious volunteer jobs ever. Now, I suppose the sacrificial victim being thrown into a volcano might take exception to that observation, and I'd probably have to concede the point, but none of that changes the fact that being a bishop is hard.

First, there's the time commitment. I've seen firsthand the hours it takes to be a successful leader of a ward. It's a full-time job—for a man already holding down a full-time job.

But it's not just time. It goes much deeper than that. Because of how most LDS people view their role in the Church, bishops are often approached to be marriage counselors, psychiatrists, employment specialists, real estate advisors, and/or givers of spiritual blessings beyond the capacity of the common Mormon man. (Sarcasm intended).

Admittedly, this is a phenomenon I've been guilty of myself. When I hit rock bottom following Marci's death, it never once entered my mind to seek out a trained therapist myself. Nope, I needed to see my bishop.

It's hard to believe that was only four months ago.

In hindsight, I don't know what I expected Bishop Lincoln to do. He has no training in grief counseling. Thankfully in our stake, the bishops are trained to provide specialist referrals when issues of depression or anxiety arise. No expectations are placed on them to shoulder the emotional problems of their wards. The spiritual problems are plenty.

Why am I even talking about this? Well, because today Bishop Lincoln—the man who referred me to Dr. Schenk—was released.

As the announcement in sacrament meeting was made, my attention became transfixed on this man who had seen me at my lowest. He was sitting comfortably on the stand with a look of serene joy. I felt happy for him. He'd served admirably, and although I'm sure he felt there were things left undone, I could see he was a man at peace.

In contrast, his replacement did not appear calm at all. In truth, I can't remember Grant Barney ever looking so serious.

Following tradition, Grant was asked to address the ward just ahead of Bishop Lincoln. Grant is an amazing speaker, and today, like always, I found myself caught up in anticipation of what he might say.

After clearing his throat, he began, "First of all, I want to express my gratitude for Brother Denton." Brother Denton had just been released as first counselor. "He helped make my transition into an already functioning bishopric very smooth. I'm privileged to call him my friend.

"I also want my friend Todd Landry to know how much I love him. I wish with all my heart that the circumstances leading to my call as second counselor had never occurred. More than anything, I wish he were speaking to you right now instead of me."

I felt my ears turn red. The fact that I had to be released from the bishopric following Marci's death still makes me uncomfortable. I know it shouldn't, but it does.

Feeling hundreds of eyes casting glances in my direction, I instinctively looked to Bishop Lincoln. He was nodding at me with a reflective grin, suggesting he echoed everything Grant had just said. My eyes filled with tears at this unexpected acceptance of my service. Embarrassed, I smiled quickly in acknowledgement before returning my attention to Grant.

"I want to express my admiration for Bishop Lincoln. He is an amazing man who has dedicated all of his time and effort these last six years to the people of this ward. The sacrifices he's made on your behalf are awe-inspiring. He reminds me of my father, who served as a bishop when I was a teenager. These men are my heroes."

Whispered sentiments of understanding filtered through the congregation. They died quickly with Grant's next declaration.

"However, to expect the same level of time and attention from me as your bishop would be a mistake."

Despite varying levels of astonishment erupting

all around me, no one appeared more stunned than the stake president. Although he recovered quickly, the image of his mouth literally falling open is one I'll carry with me for some time.

Surprisingly, the only person seemingly not caught off guard was Bishop Lincoln. The smile on his face never shifted one iota. Knowing Bishop the way I did, his lack of a response spoke volumes. Whatever our new bishop was saying, it was done so with the blessing of his predecessor.

Dropping his focus to the podium in front of him, Grant continued, "I'm sure that's not what many of you expected to hear. I hope you'll keep an open mind as I explain.

"I have a strong testimony of this Church. I wouldn't accept this calling if I didn't. But my testimony requires me to examine my upcoming service."

Throughout the congregation, not one muscle moved, not one child whimpered. Every single person's attention was centered on our new spiritual shepherd.

Raising his eyes and looking out over the crowd, Grant expounded, "When I was thirteen years old, my father was called to be the bishop of our ward. Six years later—three weeks before his release—he conducted my missionary farewell. When I called him earlier this week to tell him about my new calling, his initial response surprised me. It wasn't filled with the congratulations I'd expected. He *was* proud of me and assured me I was about to receive some of the greatest blessings of my life. But he was quick to caution me as well.

"When my dad was called as bishop, he made the decision to give his all in serving our ward. He did so with my mother's approval. But he explained to me that the day we sat in his office for my missionary interview, he was struck by how little he genuinely knew me. He was heartsick to realize he felt closer to ward members who were struggling with personal issues than to his own son. I never knew any of this, but after I left his office, he closed the door and wept. He told me he never regretted accepting his call from the Lord, but if given the chance again, he would reevaluate the amount of time spent away from his family."

Tears formed as Grant carried on. "I have a son who's turning thirteen soon. The world is a different place today, and my son needs a father, not an absent guardian who practically lives at the church building.

"So please understand—I will not come running at each and every member's beck and call. I will not respond to last-minute pleas of desperation if there was plenty of time to deal with a problem beforehand. I will not lose any of my children over neglect created by this calling. I will serve, but I will be a father first and a bishop second."

He hesitated for a moment. When he spoke again, a tone of compassion filled his voice. "As your bishop, I love each of you very much. But I love them more." He finished with his testimony of the Savior and sat down.

I have never in my life heard a family ward so quiet. Even the small kids seemed to sense something unique had just happened.

After the closing prayer, I waited several minutes for an opportunity to catch Grant's eye and wish him my best. When the moment arrived, I grinned and flashed him a thumbs-up. He smiled in return and motioned for me to join him in his office.

Once inside, he closed the door and allowed his strong façade to evaporate. He collapsed into his chair, leaned his head back, and closed his eyes.

"This is not what I wanted."

"Well, you gave it your best effort to lose the job on day one with those comments. Well said, by the way."

He opened his eyes and glared at me. "I'm not gonna be a good bishop. I don't have the patience to deal with these people."

Thinking long and hard before commenting, I finally said, "You're right. You don't have the patience. But then again, who does? Bishop Lincoln was the grumpiest old guy I'd ever met before he became bishop. I'm sure at the time he felt the same way you do now. That's why you pray. And then pray again. I'm not saying it'll be easy, but you'll be fine. In fact, you'll be better than fine."

After sitting together in silence for a while, he eventually appeared to accept my assessment and moved on. "I appreciate the compliment, but let's see how you feel once I've told you why you're here."

"You mean I'm not here to give you the pep talk you need to get out of the gate?"

"No. I need to extend a call to you."

My stomach dropped. "What are you about to do to me?"

"I need you to serve as Boy Scout advancement chair."

My reaction was immediate and highly volatile. "WHAT! Are you insane? You must be clinically insane! You know how I feel about Scouting. I hate Scouting. I hated Scouting when I was a Scout. Why on earth would you—"

Cutting across my diatribe, Grant held up his hands in defense and cried, "Whoa! Enough already. I'm perfectly aware of how you feel. As crazy as it sounds, your distaste for Scouting is one of the main reasons I need you there."

I remained highly skeptical. "Well, that makes *perfect* sense. Look, I can tell the stress of being a new bishop has gotten to you. Call me back in a week or two when you've had time to think about this rationally and we can talk then."

As I moved to stand, he waved me back into my chair, his expression one of exhausted pleading. "Todd, hear me out."

Knowing there was nothing he could present that would make his request palatable, I humored him. "Fine, say what you have to say."

"Brother Lattimore is literally going to drive people from the Church if I don't replace him immediately. Our new Scoutmaster gave us an ultimatum three days ago, saying if he had to work with that man one more month, he was done. He'd move out of the ward if he had to. I need someone dependable, but not so . . . intense."

Right then, I knew there was no getting out of this. Brother Lattimore had been in the ward for only six months, but he was already legendary. Scratch that—infamous would be a better word.

His most notorious stunt so far was standing up in the middle of a blue and gold banquet and making three eight-year-olds cry because they had jumbled the order of commands in the flag ceremony. How he avoided getting lynched that night by a mob of angry parents is still mystifying.

"Are you asking me to do this as a friend?"

"No, I'm calling you to do this as your bishop."

I huffed grumpily. "Do I have to go to that monthly meeting where everyone wears their green socks and silly neckerchiefs?"

"You mean roundtable?"

"Yeah, roundtable."

"Yes, you do."

"We're no longer friends. I hope you understand that."

"I do. So does that mean you're accepting?"

"I'm not accepting anything, but I'll do it."

"Thank you. I really appreciate it."

We stood simultaneously, and he walked me to the door. Before he could open it, I grabbed him by the shoulder and gave him a masculine hug. "You're gonna be great, Bishop Barney."

He stepped back and wiped away an unexpected tear that had escaped down the side of his cheek. "What gives you that idea? Was it the astonishing way I just managed to drive away my best friend with my first official act?"

I grinned. "No, it's in spite of that."

Growing serious, I added, "You know we're good,

right? I mean, yes, I do hate you at this moment, but we're still good."

He gave me a tired smile and hugged me again. His voice caught as he said, "Pray for me."

"Always. Good luck, Bishop."

TODD'S LANDRY LIST

It's Not You, It's Me . . .
Wednesday, April 16

ONE PERFECT MORNING is forever etched in my memory. The sky was as blue as the clearest mountain lake and the songs of a hundred birds overpowered the distant drone of traffic near my parents' home. In the early morning, the first rays of sunlight highlighted the vibrant green of freshly cut grass that can only be associated with Arizona in the spring.

It was my wedding day.

For as long as I live, some things about that day I will never forget. My first venture outside in the early dawn is one of them.

Regrettably, several other things are conspicuously absent from my fond remembrances—and one is my first kiss with Marci as husband and wife.

I blame the temperature in the room where our ceremony took place. It was so hot. I couldn't focus on anything being said or anything happening around me. My mind was in a million different places at once.

Of course, having at least one ounce of intelligence, there was no way I was going to mention this memory lapse to Marci. Conventional wisdom, combined with irrational abject terror, told me she would remember every detail.

Then, on our fifth anniversary, the moment I'd been living in fear of for years finally came. In honor of our milestone achievement, Marci wanted to record our wedding day recollections.

I was toast.

Sitting down to begin, I waited cautiously, hoping she would take the lead. I was delusional enough to believe I could survive this ordeal by simply agreeing with everything she said while providing minimal details myself. My naïve fantasy was dashed immediately.

"So," she said as we sat across the kitchen table from each other, "tell me exactly what you remember." Her eager expression made my insides churn. I had no other option but to come clean.

"I'm so sorry, babe. But when it comes to the ceremony, I don't remember anything. I'm sure that makes me the worst husband of all time, but . . ." I was so humiliated, I couldn't finish.

To my overwhelming surprise, she sighed in relief.

"Well then, what're we gonna write about? Because I don't remember any of it either. It was so blasted hot that I barely kept from passing out."

Come to find out, she'd been almost as worried about my reaction as I'd been about hers. After a good laugh, we decided to press forward and chronicle the scenes time hadn't erased.

Once we started, I realized just how full my

treasure trove of wedding memories really was. When we finished four hours later, I was content. The recollections captured in our book were of far greater value to me than anything I might have forgotten.

Each subsequent year on our anniversary, it became tradition to read through every entry. Some of my favorites include

+ My little sister, Katie, refusing to leave Marci's side the entire day. This included the time spent taking pictures. In two or three of our wedding photos, the tiniest edge of my sister's navy blue dress is visible within the frame. For some reason, my kids think that's hilarious. With the advances of digital photography, those pictures wouldn't exist today.

+ I may not remember our first married kiss, but I distinctly remember the initial pinch of my backside outside the temple afterward. When Marci thought no one was looking, she reached behind and goosed me for the first time. Of course, my brother Brock saw. That's the kind of thing Brock always sees. He then proceeded to embarrass us for the next half hour until quite suddenly he was standing silently next to my father, his gleeful smile having disappeared.

+ Our first dance as a married couple at the reception that evening. As Marci slipped comfortably into my arms, I remember truly *seeing* her for the first time all day. Everything had been so busy and rushed, and I hadn't appreciated how stunningly gorgeous she looked. As we slowly swayed in rhythm to the music, I remember thinking how fortunate I was to be married to this amazing person. With no premeditation, I kissed her. Although startled at first, her body quickly melted into mine. Choosing to ignore everyone around us, we enjoyed our first genuinely relaxed moment of the day.

The pages of our little book have dozens more anecdotes just like those, and they are some of the most valued keepsakes I own. And that book—along with everything inside—was the first thing I thought of when Dr. Schenk made his pronouncement this morning.

"Todd, I need to share my latest conclusion with you."

Having done a remarkable job of gaining my attention, he proclaimed, "It is my professional opinion that you've accomplished what you came here for."

I stared back at him blankly. "What?"

"You've done it. I've been reading through your blog postings from this last week and there's no denying it. The death of your wife has, for the most part, ceased to be a limiting factor in your mental health. I would love to take full credit for it, but in reality, you've done most of the work yourself."

Our session was less than a minute old and he springs this on me? I had no idea how to respond. "So," I stammered, "I'm done?"

The edges of Dr. Schenk's mouth turned up in a noncommitted, knowing smile. "Well, that's up to you."

Four months ago I'd have given anything to be granted clemency from this office and the weakness I felt it represented. But now?

"Well, what do you think I should do?"

"It doesn't matter what I think."

"But you said I'm over my wife."

Dr. Schenk chuckled. "Oh, Todd, that isn't remotely what I said. There are numerous things in life we never *get over*, nor should we. Your life with Marci was never meant to be left behind. You simply needed to place it in the proper perspective so you can enjoy the life you have left."

"And you think I've started to do that?"

"Well, based on your last entry regarding Emily, what do you think?"

Despite the nagging feelings of guilt prodding me to say no, the truth was—I knew better. Marci was an amazing woman who I'd been lucky enough to have fifteen wonderful years with. There was no doubt she would always be special to me. But I had to admit, I was finally starting to move on.

I'd fallen in love with Emily. And even though I still worried about what Marci might think of my new relationship, I knew in my heart there was no going back. I only hope that with her new perspective beyond this life, Marci is somehow able to be happy for me.

Nevertheless, some questions still remained. Dropping my gaze from Dr. Schenk's fatherly stare, I asked, "Then why do I feel like I'm not done?"

Dr. Schenk leaned back in his chair and looked toward the ceiling. After a few moments of consideration, he speculated, "Well, I can think of several possibilities.

"One, we have formed a bond that is valuable to you. So ending our sessions could equate to the loss of a friendship.

"Two, you are experiencing something similar to leaving the nest. Part of your problem was a fear of the unknown—of what a life without Marci would be like. Since you started therapy, you have discovered that the life you feared really isn't so bad. On the other hand, I have always been the one constant you could hold on to in case events took a turn for the worst. By ending our sessions, you will be removing your safety net. Regardless of age, that kind of prospect can be daunting.

"Three, you have overcome the issues that brought you here, but in so doing, have discovered several more. You now realize that seeing a psychiatrist is not what you initially thought it was. You understand that counseling can provide clarity and perspective, which can be refreshing. And you don't want to let it go. Any or all of these scenarios are viable."

His answer, while illuminating—and long—still hadn't answered my question. "So," I asked warily, "do you think I should continue to see you?"

"Again, it doesn't matter what I think, Todd."

"I know. I got that. But do you feel I could benefit if I continued to come?"

"As a trained mental health expert, I believe everybody could benefit from additional counseling. So, in rendering your final evaluation, take that under advisement. However, I do believe continued visits would be beneficial. I don't know that we need to continue on a weekly basis, but something on a monthly time frame would seem appropriate."

"Wow!" I exclaimed. "This is just so . . . unexpected. I guess I need to think about it."

Moving to the edge of his chair, Dr. Schenk suggested, "Why don't we do this? We have already discussed my upcoming vacation. I leave in two weeks and won't be back for a month. If I remember correctly, you are also planning a trip with your children in June. Let's make an appointment to meet the first Wednesday in July. If you choose not to return, I won't even hold you to the charge for a missed appointment."

I thought it over for a moment. "Okay, I can live with that. Should I continue to blog?"

"That is up to you, but rest assured I have no intention of reading anything associated with my practice while in the French Riviera."

"French Riviera, huh? Not doing a whole lot to fight the 'psychiatrists are pretentious' cliché, are you, Doc?"

"Have you been there?"

I snickered. "Do I look like a French Riviera kind of guy?"

"No, you do not. But that is your loss, not mine. If vacationing in the French Riviera is enough to label me pretentious—then pretentious am I."

"Fair enough, Doc," I conceded. "Fair enough."

Interlude

DR. MELVIN SCHENK couldn't help but commend himself yet again on his impeccable taste in office furnishings. The dual chair set he'd selected looked even better in person than they had in the decorator's catalog. For possibly the fourth time that morning, he acknowledged to himself how much he felt the chairs were an improvement over the couch.

However, even more impressive than his taste in furnishings was the difference in demeanor of the patient sitting before him. The Todd Landry in his office today was a far cry from the man who'd been referred to him almost six months ago.

"Todd, you look well. How was your trip?"

The doctor noticed an instant grin spread across his patient's face. "It was amazing. My kids and I had a great time. We really enjoyed being together, just the four of us. There were moments when it was a little tough without Marci, but overall it was everything I'd been hoping for."

Dr. Schenk nodded knowingly. "Excellent, and how is your daughter Alex doing?"

Todd's bright countenance darkened slightly. "During our Florida trip, I got my hopes up pretty high. But since we got home, things have gone down hill pretty quickly."

"Would you care to expound?"

"Before we left, she would rarely speak to me unless she had to. In Florida, all of that disappeared. Things were like they were before. But since we've returned, it feels worse than ever. She just seems to hate me whenever Emily is part of the equation."

Todd closed his eyes and began shaking his head slowly. "I can't seem to figure out what she wants."

Dr. Schenk smiled inwardly to himself at the irony. "Maybe now you're beginning to understand what those close to you were experiencing when you came to see me. Grief over a loss rarely makes for sound judgment."

Clearly exasperated, Todd asked, "So should I just go back to my constant state of depression so my daughter will love me again?"

"Of course not. We're merely identifying what's happening here. We're not attempting to fix it. You have to remember that this is Alex's problem, not yours."

"Well, that's lovely. But last I checked, I'm still the one who has to live with her."

"That's true. So what do you want to do about it?"

The doctor noticed how his question deflated his patient. In a much more reserved tone, Todd answered, "Force her to talk to me. Have it out with her until everything is out on the table and we can resolve some of these issues."

"So, why haven't you done that?"

Todd grinned humorlessly. "Emily and my mother both seem to think that would be disastrous. They think I should wait her out. And since I'm the only non-female involved . . . I'm choosing to accept their logic for the time being."

Nodding sagely, Dr. Schenk concurred, "I believe that is a wise course of action. My advice would be to stand back and give her space. In time, it is likely she will come around and be thankful you didn't try to rush her."

The doctor prayed his advice was accurate.

Moving on, he asked, "Meanwhile, how are things between you and Emily?"

Smiling a tad goofily, Todd confessed, "Well, I went ring shopping yesterday if that's any indication."

"I believe that says quite a lot, but it certainly doesn't address everything. Just prior to my leaving, you expressed concerns about being sealed to Emily in light of the previously expressed feelings of your wife. Have you come to some resolution on that matter?"

Dr. Schenk watched carefully as Todd took a moment to mull over his question. "Emily and I have talked about it some. To be completely honest, it still makes me a bit uncomfortable to think about, but apparently not enough to change course."

Feeling a growing sense of satisfaction, Dr. Schenk offered, "Well, good. I'm happy for you. I assume your parents are thrilled as well?"

"My dad's so excited he can't wait to leave the country. Ever since the day I introduced them to Emily, mission talk has resumed with fervor. I'm not sure we'll be able to keep him here long enough to see us get married."

"So the more things change, the more they stay the same."

"Very well put, Doctor."

The psychiatrist lowered his head in acknowledgement of the compliment before querying, "Has your relationship with your father improved?"

As Todd hesitated, unconsciously biting his lower lip, the doctor deduced at once that, no, the relationship had not improved. He was curious if his patient would have the courage to admit this.

"Of course it's better. I'm doing what he wants. Now that everything and everyone are in their proper place, he's fine. But if you're asking if we've made any progress in understanding one another, then the answer would probably be no, not really."

Dr. Schenk shook his head. Why did this poor young man insist on making things so difficult with regards to this one individual? Carefully, he asked, "Why are you so determined to be frustrated with him?"

Todd exhaled slowly. "Right after our last session, I tried to talk to him. He and I were doing much better because of Emily, so I wanted to discuss some of the things we had covered during our sessions. I thought it might help us.

"However, as soon as I mentioned your name, he immediately changed the subject. I pressed a couple of times, but he's good at deflecting.

"A few days later, I tried again without mentioning you at all. I still got nowhere. That's when I realized no conversation about feelings or introspection goes anywhere with my dad. Everything emotional has to be kept at arm's length. Logically, I get that this is just the person he is. But at the same time, I'm offended that he won't make any effort to understand or learn about who I am."

Peering over his glasses, Dr. Schenk clarified, "So, if I am hearing you correctly, you have two people close to you with whom you are struggling to communicate. Do you see any parallels between them?"

"Both of them are hard-headed."

"Or maybe you are."

"Here we go."

Ignoring Todd's declaration, Dr. Schenk continued, "Not everyone in this life is going to want to connect the way you do, Todd. All indications suggest that your father is not an emotionally driven person. Maybe he has nothing to say. Furthermore, he has no idea how to relate to what you are trying to tell him, so he chooses not to engage you."

"That's all well and good for him, but that still leaves me frustrated."

"For lack of a better term—that's too bad."

"What?"

"Just because you now are comfortable with therapy and are suddenly ready to conduct group sessions with everyone you know doesn't mean they are ready to join you. And sometimes your opportunity to talk has already come and gone. Take your daughter, for instance. She clearly will open up, but only on her terms. One of those windows opened in your car one morning before school, and unfortunately *you* weren't ready."

Todd closed his eyes. "So what should I do?"

"The answer is straightforward. You cannot change other people. So stop trying."

Todd turned his head away from Dr. Schenk and mumbled something under his breath.

"I'm sorry, I missed that last bit."

"I said I'll have to work on that."

"I'm fairly certain I heard a derogatory name for me in your initial version."

"I'm fairly certain you can't prove that."

Dr. Schenk's eyes flashed with mock warning. "Possibly not. In the meantime, is there anything else that has occurred in your life that you wish to discuss?"

Todd scratched his head and sighed. "Jason and Kimberly got married last weekend."

"Why do you say it as if it's not a good thing?"

"Because I'm not sure it is."

"How so?"

"Well, Jason has a pattern. All through high school and college he'd go after the girl everybody else wanted. But once he had her, he'd get bored and eventually move on. When he got married the first time, I really hoped things would be different, but in the end, nothing changed."

"And you are concerned this is Kimberly's fate as well?"

The patient leaned his head to one side, producing a loud pop from his vertebrae, causing the doctor to suppress a slight grin. Todd's nonverbal communication had always been so much more blatantly honest than he realized. Regardless of his answer, Dr. Schenk knew instantly that Todd had little to no faith in his friend.

"He's never done the 'save the wounded sparrow'

thing before, so initially I was hopeful. I can tell he genuinely cares about her, but those nasty little signs are showing up again."

"So what do you plan to do about it?"

"I don't know that I can do anything about it. I mean—I could talk to Jason and try to help him see where this is heading . . ." Todd let his voice trail off, belying his lack of faith in this course of action.

"How do you think that would go?"

"Not good. Jason doesn't handle constructive criticism well."

"So, once again you are left with the difficult realization that everyone gets to make their own decisions, even if those decisions will likely prove destructive."

Seemingly distracted, Todd responded, "I suppose so."

Dr. Schenk stared intently at Todd. "What is it about Jason that is really bothering you? Nothing you've said so far is branching into new territory."

Todd focused his attention on the wall. "Life just seems to get more and more complicated. Jason can be a real jerk, but, at the same time, he's a good friend. I've always been able to compartmentalize those two things in my mind. But if he follows his typical pattern and messes things up with Kimberly—the first truly nice woman he's ever had a relationship with—I'm not sure how our friendship survives."

Cautiously, Dr. Schenk said, "Todd, you do know that no amount of therapy can change a natural separation of two people who choose to be incompatible."

"I know. I mean, hopefully I'm wrong. They've

only been married a few days." Todd paused before adding. "I really do hope I'm wrong."

"I do as well. But there is wisdom in preparing for a likely outcome in spite of how distasteful it might be."

Todd nodded slightly but said nothing.

The doctor looked down to reference his notes when he was abruptly startled by his patient's return to exuberance. "Kevin's engaged."

"Wonderful!" Dr. Schenk exclaimed. "You sound much more positive regarding this development."

"I am. Caralee's pretty awesome, and she and Kevin really have a good relationship."

"Have they set a date?"

"They have. September nineteenth."

"I'm surprised the two of you haven't discussed a joint wedding."

Todd chuckled. "No, I wouldn't want to take away from Kevin's moment in any way. He deserves to have the spotlight all to himself."

"Good point."

Dr. Schenk arched his back and raised his arms halfway, signaling his belief that their conversation was winding down.

"Well, we've recapped just about everyone in your life . . . oh wait. I forgot to mention that I received a phone call from your friend Grant. It seems Bishop Lincoln passed on my contact information to him, so my connection to your ward will continue. Out of curiosity, how is he doing with his new assignment?"

"He's a little more serious at times, and he's a lot less available than he used to be, but it seems to be going okay. Of course, he and I are barely on speaking terms right now."

"Oh?"

Dr. Schenk was instantly wary. Despite his patient's much improved confidence, any additional loss of friends or family would be a cause for alarm. However, his alarm quickly gave way to annoyance as Todd began to laugh at his concerned reaction.

"I'm just kidding. Part of my new Church assignment—which he gave me—requires that I deal with the local leadership of the Boy Scouts of America. Let's just say I don't see the world the same way they do.

"Two days ago I had to go to the local BSA office for the first time. There's this woman there who made me want to pull out a crucifix and attempt an exorcism right on the spot."

Todd grimaced as he seethed. "Ms. Turcell is her name. Within five minutes of my walking through the front door, she was lecturing me about the importance of getting my paperwork right. I can't even explain how, but in a short amount of time, she associated my aversion for filling out forms in triplicate to a complete lack of concern for the well-being of teenage boys everywhere."

Dr. Schenk lowered his head in resignation. "I'm sure a mild-mannered man, such as yourself, responded with warmth and understanding as you defused the situation before it got out of hand."

Todd's eyes narrowed as he glared at the doctor for a split second. But then, as if in shame, he looked away and mumbled, "I may have implied that people like her make Scouting feel like the Hitler Youth movement of the 1930s."

"I'm sure that went a long way in establishing good relations."

"I think she barely restrained herself from ripping my head directly off my body. She told me through tightly clenched teeth that I would in no way be able to purchase awards until my paperwork was correct and not to return until I had accomplished this most basic task. Then she refused to acknowledge my presence any further."

"So, what did you do?"

"I went home and fixed the paperwork. Yesterday I went back and had no problems whatsoever. Ms. Turcell wasn't there, but the nice older lady who helped me provided everything I needed. What annoys me to no end is that she said I didn't need half the documentation I'd brought with me—the same documentation demanded from me on the previous visit—just to pick up awards. I thanked her with my sweetest smile, but the whole way home I was coming up with new and unique ways to verbally obliterate *Miz* Turcell."

"You are fully aware that you should let this go?"

"Yes."

"But you're not going to, are you?"

"No . . . probably not."

Dr. Schenk allowed a smile to play at the corners of his mouth before changing the subject. "Well, Todd, where are we as therapist and patient?"

Todd thought for a moment. "I don't know."

"That doesn't tell me anything."

"I feel like I've been doing pretty well these last couple of months. But sitting here talking with you has been . . . it's been good. I want to keep coming. Maybe on a monthly basis like you mentioned when I was here last."

"That would be fine. Should the need arise, you may call and schedule time in between our sessions as well."

"Thanks. That'd be great."

"What about the blog? Are you willing to continue with it?"

"Yeah. I obviously haven't written since our last visit, but sometimes I find myself missing it. I don't have to write as often, do I?"

"Of course not. As long as there are a few entries for me to work with in between our sessions, I will be satisfied."

"Cool."

Dr. Schenk had never considered himself a prideful man. But in truth, his ego was smarting over his patient's failure to mention his redecorated office. Unable to restrain himself any further, the doctor decided to solicit his well-deserved compliments.

"Todd, with the time we have remaining, I'd like to revisit a couple of issues we've touched on earlier, but before we do, I have to ask. What do you think of my new office décor?"

Todd shifted uncomfortably. "Please don't take this the wrong way, Doc, but it comes off a little cold. To be honest, I miss the couch."

TODD'S LANDRY LIST

If I Ever Find That Murphy Guy . . .
Friday, July 11

THERE'S A LADY who works at my firm that can't go a single day without reading her horoscope. She's obsessive about it. And not only is she obsessive about her own fate, but she's also adamant that everyone she knows be as attuned to their daily astrological predictions as she is.

Usually when I stop in at the office, I take great pains to avoid her. Learning for the hundredth time that so-and-so's moon is in somebody else's house gets tedious after a while. But when I dropped in this morning, I didn't take the proper precautions and was cornered before I'd even advanced five feet beyond the entrance.

With great agitation, she declared over and over how much danger I was in today. She didn't know what, but something horrible was definitely in my future.

Doing my best to remain polite, I nodded appreciatively as I backed away down the hall, but regardless of my subtle hints, she remained fervently in my face. By the time I reached the men's room, I was truly convinced she would follow me in. However, something about the men's room door caused reason to prevail, and I was, at last, able to complete my getaway.

Once alone, I laughed conspiratorially with my reflection in the mirror. How could an otherwise intelligent woman put that much stock in something so blatantly bogus?

Now, having lived through the day she warned me about, I'm not laughing anymore.

Emily was expecting me to pick her up tonight around six for a nothing-to-get-excited-about regular date. But to her surprise, when she opened her front door, she was met by Kevin, dressed to perfection in a rented chauffeur's uniform. He then guided her directly into the backseat of Jason's BMW, which he'd let me borrow while he and Kimberly were in Jamaica on their honeymoon.

Now when it comes to proposing marriage, most guys will go to the most expensive restaurant they can't afford. Not me. Emily's chariot pulled up to a homemade dinner of grilled chicken, salad, and corn on the cob served at a secluded table behind the local farmer's market, where a large thermostat hanging out front read 103 degrees. Thankfully, Manny, a friend of mine who owns the market, has one of the best misting systems in the entire East Valley.

Each year for Halloween, Manny hosts a corn maze/pumpkin festival. As the event has grown, he's made improvements to his property to create a more tourist-friendly environment. Two years ago he built a garden area with grass, trees, and a multitude of flowers. In the middle of his little Sonoran Desert oasis, he built a gazebo that's ideal for either live music or as a picture spot for visitors.

Tonight that gazebo, with the help of about a hundred candles and dozens of fresh wildflowers, represented my best effort at constructing a romantic hideaway. One word of advice for anyone contemplating a re-creation of my efforts: plan for the combination of candles and misting system well in advance. You'll be glad you did.

Kevin pulled up, and Emily emerged from the backseat of the car. The rays from the fading Arizona sun highlighted the gentle curls of her deep auburn hair, creating a stunning contrast with the royal-blue dress she'd chosen to wear. She was gorgeous.

For the first time all day, I felt nervous.

I met her at the bottom of the gazebo stairs with a kiss and a half dozen genuinely felt but timidly stuttered compliments on how stunning she looked. Despite my fumbled delivery, she blushed, which only made her more attractive.

Climbing the stairs hand in hand, I led her to her seat just as Caralee, our server, arrived with our menus.

Dinner was fantastic.

Okay, I don't know if that's true or not because, honestly, dinner was a blur. Everything we were served are things I enjoy, but tonight, I was way too preoccupied to actually taste anything. The only thing I do remember with vivid clarity is that with each passing moment, it became harder to fight back the nausea rising in my throat.

Following our main course, Caralee returned with our desserts, presented under silver dome plate covers. Had I been twenty years younger and asking someone to the prom, I probably would've dialed up the creativity and had the ring baked into her apple cobbler or something. Instead, I went pretty basic and had the ring box sitting open on her plate.

As Emily lifted her plate cover, I moved from my chair to kneel at her side. She sat motionless for several seconds before slowly placing the cover down on the table. In my nervousness, I started to reach quickly for the ring before something stopped me.

Emily was crying.

As I'd contemplated earlier what might happen, I felt like I was prepared for tears. But I was not ready for this. This was more than tears. This was barely controlled sobbing that left plenty of room for negative interpretation. I began to panic.

Tentatively, I whispered, "Are you okay?"

Slipping from her chair, she wiped away some of the tears streaming down her cheeks as she knelt beside me. "Oh, yes. Yes! Yes! Yes, I'm okay. Yes, I'll marry you. Yes, to everything."

With no further warning, she kissed me. I did not care for an instant that the many hours I'd spent preparing my speech were about to be wasted. I slipped my arms around her waist and passionately kissed her back.

I'm sure we made quite a picture kneeling together in the soft flickering light of a hundred candles. It was romance at its best. That's why I was so startled when Emily began to giggle.

Cocking my head to the side, I looked at her with a quizzical expression. She tried to regain her composure and apologize, but this only caused her nervous laughter to escalate. Sensing the moment had changed, I started to rise from my knees only to have her pull me back down so that our eyes were only inches apart. All traces of laughter disappeared as she said, "I love you. Thank you . . . thank you for everything."

"Emily, I love you too, but why are you thanking me? You're the one agreeing to marry beneath yourself."

A hint of vulnerability formed at the edges of her expression. "The fact you actually believe that is one more reason why I feel so lucky."

I'm not always the most observant person, but even I could tell there was more behind her words than what appeared at face value. It seemed like the perfect time to lighten the mood. "Wait a minute. You never gave me the chance to ask my question. Get back in that chair so I can do this properly."

She smiled softly and resumed wiping her eyes. "Todd, it's fine. You don't have to do that. I'm sorry I jumped the gun."

"Don't be sorry. Just straighten yourself out and get ready to do this right."

Emily chuckled lightly as she stood and began an exhaustive effort to remove all evidence of tears. Once she pronounced herself ready and had returned to her seat, I took the ring from the box, got down on one knee, and asked, "Emily Stewart, will you marry me?"

Holding back a new round of emotions, she simply nodded. It didn't matter, the tears returned anyway. I rose to my feet and pulled her gently into my waiting arms. Closing my eyes had the effect of shutting out time completely. All that mattered in that moment was the amazing woman wrapped in my embrace, weeping softly on my shoulder.

Somewhere in the distant night, a number of neighborhood dogs became alerted to an unexpected presence. On a warm evening in the desert, sound can carry for miles, and their barking was no exception. It was this unfortunate canine chorus that brought Emily and me back to reality. As we pulled away from each other, I couldn't help but smile at the ironic scene before me.

"For someone supposedly overjoyed about becoming engaged, you look pretty miserable."

She slapped me on the side of my arm in mock anger. "That's rude. Didn't anyone ever teach you not to use the word *miserable* when describing a woman's appearance?"

"Fair point. How about, you look less than thrilled?"

Something about my comment changed the mood. Emily removed her hands from mine and sat down at the table without a further glance in my direction. Not sure how to respond, I followed her lead and took my chair.

"I know I've been way overemotional, I just . . ." She stopped. Gazing intently at the ring on her finger, she finally added, "When you've wanted something so badly but have had to accept it may never happen . . .

I'm scared. I'm scared this is all a dream and tomorrow I'm going to wake up only to find out it isn't real."

Instantly, I recognized how different this moment was for her than for me. I was—happy. She, on the other hand, was experiencing something far deeper. I knew I would never fully understand what this must be like for her, so I struggled with what to do next. It turns out the answer was easy. Sit back, shut up, and listen.

"I know I haven't shared a lot about my past with you, and I appreciate you never pushing too hard, but I guess with all of my crying tonight, you deserve an explanation."

I shook my head, implying that she didn't have to say anything further on my account, but she continued anyway.

"After my mission, I felt like God had betrayed me. In fact, I felt like all men had betrayed me, and God was simply one of them. So I decided to show them all. I took out my anger on every holier-than-thou returned missionary who dared to ask me out. I was so good at being nasty—no self-respecting guy would put himself through more than one date with me. I was so blind as to what I was doing. I was so busy seeing immaturity in every guy I went out with that I never stopped to realize how immature I was being."

Fresh tears began to fall to the table.

"One day, I woke up and realized I was twenty-five years old and no one was asking me out anymore. At least not members of the Church.

"I'd just started my second year of teaching, and

a very sweet coworker was practically tripping over himself to get a date. I kept rejecting his offers until one day, I realized I didn't care anymore. I was tired of being bitter; I was tired of being alone; I was tired of everything. The next time he asked, I said yes.

"Pretty soon we were 'exclusive.' It bothered me at first that I was dating a non-Mormon, but eventually I convinced myself that I was a failure by Mormon standards anyway. So this was only the natural progression. But the longer we dated, the more frustrated he got with my *lack of commitment.*"

She smiled sorrowfully as her eyes remained lost in the past. "Finally, after a couple of months, he gave me a soft ultimatum. He said he needed more. Whether that meant marriage, or moving in together, or . . . whatever, he didn't care, but he needed something.

"That was the lowest I've ever felt in my life. Part of me was convinced that if I walked away, I'd be leaving behind my only chance for a family. But more than that, I loved him. And I knew if I let him go, I'd be alone again. Maybe forever.

"Throughout my life, I've always been close with my dad. When I finally told him what was going on, he was concerned, as any parent would be, but he took it pretty well. I know plenty of fathers who would've brought out the full-court press to try and *save* their daughter. He didn't do that. Instead, he asked me what in my life was most important. That was it. I expected a ten-minute lecture at least, but he didn't say another word. He chose to let me figure it out on my own. I broke it off with the guy the next day."

I couldn't take it anymore. Reaching over, I took her hand in mine and squeezed it reassuringly. She accepted my gesture but kept on speaking without any further acknowledgement.

"I wish I could say everything got better right away, but it didn't. If anything, the next two years were the blackest of my life.

"One night, after a particularly bad date, I went home and cried, for at least an hour. I begged God to make things better, to help me find someone. I just wanted to know my life had a purpose.

"The answer I got was not what I was asking for. For the first time in my life, I felt strongly that I needed to accept I might always be alone.

"That was three years ago. Since then, I've had to figure out who I am all over again. I've done okay, but no matter how hard I try, the one thing I've never gotten used to is the loneliness. It's always there.

"Always."

Finally, she raised her eyes to mine, and with tears streaming down her cheeks, she clarified, "So, whether you need to hear it or not, I'm still saying it, because it's not just you I'm talking to. Thank you, Todd Landry. You'll never know how much this means to me."

Out of pure instinct, I stood and took her in my arms. Tenderly, I lifted her face with my index finger and said, "Well, now that I understand, I feel I should tell you something as well. Thank *you*, Emily Stewart. Our lives couldn't be more different, but what you've done for me is equally valuable."

Her heartfelt smile pierced my soul. Unable to

resist, I slowly placed my lips on hers and kissed her once more.

It's one of life's true tragedies that moments like these can't last forever. If possible, I'd have stayed in that gazebo, and the cocoon of exhilaration I was feeling, for at least a week. However, we both knew that before it got too late, phone calls and visits needed to be made.

Emily had left her cell phone at home, so I pulled mine out of my pocket and handed it to her. The rules of chivalry demand that a newly engaged couple contact the bride-to-be's parents first. As she turned it on, her expression shifted from elated to puzzled. "Your phone says you have five messages and twelve missed calls."

"Really?"

Reaching for the phone, I added, "No one ever needs to get ahold of me that bad."

The first warning bells in my mind went off when I recognized my parents' number as the primary culprit, although the more recent calls had been placed from my brother Mike's cell phone.

Now I was seriously concerned. My parents were watching the kids. A million different scenarios flooded my brain, each more upsetting than the last.

I dialed my parents' number first, but after several rings, no one picked up. That never happens. Something had to be seriously wrong. My hands began to tremble as I dialed Mike's number.

Looking up as I waited for the connection to be made, I saw my concern reflected back in Emily's eyes.

"Hello?"

"Mike, it's Todd. What's going on?"

The panic in Mike's voice did nothing to allay my fears. "Where have you been? Why haven't you been answering your phone?"

"Emily and I were—"

"It doesn't matter. Where are you now?"

"Here at Manny's place, right off Sossaman."

"You need to get over here right away. We're at the emergency room."

"Mike, are my kids okay?"

"They're fine. It's Mom . . ."

I felt my knees go weak.

As he continued to explain, the world around me began to spin. In a single instant, my only desire was to scream, yet I found I couldn't utter a sound. It just wasn't fair. Our family could not be going through this again.

The Generation Gap
Thursday, July 17

LONG PAST THE time when the final car had pulled away from the cemetery, my father and I sat alone staring at my mother's casket. A typical July monsoon was forming around us, creating an overcast sky and a breeze that provided some relief from the oppressive summertime heat.

We had positioned ourselves several seats apart with our suit coats occupying the empty chairs between us. To the casual observer, the space between us could easily be mistaken as symbolic. But in truth, my mother's heart attack, and eventual passing, had proven to be another catalyst in our evolving relationship.

Of all my siblings, it was no coincidence I was the one sitting with him today. Together, we belong to a club no one wants to join. Everything negative between us had been put aside. We needed each other. To me, this is what families are all about.

At least an hour and a half had passed since the graveside prayer. I wasn't sure how long he intended to stay, but to be honest, I didn't care. I had enough on my mind to fill as much time as he needed to take.

I'd never fully appreciated how much my mom had been my confidant in life. When I was a teenager, we'd spend many nights talking until the wee hours about school, sports, or whatever was on my mind. In retrospect, I'm humbled to think of how many times my mother probably had to feign interest in topics she cared nothing about.

Suddenly, like an unwelcome alarm clock early in the morning, my father's voice cut through my fond memories. "How did you do it?"

Confused, I replied, "Do what?"

"How did you know what to do next? I know that today I've got family, but what about tomorrow, or the next day?"

I laughed humorlessly. "Dad, with all due respect, do you remember who you're talking to? I didn't know what to do for months. I'm still not sure I've figured it out."

Casting his eyes to the ground, my father shook his head. "No ... I don't mean what do I ..." His shoulders slumped and he sighed. "We had a plan. Your mother and I had a plan. Now she's gone, and it's all over."

He paused and inhaled sharply as the first sprinkles of rain in the distance filled the air with the creosote aroma unique to the desert. He looked toward the clouds and continued. "I thought about returning to the business, but that wouldn't be fair to your brothers. Having me around would just create friction. I don't want that. But I have to do something."

"Whoa, slow down. We need to figure out how you're going to function day to day before we begin planning the next grand phase of your life."

He snorted. "I know how to function."

"Do you, Dad? Do you really? What are you going to do for dinner tomorrow night?"

"I . . . I'm sure I can fix something."

"After the busy week you've had, I'm sure the laundry's piled up. Do you know how to use the washer you bought Mom last year? It's pretty high tech."

He opened his mouth to answer and then stopped as the realization of what I was saying dawned on him. It had been years since he'd prepared a meal for himself or done any kind of laundry.

"I don't mean to sound cold, but there are so many things you're gonna have to figure out that you haven't even thought of yet. Don't try to rush this."

Slowly, he turned to face me. He didn't say anything—he just studied me with an unreadable expression. Finally, he turned back to face the casket with a new determination. It didn't take a mind reader to know what he was thinking. He'd just relived all of my weaknesses and inadequacies following Marci's death and had determined to himself not to follow my path.

I'm sure on a normal day I would've been offended. Instead, I felt sorry for him. Today was the easy part. Sure, he'd had to experience the shock of losing his spouse, which is an emotional roller coaster no one wants to ride. But up next is the ambivalence—the day when everyone else's life starts again and yours doesn't. Having been through that, I decided to give him a little slack and save my righteous indignation for another time.

A blue sedan pulled up, and the funeral home director stepped out. He started around the vehicle, heading toward us, and then froze. It was clear he hadn't expected to see anyone still sitting at the graveside.

Watching him from my vantage point, it was almost comical as his eyes frantically searched for his employee left on-site. When he located him lounging patiently under a tree, he tilted his head ever so slightly toward us as if to ask, "What are they still doing here?"

The assistant merely shrugged as if to reply, "Beats me, but what do you want me to do about it?"

The funeral director glanced back at us with a flummoxed expression before moving to join his colleague. Feeling a little bad for them, I decided it was time to see if I could help their cause. "Dad, I think they're waiting on us. We should probably go."

Now it was my father's turn to be startled from his reflections. Spotting both gentlemen waiting on us, he acknowledged, "I believe you're right. I just . . . I don't want to say good-bye, yet."

"I understand." I stood up. "I'll be in the car when you're ready."

Ten minutes later, the passenger door opened and my dad slipped into the seat beside me. His eyes were tinged with redness, but no other evidence of emotion was on display. The matter-of-fact tenor of his voice relayed his desire to talk no more of sentimental things.

"Please tell Emily how much I appreciate all of her help."

"I will."

With a note of genuine regret in his voice, he added, "All of us should be doting on her as the newest addition to our family . . . we just haven't had that opportunity. I think we should plan a dinner next week to officially welcome her to the Landry clan."

I stifled a chuckle and shook my head incredulously. "We'll figure something out. But why don't we get through today first."

I could tell he wanted to pretend today was already over, but he simply nodded as he stared out the window. We drove the remaining miles to the church in silence.

As we pulled into the parking lot, Emily emerged from the building in tears. My heart sank, knowing at once this couldn't be good. Emily had gotten along well with my mother, but they hadn't known each other well enough to warrant tears at this stage of the afternoon.

Finding the nearest parking spot, I managed to catch her before she reached her car. As she saw me approaching, she tried to wipe her eyes but quickly realized her efforts were pointless.

I took her in my arms and held her tightly as my father approached behind me. The concern in his voice was evident as he asked, "Is everything all right, Emily? Our family hasn't misbehaved, have they?"

Emily pulled away from me and addressed my father with a manufactured smile. "No, Adrian, everyone has been wonderful. Just hearing the stories about your wife got me a little teary. I'm supposed to meet my mother this afternoon, and I didn't realize how late it was. I'm sorry to rush off. Please accept my apologies."

I knew Emily had no plans. Something was truly wrong. My father reacted graciously, but I could tell he wasn't buying this story either. "Well, once we're done here, we're all going back to the house. We'd love to have you back with us this evening."

Emily embraced my father as she said, "Thank you for the invitation. We'll see how it goes."

Returning the hug, my father offered his most genial smile before turning toward the church. Once he'd left, I gently grasped her shoulders and turned her around to face me. "That was an exceptional display of storytelling. Now, how about the truth?"

"Your daughter needs some space from me, I think."

Instantly, my blood began to boil. For the past week, Alex had taken her mistreatment of Emily to an entirely new level. More than once, I'd forced myself to remember that Alex was reacting to the loss of her grandmother. But every time I had to bottle up my anger, it only succeeded in making it that much harder to contain the next time. Despite the circumstances, I had a feeling that today, confrontation was inevitable.

"Stop! I can see in your eyes that you need to cool off before you go in there." Emily's warning and look of concern achieved their desired affect. I breathed deeply and nodded my agreement.

However, I still felt the need to argue my point. "She can't keep treating you like this."

"And she won't," she soothed unconvincingly. "It's her grandmother's funeral today. Keep that in mind when you talk to her."

Inhaling sharply, I replied, "I will."

"You better. Look, you need to be with your family. I'll talk to you tomorrow. I love you."

"I love you too. Thanks for everything."

She blushed. "I haven't done anything."

"Liar. I'll see you tomorrow."

Once Emily had driven away, I resumed my vision of storming into the church and wringing my daughter's neck. Instead, I opted to walk around the parking lot twice before heading inside.

Although Alex was the child I was looking for, I happened upon Samantha first, hiding in the north entryway, crying. I could tell she was embarrassed that I'd found her, but she raced into my arms nonetheless. At first I assumed she was emotional over the death of her grandmother, but no . . .

"Why does she have to be so mean?"

"Why does who have to be so mean, sweetie?"

"Alex."

My temper flared again before settling into a low simmer. "What did she do?"

"She's just so mean to Emily, and I don't know why."

"Sam, what did Alex do?"

"She asked her, in front of everybody, why she couldn't get her own husband."

"What?"

"When Emily came to sit at our table, Alex said it was for family only. Aunt Katie apologized and asked her to sit down, but before she could, Alex asked her why she didn't go find a husband of her own and leave our family alone."

Now I was boiling. I was willing to accept she had suffered a loss, but so had the rest of us. It didn't give her the right to treat another human being like garbage. "What did Emily say after that?"

"I don't know. She just looked so sad it made me cry. I didn't want anyone to see, so I ran."

Reliving the memory caused her tears to return. Between sobs she asked, "Why does Alex have to be that way? I like Emily. She's so nice to us. I don't get it."

I held her close as I murmured, "I don't know, baby. But I plan to find out."

Based on Samantha's description, it appeared Alex hadn't moved at all. As I approached the table, I heard a small voice in the far reaches of my mind reminding me that I was the parent and needed to proceed cautiously, but by this point, I was beyond rational.

I was less than ten feet away when Alex finally noticed me. My expression must have been a giveaway because she immediately attempted to make her escape.

"Not so fast, little girl. We need to talk," I seethed as I intercepted her. My volume never rose above a normal speaking level, but my tone left no mystery as to my state of mind. Exiting out a side door, we found an empty classroom far away from the familial clamor.

As the door shut, I turned to face her. "What in the . . . what is your problem?"

A defiant look of contempt greeted me as she refused to acknowledge my presence. I felt like I'd been slapped across the face. Never once had I seen this demonic look of hate cross her beautiful features before.

"Fine, I can't make you talk, but I can make sure you listen. Sam told me what you said to Emily, and it is beyond unacceptable. What you did is disgusting."

I could feel myself losing control and knew I needed to dial back my antagonism before I did some serious damage. Leaving aside everything else I'd intended to say, I uttered the only appropriate thing I could think of. "Is this the person you really want to be?"

That comment got a response. Her look of insolence turned to pure rage as she fiercely whipped her head around and screamed, "Who even cares what kind of person I am? Not you. All you care about is Emily. Not Mom—she's gone. And now the one person who did care is dead. So, if no one else cares, why should I?"

Her words were a knife being thrust through my heart. "Is that really what you think?"

Turning away from me once more, she resumed her silent treatment. I started to move toward her, but she immediately backed away. Through all of this, the most disturbing aspect was her lack of tears. It was like a bizarre version of the night her mother died.

I retreated to indicate I was accepting her terms. Finding a chair, I sat down and contemplated my next move. Unfortunately, no amazing burst of inspiration hit me, so I said, "Alex, I love you. I'm sorry you don't believe that, but you mean more to me than anything in this world."

No response.

"Honey, you've been through two majorly traumatic experiences. You need help. I want you to come see Dr. Schenk with me next week."

Her eyes continued to focus on the wall far to my right. I was afraid she had chosen to close herself off for the rest of the day when all of a sudden she said, "No. I won't go."

"Sweetheart, you can't continue bottling everything up. I'm not asking if you want to go. I'm telling you. We're going."

"You can't make me." Her declaration was delivered with a fury bordering on hatred. I was starting to get a little scared. Now was clearly not the time to escalate any battle, regardless of my intentions.

"Alex, I'm sorry. You're right. I can't make you. I just want what's best for you. Life has treated you pretty badly over the last year, and I just want you to be happy."

There was just a moment's hesitation before she said, "Then get rid of her."

I felt myself go numb. "What?"

As she turned to meet my stunned gaze, the determination in her eyes was rock hard. "Get rid of her. Get rid of Emily and I'll see Dr. Schenk. If you don't . . ." She never finished the sentence. She didn't have to.

The Casualties of Keeping the Peace

Friday, July 18

I'M SOMEWHAT ASHAMED to admit this, but today I experienced full-fledged resentment toward my child. I've been angry before and I've been frustrated, but today was different. Today, I wasn't sure how I could ever forgive Alex for placing me in this position. It felt so unfair. Of course, then I had to remind myself that playing fair isn't generally high on a teenage girl's priority list.

Late this afternoon, I called Emily and asked if I could come over. I didn't know how I intended to handle Alex's challenge, but either way, I wanted Emily's input.

But before I could leave, I needed to let Alex know she was in charge while I was gone.

As I stood in the hallway preparing to knock, I heard a sound inside her bedroom that melted me from the inside. It was my daughter weeping.

In that instant, my path forward became clear. I knew what had to be done, and the realization caused a knot to form in my stomach.

Even through her closed door, I could tell I had startled her. Rustling papers were clearly audible as Alex's panicked voice called out, "Just a second."

After something more like a full minute, she invited me in and the cause of her delay was immediately clarified.

Just visible from under her pillow was Alex's photo album. It had been a present from Marci on her eighth birthday. Every important photograph from Alex's life can be found in that album, but I knew which pictures she'd been looking at.

Inside the back cover are two of my daughter's most cherished keepsakes. One is a photograph taken with Marci two weeks before her death. The other is a picture strip from a mall photo booth taken with her grandmother two years ago.

Alex was doing her best to appear nonchalant. The latest book in some teenage literary series was supposed to be her alibi, but the redness in her eyes made it clear she'd been crying. I pretended not to notice.

"I'm headed out."

Without looking up, she retorted, "Fine." I got no further acknowledgement. Closing her door quietly behind me, I set out on the longest journey of my life.

As I pulled up in front of Emily's house, my emotions were a mixture of sheer terror and overwhelming grief. I did not want to do this.

Emily's warm smile should have been comforting. But now the gleam in her eyes—the same eyes that had entranced me from the moment I'd first met her—made me feel sick to my stomach. I wanted to throw up.

Her smile slowly faded as she noted my discomfort. "Todd, is everything all right?"

I looked away. The sight of her trusting face was more than I could handle. "No. Not really."

Almost instinctively, Emily stepped out of her house and slowly shut the door behind her. Stealing a glance in her direction, I saw panic beginning to cloud her expression. "What's happened?"

"It's Alex."

"What about Alex?"

"Emily . . . I don't know how . . ."

"What about Alex?"

I couldn't take it any longer. I raised my eyes to meet her tortured gaze. "She's not handling things well."

"Did you talk to her about seeing Dr. Schenk?"

"Yes, but . . ."

Emily's voice grew smaller as it rose in pitch. "She won't go see him?"

"She will, but only under certain conditions."

Emily closed her eyes as she appeared to accept the inevitable. "What are you trying to tell me?"

"Alex agreed to see Dr. Schenk, but only if I agree to stop seeing you."

I don't know what I expected to happen. If I were honest, I would have to say I'd pictured this being the moment where Emily collapsed in my arms amid a flood of tears. That didn't happen.

Instead, she whispered, "What does that mean for us?"

"I guess we just need to take a break from each other for a while. I really hope it's not for long . . ." I let my thought go unfinished since anything else would be meaningless.

"So you're here to . . ." Her voice caught in her throat as tears began to fill her eyes. Inhaling deeply, she tried again, "So you're here to say good-bye?"

The finality of her words felt like a whip across my face. "Not forever. I still want to marry you, I just . . . I can't see you for a while."

"For how long?"

My vision blurred, and through my own tears I softly admitted, "I don't know."

Emily's gaze never left my face as she stepped forward to tenderly stroke my cheek. I couldn't help myself. Even though I was the one responsible for this mess, I broke protocol and hugged her. For several minutes we stood motionless in each other's arms as the warm afternoon breeze stirred a wind chime in the distance.

Finally, Emily released me and retreated. Without speaking, she began to slip the ring from her finger.

"Emily, don't," I pleaded. "That's not what I want at all. I want to be with you. I just have to take some time to help my daughter."

"I understand." Once again, her voice caught and she closed her eyes to keep emotions at bay. When her eyes reopened, I saw a new determination staring back at me.

"But, Todd, this isn't something you can do halfway. If this is truly what you're committing to, you can't keep me tucked away in your back pocket. Alex has to know you're fully in. If we try and have some secret pact, she'll know. That's why I'm going to make this easy for you."

With one final twist, the ring came free and fell into her open palm. Emily stared at it for a long time before, finally, raising her eyes to mine. Gingerly, she lifted her hand and offered it back to me.

"Emily, I'm sorry."

Fresh tears escaped her eyes and ran down her cheeks as she acknowledged, "I know. I'm sorry too."

Slowly, I took the ring from her hand and held it in front of me, dumbfounded. Shifting my gaze from the ring to Emily, I asked, "Is this it?"

A solemn smile touched the corners of her mouth, leaving the pain in her eyes untouched. "I think so. Although, can I ask a huge favor?"

"Anything."

"Can I say good-bye to Samantha and Drake?"

"Of course. I'll bring them by anytime you want."

Emily looked out toward the setting sun. "Actually, I was hoping you'd drop them off at Grant and Stacy's and not be there when I come. That is, of course, if they're okay with that."

Confused, I asked, "Why don't you want me there?"

"Because when you leave here today, I'm gonna cry—a lot. I'm gonna lock myself away in this house for at least a week, and it's guaranteed that I'm gonna eat way more chocolate than I should."

Closing the space between us, Emily murmured somberly, "You were the *one*."

She let all of the implications of her last statement hang in the air as she hesitantly raised her hand to touch my cheek once more. "And standing here, looking at your wonderful face . . . it's almost more than I can bear. I can't do this again. When you leave—you have to be gone."

Overwhelmed with heartache, I whispered, "I get it. I'll have Stacy call you with the time."

She nodded. "Thank you."

As she turned to go back into her house, she opened the door and then stopped. "Take care of yourself, Todd. And take care of those beautiful children. They're lucky to have you as a dad."

She didn't wait for me to reply as she slipped inside and closed the door. In a choked whisper, I answered anyway. "Good-bye, Emily . . . I love you."

Walking back to my car, it hit me with all the weight of a millstone. I was alone. Again.

What had just happened in no way compared to losing Marci, but in some aspects, it was worse. With Marci, I never had a choice.

As a natural reaction, I reached for my cell phone to call my mom. A split second later, reality set in. That's when I realized how alone I truly was.

A River in Egypt

Wednesday, July 30

SITTING IN DR. SCHENK'S office this morning, I felt like an exhibit in a zoo. For several minutes, I sat quietly looking at the good doctor as he casually stroked his beard and stared back at me.

Finally, I couldn't take it anymore. "Doc, if this is some new form of therapy, I have to admit, I'm pretty unimpressed."

His eyes never left my face as he continued to study me without speaking. Eventually, I gave up out of sheer boredom and began scrutinizing his new office décor.

As my interest fell upon a lousy re-creation of a Native American kachina doll, Dr. Schenk finally relented. "I have to say, I am truly impressed."

I glanced back at him with a quizzical expression, clueless as to what he was talking about.

"Despite all that has happened since we last met, you seem far less despondent than I would have expected."

Sensing the potential for an ambush, I hesitated. "Is that a . . . good thing?"

"Very much so. Well, as long as you're not in denial, I suppose."

"Do you think I'm in denial?"

"How would I possibly know that? We haven't spoken two words to each other since you arrived."

I consider Dr. Schenk a brilliant therapist and, beyond that, a friend, but he still has the ability to aggravate me a great deal. "Hey, I'm not the one who's been doing a fantastic impression of an uninterested statue."

Dr. Schenk reclined in his seat with a continued air of indifference. "True. And I take full responsibility for our lack of communication. I simply wanted to observe you for a moment before we began our visit. A therapist can learn a great deal through body language without ever having to hear a patient utter a word."

I was quickly tiring of this inane teacher/student dynamic.

"Is there a point to all this, or what?"

Retrieving his pen, Dr. Schenk made a notation on the pad in front of him. "Hostility," he murmured to himself. "Interesting."

That was it. "Seriously, Doc, I do not have time for this. Are we going to talk about my problems or not?"

Suddenly, his whimsical attitude vanished as he leaned forward and glared at me with a ferocity I found startling. "Todd Landry, you would be wise to figure out how to make time. Everything I do has a purpose, and despite your desire to appear completely in control of your emotional well-being, you have a real problem as I see it."

If anyone else had confronted me that way, I'd have instantly lashed back. But with Dr. Schenk, I felt ashamed, and a little scared. His next statement did nothing to remedy my fear.

"Your impatience mixed with a nasty touch of anger has me more than a little concerned. Tell me, what's your hurry today?"

My mind went blank. "Well, I want to . . . get better." Wow, even I was embarrassed by that answer.

Dr. Schenk lowered his reading glasses, raised an eyebrow, and asked, "Get better? Are you sick?"

"No," I confessed. "You know what I mean. When I first came to see you, my life was a wreck. Thanks to you, I was able to experience hope. In light of everything that's happened to me over the last three weeks, I could use a little hope."

Dr. Schenk shook his head as he made an additional notation. "Very nice effort, my friend, but you and I both know your explanation is completely fabricated."

I gave up. Dropping my eyes to the carpet in front of me, I signaled my surrender.

In a much softer voice, Dr. Schenk said, "I know you're dying to know how my visit with Alex went earlier. I also know you're smart enough to realize I can't share any of that with you. Yet I'm still curious as to *what* it is you would like to know."

I remained transfixed on the tan berber carpet without answering. Somehow, I'd interpreted his interest as rhetorical.

"I'm serious. If you could ask me anything, what specifically would you want to know?"

"Oh . . . well, is she going to be all right?"

"I believe so. It's early, but to your credit, she is a smart, well-adjusted girl who needs time to adjust to her new reality. Is that all?"

"Um, yeah. I guess."

"Ask it, Todd."

"What?"

"Ask it."

I shut my eyes and breathed deeply. "How long?"

Receiving no reply, I opened my eyes and stole a furtive look in Dr. Schenk's direction. Inclining his head, he raised his eyebrows as if to say, "Keep going."

"How long is it going to take?"

"How long is *what* going to take?"

"Just stop," I demanded tiredly. "You know what I mean."

"How long will it be until she is ready to accept Emily?"

"Yeah, that."

Dr. Schenk pursed his lips and exhaled slowly through his nose. "May we review a few things?"

I nodded.

"In the span of twelve months, Alex has lost two major female role models in her life. During that time, she saddled herself with the burden of being a surrogate mother to your other children due to a misplaced obligation unknowingly created by you. Then you commit the ultimate betrayal, in her eyes, by attempting to replace her mother. So I guess I would turn the question back to you. How long do you think this is going to take?"

In a whisper, barely audible above the ticking of his clock, I acknowledged, "Quite a while."

"I would agree. Especially when factoring in that your aversion to therapy must be genetic. Alex is experiencing the same feelings of guilt that you did, simply for being in my office. I would love to help her, but I am not specifically trained to treat adolescents. I intend to refer her to a certified child therapist. I believe this change will greatly benefit your daughter."

I nodded in agreement. To be truthful, I'd have agreed to anything. Watching what little hope I had of holding on to Emily fade away had left me feeling defeated and entirely accommodating.

As if reading my thoughts, Dr. Schenk said quietly, "I'm sorry, Todd. It gives me no pleasure to dash any dreams you may be harboring, but it would be unfair of me not to be honest with you."

"I understand."

"It is probably of little value at the moment, but I am impressed with how you are handling the passing of your mother."

"I guess practice makes perfect," I muttered bitterly.

At the conclusion of my session, I walked out to find Alex waiting impatiently for me in the lobby.

She and I have been in an uncomfortable place since I'd ended things with Emily. I'm certain she never expected me to submit to her demands. But now that I have, she's gaining a true appreciation of the phrase, "Be careful what you ask for."

More than anything, I think she's beginning to realize that getting rid of Emily didn't fix anything.

For one, her attitude has severely damaged our relationship. She's my daughter and I love her, but I feel like I'm going through a mourning process all over again, and I can't help feeling like it's her fault. I know things will get better between us, but it's going to take me some time. I don't think she counted on that.

Walking to the car, I decided to attempt an outreach. "How did it go?"

She shrugged. "About what I expected."

"Really?" This time she didn't respond. "Alex, Dr. Schenk didn't tell me what you talked about, but he did tell me you made it clear you didn't want to be there."

Without looking at me, she scoffed, "Well, duh! I told you that already. I don't need this. I'm not crazy."

We'd reached our car, so I allowed the conversation to pause as we climbed inside. Once we were settled, with the engine running, I turned to her and laid it out as plainly as I knew how.

"I know you're not crazy. I never said you were. But you are not okay. You're angry, and you're nothing like the daughter I knew up until a few months ago.

"Now, if you choose to present nothing but attitude to your new therapist, we can end this now. You don't have to go. But you better understand exactly what that means. If you won't see this new doctor, I will drop you off at home right now. Then I'll drive straight over to Emily's house and beg her to take me back. It's that simple.

"I love you. In fact, I love you so much I chose to hurt someone I care about deeply. And I did it for you and you alone. But if you're not going to meet me halfway, then I'll worry about my other two children, who happen to love and miss Emily very much, and you can figure this out on your own."

Of course I was bluffing. I only prayed she didn't realize it.

What happened next broke my heart. For the first time in a long while, my daughter cried in front of me. It wasn't much, but two or three tears escaped and streaked down her cheek. I wanted to hug her, but I knew we were at a critical juncture.

"So, what's it going to be? Will you give this your best shot or are we done here?"

I waited patiently, listening to the sound of the vehicle's air conditioning unit as it struggled to provide relief to our stifling vehicle. Finally, I gently pushed once more. "Alex, I need to know."

She wiped her eyes with the back of her hand as she looked out the window. "I'll try."

Leaning over, I kissed the top of her head. "I love you, sweetheart. I promise we'll get through this."

Nothing Says Family like Potlucks and Arguing

Sunday, August 3

WHAT MIGHT A LAST meal be like? I can't imagine it would be very good. I mean, no matter how much I love what's being served, as soon as it's over . . . I'm dead. Under those circumstances, I think I'd automatically hate anything showing up on my tray because of what it represents. Am I wrong?

These were the thoughts running through my mind as I drove to my father's house tonight for an extended family dinner—the dinner I'd been anticipating about as much as I would my last.

At the time of my breakup, I honestly wanted to believe that my situation with Emily was temporary. Therefore, I never mentioned a word to my family. Now, three weeks later, I still hadn't told them my engagement was off. Tonight, I knew I was walking into a buzz saw of questions I couldn't answer, sympathy I didn't want, and advice I wouldn't heed. Worst of all, I had no idea what to expect from my dad.

Brock greeted my family and me at the front

door. Once my children and I were inside, he continued to hold the door open in anticipation of someone who wasn't coming. A split second later, the dreaded questions began.

"Where's Emily?"

"She's not here."

"How come?"

"Um . . . well, we broke up."

I don't think his face could have registered any additional shock. "Are you kidding? What happened?"

From the corner of my eye, I could see Alex's panicked expression. "There were some things I needed to deal with and . . ." I shrugged my shoulders. "It just didn't work out."

"Whoa. Sorry to hear that, bro. I really liked her."

Brock gave me a conciliatory backslap as he passed me on his way to the living room. Taking a deep breath, I braced myself for what was coming next.

Once I was in the kitchen, I barely managed to set down my chips and homemade salsa before my sister burst in followed closely by my father. His annoyed countenance told me he'd have preferred to come alone, but when it comes to family gossip mixed with matters of the heart, Katie has never really cared what he prefers.

Katie was already in tears as she rushed forward to hug me. "Oh Todd, I'm so sorry."

"Katie, relax. I'm fine."

Releasing me, she gently swatted my arm. "You're such a liar. And who cares if you're fine? What about the rest of us? I *adored* her."

Awkwardly, I admitted, "I know. She was pretty great."

"Then, why isn't she here?"

"I guess it just wasn't the right time for us."

The remaining questions lingering in her eyes were suddenly put on hold as my father softly, but firmly, interrupted, "Katie, could you give us a moment alone?"

Her frustrated scowl suggested she was ready to fight over this, but my father's stern demeanor won the battle before it ever began. "Fine. Todd, I want to talk before you leave tonight, okay?"

"No problem, sis." Placated, she stepped around my father and disappeared.

Once he was certain no prying eyes or ears remained, he leaned against the island counter and asked, "So, how about some real answers?"

I shrugged. "What do you want to know, Dad?"

"When did this happen?"

"The day after Mom's funeral."

My father closed his eyes as he began rubbing his forehead with his index and middle finger. "Why didn't you tell me?"

"I'd hoped it wasn't permanent."

He nodded his understanding, although his furrowed brow insinuated he still would've preferred to know sooner. "So, I guess you now consider this permanent."

"It looks that way."

"Is this what you want?"

"Not necessarily."

"Is this what she wants?"

I sighed deeply. "I can't speak for her, but if you're asking if this was her idea, the answer is no."

"So, if neither one of you wants this relationship to end, why has it ended?"

"It's not that simple, Dad."

Waving off my explanation, he scoffed, "Sure it is. If you don't want to break up and she doesn't want to break up, then there has to be a pretty good reason why you are breaking up."

"The timing was just bad. It's just one of those things."

"See, those vague answers you were giving your sister are what I would like to avoid. How much does Alex have to do with all of this?"

I raised my eyes to the ceiling and took a deep breath. But before I could speak, I was cut off. "Don't try to sidetrack me, son. You've never been very good at it, and your patented 'look up and breathe deeply' routine has been your signature giveaway since you were four. Tell me straight—how much of this has to do with Alex?"

There was no point in denying what he already suspected. Lowering my focus to the jar of salsa sitting in front of me, I admitted, "Pretty much all of it."

"Oh, Todd. Are you sure you know what you're doing?"

Instantly, my hackles were up. Did he really think I would go and shoot my barely recovering life directly in the foot without giving it some thought first?

With the intensity in my voice rising, I snapped, "Dad, I don't think I have an option here. Alex is confused and she's hurt. She's been storing up a ton of anger, and ultimately, Emily provided the perfect target for it. This is nobody's fault; it's just life. Alex needs me right now, and she doesn't need all of the distractions that come along with a fiancée and a wedding. I've barely been able to convince her to see Dr. Schenk. Thank heavens he knows a child psychologist that will hopefully help her."

Disgusted, my father shot back, "Well, of course he does. Dr. Schenk knows just what to do about everything, doesn't he? I suppose he's the one who convinced you that ending things with Emily was the right course of action."

Now I was really upset. "No, Dad. I made that call on my own when Alex basically told me it was either Emily or her. Did I not make the right decision? What is it about Dr. Schenk that's so threatening to you anyway?"

Completely ignoring my second question, he replied, "Obviously you'd choose your daughter, but she's thirteen. Give her some time and I'm sure she'll be fine. Children only see what's right in front of them, but in the end they recover quickly."

"I'm sorry, but what evidence do you possibly have to support that?"

Shaking his head impatiently, he said, "You're not listening to what I'm trying to say. What she needs is God's basic design—a mother and a father in the home. Maybe right now she has problems with Emily, but eventually she'll come to appreciate her. What she doesn't need is to be hauled off to some atheist shrink every time something bad happens in her life."

"Psychiatry does not equal atheism," I retorted.

"Close enough."

Despite my intense desire to scream, I managed to keep my voice at a controlled volume as I hissed, "This isn't a sprained ankle or a bad grade we're dealing with here. She's lost her mother and her grandmother in less than a year. Not only that, she sees my wanting to get remarried as a complete betrayal. These are problems I need to face head-on, not circumvent as if they don't exist."

Things were escalating quickly. Anticipating another round of Adrian Landry's "here's what you would do if you were righteous" logic, I stiffened my back and put on my battle face. Instead, I was stunned to see my father's whole posture slump.

Sighing deeply, he lamented, "That woman just seemed to make you so happy. I would hate for you to throw that away. She made you better. Watching you wrestle with your demons after Marci died was almost unbearable. I don't want you to go through that again."

How was I supposed to stay angry after an admission like that? My dad was still trying to cope with his own loss after being forced to watch me suffer through mine. His concern touched me.

Walking around the island, I placed my arm across his shoulder and softly said, "Dad, I really do appreciate what you're saying. I am listening. But I'm asking you to trust me. I may be wrong, but I feel like I'm doing what I have to."

For several seconds, he stood stoically, staring straight ahead. Finally he turned toward me and, looking directly into my eyes, declared, "Okay, I'll leave it be and not mention it again."

I couldn't believe what I'd just heard. Unable to help myself, I hugged him. Not being a touchy-feely kind of guy, his body went rigid at first, but gradually he relaxed and returned my embrace.

However, that doesn't mean it lasted very long. After two solid slaps on the back, we immediately backed away from each other. But regardless of how abbreviated our show of affection may have been, my feelings of euphoria remained. At least until he opened his mouth again.

"Well, I suppose there is a silver lining. There's a single adult conference in three weeks, and I was nervous about going by myself. Now that no longer appears to be a problem."

I'm pretty sure my jaw didn't actually hit the floor, but that's only because of its physical impossibility. "Dad, what are you talking about? Mom's only been gone a few weeks. Don't you want to take some time to ease in to your new life before rushing off headfirst into the singles' scene?"

A tired smile crept across his face. "Son, I have so much time on my hands right now that I'm drowning in it. Your brothers don't need me. I taught them everything I know, and they learned it all too well. You don't need me, and neither does your sister. To add insult to injury, you know all those home remodeling projects I swore I'd get to? Well, without your mother, it turns out they were all things I never really wanted to do in the first place."

Listening to his painful confession was

heartbreaking. I wanted to tell him everything was going to get better, but I knew how empty those words had sounded when others had shared them with me.

"So, in answer to your question: no, I don't really want to rush off to a singles' conference. What I want is your mother. But it would seem that the Lord has other plans for me. And as much as I may not care for it, I'm single and this is what singles in the Church do. If you're an elder, you go to elders quorum activities. If you're a high priest, you attend high priest functions. Now, I'm a single, so that conference is where I'm supposed to be. Unfortunately for you, it seems you're determined to remain single too."

Now my shoulders slumped. I'd already met my day's quota of battles won, so it was time to accept the inevitable. "Is it even worth the effort to try to say no?"

"Not really."

"Tell you what. I'm not going to the entire conference, but I'll agree to attend any two of the events that you choose."

"You really should go to the whole thing."

"Two events, Dad."

Like an auctioneer sensing an end to the bidding process, he jumped at my offer. "You've got a deal. We'll go to the service project and the dance."

"Fine," I said out loud. The swear word that followed, I kept to myself.

TODD'S LANDRY LIST

Who Would I Be If I Weren't Me?
Tuesday, August 19

I'M NOT A big fan of the "what if" game. Not being someone who has grand desires to change the world, that phrase can only mean one thing for me: I'm worrying about things I can't change. I don't like to do that.

However, I have some valid "what if" questions I wish I knew the answers to. For instance, what if I weren't such an idiot?

From the day I received my new calling as Boy Scout advancement chair, one of my least favorite responsibilities has been visiting the local Scout office. In reality, it isn't so much the place as it is *her*.

The "her" to whom I'm referring, according to her official Scout name badge, is Ms. Turcell, and she's the only woman I've met who clearly missed her calling in life as an IRS auditor. Her face carries a perpetual look of contempt that just screams, "By having to acknowledge your presence, precious moments of my time are being sucked into a vortex, never to return."

To be fair, I don't know if she treats everyone

the way she treats me. I can't imagine that she does. I would think even the Scouting organization would have some sensitivity toward customer service. But then again, I could be wrong.

I think the main problem is . . . we just don't click. Of course, my disrespectful observations regarding her job performance the last time I saw her probably didn't help things. However, I don't think I'm the only one to blame here. In truth, I can't remember the conversation leading up to my over-the-top critique, but I do remember feeling quite clearly that it seemed more than justified.

Regardless, since that day, I've done my best to avoid her. It took a couple weeks of extensive reconnaissance, but I discovered she rarely works mornings.

So, this morning, I took for granted that she wouldn't be working and I'd get in and out of the BSA office with relative ease. I was scheduled to meet up with Kevin and Jason for tux fittings and was already running a bit late.

If Ms. Turcell had been visible when I entered, I probably would've snuck back out, praying I hadn't been noticed. But, as it was, the entire place felt deserted when I walked in.

I'd just reached the back counter when Ms. Turcell appeared from behind a curtain leading to the Employees Only section. The sudden and unexpected sight of her caused my pulse to quicken as I anticipated the probable confrontation about to occur.

In hindsight, I suppose it's possible my defensive attitude played a large role in what happened next, but giving myself the benefit of the doubt, I'd say those odds were fifty-fifty at best.

Sensing the presence of someone behind her, she turned to greet me. I vaguely recognized the look of genuine kindness that graced her sharp yet attractive features. It was the same expression that had initially welcomed me during my first visit a few months back. For one instant, and one instant only, I found myself taken aback by her natural, makeup-free beauty.

Then she recognized me. With incredible speed, the nasty librarian face that I remembered with amazing clarity returned.

In a terse voice, dripping with disdain, she asked, "How may I help you?"

Being challenged with a blast of condescension didn't help my mood in the least, but I was determined to make this as quick and painless as possible. Handing her a list, I said, "I need to pick up these merit badges and get instructions on how to register a new Scout leader online."

Without acknowledging my list, she responded, "Registration of new leadership cannot be done online." With the speed of a viper, she produced a leadership application and placed it on the counter in front of me. "You need to fill out this form and return it to this office once the individual has completed his or her online youth protection training."

Ignoring the throbbing sensation beginning to manifest itself at the base of my skull, I countered, "How does he get online? I thought you had to be registered in order for any of your online training to be recognized."

"Technically yes, but in situations like this, he'll have to log in under someone else's password and take the training. Then you will have to fill out this form verifying that the person in question has, in actuality, fulfilled the training himself." I'm not sure how she did it, but a second form had suddenly materialized on the counter next to the first.

"So wait, our new assistant Scout leader has to get online, under somebody else's password, and do a training session with me in attendance before we can fill out this application." With each word, my voice mirrored my growing irritation. "Meanwhile, this is an application that, if I understood you correctly, can't be done online. So then I have to waste another hour and physically bring both forms back to you.

Ms. Turcell made a poor attempt at hiding an eye roll. "If you'd followed procedures, this wouldn't be an issue. But let me guess: you're representing an LDS unit, and you didn't bother to submit this individual's name for a background check before he was called, did you?"

I really hate being lectured. Especially by someone who knows they're right.

"You're absolutely correct. We didn't submit his name, and yes, he's already been called. In our defense, we didn't have the luxury of waiting six months, assuming you all take as long to do a background check as you do to approve an overnight camping trip. Bottom line, I need to get this guy registered, so if I need to play your stupid little games regarding this form and that form, so be it. Now, are there any other land mines waiting for me, or am I good to go?"

As I spoke, a pulsing vein appeared in her neck where I hadn't even known a vein existed. Through gritted teeth she replied, "You have everything you need."

"Great. Then can I get my merit badges and be on my way?"

She continued to glare at me for a few moments before looking down at her computer screen. In a tone laced with contempt, she requested, "Your troop number, *please*."

"Fifty-one, ninety."

She typed in the number and then promptly closed her eyes. I did not interpret her reaction as a positive sign.

"My records indicate that your troop has a leader who has not received his leadership-specific training. Unfortunately, the grace period he was allowed to receive that training has expired. We sent out a district directive stating we would not be able to provide any supplies, including merit badges, to any troop out of compliance with regard to this training."

The dull throbbing from earlier was now threatening to explode through my forehead. I stared at her with a mixed expression of disbelief and disgust. "So you're telling me I can't get the merit badges I need for our court of honor tomorrow night."

"Not until Russell Donagee gets his leadership-specific training done."

"Can he do that online?"

"We're working on that and hope to have it available by early next year, but as of right now . . ." I could tell it was causing her great anguish to finish this sentence, ". . . no."

I took a deep breath. "When is the next available training?"

"The trainings are held on the first Saturday of each month."

I had to hand it to her. She was holding her ground quite admirably. Her tone left no doubt as to whom she considered at fault here, and it wasn't her.

"So . . . what you're saying is that there's no way I can get the merit badges I need until next month, at the earliest."

"That's correct."

"Okay, well, I'm so glad to know everything I heard at *my* training session about Scouting being entirely for the boys was complete and utter nonsense."

That comment finally broke her smooth veneer. Her cheeks flushed and her voice shot up an octave as she cried, "Just what is that supposed to mean?"

"It *meeeaaannns* all of your idiotic rules are basically going to keep several young men in my ward from receiving the recognition they deserve. I have a hard time believing this would occur if we were really *focused* on the boys right now. Which begs the question—is everyone here at the district level as rigid as you are, or is this your petty way of punishing me for referring to you as a Nazi the first time we met?"

"I think you need to leave."

For the first time since I'd arrived, rational thought started to infiltrate my brain as I felt the first inklings of embarrassment caused by my behavior. In my most apologetic voice, I quickly began to backtrack. "I'm sorry. That was over the top."

"I do not accept your apology, and I am serious

when I say I think you should leave. You have the forms you need, and there is nothing more I can do for you."

"Fine," I muttered as I grabbed the documents off the counter and turned to go.

Maybe this is wishful thinking on my part, but with my final glance in her direction, I thought I saw the tiniest hint of remorse crossing her expression.

Admittedly, I only saw it for roughly one tenth of a second, and the far more logical conclusion would be that I have no idea what I'm talking about. But I don't think so. In my heart, I believe both of us are a little ashamed of that entire exchange.

Regardless, the whole episode threatened to cast a pall over the rest of my morning, which was exactly what I'd been hoping to avoid.

Today was my best friend's tux-fitting day. If he were twenty-two, this exercise might be considered a nuisance. But at thirty-eight, it was just one more excuse to hang out with friends. So, as I exited the Scout office, my immediate goal was to get my mind right before picking up Kevin and meeting Jason at the tux shop.

Fortunately, all anger remaining faded as soon as Kevin hopped in my car. He was absolutely giddy. In fact, if we weren't such good friends, I'd have sworn he was almost too excited. After ten minutes of his jabbering, I had to interject for my own sanity's sake.

"Whoa there, pardner! What is this?"

"What's what?"

"The nonstop chatter I'd expect more from one of Alex's friends instead of my own."

"Ahh . . . shut it. I'm getting married. I can say or do whatever I want, and, as best man, it's your job to deal with it."

"I don't remember that in the contract."

"It's there. Trust me."

It was awesome to see him so pumped. With all of the near misses he'd been through, I'd almost given up hope that a day like today would ever exist.

"Look, I don't want to go all mushy on you, but it's good to see you this way."

"It's good to be this way."

"Are you nervous?"

To me, the question had been traditional small talk between a groom and his best man. I'd expected him to shoot back something along the lines of "a little, but not too bad." Instead, he was contemplating my question with far more gravity than I'd intended.

Finally, he slowly nodded. "I think I'm good. No . . . I'm sure of it. I'm good. No nerves at all."

Okay, that wasn't a bizarre reaction at all. But it certainly wasn't the most peculiar thing I'd ever heard from somebody preparing for the big plunge, so I let it go.

As for the rest of the morning, I had no idea getting fitted for tuxes could be so fun. I certainly hadn't enjoyed it this much when I got married. The three of us laughed so hard my stomach hurt. Thinking back over the last year, laughing is something I haven't done nearly enough of.

Upon release from the confines of fabric, measuring tapes, and straight pins, we were ready for food. With our appetites raging and no other options visible, the Chili's across the street became our new favorite restaurant.

At first, our conversation during lunch was unremarkable. But then things got quirky when Jason became preoccupied with the people sitting across from us.

In and of itself, preoccupation from Jason isn't unusual, except that generally, his loss of focus is caused by twenty-something-year-old females wearing clothing made from fabric measured in inches rather than yards. Today, he kept staring at a couple of older guys who had to be in their sixties. After fifteen minutes and countless glances in their direction, I couldn't take it anymore.

"Yo, Jason!" I said, snapping my fingers in front of his face. "I'll admit the one in the velvet tracksuit is pretty cute, but frankly neither one of them really strikes me as your type."

Flinching, as if he were startled out of a trance, Jason spluttered, "What . . . excuse me?"

"What is it about those two retirees that has you so fully enraptured? Are they famous or something?"

Jason looked a little sheepish as he confessed, "No, I was just checking out their drinks."

Now I really was confused.

"Their drinks?" I asked. Glancing over, I acknowledged, "I'll admit they've got a weird color, but . . . Huh?"

"I've just never seen a drink like that before."

Random thoughts from Jason were certainly nothing new, but even so . . .

"Um, I'm pretty sure there are thousands of

drinks we've never seen before. We don't drink alcohol, remember? So when it comes to beverages being served in a sports bar, there's a good chance we're gonna be a little naïve."

Puffing his chest out slightly, Jason retorted, "Actually, I know quite a bit about libations. You guys never knew it, but I seriously considered bartending in college . . . for the money. Obviously I didn't, but I learned a lot about different drink combos, and the whole thing fascinated me. I can identify most everything they're serving around here, but whatever they're drinking, it's something I've never seen."

Kevin and I stared at him, dumbfounded. After a couple of seconds, he started to get a little defensive. "Come on, it's just a hobby. I don't drink, and I certainly don't moonlight as a cocktail waitress on the weekends. It's just something that interests me. And besides, it's not like we all haven't wondered what alcohol tastes like at some point in our lives, right?"

If it were possible, I felt my eyebrows rise another inch up my forehead. "I haven't."

"You're lying. Are you telling me you've never been curious about . . ." He shrugged his shoulders, implying we should all know how his question ended. When Kevin and I refused to rescue him, he decided to finish his thought. " . . . you know, stuff we'll never experience because we're Mormons?"

Kevin recovered first. "Are you serious? Are you seriously asking if we daydream about alcohol?"

Watching Jason try to recover from the hole he'd dug himself was almost painful. I couldn't help but feel bad for him, so I offered an olive branch.

"Fine, a couple of years ago I tried the Bailey's Irish Cream flavor of Häagan-Dazs ice cream. Afterwards, I couldn't help but wonder what a real Irish Cream would taste like. And if we're truly lining up at the confessional, I'd also have to admit to having an interest in knowing if rum actually makes eggnog drinkable."

A look of relief spread across Jason's face. But instead of retreating from the subject, it was almost as if my admission empowered him.

"Exactly! That's all I'm saying. And it doesn't have to be alcohol. Don't you ever wonder what your life would be like if you weren't LDS?"

I was about to laugh the whole thing off when Kevin spoke up with his own revelation. "I don't have to wonder at all. Based on my love for all things mocha flavored, I'd probably own my own Starbucks by now."

With an almost gleeful look in his eye, Jason turned to me. "Come on, Todd. What about you? The rum-in-the-eggnog thing doesn't cut it. What would your vice be?"

I pretended to ponder the question, but I already knew my answer.

"Gambling. If we weren't LDS, I'd be the one constantly pushing for weekend trips to Vegas. Now, since my children like to have food to eat and clothes to wear, I'm actually very grateful to have been spared that heinous addiction."

Despite my hope that we had exhausted the subject and might be ready to move on, Jason pressed forward.

"Do you think you'd have waited until you were married?"

This was too much. "Come on. Really?"

"No, seriously. Do you think you'd have the same morals if you hadn't been brought up in the Church?"

As I prepared to retort, I noticed a deep frown settling over Kevin's face. I didn't know why—nor did I want to—but somehow I knew I needed to put an end to this right now.

"How am I even supposed to answer that? If I weren't LDS, what would I be? This whole conversation is irrelevant, and frankly, a little stupid."

Raising my index finger to cut off Jason's next question, I added, "And before you even think about taking it a step further, which I can see in your eyes you want to, I'm not going to answer any questions regarding curiosity about other women. It would be highly inappropriate and show a complete lack of respect for my wife."

My rebuke led to different reactions. Jason recoiled and sat back in his chair, looking properly chastened. Meanwhile, Kevin's face registered relief quickly masked by an air of ambivalence.

Leave it to Jason to take a completely enjoyable afternoon and devolve it into an uncomfortable mess. All I wanted was to get back to the camaraderie we'd been experiencing earlier. With that in mind, I offered the one thing I knew would diffuse our problems instantly.

"Now, if everyone can agree to talk Diamondbacks baseball for the next ten minutes, dessert is on me."

As our conversation turned to pitching staffs and batting averages, the positive energy of our day returned. But more than once, I caught Jason's eyes returning to the table across from us, and something told me that wasn't good.

TODD'S LANDRY LIST

Everyone Here Is
Feeling the Way I Do
Saturday, August 30

I USED TO believe the worst moment in my life would be the day my son surpassed me in either athletics or intelligence or . . . something. It's not that I wouldn't be proud of him. It would just be the ultimate validation that I'm old. But today I learned that will not be the worst moment of my life. Because there is virtually no way possible for something to be worse than what I experienced tonight.

The day I'd been dreading for more than a month had finally arrived. From the moment I'd agreed to go to the single adult conference with my dad, August 30 had been haunting me like a prearranged date with the guillotine.

Per our original agreement, the two events we attended were the service project and the dance. As far as service projects go, I have to admit, I enjoyed this one a lot. It was cool to be one of the hundreds of LDS singles descending on Phoenix metro food banks like a swarm of locusts. When these organizations agreed to let us come, I don't think they had any idea of the number of volunteers they'd be dealing with.

Dad and I were assigned to the group going to St. Vincent DePaul. For four hours we served, visited, and gained a greater appreciation for charitable organizations in our valley. When we were finished, it took every ounce of remaining energy to load our tired, aching bodies into my van for the long drive home. As I pulled onto the freeway, I glanced over to the passenger seat and saw contentment in its purest form.

Earlier, as our assignments within the food bank were being handed out, my dad had been chosen as a volunteer supervisor. In almost no time at all, he'd reassembled the entire work-flow process. Initially, the food bank's director tried to correct what was happening. But after observing the effectiveness of Dad's changes, he ended up taking notes for future implementation. It's a good thing we were only there four hours. Given a full day, my dad likely would have had the director's job.

With my focus directed toward the weekend traffic in front of me, I offered my passenger the validation he deserved. "You know, Pops, that was fun today. Thanks for making me come."

From the corner of my eye, I saw his chest puff out ever so slightly. "I am not your *Pops*. But you're right, there's nothing like a good day of service done together as family."

Quickly, I directed my attention to the driver's side window so that my massive eye roll would go unnoticed.

"It was good, Dad. Brought back a lot of memories."

"Thank you, son. I know this wasn't your preference for today, but it made the experience much more fulfilling to have you here."

And thus ended our father/son bonding moment. Taking a deep breath, he leaned back, closed his eyes, and drifted off. I chuckled to myself as I reached over and turned on the radio.

As we pulled up in front of his house, I tried once more to get a reprieve from the dance. His rejection of my request was quick and painless—as I knew it would be—but I had to try.

At home, I decided to find something to eat before cleaning up for the night. With my fingers crossed, I searched my fridge, only to be disappointed when I couldn't find any expired eggs I could use to make an omelet. Salmonella ended up being just one more potential alibi to let me down.

Then, before I knew it, my father and I were sitting quietly in my van, staring at an unfamiliar stake center. Although I'd attended my first dance months earlier, a large rabble of butterflies had still managed to find a nesting ground within my stomach. The only thing making it bearable was seeing my normally unflappable father displaying his own severe case of nerves.

Finally, accepting that no one was coming to save us, we stepped out into the balmy August night.

As we strode toward the entrance, I was struck by a thought. When I'd come to my first dance five months ago, I'd been away from the singles' scene for a little more than fifteen years. Tonight, my father was back after an absence of over forty. I had to admire his guts of steel.

However, in spite of his impressive intestinal fortitude, his face still had the appearance of a ghost as we reached the door. I leaned toward him as we entered and asked, "You doing okay?"

"I suppose. I keep telling myself that they can't kill me, right?"

"I've never heard of that happening, but don't be surprised if, at times, you have thoughts of killing yourself."

He spun to face me with a stunned look of horror in his eyes. Clearly the stress of the situation had dulled his ability to appreciate sarcasm. In a voice filled with panic, he blurted out, "What is that supposed to mean?"

"Dad, I'm just kidding. Don't worry. Everything will be fine."

I heard him mutter under his breath, "We should've gone to the seminars this morning."

As we entered the cultural hall, I was already wondering how long I should let his misery fester before suggesting we call it a night and head to Dairy Queen. As it turned out, I never got the chance. The moment my father walked in, several people we'd met that afternoon surrounded him. Within seconds, the poor newly-minted widower was whisked away by a mob of concerned well-wishers, leaving me standing alone by the door.

I was flabbergasted. No benevolent bunch of groupies had done that for me at my first dance. I'd been left to fend for myself. The longer I stood there, looking on in disbelief, the more incensed I became.

Eventually, I realized he wasn't coming back, so I found my favorite chair in the corner and sat down. Two or three songs later, I finally spotted him again. He was dancing with a woman at least ten years his junior and was sporting the biggest smile I'd seen on his face in weeks.

As the DJ's voice came over the speakers, I stood in anticipation of intercepting Dad as he exited the dance floor. But I shouldn't have bothered. The song's conclusion caused a throng of females to materialize at my father's side.

That's when the undeniable truth came crashing down on me. My father was already more success-ful at "being single" than I'd ever been. I suddenly felt ill.

But as I continued to watch him, I found myself mesmerized. I couldn't get over how genuinely cheer-ful he looked. As I compared his visible joy to the gloom I'd experienced months earlier, I couldn't help but ask myself—why the difference?

Even as the question formed in my mind, I had to laugh. I knew perfectly well what the difference was. I just didn't want to admit it. I mean, who really wants to acknowledge that they're a snob.

When I'd come before, I was convinced I didn't belong with people like this. In my flawed think-ing, I'd believed most people attending these events were responsible for their own banishment to this LDS version of purgatory. I, on the other hand, had received my sentence through no personal fault of my own. Using that line of logic, I had felt quite comfortable justifying my feelings of superiority.

Tonight, though, I was staring at hard evidence that suggested otherwise. My father—who by my own analysis should have fit in even less than I did—was adapting and even enjoying himself. He hadn't approached tonight as if he were coming off the mountain to walk among the peasants. He was spending a pleasant evening rubbing shoulders with equals. He was busy exemplifying the love of the Savior while I'd been concerned with channeling my inner Pharisee.

The longer I sat there, the worse I felt. This personal examination was causing me to ask myself some uncomfortable questions. Did my attitude mean I thought I was somehow better than Kevin? I knew that wasn't true. How about Emily? Each new comprehension just kept pouring over me, burying me deeper and deeper.

To save myself from the onslaught of self-flagellation, I once again focused on my father. He was effortlessly gliding a middle-aged woman I would've described as "frumpy" around the dance floor. Even from my distant vantage point, I could see the delight in her eyes. And my father? His entire focus was on her. As they chatted, his countenance radiated an uncomplicated love for this fellow child of our Heavenly Father.

In that moment, parts of my world came full circle. My father regained his title of "Man I Most Admire," and I discovered within myself an almost desperate desire to emulate him. I wanted to see people the way he did—the way he always had.

Feeling as if I'd attended a motivational seminar, I stood with a new determination to enjoy myself regardless of what I might encounter. But first, I needed a trip to the restroom.

As I entered the hallway, my enthusiasm vanished. Emily was just ten feet away, exiting the kitchen with a tray full of cookies. In the second before she saw me, my mind rifled through a dozen escape options, each more doomed to failure than the last.

When our eyes connected, her good-natured disposition melted as she closed her eyes and inhaled sharply. We stood opposite each other without moving.

"Hey," I said weakly.

She nodded stiffly in response but made no effort to reply. "Interesting little déjà vu thing we have going on here." I laughed uncomfortably at my lame attempt at humor. It was greeted with a halfhearted smile in return.

If it were possible, she was more beautiful than ever. I wanted to throw her cookie tray to the ground and take her in my arms. Even though six weeks had passed since that awful afternoon on her doorstep, it still felt like the natural thing to do.

I also wanted to beg her to take me back, but I didn't. Nothing had changed. Alex was thawing, but it was an agonizingly slow process. As such, I had nothing new to offer.

Since neither of us had anything to say, she stepped to the side to go around me. If I could do it over again, I probably would've just let her go, but for some reason I couldn't.

"How are you doing?"

She stopped, and, without looking up from the tray in front of her, she said evenly, "I'm seeing someone."

Those three words ripped my heart directly from my chest.

"What?" My shocked comeback landed a little more forcefully than I'd intended.

She whirled toward me and, with obvious pain in her eyes, demanded, "Just what is that supposed to mean?"

The sheer force of her tone caused me to back away a step. "Nothing. I . . . I meant nothing by that at all."

As quickly as it appeared, her anger retreated. "I'm sorry. I didn't mean to lash out that way."

Still stunned from her outburst, I tentatively replied, "No problem."

"Look, the last time we talked, I was sure I would never see you again. I mean, I knew it was always possible, but I didn't think it would be this soon. I'm moving on, but you're still an emotional topic for me—one I try to avoid. Seeing you tonight . . ." She stopped as if searching for more to say.

Before she had the opportunity, I softly replied, "I understand. I was just surprised, that's all. And for the record, I'm not seeing anyone."

Her face registered a smile that tried to mask the pain in her eyes. "Well, hopefully you've come to the right place for that. I need to go."

She turned and walked away without another word.

Unsure of what to do, I continued my journey to the restroom, my resolve from earlier completely shattered. Standing in front of the mirror, I stared at my reflection for what felt like hours. I wanted to feel anger, or sadness or . . . something. Instead, all I felt was numb. Numb, and unbearably alone.

When an older burly gentleman came into the restroom for the third time, eyeing me suspiciously, I decided it was probably time to leave. I verified that the hallway was empty before slipping through the door and eventually landing back in my favorite dark corner.

Casting my eyes toward the dance floor, it didn't take any time at all to locate my father. He was exactly where I'd left him, except this time I recognized his companion. He was dancing with Maureen—the cookie lady. I don't know why I always think of her that way, but I do.

They were slowly gliding among the multitude of couples, engaged in what appeared to be lively conversation. Every few seconds she would break into laughter, and my dad would beam at her enthusiastic response to his latest joke. Personally, I've heard his jokes, and I couldn't help but think she was laying it on a little thick.

The song ended and another began, but this time no groupies appeared. Instead, without breaking rhythm, he and Maureen settled into a foxtrot and their banter continued.

That insignificant detail depressed me. Actually, sitting alone in my dark corner, everything depressed me. Seeing my father with Maureen, my devastating interaction with Emily, the music that hadn't been popular in decades—everything.

Standing up, I walked out the front door and straight to my car. A last-minute pang of guilt forced me to call Mike, verifying he could pick up Dad. But once that was settled, I drove home.

I know the next time my father and I talk, I'll be severely chastised for leaving him. But tonight, that was a price I was willing to pay.

I Have Met My Enemy
and She Is Me
Tuesday, September 9

EVER SINCE THE Hindenberg-level disaster that
occurred during my last visit to the Boy Scout office,
I've been trying to find a plausible excuse to keep me
from ever having to return. So far, nothing. Therefore,
this morning, with our ward's rescheduled court of
honor bearing down upon me, I was left with thirty-
six hours to either get my hands on a pile of merit
badges or make a hasty escape to a non-extraditing
country.

For five minutes, I stood outside the door to the
BSA office trying desperately to convince myself the
boys would be satisfied with whatever I could make
out of cardboard and computer printouts. Eventually,
though, sanity prevailed, and I mustered what little
courage I had to step inside.

Opening the door just wide enough to slip
through, I entered the office as quietly as possible. I
spotted her instantly.

Ms. Turcell was behind the counter, examining
some sort of document. A strand of her dark brown

hair had escaped her ponytail and was hanging down in a crescent shape, framing her delicate features. As on previous visits, I was struck by how attractive this woman could be if she'd just ditch the khaki and the attitude.

Shaking free from my momentary lapse in judgment, I redirected my focus to the business at hand. It appeared she hadn't heard me enter. I stood silent, unable to move, as my initial surge of bravery abandoned me.

Today had the potential for real bloodshed. Aside from the merit badge and registration issues leftover from my last visit, another matter had arisen that was equally pressing. It was time to start on my ward's charter.

Each year, the Boy Scouts require every ward, or troop, to basically reregister each leader and boy. This is known as the chartering process. In theory, it shouldn't be that big of a deal. But as with all things BSA related, don't follow procedure and anything can quickly become a big deal.

I was supposed to have picked up my charter packet at the last roundtable—the monthly meeting where all area Scout leaders gather for training/boredom. It's also the place where business, such as handing out a troop's charter packet, occurs. And since I'd missed that opportunity, I was now forced to come and beg for it from the Scout office.

When I mentioned my predicament to a fellow chartering officer from another ward, she visibly backed away from me as if I'd contracted the plague. Apparently, our local Scout office officials relish any opportunity to lecture those who don't abide by the all-important roundtable PPP (packet pickup protocol). In a somewhat terrified manner, my friend explained that you never want to give anyone from the Scout office an opportunity to lecture you. From my own firsthand experience, I could see why.

What was most frustrating to me about my predicament this morning was that I knew Ms. Turcell would automatically assume I'd blown off the September meeting. Nothing could be further from the truth. I'd taken the time to clean up, provide a meal for my family, and drive seven miles to the appointed location. I'd even arrived five minutes early.

Once I'd found a seat, everything was fine for at least . . . ninety seconds. Then, a woman in full Scout regalia stood to hype the joys of selling popcorn as a troop fund-raiser. That, by itself, was not a problem. My issues arose when she put on a corncob hat.

To be clear, this wasn't a hat made out of corn or a hat woven from corn shucks. This was a Styrofoam hat made to resemble an actual half-opened ear of corn.

I recognize that I'm probably blowing this out of proportion, but I was staring at a lady, whom I was expected to take seriously, wearing a corncob hat. If I had been eight years old, I probably wouldn't have found this quite so patronizing, but I was one of the youngest people in the room. To make things worse, she insisted on using a wide variety of corn-related puns.

By the time she wrapped up with, "If your boys have a *kernel* of desire and are *stalked* full of enthusiasm, they can experience a *cornucopia* of success," I'd tuned her out in favor of counting holes in a ceiling tile.

Following the corncob lady, another gentleman stood to recognize those individuals who'd completed a week of leadership training called Wood Badge.

Each Wood Badge graduate was presented with a new neckerchief. The whole presentation was ceremonial and grand, which, in my cynical view of the world, translates into long and drawn out.

Nevertheless, to finish the formal ritual, every person who'd ever completed Wood Badge training stood and sang a song about forest animals. I'm sure it was important to those taking part, but I was done. Easing as quietly as possible to the back of the room, I grabbed the informational flyers regarding upcoming events and snuck out the back door. I completely forgot about the charter packet.

And that is why I found myself standing in the front of the Scout office this morning with no one to blame for my predicament but myself. However, in order to maintain my perch on the moral high ground, I've chosen to ignore my own personal responsibility, and instead have placed the blame squarely on the writers of the Wood Badge song.

As the digital clock in the corner registered the passage of another minute, I realized my entire day would be wasted if I continued to stand there. Willing myself forward, I set off toward the back counter, weaving through myriad clothing racks packed with colors not sold in any other retail location.

For some unexplainable reason, I continued to

operate in stealth mode. As such, she never heard me coming. I wasn't sure if that was good or bad. Now standing only five feet away, and uncertain of how to proceed, I selected my worst possible option.

"Ahhh, we meet again Lord Vader."

Wow! That line looks even worse in print than when I said it out loud.

Slowly, Ms. Turcell raised her head with an unmistakable expression of loathing darkening her face.

Placing the piece of paper she'd been reading aside, she glared at me as she asked, "What may I do for *you*?" The stress on the word "you" came across as less than complimentary.

Gulping nervously and trying to sound as contrite and pleasant as possible, I replied, "I don't know if you remember the conversation we had a couple of weeks ago, but I'm back with all of my documentation in order. Our court of honor is scheduled for tomorrow, and I was hoping I could get the merit badges I need."

After taking my completed forms and giving them a cursory glance, she retreated to the back of the store to fill my order. When she reemerged, she handed me a bag without speaking and then returned her attention to the document she'd been studying earlier.

"How much do I owe you?"

Keeping her focus on the paper in front of her, she replied, "Don't worry about it. We'll bill your unit directly."

I shrugged but didn't move.

Irritated, she forced herself to meet my gaze once more. "Is there something else?"

"I need to pick up my troop's charter packet."

Ms. Turcell did not move a muscle. The only indication she'd heard me was the twitch forming directly over her left eye that hadn't been noticeable seconds earlier.

"You were supposed to pick it up at roundtable."

I knew it. She'd already judged me. My temper flared from zero to sixty in a flash.

Pronouncing each word with a heightened level of diction, I set out to defend myself. "I am aware that I was supposed to pick it up at roundtable. However, I was unable to. I would like to pick it up now. Please." In hindsight, I probably shouldn't have packed four cups of sarcasm into the word "please."

Through a clenched jaw, she asked, "May I ask why you didn't pick it up at the designated time and place?"

"You may ask, but I'm not sure you'll appreciate my answer."

Assuming an expression of utmost superiority, she launched into her well-prepared dress-down speech. "I'm not going to assume that you care about any of this, but we have processes in place for a reason. We have people pick up their packets at roundtable because that is where we provide specific instructions on how it is to be completed. Those who don't pick it up at roundtable are almost always the same people who complete it incorrectly, turn it in late, and end up wasting a whole lot of people's time, up to and including mine. So if you were unable to pick it up when you should have, I would hope you'd have a good reason as to why. If not, then I would *try* to impress upon you the importance of adhering to our processes."

"You mean if I tell you why I didn't pick it up and you don't like my answer, I get to hear everything you just said again? Or would this be like everything else in Scouting and require me to sit through an hour-long PowerPoint presentation?"

The eye twitch increased its speed drastically. At the same time, her eyes narrowed slightly as if to more accurately pinpoint the laser she intended to use to blow a hole through my forehead. In a venomous whisper, she asked, "Why do you bother?"

"Excuse me?"

Her voice returned to its regular volume as she elaborated, "You clearly despise everything about Scouting. Why would a bishop call you to be an advancement chair? And furthermore, why would you accept?"

Without thinking, I shot back, "I do it because I love the boys."

"Well, that's nice. Go for the most cliché line in the Church."

Whoa! That actually stumped me. She was right. *The boys* had nothing to do with why I was here. Caught completely flat-footed, I hesitated before sheepishly admitting the truth. "I was raised to never turn down a calling, regardless of how I felt about it."

My candid answer caused her expression to soften. "I suppose I can understand that, but why accept a calling you aren't going to fulfill?"

Although I could tell she didn't mean it

insultingly, I still took it that way. I lashed out defensively, "I fulfill every bit of this calling. I do everything that's required regardless of how stupid or pointless it is. And believe me, with Scouting, there's plenty that's stupid and pointless."

The look in her eyes following my outburst was not what I expected. If anything, I'd anticipated another volley of fury and fire. Instead, she looked hurt.

"I was taught there's more to fulfilling a calling than meeting the letter of the law."

Her subtle rebuke was no louder than before, but this time all traces of venom were gone. I think that's why it stung so much. As someone who likes to play the "spirit of the law versus the letter of the law" card quite regularly, I felt incredibly small. And the worst part of it? She was right.

Feeling completely humbled and desperate for something to say that would ease the tension, I proved yet again that I may be the world's biggest moron.

"Would you go out to dinner with me sometime?"

To a certain degree, that one even caught me off guard. But my feelings of surprise were nothing compared to the look of shock, mingled with horror, that registered on her face.

"WHAT?"

It was at this precise moment I realized, I had no idea if this woman was even single. I'd always assumed she was single because . . . why did I always assume she was single? She'd never worn a wedding ring, but that doesn't mean anything. I was lucky if Marci remembered to wear hers half the time. Racking my brain, I stood there, dumbstruck, wondering what lead me to make such a leap. I felt humiliated. I don't have any idea what came over me.

Okay, that's a total cop out. I know exactly what came over me. She's quite attractive, I hurt her, and I hate providing people a reason to hate me. Combine all that together and let the fun begin.

But why had I assumed she was single? And that's when it hit me. The most powerful thing attracting me to her was the same reason I'd assumed she was single. Ms. Turcell was lonely.

A year and a half ago, I never would've noticed. All I'd have seen was a tough-minded woman who, despite her good looks, was annoyingly rigid. But now . . . now I was all too familiar with what lonely looks like. I see it every day in the mirror. And that same look had been staring back at me from across a counter holding displays of Scout books and Camp Geronimo pamphlets.

But what if I was wrong?

"Please tell me you're not married."

My question caused her stunned expression to give way to bewilderment. "Uh, no . . . Are you crazy?"

I took a step toward her in an effort to assure her I wasn't crazy. Looking back, maybe an aggressive move forward wasn't my best play. She backed away as she continued, "No really . . . are you crazy?"

Little by little, the reality of what I'd just done pieced itself together in my still spinning brain. In an effort to avoid a full-on panic attack, I did the only thing I could think of. I started talking.

"Look, from the beginning we got off on the

wrong foot. I'm sure every impression you have of me is just horrible, but . . . let me start again. I'm recently widowed. Not recently enough that I should still be a certifiable lunatic, but fairly recent. My wife discovered me in a cabin, far from civilization, where I'd lived without language or social skills. Clearly she taught me how to speak, but we only got so far when it came to human interaction . . ." I stopped. It occurred to me that incoherent babbling was probably not going to help me.

"I'm sorry. I should probably go. I don't know what came over me."

In my final defense, I looked directly into her eyes and added, "What you said about the letter of the law was dead on, and I realize what an idiot I've been. An irrational train of thought from there led me to believe that you could be an interesting person I might enjoy getting to know. Please forgive me. I'll pretend this never happened, assuming I ever have to come back here. I suppose I could beg for an assistant whose sole job is to come here, if that would be better for you. I really should—"

"Do you ever plan to shut up?"

"As a matter of fact, yes, right now."

Her eyes dropped back to the sheet of paper in front of her as she contemplated her next move. I stood motionless, worried that the least provocation might incite her to pepper spray me. Without raising her head, she asked, "So when would we go?"

My mouth fell open in sheer astonishment. I quickly tried to recover before she noticed. "Umm . . . Friday?"

"You do realize that having dinner with you in no way commits me to liking you as a person?"

"Totally understood."

Her eyes never left the counter as she continued, "Somewhere in all that gibberish, you convinced me that you might not be the anti-Christ after all. Heaven knows I could use the illusion of having a life, even if it is for only one night."

From the change in her voice, I was pretty sure that last statement was not for my benefit. Abruptly, she came back to reality and looked me square in the eye. "Pick me up at seven. And if you're more than ten minutes late, I don't ever want to see your face again."

To me that seemed fair. I agreed, got her address, and escaped quickly before she had a chance to reconsider. And I discovered Ms. Turcell's first name is Abby.

TODD'S LANDRY LIST

I'm Not a Rock,
I'm Not an Island
Wednesday, September 10

"TELL ME ABOUT this woman."

Being somewhat taken aback as Dr. Schenk and I usually began our sessions with some sort of pleasantries, I genially countered, "And a good day to you. My children are well, thanks for asking. And how might you be?"

My hostile interrogator (formerly known as my therapist) didn't bat an eye. "I'm fine. Tell me about this woman."

Okay, Dr. Schenk had definitely woken up on the wrong side of the bed this morning. I have to admit, it was disconcerting not to have the calm, welcoming therapist I was used to.

"I apologize, but there's not much to tell. Obviously you've read what I wrote about her, and that means you probably know as much about her as I do."

"Why, then, are you asking her out?"

Although I didn't want Dr. Schenk to know it, I'd actually been asking myself the same question. "I don't know how to describe it, except to say . . . at that moment, it felt like the right thing to do."

"How does it feel now?"

I'm not sure how he does it. In less than three minutes, Dr. Schenk, with his menacing tone and direct questioning, had shattered my self-confident façade. Placing my head in my hands, I rubbed my eyes in such a way that my palms covered my face.

"Not the right thing to do."

I was hoping a vulnerable admission of the truth might gain me a certain level of sympathy. He wasted no time in putting those fantasies to bed.

"Of course it feels that way. Tell me, had you given any thought to asking this woman for a date prior to the moment you verbally vomited all over yourself in front of her?"

"No," I admitted sheepishly.

Dr. Schenk stared at me, baffled, before looking away with an exasperated shake of his head.

"Todd, I've never thought of you as impulsive. Yet reading your blog over the last month or so, I feel like I'm reading the words of a complete stranger. You seem to be making one nonsensical decision after another."

His declaration flummoxed me. My jaw worked itself up and down several times before finally finding a voice to accompany it.

"Why would you say that?"

"Well, let's begin with this question. Who is the person most responsible for helping you through your grief following the loss of your wife?"

"You, I suppose."

"Balderdash! Why don't you try again when you have a real answer."

Properly chastened, I hesitated before venturing, "Emily?"

"Why are you placing your answer in the form of a question? Of course it's Emily. She possessed all the qualities necessary for you to break through your shell of depression. Factor in her need for a hero on a white horse, and you had your perfect elixir."

The mere mention of her name was bad enough. Unfortunately, he wasn't done.

"You bond with this woman to such an extent that you are ready to commit the rest of your life to her. Then at the moment when you should be turning to her for comfort and support, you decide to abandon rational sense and submit to the terrorist demands of a thirteen-year-old."

"Wait a minute! You seemed to be in total agreement with that decision when I was here last."

"I'm sorry, but that is the epitome of self-delusion. I agreed with your rationale that getting Alex into therapy was vital. We discussed your unrealistic view of her recovery, and then, apparently, we sat in this office together making small talk for forty-five minutes."

"Wha . . . Huh?"

"Funny, I had the same reaction when I read your blog post recounting our last visit. You covered in great detail our discussion regarding Alex, and then suddenly you're walking out to greet her in my lobby. That conversation ended within the first fifteen minutes of our session. For the next forty-five minutes, I tried desperately to get you to recognize the flawed judgment you employed when you ended your relationship with Emily."

Stupidly, I answered back without thinking, "I don't remember that."

"Apparently! I'm curious, what *do* you remember from the remainder of that session?"

Rifling through my memories, I felt a flush of embarrassment rising quickly from my neck up to my cheeks. I could remember that initial exchange dominating my thoughts to such a degree that I found it hard to focus after that. As if sensing my dilemma, Dr. Schenk proffered an answer for me.

"You don't remember it at all, do you?"

Not wanting to admit to my own failures, I retorted defensively, "Well, if it was so important, why didn't you just come out and tell me what I was supposed to do?"

Dr. Schenk snorted in derision. "Because that is not how this works. I don't *tell* my patients what to do. I provide clarity and then allow people to make their own decisions. At the time, I thought it imperative that you discover for yourself how important your relationship with Emily is . . ." Dr. Schenk closed his eyes and exhaled before correcting himself. ". . . was."

"So why are you telling me this now? What changed?"

It was incredibly disheartening to see my therapist's shoulders slump in response to my question.

"Two things. One, a month ago, I was not aware that irrational decisions made on the spur of the moment were going to become a trend for you. And two . . ." He paused as if he truly wished to avoid his next statement. "I'm afraid it's my belief that your opportunity with Emily may have passed."

Realistically, I'd already come to that conclusion on my own. Yet hearing him say it out loud felt like a stinging slap to the face. Tears flooded my eyes as I whispered, "I'm afraid you're right."

Dr. Schenk offered me a tissue before settling back in his chair. Once I'd cleared my eyes, he quietly said, "Todd, I rarely admit to a patient when I believe I've made an error. It's generally not a good practice, and, in most cases, there is nothing to be gained.

"However, in light of your earlier question, I feel it would be disingenuous of me not to acknowledge an oversight on my part. If I could go back to our previous session, I would have been more forceful in suggesting you try and salvage your relationship with Emily."

His words felt like anvils on my shoulders. It wasn't that I blamed him—I just never should've let her go. I should've tried another avenue to help Alex and not been so rash in reacting to her demands. What had I been thinking?

Again, Dr. Schenk seemed to be ahead of me. "As much as we may want to dwell on our shared failings, we have more to discuss."

I breathed in deeply. There was no telling where the conversation was headed next.

"Your abrupt dismissal of Emily is one thing, but you may be surprised to know I find your proposition of a date to this . . ." Dr. Schenk consulted his notes, ". . . Abby, to be equally troubling."

"Why is that?"

"Right up until the moment you asked her out, your writings displayed only feelings of intense loathing for this woman. What changed, and how did it change in such a dramatic fashion?"

I took several moments to ponder his question. I knew the answer, but I'd never attempted to put it into words.

"I hate the thought of someone not liking me. I mean, it's not that I can't handle being disliked. I just . . . I just hated that *I* was responsible for her not liking me. Does that make sense?"

"Possibly. Continue on and see if you can't be a little more specific."

"I don't think I'm a mean person. So if someone genuinely detests me, I have to assume my personality simply doesn't jive with theirs.

"However, with Abby, I'd given her a legitimate reason to hate me. I was really mean. And I knew what I was doing, but in the heat of the moment, I didn't care. Yet, once I saw that look of pain in her eyes when I snapped at her the last time . . . I had to do something to fix it. Asking her out was the first thing that popped in my head."

"How does the fact that she accepted make you feel?"

"Um . . . a little frightened, to be honest. I mean, what woman in her right mind goes out on a date with a guy who acts like I did? Doesn't that seem a little crazy?"

"A little, yes. Nevertheless, in your defense, you did seem to recover nicely following the date suggestion."

I scoffed dismissively, "Maybe, but I can't help feeling this is going to end in disaster."

"When you left Emily's house for the last time, you expressed a desire to talk to your mother. Why is that?"

I wasn't sure what this had to do with anything, but deciding to trust Dr. Schenk, I directed my thoughts back to that horrific day.

"I guess I've always talked to my mom when things get tough."

"Why is that?"

I stared at him, trying to determine what he wanted me to say. "Because she's my mother. I'm sorry. I'm not sure what you're after."

"Would you say she was a stabilizing force for you? Was she someone who provided a sense of calm in the midst of life's storms?"

"Very much so. No matter the problem, she always had a way of helping me see the big picture."

Dr. Schenk removed his glasses and held them by one end as he gazed at me. "Since her passing, it appears to me you have been doing your best to live up to the Landry persona. To coin a phrase from your culture, you've picked up your handcart and pressed forward.

"But this belief you seem to harbor that you're not experiencing any lasting repercussions resulting from your mother's death is a fallacy. Every loss has its consequences."

"Believe me, Doc, I understand that."

"I'm sorry, but I don't think you do. And I would submit your recent behavior as evidence."

Exasperated, I fell back into the chair behind me. "I can't win. With Marci it was, 'you need to be strong and move on with your life.' Now you're trying to tell me when it comes to my mom, I'm being too strong? Forgive my stupidity, but which is it?"

"Your strength is immaterial. The death of your wife and the death of your mother are two different things. With Marci, you almost ceased to function. That's understandable as your life was completely interwoven with hers. To heal, you needed to find a new foundation—a new reason for living, if you will.

"The passing of your mother created different issues. You loved her and cared about her, but she wasn't integral to your daily life. Yes, she may have watched your children on occasion, but that role is relatively easy to replace in the grand scheme."

Dr. Schenk moved to the edge of his seat. "Because of this fundamental difference, you processed her passing quite differently. I believe when your mother's death didn't cause the same emotional paralysis as your wife's, you mistook that as a sign of full emotional health. You convinced yourself that it was your turn to be the rock everyone leaned on and never took the time to recognize exactly what you'd lost."

"And what was that?"

"Why don't you tell me?"

My reclined position remained unchanged. I'd been at this therapy game long enough to recognize that the smart-aleck remark dancing on the edge of my tongue would only come back to bite me. So I went with honesty.

"I lost the one person I knew would never judge me." Smiling sadly, my voice caught as I added, "I lost my safe harbor."

"That is insightful. You have probably never expressed those feelings verbally before, but I'm sure you've contemplated them several times. Have you ever felt a sense of homesickness while thinking about her?"

Almost unconsciously, I lifted my head up and leaned forward, nodding. "Yeah. I never put that together before, but that's exactly what I feel."

"Regardless of age, almost every child experiences something similar when he or she loses a parent. It's not uncommon for those feelings to continue for years. Unfortunately for you, the loss of your mother was complicated by your wife's passing."

"How's that?"

"Ever since your wife's death, you've felt weak. Even worse, you believe everyone else sees you as weak. Because your last name is Landry, that has haunted you for months. Do you disagree?"

My gaze shifted to the floor. He was right, but I wasn't ready to admit it out loud. Recognizing my silence for what it was, he continued, "Your mother's passing provided the opportunity to be the Landry you always felt you should've been. So you buried everything else and embraced that role.

"However, those manifestations of grief that every child experiences when a parent dies don't go away because you refuse to have time for them. They are like water. They'll simply find the next path of least resistance."

Shifting uncomfortably, I interjected, "What does this have to do with Emily or Abby?"

"I'm getting there. First, answer this question: when Marci died, what words would you use to describe the resulting relationship with your mother?"

I hesitated. "Confidant. Friend. Something along those lines."

"Interesting. Early on in our blogging experiment, you used a different word. You referred to her as your *protector*."

"I did?" My mind was racing, trying to remember such an admission. "When was that?"

"You were anticipating an upcoming dinner with your parents following your first venture into the world of single life. Your father had made his intentions clear to interview you regarding your encounter with Emily. The only thing that brought you peace was, in your own words, 'At least I know if things get too bad, I can always count on my mother to protect me.' That admission was more telling than you knew."

Moving forward even more, I perched myself on the edge of my chair. I could sense what Dr. Schenk was about to say was important. Of course, being the therapist that he is, he diverted from his revelation to a question.

"What happens when people no longer feel protected?"

"Chaos?"

"Close. I believe a more appropriate description would be desperation. People who feel vulnerable will resort to almost anything to regain a sense of safety. Unfortunately, one of desperation's first victims is rational thought. Think of the drowning person who fights against their rescuer out of panic. That's just one example out of thousands I could give."

And here we were. We'd rounded the corner, and I could see the finish line ahead. "Are you saying that because I've lost my protector, I'm now acting out of desperation?"

"You tell me. When Alex laid down her ultimatum that led you to end your relationship with Emily, who would you have normally gone to for advice?"

My eyes dropped to the floor. "My mom."

"So, with her unavailable to you, to whom did you go next?"

"I didn't. I made the decision on my own."

"And what caused you to make that decision?"

Without even realizing the blatant trap I was walking into, I replied, "It felt like the right thing to do at the time."

"Do you realize that is the exact same reasoning you expressed to me earlier with regard to asking out Ms. Turcell?"

I closed my eyes and took a deep breath. "No. No, I didn't."

"Todd, it's my belief that you're afraid. You're afraid of what life will be like without a protector—a safe harbor. And because you're feeling afraid and vulnerable, you're abandoning reason to a certain degree and functioning on a strictly instinctual basis. Now while it's true that a person's instincts can be valuable, when employed under these types of circumstances, they can also be destructive."

"So, what are you suggesting that I do?"

Dr. Schenk smiled sheepishly, as if embarrassed to say what he was thinking. "I could go into a long psychological explanation, but really the answer is very simple. You need to start thinking before you act."

What's the Spanish Word for Uncomfortable?

Friday, September 12

THERE'S A GREAT quote from a guy named Cato the Elder. It goes: "Wise men profit more from fools than fools from wise men, for the wise men shun the mistakes of fools, but fools do not imitate the successes of the wise." Every day I pray that my kids grow up to be wise, because heaven knows they could profit greatly from this fool they have for a father.

For an example, look no further than my date tonight with Abby. All along, I'd planned on taking her to a nice Italian bistro I knew of in Chandler, but when I called to get a reservation during a quick stopover at my office this morning, I was informed they were hosting a wedding and would be closed after 2:00 p.m.

Hanging up the phone, I began to panic. I needed plans. In hindsight, this was the time I should've heeded Dr. Schenk's advice from our last session about thinking first, acting later. As an alternative, I chose insanity.

I've worked with Cal for about six years. In that time, I can count on one hand the number of times Cal has made a personal decision that makes sense. If anything, he's been my barometer of what not to do in my own life. So I'm clueless as to how I suddenly forgot all of that when he wandered over to my desk, interrupting my frantic search for a restaurant in the yellow pages.

"Hey, dude, you look stressed." Pushing aside my family pictures, he perched himself on the edge of my desk. "What can Cal do to ease your burden, my friend?"

"Unless you know of a way to break up a wedding in the next six hours so I can get a table at Naples, I think you're pretty much useless to me."

"Naples? Why would you want a table at Naples? That place is tired, man."

"I happen to like Naples. The fact that you don't makes me like it even more."

"Buddy, don't get me wrong. Naples is a fine eatery, but it has . . . a married vibe to it. That's the kind of place people go to celebrate the death of fun."

Oh, the opportunities I had to avoid disaster. I've never gone wrong with Naples, yet for some reason, Cal's description planted a seed in my brain. I should've aborted the conversation right then. Instead, I let him continue. "If you're going on a date, you want to go to a place that has a little more excitement, you know, pizzazz."

He looked me up and down as if he were my personal shopper trying to identify which colors would bring out my true summer aura. Finally, he reached his verdict. "What you want is Taraza."

"Taraza?" I asked, with no attempt to disguise my skepticism.

"Yeah, man, Taraza. It's a swanky joint up in Scottsdale that serves the best Colombian food in town. You've had Colombian food, haven't you?"

"Can't say that I have."

"Ohhh man, you haven't lived. Colombian food is to die for." Right then, the last remaining barrier protecting me from lunacy fell. Between his ravings about Colombian cuisine and my fanatical need to impress, the craziest of notions began to form. I was about to seek advice from Cal.

"How busy is this place?"

"It's fairly new, so you shouldn't have any trouble getting a reservation."

"Is it pricey?" I asked. But before he could answer, I continued. "Never mind. That doesn't matter."

My mind was already conjuring up an extremely romanticized version of what this mysterious place must be like. Just to be sure, I narrowed my gaze to ensure he understood we were one step away from pinky swearing. "You promise this place is good."

"It's amazing, buddy. You will not be sorry you took ol' Cal's recommendation on this one." As it turned out, ol' Cal couldn't have been more mistaken.

When Abby and I walked through the front door of Taraza, several things about Cal came quickly to mind that would've been helpful had I remembered them earlier. One, Cal isn't LDS; two, Cal is single; and three, Cal has never matured beyond junior high.

Abby and I were greeted by a hostess identifying herself as Carla. Carla was wearing a dress (and I use that term only because I don't know what else to call it) with a neckline that plunged to her navel. My personal humiliation couldn't possibly get any worse.

Then Carla stepped out from behind the hostess station.

That's when it was revealed that had the neckline dropped a mere eight inches more, it would've reached the bottom hem of her garment. I should've turned around and walked out right then.

Nevertheless, I let her lead us to a table located directly in the center of the floor. Once we were seated, I had to avert my eyes as Carla placed our menus in front of us. However, as I turned to my left, I found my line of sight completely blocked by the backside of a waitress serving the table next to us. She had perfected the same leaning technique as Carla, only wearing a skirt that was even shorter.

In a nanosecond, I realized how the posture of the waitress and the position of my head could be misconstrued. Hastily, my eyes darted around for any kind of view that was safe. I settled for a ceiling fan ten feet away as Carla recited the daily specials.

When it was finally safe to look down, I glanced across the table expecting to find daggers waiting for the opportunity to skewer my retinas. Instead, Abby was smiling.

"You know, you could've planned the perfect evening and not come off as good as you did just now."

I stared at her stupidly. "I'm sorry?"

"There isn't a man alive who could fake how uncomfortable you look."

"Please forgive me," I stammered. "Someone I should've known better than to trust highly recommended this place, and I was too stupid to check it out first. I'm—"

She cut me off. "Don't sweat it. Of all the crazy coincidences, a friend and I were planning on coming here next week. So either way, I would've ended up here eventually. But this way, I get dinner and entertainment."

"Do you want to leave?"

"I hope you don't think less of me, but I'm kinda curious about the food. It's supposed to be really good. If you want to, we can go, but I'm okay."

"Tell you what. If we can get that booth over there," I pointed to a table near the back with privacy walls extending to the ceiling, "I think I'll be able to manage."

"Deal."

I intercepted Carla on her next trip through the dining room and made my request. She flashed a smile filled with overly whitened teeth and accommodated us without a hint of annoyance. Whatever the staff may have lacked in clothing, they definitely made up for in customer service.

If I had to do it all over again, I would still choose a different restaurant. However, those opening minutes of awkward torture proved to be an excellent icebreaker for us.

Once we'd ordered and as we waited for our food to arrive, I learned that Abby was originally born and raised in Preston, Idaho. Upon graduating from high school, she attended Ricks College, where she met her eventual ex-husband. His desire to become a doctor eventually brought them to Tucson where he attended medical school at the University of Arizona.

At this point in the narrative, Abby paused as our waitress returned with our meals. All dialogue between us stalled as we immersed ourselves in the exquisite flavors of our entrees.

As much as I may have wanted to bury Cal somewhere in the desert earlier, I had to grudgingly admit he was right about the cuisine. My dish of bandeja paisa was amazing. After three bites, I was ready to quit my job and join a Colombian drug cartel if I could eat like that every day. Abby expressed similar enthusiasm for her sancocho de gallina, minus the desire to traffic in illegal narcotics.

A brief time later, the burden borne by the wooden plates in front of us had lightened significantly. Placing my fork on the table, I decided to pose the question I'd been harboring all evening.

"Please understand, I'm not trying to pick a fight by asking you this. And if you don't want to discuss it, I will back off. But how did you become so involved with and *into* Scouting?"

Her eyes, which had been watching me with wary interest, slowly registered a suspicious smile. "You really think that's a safe subject?"

"I promise to sit silently and not argue with anything you say."

She laughed and let her gaze drift out onto the

main floor. For at least a minute, she sat quietly. I can only assume she was evaluating how much she wanted to share. As promised, I didn't move a muscle.

Without returning her eyes to our table, she said, "When you asked me out, you said you were recently widowed, right?"

"Correct."

"How long ago was that?"

"A little over a year."

"How's the single-parent life working out for you so far?"

"It's hard," I admitted honestly. "But I'm pretty lucky to have my family nearby. Without them, I don't know how I would've survived."

She continued to stare into the distance. "I understand that. I thank God every day for my parents."

Sensing she had finally reached a verdict, I held my breath and sat motionless. Slowly, she turned back in my direction and leaned forward with her eyes boring into mine. "I have one son. He's seventeen, and he's just starting his senior year. I got pregnant right after I was married, and within two years of graduating high school, I was a stay-at-home mom."

I leaned forward just slightly, as if to say, "Please continue." Somewhat embarrassed, she looked away from me but continued with her story.

"The staying at home thing didn't work so well for me. I think I got depressed. I gained weight and discovered what a lousy housekeeper I am. My husband would drop hints about the pounds I was putting on, but since he wouldn't say anything directly, I ignored him. Six years later, he was done hinting. In fact, he was just done. Right after medical school, he left me and married one of his classmates."

I sat still, unsure of what to do. Never did I think a simple question about the Boy Scouts would lead to such personal revelations.

"My parents had already moved to Mesa a couple of years before to be closer to me and James. That's my son, James. Anyway, after my husband left, I moved up here so my parents could help me get back on my feet.

"To my ex's credit, he's never tried to get out of paying child support or anything, but when he decided to leave, he really decided to leave. He didn't seek any custody and didn't see his son again for four years. It didn't take long to figure out I was going to raise my boy alone."

I'd never anticipated that our conversation would go this deep. I wanted to say something supportive, but I wasn't sure if it was my place to do so. Nevertheless, I decided to try.

"That must have been hard."

A dismissive expression crossed her face accompanied by a shrug of her shoulders. "It's life. Like you said, I was blessed to have my parents here. It would've been impossible without them."

She stopped suddenly, and her eyes filled with intensity. "Just to be clear, I'm not after sympathy. I'm just answering your question."

I raised my hands in mock surrender to let her know I understood. She nodded vaguely before pressing on.

"My dad did everything he could, but he was powerless to change two things—his age and his health.

"By the time James was eleven, I was starting to lose him. He didn't click with any of the boys in our ward, so he found friends where he could. I knew I had to do something."

Out of the corner of my eye, I saw our waitress returning to check on us. Fortunately, I was able to indicate with a slight shake of my head that now was not the ideal moment, and she retreated without Abby noticing.

"I'd heard good things about a charter school in Gilbert, so I looked into getting James enrolled. At the same time, I got a better job, which meant a better apartment in east Mesa. That move was the best thing that ever happened to us.

"Within a week, the Scoutmaster from our new ward was at our door. My son still had a month before he turned twelve, but Brother Hart was a real go-getter. He said he just wanted James to feel welcome. I've known a lot of good men in my life, but Bruce Hart is special. I'll always consider him the man who saved my son.

"Anyway, with Brother Hart's help, James took to Scouting like a duck to water. Seeing my son so happy and headed in such a positive direction, I couldn't help but get sucked in. I started volunteering for everything, and the next thing I knew, I was being invited to sit on the council. A couple of years later, they offered me the job I have now.

"So, in a nutshell, I think Scouting saved my son. Does that answer your question?"

"And then some."

I smiled to indicate I was joking. She chuckled softly in return.

"No, seriously, thanks for sharing. I hope I didn't pressure you to talk about anything . . . I don't know . . . uncomfortable."

Abby shrugged her shoulders again. "I tell that story as often as I can. Maybe not in that much detail, but I love the Boy Scouts, and I don't mind if people know why. But since we're on the subject, I think it's only fair you tell me why you hate Scouting so much."

Instantly I felt my neck heat up under my collar. I wasn't angry; I was just extremely self-conscious.

"Can I ask you something first?"

"Sure."

"Feeling the way you do, why'd you agree to go out with me?"

Abby puckered her lips as she considered my question. "The one thing I couldn't deny was your passion. You were genuinely trying to help the boys in your ward. I couldn't help but admire that, even if you were the biggest horse's rear end I'd ever met. So when you finally dropped the attitude . . . I don't know. Opportunities to get out don't come along all that often for single moms in their late thirties. I'm not sure if that's the answer you're looking for, but I wouldn't really read too much into it. I'm up for just about anything once."

She was right: that wasn't the answer I'd been expecting. But before I could dwell on it any further, she pressed again. "But you still haven't answered my question. Why do you hate Scouting so much?"

"Well, I certainly don't have a story to match yours. It's kind of simple really. Scouting and I have never gotten along, even when I was young. I certainly didn't feel the animosity toward it I do now, but it was never really my thing."

"Why the animosity now? What did Scouting ever do to you?" Her second question was asked with a playful smile and a twinkle in her eyes, conveying that our truce remained in place.

"Are you sure you really want to hear this?"

"It would be unfair of me not to after you were so polite."

"Okay, but please remember I gave you every opportunity to avoid this."

She smiled again. "Understood."

"I would have to say my biggest hang-up with Scouting now, as an adult, is the time commitment and the bureaucracy."

Abby cocked her head to the side in curiosity but stayed true to her word not to interrupt.

"I mean, requiring a person to sit through eight hours of training on a Saturday, when the necessary information could be covered in two. That drives me crazy.

"And the nitpickiness over every bit of paper-work, which there is tons of, just grates on my nerves. I feel like, sometimes, the rules and the pro-cedures and the forms in triplicate are getting in the way of exactly the type of things you love about the program."

I paused, took a deep breath, and leaned back in my seat. "I realize that isn't a great answer, and it in no way accounts for my highly obnoxious behavior, but that's it. I do appreciate what you told me about your son, and I do believe Scouting has a lot to offer, but . . . it's just not my cup of tea."

My admiration for this woman rose tremendously over the next ten seconds. Instead of rising to my challenges, she sat reflectively, obviously mulling over everything I'd just said. When she did speak, it was in a gracious and conciliatory tone.

"You raise some good points, and in some ways, I can agree with you. On the others, we'll just have to agree to disagree. But I'm still curious, why would your bishop call you to serve as advancement chair if this is how you feel?"

"Because my bishop also happens to be a close friend, and he's the only person on earth who could convince me I'm needed in this position."

Abby raised her eyebrows in surprise but chose to focus on her napkin rather than comment.

Worried that I'd offended her, I tried delicately to ascertain the damage. "Up until my rant just now, I felt like we were having a pretty good time together. I hope I didn't ruin that."

Continuing to play with her napkin, she responded, "No, like I said, I'm just taking in everything you had to say. But beyond that, I'm amazed at the twists and turns of life. If someone had told me a week ago that I'd be out on a date with you, and I'd actually be enjoying myself, I'd have thought they were crazy. And yet here we are."

Feeling emboldened by her admission, I decided to press my luck. "And where exactly are we?"

"Well, besides in a restaurant that has amazing food and incredibly tacky waitresses . . . I'm not sure."

"If I promise that next time I'll find a place with amazing waitresses and incredibly tacky food, can we try it again?"

"As long as you understand that if I accept, it still doesn't mean I have to like you."

I smiled. "I can live with that."

You Think You Know a Guy
Friday, September 19

"YOU'VE REACHED THE cell phone of Kevin Brockbank. I'm not available at the moment, but if you'd leave a message, I'll be happy to return your call at my earliest convenience." (Pause) "If you're a member of my wedding party and you're wondering where I am . . . I'm not coming. I'm really sorry." (Pause) "Caralee, I really am sorry."

Slowly, I lowered the phone from my ear. The small crowd around me was already impatient with curiosity, but I was at a complete loss as I tried to grasp the implications of what I'd just heard.

"Todd, are you okay?" Christy, Caralee's maid of honor, was standing close by and asked her question in a hushed tone. She had no idea what was wrong, but my reaction to whatever I'd heard implied it wasn't good.

I tried to appear nonchalant as I grabbed her elbow and bent down to whisper in her ear. "Christy, you need to get Caralee out of here as quickly as possible. Kevin isn't coming. I don't know why or . . . really, I don't know anything, but she needs you to get her away from the circus that's bound to erupt. And hurry, because if anyone else calls that cell phone, we're done."

Christy raised her eyes to mine with a horrified expression but quickly recovered and hurried off to protect her friend.

Turning back to face the small congregation surrounding me outside the Mesa Arizona Temple, I raised my voice to ensure everyone could hear me. "Okay, Kevin didn't answer, but that's really all we know at this point. Why don't you all head back inside, and I'll continue trying his phone. When I know more, I'll be straight in with an update."

"What'd you say to Christy?" a cocky twenty-something with a faux-hawk asked. "How come she ran off so quick?"

Recalling that this joker had been introduced to me as Caralee's brother, I held my sarcastic tendencies mostly in check. "I don't know. I thought it might be important to keep the bride informed first and foremost."

A suspicious murmur rustled through the group, but with nothing else to go on, my explanation was grudgingly accepted, and each person around me gradually made their way back up the steps and into the temple.

Once I was certain no prospective cell phone vigilantes remained outside, I slumped down on the closest bench and groaned. When it came to screwups with fiancées, Kevin was no slouch, but this was his worst by far.

One by one, I searched my memories from the

night before to see if I could recall any signs of this brewing. Kevin had been a little quiet, but I'd chalked that up to typical night-before-the-wedding jitters. I mean, heck, it was a Mormon bachelor party. We were all a little subdued.

Faux-hawk's nasally whine interrupted my thoughts. "You said you were gonna keep calling. How come you're just sitting there? My sister's supposed to be getting married in half an hour."

"I just called and there was still no answer."

"No you didn't. I've been watching from just inside the door."

That was it. Caralee's brother or not, I was finished with this snot-nosed college-aged brat. Without ever breaking eye contact, I took my phone from my pocket, pressed the speaker button, and hit redial. With each unanswered ring, his confidence seemed to waver more and more.

Finally, Kevin's message began blaring through the muggy heat of the mid-September afternoon. As soon as it was clear we were listening to a recording, I disconnected the call.

"As I said, there's still no answer. As soon as I get one, I will make sure you are the first to know."

His scowl left no doubt as to his feelings regarding our new arrangement. However, he'd just suffered a bruising shot to his ego and needed time to recover. He retreated back into the temple without another word.

Standing up from my bench, I began walking. I knew it was pointless, but once more I opened my phone and dialed. This time I let the message play to the end. Listening to his final apology again was almost too much. I silently prayed that whatever had driven him to make this decision would resolve itself soon, because recovery from this was going to be tough.

My aimless wanderings had led me to the temple's northeast corner. As I stood in the shade of an orange tree, contemplating what to do, I saw Caralee and her mother emerge from the baptistry door with Christy a step behind. Even from a distance of fifty yards, the devastation on Caralee's face was obvious. I was grateful neither she nor her mother saw me. This whole thing was uncomfortable enough already.

Just before she turned to follow them to the parking lot, Christy caught sight of me and stopped. Shrugging sadly, she waved before hurrying down the sidewalk after her friend.

I continued to stare after them for several minutes. I knew I needed to get back inside and reveal the truth, but I really didn't want to. More than anything, I hated the thought of facing Kevin's parents.

Thankfully, by the time I arrived in the temple's chapel, Caralee's father had broken the news to everyone assembled. Standing at the back of the room, I couldn't help but feel for the man. He stood alone, the sole target of questions he had no answer for. Prodded by compassion, I walked down the chapel's center aisle to stand next to him.

I stood silently, with my hand raised, and waited until everyone accepted that the Q-and-A session had effectively ended.

"Look, here is what we know. Kevin isn't here,

and he isn't coming. We don't know what happened or what will happen. I'm sure everyone has more questions, but I would ask that we all remember where we are, and that we head outside for any further discussion."

Caralee's father put his hand on my shoulder and whispered, "Thank you." With that, he walked toward the exit with no further acknowledgment of anyone. His hunched shoulders and bowed head gave him the appearance of a man defeated. As I envisioned my own two daughters, I was swept up in a wave of anger. How could Kevin do this?

Within minutes, the chapel was empty, save for a couple near the back. Kevin's mother was weeping into her husband's shoulder as Brother Brockbank did his best to hold himself together. But his voice betrayed him several times as he softly comforted his wife.

I forced myself to make the short walk to their side. Sitting down in the seat next to them, I placed my hand lightly on Sister Brockbank's back.

It took a moment for this woman who had been like a second mother to me to recognize who I was through her tears. Once she did, she pulled me close and clung to me as she continued crying. As I embraced her with one arm, I offered my free hand to Brother Brockbank, who grasped it tightly as his tears refused to be held back any longer.

No words passed between us for quite a while. None needed to. No amount of consolation was going to dampen the pain we were feeling. He'd come so close, only to have it slip away once more. There was absolutely nothing left to say.

After a time, the Brockbanks became conscious of where they were, and we all stood hastily, preparing to exit the chapel. As I turned to go, Sister Brockbank clutched my arm, her red-rimmed eyes overflowing with concern.

"Todd, thank you. Thank you for being such a good friend to our Kevin. I don't know what happened or where he is, but I know he's hurting. Please find him. He's always been more comfortable talking to you than anyone else. Tell him we love him . . ." Her voice broke, and she was no longer able to continue.

Putting my arms around her once more, I consoled, "Sister Brockbank, he knows. Trust me, he knows."

Faintly nodding, she turned, took hold of her husband's hand, and edged past me, moving toward the exit.

Once I was outside, I let my fury take hold. No longer was I walking slowly with the stride of someone engulfed in sadness. Now I was moving at a pace propelled by rage. I knew where he was. And heaven help him when I got there.

When Grant, Jason, Kevin, and I were attending ASU, we came up with the concept of an escape spot—a place to go when girlfriends got too clingy or homework got too hard. We all made a pact, forbidding the revelation to anyone of our escape spot's location. The place we decided on was Casey Moore's Oyster House just off Mill Avenue in Tempe.

Casey Moore's is an old Irish-style pub within walking distance of the main ASU campus. We figured no one would go looking for four nice Mormon boys in a pub hidden off the main roads.

After we graduated, none of us ever really needed Casey's anymore, at least as far as I knew. But within a few weeks of Marci's passing, I'd started making regular visits again to get away from a life that no longer made sense to me.

Eventually, my routine disappearances caused my mother to panic, so she called Kevin. When he found me a short time later, neither of us said anything. He simply sat down, and for the next two hours we drank Dr Peppers and stared at a Suns game on the television overhead that neither one of us cared about.

I'm sure I made quite the spectacle walking into a bar on a late Friday afternoon in my best suit. The fact that I'm in my late thirties probably created more of a stir in this college hangout than my suit did, but I chose not to think about that as I scanned the room for my friend.

It didn't take long to find him.

A waitress was coming out from behind the bar with a dark, carbonated beverage that, to my admittedly inexperienced eyes, didn't look like beer. I followed her to a table in the back where Kevin sat alone. He'd also been wearing a suit, but now the jacket was draped casually over the chair next to him and the sleeves of his white shirt were rolled up. His tie hung loosely beneath his top button, which had probably been the first thing to come undone when he'd arrived. His eyes stared vacantly toward a screen presenting some kind of poker tournament.

As I approached, he glanced in my direction

before returning his attention to what has got to be the most boring thing to hit ESPN since billiards. I walked up to his table and turned to face the television as well.

"Well, it would've been a close call, but I think you got it right. In retrospect, I'd have chosen to watch a mindless card game on TV over my wedding too."

Ignoring my sarcastic intro, Kevin's eyes never left the screen as he asked, "How bad was it?"

I moved around the table and placed myself in the chair facing him. Dropping his eyes from the television above, he dejectedly met my gaze.

"Pretty bad." At my honest declaration, his eyes continued downward to the drink in front of him. "Whatever you're imagining, I'm sure it was that bad or worse."

"I'm sorry—"

Before he could continue, I cut him off. "Look, I'm not here for apologies. You're gonna have to hand those out like Halloween candy to a lot of people more deserving than me. I just want to understand what happened today. I want to understand what's been happening for the last fifteen years. You're my best friend, and I think I know you as well as anyone. But for the life of me, I can't figure out what would cause you to do what you just did today."

As if I hadn't spoken, he asked, "Did you talk to Caralee?"

"No. Christy and her mother whisked her out the back door so she wouldn't have to face anyone."

"Well, that's good," he replied softly.

"No, Kevin, that's not good. She may have avoided having to face her friends and family today, but she's gonna have to face them all eventually. This is going to be highly traumatic for her. And did you think about your mom and dad?"

At the mention of his parents, Kevin closed his eyes. Part of me wanted to back off as I saw a couple of tears escape and roll down his cheeks, but the frustration I'd allowed to build over the last few hours urged me on.

"I'm the one who had to console them when you didn't bother showing up. And as you might expect, they're not handling it well. Although you should know, your mother figured I'd be the one to find you, so she asked me to pass on how much they love you."

"We'll see," he muttered.

That made me come unglued. Raising my voice, I demanded, "What's that supposed to mean?"

With his own anger flashing, Kevin declared, "I'm gay, Todd. That's what it's supposed to mean."

All the blood in my veins froze. Whatever I'd been feeling up to that point was immediately erased by shock. "What do you mean you're gay?"

"I thought it was pretty self-explanatory."

"But . . ." I placed my hands over my eyes, trying to block out everything he'd just said. "I don't understand. This suddenly hit you today?"

"I've known for a while. I've been meeting with my bishop for over a year, and I thought I was ready for this. But I woke up this morning, and . . . I wasn't."

My astonishment was quickly returning to anger.

"You mean you've known about this for over a year, and this is the first I'm hearing about it?"

"Todd, let me—"

"You knew, and yet you put your parents, Cara-lee, Grant, Jason . . . *me*, through all of this? You let me—" I had no way to express what my brain could not comprehend. I felt hurt and angry, but most of all, I felt betrayed. I stared across the table at the person I had thought of as my best friend. His tears were flowing freely now, but because of my growing rage, I didn't care.

Slowly and deliberately, I stood and pushed my chair back to its original position. Staring down at him, I felt an intense desire to say something that would hurt. But his obvious suffering stopped me. Finally, I just turned and walked away.

Through his sobs I heard him call after me. "Todd, please . . ."

Years of devoted friendship demanded that I turn around. Instead, I never broke stride as I walked out the front door.

TODD'S LANDRY LIST

We're Burnin' Daylight
Saturday, October 4

I'M NOT A mirror guy.

For clarification's sake, I'm not Count Dracula or anything. I just don't spend near the amount of time in front of them that I used to in my younger years. I figure, what's the use? Those crow's-feet are going to continue to expand whether I choose to look at them or not. It's just not worth the stress.

However, over the last two weeks, my bedroom mirror and I have gotten reacquainted.

The looking glass in question hangs over my dresser that houses my cell phone charger and, subsequently, my cell phone at different times. That would be the cell phone I'm not using.

This evening, as I was getting ready to attend the priesthood session of general conference, I stopped in front of that mirror and reached for my phone. Pressing the preset button for Kevin's number, I placed my thumb on the call button. But as I've done dozens of times over the last two weeks, I hesitated.

I don't know what to say to him.

I mean, I'm ashamed of how I treated him the last time we spoke. But, on the other hand, I'm still hurt, and I don't know how to get over it. And that's what stops me every time—what do I say if he picks up?

So there I stood, staring at my reflection, unable to convince myself to make the call. With a small shift, I moved my thumb to the cancel button and pressed down. The eyes staring back at me from the mirror chastised me accusingly.

Shame on you.

In a voice far too animated for a man arguing with himself, I shot back, "Yeah, well shame on him. He hasn't called me either, and I'm not the one who started this." Inhaling deeply, I forced my eyes away from the glass and tossed my cell phone back onto the dresser before walking away.

Fortunately, I was able to drag my mind to other thoughts as I finished getting dressed in anticipation of the evening's festivities. Tonight, following general conference, traditions would continue and I would head to dinner at Joe's Barbeque along with the rest of the Landry men.

But tonight, something different was in the air as I walked into Joe's—the scent of my sister's perfume.

Seeing Katie in the waiting area as I entered was so unexpected, I stopped dead in my tracks halfway through the door. Somehow this inadvertently caused Brock to walk face-first into the glass behind me. I'm still not clear on how the one action led to the other, but Brock swears it was my fault, so . . .whatever.

Regardless, I almost had to walk back outside and check the sign to make sure we were in the right place. Not once in over twenty-five years had any female from our family ever invaded the inner sanctum of Joe's on conference weekend. What was even more bizarre was seeing the person seated next to my sister—Maureen Littleton, the cookie lady.

Before I could ask all of the questions bouncing around my head, my father pushed past me to greet them. "Ahhh, Maureen, Katie. I'm so glad you could both make it. Are Linda and Natalie here yet?" Katie explained that both of my brother's wives were indeed present, but had made a quick visit to the ladies' room.

Something reeked of a setup. Why would my father fail to mention this obvious breach in protocol? From my brothers' puzzled expressions, I gathered they were as clueless as me.

For half a second I thought about confronting my father, but almost immediately I decided against it. My life experience had taught me the best course of action was to let whatever plans he had play out. He'd never been one for the spotlight, but on those rare occasions when he did want to produce a *moment*, no amount of coercion would force him to reveal his hand before he was ready.

Once we were seated, conversations sprang up all around the table as everyone relaxed. Everyone, that is, except Katie. She continued to sit rigidly in her seat, a look of extreme apprehension clouding her features.

From across the table, I couldn't determine the source of her distress. Finally, I was able to catch her eye.

"Are you okay?" I mouthed anxiously.

Very subtly, she shook her head. It was then I noticed she was on the verge of tears. I furrowed my eyebrows as if to ask, "What's up?"

In response, she faintly shrugged her shoulders and inclined her head toward Dad. I felt my stomach begin to tighten.

At the precise moment I lost my appetite, our server arrived and the long process of ordering commenced. What had traditionally taken three to four minutes for the men stretched into ten and beyond with the inclusion of spouses. Generally I'd have been aggravated by my sisters-in-law's inability to make a decision, but tonight I took the opportunity to scrutinize my father and his new lady friend.

The longer I observed, the larger the knot in my stomach grew. The familiarity they were exhibiting had increased dramatically from the last time I'd seen them just five weeks earlier at the single adult conference. I was hoping against hope I was wrong, but suddenly there was no doubt in my mind what we were in for.

Once our server had retired with our orders, my father tapped his glass with his spoon to gain everyone's attention. "Everyone, I'm sure you're all wondering why I've invited our better halves tonight. Few people value tradition more than me, but in light of an announcement I have, I hope you'll all forgive me, just this once."

As he spoke, I scanned my family's faces. Based on my quick and definitely unscientific assessment, almost everyone had a fair idea what they were about

to hear. The one exception was Brock. Katie was looking down, still doing her best to contain her emotions,
while Mike's face wore an expression of "Please don't
let him say what I know he's about to say."

"I want you all to know that losing your mother
was very difficult for me. She and I had lived our lives
side by side for just shy of forty-one years. But for his
own purposes, the Lord has called her home, leaving
me a lone man."

I know I can be overly cynical, but seriously, this
was getting to be a bit much. Unfortunately, he was
just getting started.

"The scriptures state it is not good for man to be
alone, and having been just that for these last couple
of months, I have to say, I firmly agree. With that in
mind, I wanted the family together tonight so that I
could introduce you to Maureen Littleton. Todd has
met her before, but as far as I know, the rest of you
have not."

He paused and looked at Maureen. Each of us at
the table knew the etiquette that would follow. Maureen would graciously acknowledge us with a slight
nod and maybe even throw in a softly spoken "hello"
or "nice to meet you," following which my father
would then continue with his remarks. Everyone
knew this—except Maureen.

"And we're getting married," she blurted out in a
voice far too loud.

Had her pronouncement not carried such life-
altering repercussions for our family, I might've burst
out in a fit of laughter. My father had returned his
attention to the full gathering and had even opened

his mouth to continue speaking when Maureen jumped in. For just a fleeting moment, a look of horror I'd never seen before registered on my father's face. To his credit, he disguised it instantly and smiled graciously at his new fiancée.

Meanwhile, the reaction from the rest of the family was excruciatingly awkward to say the least. Brock broke the "don't make a scene" rule by jumping up and bounding around the table to give Dad a hug. For his part, Dad hadn't fully recovered from the abrupt loss of the spotlight and, as such, was only able to make it halfway up out of his chair by the time Brock arrived. The unnatural embrace that followed would've received one million hits on YouTube in under an hour had someone had the presence of mind to film it.

Once again, my father's irritation flashed briefly, but as before, he was able to mask it before most people would notice. Untangling himself from Brock and his chair, he stood and engaged in a proper embrace with his youngest son. After a couple of solid back slaps, they separated and Dad turned to face the rest of us. If he'd been hoping for a line to form behind Brock, he was sadly mistaken.

Katie's head had never risen, and multiple tears had finally escaped. Her husband, Scott, was doing his best to comfort her while trying to avoid attention for the both of them. Mike was holding his head in one hand with his elbow resting on the table. His eyes were shut and he looked as if he were trying to ward off a migraine with little success. The glances being exchanged between my two sisters-in-law suggested they would've been much more at ease having dinner with a mob family than be involved with the current meal underway with the Landrys.

The most dramatic thing of all was the silence shrouding our table. The tension was palpable. Every second that ticked by without someone speaking caused the look of triumph on my father's face to give way to a hardened look bordering on sinister.

As I've mentioned before, Adrian Landry isn't used to dissension. He's not a tyrant by any means, but he's definitely used to a certain amount of conformity from his children. Over the last year and a half, I've bucked that trend repeatedly, and it has led to some unintended consequences.

When Dad heads down a path the family isn't comfortable following, I've become the designated voice of opposition. I recognize how and why this happened, but in that moment, sitting around a table in a public place, it was the last responsibility I wanted to live up to. Nevertheless, I knew I had to say what everyone else was thinking.

Sighing, I leaned forward preparing to speak, when suddenly, the opportunity was taken from me. For the first time in my life, my brother Mike took the lead role in challenging our father. "Um, Dad . . . with all due respect to . . . Maureen, is it?" His wife, Natalie, nodded quickly without looking at him. "With all due respect to Maureen, don't you think this is a little quick?"

It was obvious Dad had been expecting it from me. When I'd leaned forward, his focus had been trained specifically in my direction. We'd reached a comfort level where some mild insubordination on my part was not preferred, but was at least expected. When Mike was the one to speak up, I could tell it rocked Dad's world to the core.

"Excuse me, son?"

Mike's lack of confidence in this new role was evident. However, despite a nervous hesitation in his voice, he didn't back down. "Isn't this a little fast? No one at this table, except for Todd, has ever met this woman before. I'm not trying to be rude in any way, but don't you think there are some things that might warrant consideration within our family before you commit to remarrying?"

"Well, son, whether you mean it or not, rude is exactly what you're being. Maureen is my welcome guest this evening and my fiancée. I have to admit, I'm a little surprised at everyone's lack of manners right now, with the obvious exception of Brock." He nodded at Brock, who by this time looked thoroughly unsure as to which side of this argument he wanted to land on.

No longer able to control my tongue, I spoke up in Mike's defense. "Come on, Dad. That's not fair. You're the one who put Maureen in this situation, not Mike. And frankly you should be the one apologizing to her for forcing this issue on us in a way that we now have to speak about her as if she isn't even here."

I then acknowledged Maureen with a nod of my head to reinforce my declaration. Oddly enough, she didn't seem to mind at all. She didn't look thrilled by any stretch, but neither did she look all that uneasy.

Before my father could retaliate, our food arrived. The next several minutes played out like a ridiculous Spanish-language telenovela. Dad sat glaring at everyone, waiting to unleash the second it was socially acceptable to do so. Mike, on the other hand, was plainly using the time to psych himself up in preparation against the verbal barrage obviously headed our way. I'd never been so proud of him in my life.

However, for the sake of family harmony for years to come, I decided to play peacemaker. A fraction of a second before the last waiter stepped away, I spoke up.

"Look, Dad, you know everyone here only wants what's best for you. Once we've had a chance to get used to this, I'm sure you'll find that your family is supportive of you and Maureen. Frankly, we're just shocked. No one here saw this coming. And while we want you to be happy, we're also just a tad concerned for you. Whether you want to admit it or not, this is pretty fast. Which begs another question—have you guys already settled on a date?"

"November first," Maureen piped in.

An audible gasp went up around the table. Unable to contain herself, Katie exclaimed, "That's only four weeks from now!"

For the second time that night, I saw a crack in my father's smooth veneer. He shot an aggravated glance in Maureen's direction but quickly replaced it with his trademark expression of goodwill.

I continued, "Now see, Dad, to me that's really soon. I, personally, am going to need some time to get used to that. And Mike is right. We need to discuss and deal with a lot of things.

"However, having said that, why don't we use tonight to take a deep breath and agree to let those other items sit? We can spend the rest of our evening getting to know Maureen with the understanding that come Monday, we'll begin dealing with the logistics of your announcement. Is that fair?"

Maybe I'm letting wishful thinking cloud my judgment, but as my father contemplated my suggestion, I thought I saw a newfound respect for me in his gaze. When he finally delivered his verdict, his voice carried a new tone of humility.

"I do think that's fair, and Todd does make some good points. I'm sorry I forced this on everyone. It seemed like a good idea when I was planning it, but now I can see how maybe I should've thought it through a little more. Maureen, I do apologize for putting you in this unfortunate situation and hope that you'll forgive me."

Maureen inclined her head in acceptance of his apology.

Dad then looked back at us and said, "I want you all to know how much I love you and how much you mean to me. Saying that, I hope you'll trust and support me and give Maureen a chance."

Despite varying levels of enthusiasm, agreement was offered from everyone at the table.

Satisfied, my father smiled and declared, "Thank you. I appreciate that. Now, let's eat."

Simultaneously, nine people turned their attention to the barbecue in front of them, and the mood surrounding our table eased considerably. After a few minutes, I looked in my father's direction and found him waiting to catch my eye. He smiled at me and nodded. In true Landry style, I buried the waves of gratitude and pride I felt and simply nodded and smiled back.

TODD'S LANDRY LIST

The Lights Go Down on the Party That Never Ends
Friday, October 10

BEFORE MARCI PASSED away, I was the typical dad—gone Monday through Friday from 7:30 in the morning until 6:00 at night. These days, I'm the dad who drops my girls off at school before heading home with Drake for some precious father/son time.

Even on days when I go into the office, I don't have to be there until 9:00, so my son and I still get our mornings together.

Our typical morning, when I'm not working, consists of pancakes, reading books, and watching his favorite movie of the moment. For the last three weeks we've been stuck on *Finding Nemo*, and Nemo's dad is really starting to get on my nerves. But in spite of my desire to see that annoying little clown fish impaled by a stick, I'll sit quietly and take it all in for the forty-first time because Drake wants me to. Next year, when he goes to school, these days will be gone forever.

This morning, my patience with clown fish in general was reaching an all-time low. I was sitting next to my son, harboring fantasies of Bruce the shark swallowing both Nemo and his father whole, when the doorbell rang. Doorbells that early in the day generally mean one thing—salesmen. Hopping up without a moment's hesitation, I headed for the door. I'd never been so thankful for the opportunity to tell some schmo I had no interest in buying life insurance from him.

I opened the door, primed for battle, when I was stopped cold. Jason was standing on my porch, and he looked terrible.

His normally perfect hair wasn't combed, and he obviously hadn't shaved in days. But most shocking was his wardrobe—cut-off sweatpants and a T-shirt that had seen better days. The departure from his normally perfect appearance dumbfounded me. Nevertheless, I recovered quickly enough to invite him in before I came across as rude.

Once I'd verified that Drake was still firmly planted in front of *Nemo*, I led Jason back to my kitchen. He sat down at the table while I skirted around my island counter to take stock of what my refrigerator had to offer him.

"Can I get you something to drink? Dr Pepper? Water? Pickle juice?"

The last option earned me a smile, but not much of one. "No, man, I'm good."

"You sure?"

"Yeah, I'm fine." His dejected tone gave me pause. Closing the fridge, I leaned forward on my countertop to take a closer look at my friend.

"What's going on?"

Jason inhaled deeply. "I've come to say good-bye."

My eyebrows shot up as I backed away from the island to lean on the stove behind me. "Come again?"

"I've been offered a job as regional sales manager for some insurance outfit in Austin, Texas. It's better money and"—he shrugged, looking away—"it'll be a good change of scenery."

"Wow! Well then, congratulations, I guess. Hopefully it'll be a good thing for you. How's Kimberly with all this?"

His eyes remained riveted on something outside my bay window. "She's not coming."

My heart dropped into my stomach. "What?"

"She wants a divorce."

From day one I'd been worried about their marriage, but even still, this sudden revelation caught me completely by surprise.

"Jason, you've only been married for what... three months? What could possibly go so wrong so fast?"

"I don't know. I suppose her discovering my secret affair with alcohol didn't help."

I sighed. "I knew it. That day we were at lunch, I just knew it. When did this start?"

"Do you mean originally or when did I start again?"

I just stared at him with a look of frustration.

"Come on, Todd. You had to know what was going on before our missions. All those times I blew you guys off to hang out with the basketball team? We weren't goin' to church."

He was right. It was obvious what was going on

with him back then. But we were eighteen and had no idea what to do. So we pretended and we ignored.

"When I decided to go on a mission, I stopped, but I never forgot. It would be awkward sometimes, walking down the streets of Buenos Aires with the hot sun beating down on us, and all I could think about was how much I wanted a cold beer." He chuckled to himself as he added, "They never covered that in the *Called to Serve* video. Anyway, I got it under control, but like I said, I never forgot."

"Then let me clarify my question. When did you start again?"

"Right after Tiffany left me. I guess you could say I've never stopped since. I'll go weeks, even months without a drink, but eventually stress will get to me or I'll be hangin' out with some guys at the office and . . . you know."

"So you're going to throw your life away over this?"

"No, Todd. I'm gonna throw away the life *you* think I should have over this. You, my parents, Kimberly . . . everybody but me. I'm gonna throw away *your* life for me, because I don't want it anymore. I don't think I ever wanted it."

I don't know if it was the sheer volume of times I'd been disappointed in Jason or the shock of hearing him being truthful about himself, but the anger I would've expected never came. Instead, a gloomy sense of fatalism seemed to numb my emotions.

"Why now? Why, after all these years, are you telling me this now?"

The question seemed to stump him, and he sat

reflecting for quite a while. Finally, he offered, "I guess the stars aligned, and now's as good a time as any."

"That's fluff. I don't even know what that means. I want a straight answer."

"Look, I'm just being honest. In fact, for maybe the first time in my life, I'm being totally honest with myself. And by the way, none of this was necessarily my choice. But now that it's happening, I feel like rollin' with it."

"What about your boys?"

"They hate me. They'll be glad I'm gone. Tiffany has 'em so poisoned against me—trust me, it's probably for the best."

I couldn't believe what I was hearing. "What a coward you are. They probably wouldn't hate you so much if you wouldn't blow off your visitation half the time. You are such an unbelievable coward."

With eyes blazing, he launched from his chair and sent it crashing to the floor behind him. For a moment, I was afraid he was going to punch me in my own kitchen. But once he was standing, he froze. His eyes were on fire and his chest was heaving rapidly, but he didn't move. Finally, as his breathing became more measured, his eyes took on a look I'd never seen before.

"You didn't figure that out just now, did you? I've been a coward my whole life. A coward, a failure, a disappointment—you name it."

Hearing him describe himself so negatively broke my heart. Something snapped inside me, and suddenly I had to help him. I had to make him see what a huge mistake he was about to make. "It doesn't have to be this way, Jason. I'll help. Kevin'll . . ." I stopped, reminded of the uncertainty that still existed on that front.

"Kevin'll what? Help me get my sins under control? Last I heard, the Church doesn't consider homosexuality to be a good starting point for reaching out to the fallen."

"Have you talked to him?"

"No. And I'm not going to. Let's face it, he and I were only friends because of you. Without you, we'd have parted ways years ago."

I was becoming desperate for ways to talk sense into him. Every argument seemed to be unraveling around me.

"I could talk to Kimberly. Maybe we could find a way to work this out. I'll go with you to visit with the bishop." I sighed. "Don't do this."

"Kimberly's done with me. I can't say I blame her. If I had her track record with men, I'd be done with me too."

"Then how about you and I go see your bishop? I'll be there. I'll support you. I'll do whatever you need me to do."

"You're not listening, Todd. This right here"—he gestured with his hand back and forth between us—"this is my confessional. When I walk out of here, I'm packing my car, and I'm not looking back. Not to the Church, not to Kimberly, not to my parents . . . not even to you. My life begins tomorrow, and none of those things will matter anymore."

"Then why me?"

Jason looked at me quizzically. "What do you mean?"

"If you're leaving and none of this matters, why'd you come to me?"

His eyes dropped to the floor. "Because you deserve better."

If he was expecting some response, I had none. Eventually, he continued.

"Time after time you've been there for me. You've overlooked the lousy way I've treated you, and you continue to try to be my friend. I'm not a good person, Todd. But it's not from a lack of effort on your part.

"You were right about me being a coward. Like I said, I've been one my whole life. If you want to know the truth, I planned on leaving without talking to you. But despite all the things I've done and the rotten person I've turned out to be, even I couldn't have lived with the coward who couldn't face you and say thanks. Thanks for being my friend. I'm sorry I wasn't a better one to you."

Tears were streaming down both our faces when he finished. I walked around the island and stood face-to-face with him. A thousand conflicting thoughts were swirling through my mind. I was angry and I was hurt, but, most of all, I was in despair at the lack of value my friend placed on himself. I couldn't bring myself to gloss over everything, but I knew I needed to say something positive.

"You're right. For most of my life you haven't been a very good friend. But you've been a friend, and for me that was always enough. I guess there's nothing I can do to stop you, but there are a couple of things I want you to remember. If this new life of yours turns out to be as lonely as I think it will, my door is always open. And don't forget who you are. I know you don't believe it right now, but you are a worthwhile and valuable son of God. And His door's open too. If you're gonna make me take your confession, then promise me you won't forget that."

He grabbed me and we hugged.

As we stepped away from each other, I couldn't resist. "By the way, I still hate you for messing up my best golf round ever."

Jason smiled and put his hand on my shoulder. "If that's the worst thing you hate me for, I'm in better shape than I thought. Take care of yourself, Todd."

"You too, my friend."

I walked outside with him and stood watching from my porch as he got in his car and drove away. Long after he was gone, I continued to stare at the spot where his taillights had disappeared. Finally, inhaling deeply, I stepped back inside.

My son had not moved since I'd left him. So I sat back down and watched as Nemo faked his own death, not realizing that his father was looking on.

Drake looked up and, with a great deal of concern in his voice, comforted, "Dad, don't cry. Nemo's only pretending."

I wiped away a tear and smiled at him. "Thanks, buddy. I'm glad you told me."

TODD'S LANDRY LIST

Isn't That Against the Hypocrite Oath?
Wednesday, October 15

"MY GOODNESS, SO much has happened that I don't have a clue where to begin."

Dr. Schenk sat across from me—reading from a file I could only assume was mine. The mass of documentation was disheartening. With over two inches worth of paperwork, his records of our time together now warranted a large three-ring binder.

Staring at the binder in his hands, I failed to notice he had asked me a question.

"I'm sorry, did you say something?"

Dr. Schenk sighed. "Yes, I asked if you had any preference as to our first topic today, but . . ."

"Is that my file?"

Dr. Schenk looked down with open puzzlement at the binder now sitting on his coffee table. "Yes . . . would you expect me to have another person's file here?"

I looked up at him, nonplussed. "Well, no . . . it's just so big."

"Is that a problem?"

"Am I really that crazy?"

His eyes danced in amusement. "What do you think I have in there?"

"I don't know. Notes from our sessions?"

He laughed. "That's simply all of your writings from the blog."

My mouth dropped open in surprise. "I wrote all that?"

"Every word."

"How on earth could I have had that much to say in . . . what, a year?"

"Seven months, to be precise, but are you taking into account all that has occurred in that period? If so, I'm surprised you're not wondering why it's so small."

My mind began to filter through time, and just as Dr. Schenk had predicted, my perspective began to shift. Day to day, my life had seemed relatively monotonous. Looking at the last seven months as a whole told a much different story.

"I see what you're saying. So normally, a person wouldn't be writing this much?"

Dr. Schenk smiled and shook his head. "That's not what I said at all. Our days are filled with events we deem noteworthy in the moment, but over time their importance begins to fade. While I would certainly acknowledge that these last few months have been more eventful than most, I would suggest that if you continued writing consistently, a comparable number of pages would be filled in the seven months that are to come.

"For a further example of just how flawed this reasoning is, we need not look any further than within your own sphere of influence. How expansive do you suppose your friend Kevin's writings from the last year would be?"

That observation stopped me short. I had never even considered that. I nodded to acknowledge my understanding. But Dr. Schenk wasn't done.

"Much of your writing deals with the changing relationship you're experiencing with your father. Did your knowing look of comprehension just now take into account the dynamic shifts undoubtedly occurring between Kevin and his parents?"

It hadn't. Picturing him seated at his computer chronicling that aspect of his life was sobering.

Not one to let me get comfortable, Dr. Schenk continued, "You also have a great deal written here about Emily. Is it not safe to assume Kevin would have an equal number of pages dedicated to Caralee? His highs, his lows, his regrets . . . his pain. Would you not imagine them to be somewhat equal to your own?"

My feelings of understanding from earlier disintegrated as a more humbling realization set in. "Yeah, I suppose they would."

"You know what I find most interesting when it comes to you and your friend Kevin?"

"What's that?"

"I'm perplexed at the level to which you berated him for his numerous betrayals. Of course you mentioned yourself most of all, but you seemed equally incensed at his treatment of Caralee."

"Well, sure. He said he'd known for a year how he . . . is. If that's the case, it seems awfully insensitive to take their relationship to such a level if he knew there was a chance he would have to break her heart."

"You knew from the beginning how opposed Alex was to Emily."

I suddenly couldn't breathe. "Wait . . . that's not fair. You aren't seriously comparing my situation to what Kevin did, are you?"

"It seems an apt comparison to me."

I stuttered several times before accepting I had nothing to say. Leaning back in my chair, I cast my eyes up to the ceiling. That was when Dr. Schenk delivered the deathblow.

"I'm not seeking an answer. I only want you to consider something. Is it possible a good portion of your anger that is keeping you from contacting your friend is actually misdirected anger at yourself?"

Indignantly, I shot straight up in my seat and angrily responded, "His mistreatment of Caralee is not the only issue at play here. I—"

Dr. Schenk raised his hand to cut me off. "As I said, I'm not interested in your answer. Whether you choose to accept it or not, the resentful tantrum you were about to throw speaks in volumes far louder than you ever could. But understand this—I don't have a relationship with Kevin. He's your friend, not mine, and whether or not you repair this rift has no bearing on my life whatsoever. I'm simply stating some observations I believe you should consider."

Somewhat abashed, I still felt a need to differentiate myself from Kevin. In a calmer tone I tried again. "I understand that, but, Dr. Schenk, you can't seriously compare me to Kevin. He came out. He's said he's gay. My issues with him go a lot deeper than whether we both treated our respective fiancées correctly or not."

"Why?"

I gasped. "*Why?* Isn't it obvious?"

"Not to me. Why don't you attempt to explain?"

"He's gay!"

"Yes, so you have mentioned repeatedly. Once again, we are here to treat your issues, not someone else's. I have given you what I believe are some serious insights into what may be fueling your anger toward Kevin, and now I have no desire to go any further down that path. I do not treat Kevin, nor am I convinced that I need to. I believe it would be best to end our discussion on this matter right here as my beliefs on homosexuality do not generally coincide with those espoused by members of your church or most Christians in general."

I stared at him, astonished. This was the first time I could ever remember Dr. Schenk telling me a topic was, in essence, off limits. "Fair enough, I was only asking about the size of my file. You're the one who brought up Kevin."

Dr. Schenk removed his glasses and cleaned them while shaking his head. "Defensiveness cloaked in immaturity. I'm so proud of the progress you've made, Todd."

Instantly, I felt ashamed. "I'm sorry. You're right. That was uncalled for."

"Don't be. Regardless of how little I shared, I shouldn't have allowed my personal opinions and beliefs to enter our discussion. You have a tough job ahead of determining how your friendship with Kevin moves forward. It is a task I do not envy, but I also recognize it is something you will have to work through on your own, or with someone other than myself. For what it's worth, I truly hope you're successful."

"Thanks . . . I guess."

"Moving along, how are you coping with the turn of events regarding your other friend Jason?"

"Would it make sense if I said I was shocked and saddened by his leaving but, at the same time, completely unsurprised at his decision?"

"It would make perfect sense. I think you anticipated this outcome months ago. Or would it be more appropriate to say years ago?"

"I think I'm more surprised it didn't happen sooner. It still makes me sad though."

"As it should. It sounds to me as though he believes he is finally being honest with himself and others. Yet his lack of concern over leaving his new wife and his children suggests he is as deeply entrenched in denial and destructive self-serving behavior as ever."

I couldn't have agreed more. However, with nothing more to add, I simply nodded in concurrence.

"How are you feeling about your father's engagement?"

"I think it's rushed, but I also think there's nothing I can do about it so . . ." I shrugged.

"Interesting. Is this a commonly held view within your family?"

"Uh, no. What's funny is that over the last year, I've been the one to butt heads with my dad constantly. Now, I'm sitting back, content to let things happen, while my brother Mike and my sister, Katie, are doing everything within their power to talk Dad out of his decision."

"If you agree with them, why aren't you getting involved?"

"It's like I said, I don't think there's anything I could say to change his mind."

"Is that the only reason?"

I considered his question for a moment. "I don't know. Why?"

"It really doesn't matter. I simply have another theory."

I sat back in my chair with a guarded grin. "Let's hear it."

"Since your wife died, you've had your father constantly giving you unwanted advice. At its worst, it became so problematic that it almost ruined your relationship with him. Would you agree?"

"Yeah."

"But in recent weeks, your relationship with your father has dramatically improved. Why is that?"

Expecting a monologue only, the question startled me. "I don't know. Maybe we just needed a little time?"

"You can do better than that."

This time, I contemplated what he was asking and tried to pinpoint just when our relationship had changed.

"Ever since my mother passed away, he seems to respect me more."

"Precisely. Once again, he hasn't changed as a person a great deal. He has simply gained a greater respect for what you had experienced. What's even more interesting is that he is taking his own advice with regards to handling the loss of his wife, but he seems more content in now allowing you to choose your own way."

I hadn't put those two things together before. Dr. Schenk was right. Dad had lightened up considerably on his lectures, and our relationship had been improving ever since.

"So my theory is this—whether you realize it or not, receiving latitude from your father has led you to reciprocate and extend that latitude back to him. It's not about whether he's making a mistake. For you, this is about building upon the mutual respect that has formed between you and your father. In the end, you've come to realize that a solid relationship is more important than being right."

His analysis was like a ray of sunshine breaking through the clouds. "I think you have a point, Doc."

"Well, thank you, Todd. I just find it a shame that you seem unable to apply this same principle to all of your relationships."

TODD'S LANDRY LIST

The Heart of the Matter
Tuesday, October 21

AS A PARENT, one of my main goals has been to develop a strong relationship with each of my kids. When I was a brand-new father, I would sit and rock my infant daughter for hours, daydreaming of all the bonding moments our lives would bring. Many of those musings included late night chats complete with homemade chocolate chip cookies and milk. It had worked for my mom—surely it would work for me.

Unfortunately, over the last three months, reality has proven to be far different from those dreams of days gone by. My relationship with Alex has continued to deteriorate since her entry into therapy. I don't know what I'd been expecting, but it wasn't this.

To make matters worse, ending my relationship with Emily has directly led to my other daughter, Samantha, withdrawing from me as well. She's always been my "quiet" child, but now her silence is accompanied by an unmistakable sense of despair. It's clear to me she needs help. I almost wonder if I should talk to Dr. Schenk about the possibility of a Landry group rate.

All of this silence and all of this despondency permeating our lives has created a pretty gloomy atmosphere around our house. However, tonight may have provided the first glimpse of light at the end of our tunnel.

Not that the glimpse of light was visible when we sat down to dinner. If anything, our typical daily grind had been more churlish than usual. Sam, who up until recently would never think to pick a fight with anyone, seemed intent on making Drake's life miserable.

Multiple times, she snapped at him for nothing more than perfectly innocent four-year-old behavior. I tried to let it go, but after the fifth time, I'd finally reached my limit.

Slamming my fork down, I barked, "Leave him alone."

"But, Dad, he's—"

"I said, LEAVE HIM ALONE!"

I delivered my rebuke more forcefully than I'd intended. Sam stared at me in shock for a couple of seconds before bursting into tears. In a dynamic I've never understood, Drake immediately jumped to Sam's defense and yelled at me, begging me to stop being mean to his sister. Desperate for an ally, I glanced across the table pleadingly in hopes of receiving Alex's support. But her eyes never rose from her plate.

Within a few minutes, order was restored, but animosity continued to bubble just under the surface. Over the next two hours, mayhem threatened to break loose again several times, but we were able to escape with minimal damage.

Finally, around eight thirty, I kissed Sam good night and got Drake tucked into bed after his third and final "last drink." I stopped by Alex's room to say good night but hesitated. Her light was out.

Standing in the hall outside her door, I grieved over how our family dynamic had fallen so apart. Following dinner, Alex had disappeared to her room to supposedly work on homework. She'd been in there ever since, with the exception of the few minutes it took to join us for family prayer. We'd been following this same pattern for weeks. I was no longer aware of when she went to bed because she'd long since stopped checking in with me before doing so.

Feeling like a failure as a father, but unsure of what else to do, I leaned in close to her door and softly called out, "Good night, Alex." I waited silently for a response. None came.

I walked back into the living room and gave a fleeting thought to the disaster waiting for me in the kitchen. Part of me knew if I didn't deal with the mess tonight, I'd be cursing myself in the morning. But the silence was too blissful to resist. Assuring myself it was only for a minute or two, I sat down on the sofa and relaxed.

I know it wasn't real, but the couch cushions felt softer than usual. Before I knew it, I'd closed my eyes and drifted off. I'm not sure how long I'd been there when a timid voice jarred me back to reality.

"Dad?"

I bolted upright, looking around frantically. Alex was standing at the end of the couch, gaping at me with an expression of doubt and anxiety. I think I scared her as much as she'd scared me.

Her apprehension flustered me, and I suddenly felt a need to explain. "Hey, sweetie! I'm sorry—you startled me. I think I might've fallen asleep."

"You did. You were kinda snoring."

"Well then, there you go." I probably should've been more embarrassed, but what was the point? Besides, I was too caught up in the fact that my teenage daughter was initiating a conversation with me. "What's up?"

Alex stood unmoving as she tried to summon the courage that had propelled her thus far. I sat motionless, worried that any further encouragement on my part would only serve to push her away. It was when my eyes began to lose focus that I realized I'd been holding my breath.

As I exhaled sharply, a look of determination stole over Alex's face, and she formally addressed me, "Dad, I need to talk to you. Would now be okay?"

The primness in her voice almost made me chuckle, but I stifled the impulse quickly by reaching over and patting the cushion on the opposite side of the couch.

Awkwardly, as if she were concerned it might bite, Alex took the seat I offered. From the look in her eyes, I could see that her plans had extended this far, but no further. I returned her gaze without speaking, allowing her the time to formulate her thoughts.

Suddenly, she blurted out, "Do you even think about Mom anymore?"

The intensity in her voice coupled with the

unexpected question took me back. "Sure . . . uh, I mean yes. Of course I do."

"Because you don't act like it!" The accusation felt like a slap across the face.

"Honey, I'm sorry. I don't mean to give off that impression, but I'm not sure I know what you mean. How do I not act like it?"

When she replied, her voice had softened and she sounded more hurt than critical. "You never talk about her anymore."

I still wasn't sure I understood exactly what she was driving at, but deep down, I sensed she needed me to grasp her meaning without further explanation. I inhaled slowly and prayed for help to say what she needed to hear.

"Alex, I think about your mother every day. I realize you can't hear my thoughts, but I'm constantly thinking about her, missing her—wishing like crazy she was here."

My voice caught in my throat. It had been months since I'd broken down over Marci, but, without warning, a thousand emotions I'd battled and supposedly conquered were once again bearing down on me. Despite my best efforts, a tear leaked out of my eye and rolled down my cheek. Alex was mesmerized by its slow descent.

That lone tear falling from my chin seemed to crash through a wall on its way to splashing on my collar. Alex's eyes welled up, and she closed the distance between us in a heartbeat. Her arms around my neck were the sweetest thing I'd felt in days, and her tears, hot on my face, caused my own to fall more freely.

Silently, I thanked God for His understanding beyond my own. I'd been so worried about saying the right thing—it never occurred to me that no words would've ever been enough. She simply needed to see some sort of proof that I still cared about her mother. A single tear was the exact prescription she was looking for.

Minutes later, I pulled back and self-consciously wiped my eyes while Alex returned to the opposite side of the sofa. It was clear not everything had been resolved as she suddenly found a tassel on the throw blanket draped over our couch to be the most interesting item in the room.

I waited patiently to give her a chance to continue on her own. Once I realized that wasn't going to happen, I prodded, "Honey, is something else bothering you?"

Her gaze fell as she quietly whispered, "Dad, I'm sorry."

"Sorry for what, sweetheart? You don't have anything to be sorry for."

"Yes, I do. I screwed everything up. Sam hates me. You hate me . . ." Her words trailed off as she found it impossible to express the mountains of pent-up anguish and guilt.

"Alex, I don't hate you. I've never hated you. You're my daughter. Sure, you frustrate me to no end sometimes, but that's just part of being a family. And I'm sure Sam doesn't hate you either."

"Yes, she does. She told me so. She hates me for getting rid of Emily, and she told me everything in her life would be perfect if I wasn't her sister. She hates me, Dad . . . and I don't know how to fix it."

My heart broke as I watched Alex draw her knees into her chest and hug them tightly as her tears started flowing once more. This time, when she dared to look at me, I no longer saw the anger and resentment I was used to. Instead, I saw a vulnerable little girl carrying far too much baggage for someone so young.

At that moment, everything about my faith suddenly made greater sense. There was no denying that Alex was responsible for Emily not being a part of our lives. I certainly couldn't downplay my role in everything, but, in the end, she was right—that particular opportunity for our family was gone and it had been her call.

But she regretted it. And she wanted desperately to fix it. But she had no ability to do so. She needed help. More than that, she needed my help. She needed to know that even though she'd made choices that had possibly hurt our family, she was still loved and, more important, forgiven.

The interesting thing was that I'd forgiven her completely weeks earlier. All I wanted was my daughter back. And right then—if I could somehow convince her of my love for her—I could have it. Something told me the old Alex would be back. Not the Alex from six months ago, but a deeper, more mature version of the sweet girl I'd known before Marci died.

Easing off the couch, I knelt directly in front of her. Her tear-filled eyes, which had returned to their downcast position, slowly looked up into my own. I smiled and pulled her into another embrace.

"I want you to listen to me and listen closely. I love you. I will always love you. I will always love your mom, and no way could I ever hate you for acting out of loyalty and love for her.

"Now, sweetie, I'm not gonna lie. Sometimes I do miss Emily. And to be honest, I don't know how we're gonna fix things with Sam. But right here, right now . . . you and me—we're good."

Alex's arms tightened around my neck as I finished speaking. At the same time, there was a subtle but unmistakable shift in her sobbing. The tears, which seconds before had been shed out of sorrow and pain, were transforming into tears born out of relief.

I kissed her forehead and settled in. I had no idea how long she intended to hold me, but if the Lord could supposedly pick me up and carry me as He and I walked along some sandy beach, I could certainly stay on my knees in a dimly lit living room for as long as my baby girl needed me to.

A Reality Check from My Personal Dalai Lama

Monday, October 27

BEFORE HER PASSING, my mom had been Drake's regular sitter when I needed to work, with my sister as the backup. These days, Katie has become the primary, and Grant's wife, Stacy, has been kind enough to accept the on-call duty. Before today, Drake had only been to the Barneys' once before, and let's just say it could have gone better. Consequently, as I pulled up in front of Grant's house, I was quite anxious as to whether I still had friends living there.

As I stood outside their front door, I was more than a little relieved not to hear any screaming. I waited for a couple of seconds before knocking, just in case my ears hadn't tuned into the right frequency, but the only sound that greeted me was blessed silence.

Smiling, I knocked.

My thoughts had already turned to the multitude of errands I still needed to run when suddenly the door opened and Grant stepped out to greet me.

Right away, my hackles were raised. My natural

instincts couldn't quite place it, but something was off.

In his best attempt at keeping things casual, he asked, "So, a full day today?"

Warily, I peered around the doorframe and back into the house, trying to piece together what was happening.

"Yep. Doesn't happen often, but we had a big project fall behind, so the boss called for all hands on deck."

Grant nodded knowingly as he closed the door behind him, and that's when everything clicked. My eight hours had started at seven this morning, which meant it was only a little after four. I knew Grant rarely made it home before five. Also, I was here to pick up my son, and after several minutes there was still no sign of him. Based on his last experience at this house, that seemed highly out of the ordinary.

"Is this a setup?"

"What do you mean?" Grant asked, his expression reeking of guilt.

"It is, isn't it? You've been waiting for me."

"Well, if I ran into you—"

"Oh my gosh! This must be serious if you're pulling the 'well since I ran into you' routine. Is Drake even here?"

Sheepishly, Grant looked away and squinted toward the horizon. "Uh . . . no. Stacy took him and my boys to get ice cream."

"He was that bad?"

"No, Stacy said he was perfectly fine today. I just wanted to talk to you."

All of my personal defense mechanisms locked

firmly into place. After all, friendship or not, he is my bishop. "Am I speaking on Sunday, or have you lost your mind completely and decided to make me the full-fledged Scoutmaster?"

He chuckled. "It's nothing like that."

Had his response been sincere I would've relaxed, but the laugh was forced, and Grant seemed genuinely uneasy.

I dropped all pretenses of jocularity. "Then, what?"

"Have you talked to Kevin yet?"

I wish he'd have just hit me in the stomach. I think it would've hurt less. His tone was certainly not judgmental, but it didn't have to be.

"No, I haven't."

"Are you waiting for something in particular?"

With a sarcastic cock of my head, I countered, "Uh, yeah—like some idea of what to say. Besides, I'm still angry, somewhat. I think it'd be best if I waited until I can approach him calmly."

"What a load! It's been a month and a half. What could you possibly still be mad about?"

Almost like a recording, I began reciting my all-too-familiar line. "I'm having a really hard time with how he deceived everyone. Especially Caralee."

I winced inside as I said the last bit. Since my visit with Dr. Schenk, using that reason with even an ounce of authenticity was getting increasingly difficult. Grant didn't react at all. He just stood there wearing me down with a fixed stare. Before long, his scrutiny proved too much, and I looked away.

"You're slipping, buddy. Besides, have you

forgotten who you're talking to? What's really going on with you?"

Angrily, I lashed back, "What is it you want me to say?"

Grant took a step forward, invading my personal space. With him so close, I had no choice but to look him in the eyes. "I want you to admit this is about your issues with homosexuality and to stop blaming your problems on Kevin."

"Fine. I admit it. It's a huge problem for me. Isn't it for you? You're a bishop, for heaven's sake."

Neither of us moved. Finally, Grant took a step back. However, his eyes never left my own. He seemed to be analyzing me, as if he were looking deep into my soul and finding something he'd never realized was there.

"What has he done wrong, Todd?"

"Are you kidding me? He's attracted to men. That's a pretty big deal, don't you think?"

"So I guess that makes me a pretty lousy person then too. I've been attracted to other women since I've been married to Stacy. I haven't acted on those attractions, but, by your standards, simply admitting those feelings exist makes me just as guilty as if I had."

"That's ridiculous."

"Is it?"

Twice I started to counter only to cut myself off. Finally, I just shrugged and said, "Fine, you win. I'm a judgmental jerk, and Kevin is as pure as the wind-driven snow."

Grant snapped back, "Knock it off. This isn't about winning or losing. This is about our friend. This is about the guy who basically put you on his back and carried you through the last year of your life. Now, he sits alone every night in his apartment because you, and just about every other person that matters to him, has walked away. Stacy and I are doing what we can, but he needs his best friend. He needs *you*."

Frustration burned inside my chest. I knew he was right. Kevin was my best friend and had done more for me than anyone, outside of my mother, when it came to dealing with Marci's death. Of course, I hated how this whole mess was playing out.

But it wasn't my fault. I'd never heard anything but fire and brimstone regarding homosexuality. God had supposedly destroyed cities over this stuff, and now my best friend was forcing me to be accepting of a behavior I'd been taught to abhor. I wasn't the bad guy here, yet I was the one being made to feel guilty. The whole situation felt upside down.

As if sensing my thoughts, Grant quietly continued. "It's hard, isn't it? All the lessons we had on morality and repentance as teenagers that never included a mention of homosexuality. We all knew why. It wasn't like having premarital sex with a girl. Being gay was a death sentence. A plague you never came back from."

"Isn't it still?"

Grant paused before answering. "I guess if we want it to be."

I shook my head and scoffed. "Look, we don't get to rewrite the rules. They're black and white, and we both know it. And so does Kevin."

"Who's asking you to rewrite any rules? All

I'm saying is that I believe that far too often, we as Church members like to take what's black and white and stretch it to cover a whole lot of areas that are gray." Grant paused and then started in again with a different tack.

"What if it was Drake? How would you feel then?"

My shoulders slumped as the fears I'd been holding at bay came crashing through my defenses. What would I do? I certainly wouldn't be treating him the way I was treating Kevin.

I turned to face Grant and, in a voice just short of pleading, asked, "Why? Why did he have to do this? Why did he put us in this position?"

Grant sighed. "Can I tell you something and trust that you'll keep it confidential? I can't share any names, and I'm seriously begging you not to guess, but I'm working with a young man right now who's struggling with these same issues."

Grant opened his mouth to continue, but his voice caught in his throat. Finally, he went on, despite fighting back tears. "He hates himself. He thinks he's some kind of monster. Worst of all, he believes God hates him too. I mean, that makes sense, doesn't it? If God loved him, he certainly wouldn't have these feelings."

As he spoke, I couldn't picture any of the young men in our ward. I could only see my son. It ripped my heart wide open. I wanted him to stop talking, but he didn't.

"I love this kid. I was his deacons quorum advisor. And every time we visit, I feel a massive weight of guilt on my shoulders. Not because I didn't try harder to fix him, but because of what I didn't do on a camp-out years ago."

Grant leaned against the pillar adjacent to his front steps and cast his gaze out toward the street.

"I don't remember how it came up that night, but me, the Scoutmaster, and all the boys were sitting around a campfire roasting marshmallows when it happened. Out of the blue, the Scoutmaster went off on gays. *Queers* was what he called them. He ranted and raved for a good ten minutes about how worth-less every single one of them was. Even now, I can see it in my mind like it was yesterday. It was one of the most uncomfortable experiences of my life. Here were these six little twelve- and thirteen-year-old boys sit-ting there silently staring into the fire—scared out of their minds as this man they'd been taught to respect spewed horrible things that just felt ugly.

"If I live a thousand years, I'll never forget his final words on the subject. He said, 'They oughta round up every single one of them queers, take 'em out in the desert, and beat the hell out of 'em.'

"Later that night, he apologized for his language, but I could tell he thought he'd done a good thing. He'd 'scared 'em straight,' and if a curse word had to be used to drive his point home, so be it."

At some point, Grant had stopped talking to me and had begun unburdening himself of a weight he'd carried far too long. "I should've stopped him. I should've put an end to it right away, but he was so much older than I was and had been the Scoutmaster for years. I was intimidated."

As if coming out of a trance, Grant blinked and turned back to face me. "So now, when I hear this young man describe himself as worthless and evil, how far do I have to dig to find his inspiration?"

"It wasn't your fault," I offered quietly.

Grant laughed scornfully. "Of course it was. At the time, I knew what he was saying was out of line, but that doesn't mean I disagreed with him. I mean, the beating them senseless part was way over the top, but didn't he say what we all believe? I mean, isn't it black and white?"

Humiliation coursed through my veins as my own words were thrown back at me. "No, I suppose not."

Stepping closer and placing his hand on my shoulder, Grant softly added, "Todd, you asked me why Kevin is doing this to us. Answer me honestly—do you think this young man I'm working with would choose this voluntarily? Kevin's father won't speak to him. His mother can't without crying. His best friend since childhood hasn't contacted him in over a month. Do you think Kevin is choosing this because he wants to?"

With my eyes cast down, I slowly shook my head.

"Me either. Which, in my mind, changes everything about your question. Why is Kevin doing this?"

Raising my gaze to meet his, I answered, "I don't know."

Grant leaned back against the pillar and, without looking at me, admitted, "I'm not going to pretend that I have any idea either, because I don't. But I do have a theory. No one in Salt Lake has endorsed it yet, but living by it has sure lifted a huge burden from my soul. And who knows, maybe it can help you find a way to reach out to our friend."

A lifeline—any lifeline—sounded good. I was tired of living with the guilt that weighed me down each and every time I thought of Kevin.

"Let's hear it."

"How differently would we act if the 'Golden Rule' was the only rule? What if the only question on the final test is how did you treat other people?"

Grant's eyes bored into my own as he delivered his final blow.

"What if Kevin's homosexuality isn't God's test for Kevin? What if it's God's test for us?"

TODD'S LANDRY LIST

Solitary Man
Saturday, November 1

WOW, A MERE twenty-eight days had passed since my father's unexpected wedding announcement, and this afternoon my family and I were gathered on the steps of the Mesa Arizona Temple, taking pictures following the ceremony. Even though the marriage was not a sealing, my father still insisted it take place in the temple to provide a positive example for his grandchildren. His logic was sound, but all week I'd been teasing him about lost opportunities.

At a Landry family dinner last Sunday, I'd presented my best argument to date. Gaining everyone's attention, I suggested, "Dad, you should try one of those weddings on the beach in Hawaii. That way, the whole family could enjoy a nice vacation, and we'd be able to see you get married in your bare feet with a floral arrangement around your neck. Isn't that referred to as a win-win?"

Despite a huge swell of support from other family members, Dad merely frowned and grunted something under his breath that included the words *ridiculous* and *unbecoming*. It was a fun, lighthearted moment until Maureen got hold of the idea and ran with it.

"You know, Adrian, that's not a half-bad idea."

Every person seated at the table would've been less shocked had Maureen stood up and fired a shotgun into the ceiling. All talking stopped, and every eye turned to my father.

I swear his face turned a sickly shade of green in less than a second. Using every ounce of restraint, he deliberately lowered his fork and turned to face his fiancée.

"Excuse me?"

Maureen, completely oblivious to the tension she'd created, kept on. "Think about it. It could be fun. Plus, my kids have never been to Hawaii, and something like this might be their only opportunity."

I couldn't believe what I was hearing. Did this woman know my father at all? Lavish spending combined with travel was kryptonite to my father's soul. Deep down, I felt a little bad about putting him in this position. But not bad enough to resist the temptation I felt to make it worse.

"I could check in with the travel agents we work with at the office, Dad. It'd be no trouble at all!" I smiled broadly at him with my most innocent expression. Brock snorted in laughter but then quickly grabbed his napkin and tried to play it off as if he'd sneezed.

Following a quick glare in my direction, Dad let a smile replace his frown before turning back to Maureen. "Sweetheart, everything is already set for this Saturday. The reception arrangements are underway and . . . I think we're fine to continue as planned."

"But, Adrian, nothing has happened that couldn't be undone. We could—"

"I don't know that now is the best time to discuss this. Let's finish eating and you and I will talk about this, if we *need* to, later." My father's smile remained in place as he cut her off, but all signs of sincerity had vanished.

Today, however, it was clear Maureen had put her recent defeat behind her as she stood beaming for photo after photo. Dad, on the other hand, was not faring so well.

As we posed for a full family shot, I leaned over to Mike and whispered, "How much longer do you think Dad can last?"

Mike remained stock-still as he whispered back, "Five minutes max. I'm surprised he's made it this long."

Mike's estimation proved more than generous as just three minutes later, Dad informed the photographer we were done.

As family members dispersed, I asked Mike quietly, "Do you sometimes wonder if Maureen knows our father at all?"

Mike scoffed, "Every day. And frankly, he's not making it easy for her. These last couple of weeks, we can't seem to get him out of the office. He's retired, for heaven's sake. There's nothing for him to do, but he just hangs around finding odd jobs for himself. I have no idea when they even see each other."

That seemed odd, but then I was struck by a thought. "Do you think he might have been avoiding the reception planning?"

"Good point. If that was his problem, then maybe things can get back to normal now that it's about over. Of course, if tonight's party is any indication, he may have to come back to work just to support his new bride's expected lifestyle."

I recoiled in astonishment. Mike was not the brother I was used to hearing snide comments from. "What're you talking about?"

"Have you not heard how much this reception is costing?"

"To be honest, I've tried to stay out of it. How bad is it?"

Mike laughed humorlessly. "I don't know if bad is the right description, but suffice it to say that the new Mrs. Landry is not shy about showing off her new financial station in life."

"Uh-oh." I chuckled. "Sounds like it's time to set up guards around the family vault."

"I wouldn't laugh. I've spent the last month making sure Dad no longer has any vested interest in the business. I've also set up trusts and worked non-stop to get a prenup signed."

I turned and stared with my mouth agape. "Dad signed a prenup?"

"He was adamant that he wasn't going to. But the morning after your Hawaii comments at dinner, he came in and agreed to sign anything I put in front of him. I don't know how he got Maureen to sign, but two days later, she did."

I grunted in surprise. "Well, thanks, little brother. None of that even occurred to me."

"Don't worry about it. You were too old to know any of Maureen's kids, but a couple of them were near my age in school. The night I found out Dad was getting serious with her, I freaked. I started working on all of this the next day. Bottom line, if this is what he wants to do with his life, so be it. But the rest of us shouldn't have to suffer if this turns out to be a bad decision."

I had an overwhelming desire to hug Mike right there on the temple steps, but instead I slapped him on the back and said, "For my kids' sake, I appreciate it. You really are a good brother."

Unexpectedly, Mike turned and grabbed my shoulder. With startling emotion, he declared, "So are you, Todd." He looked away, embarrassed, but continued, "I don't know if now is the right time, but I keep waiting, and the right time never seems to come. So I'm just gonna say it now.

"You're my hero. And I feel really bad about everything you've had to go through lately. It's not fair. But, I want you to know I love you . . . and I'm always here if you need me."

Suddenly, both of us were blinking back tears. Although Mike is my next oldest sibling, the five years difference in our ages has never lent itself to a close bond. We'd never said the words "I love you" to each other before. It's just not what we do. But if this was a new tradition we were starting, I realized right then, it was one I could definitely get on board with.

After a couple of hard swallows, I replied,

"Apparently you've been busy doing a ton already. Thank you. And Mike? I love you too."

He smiled self-consciously as he pulled a hand-kerchief out of his pocket to wipe his eyes. "Well, since the money's already spent, we might as well go and enjoy this thing. Are you headed straight over?"

"Kind of. I'm sending my kids over with Katie and Scott while I go pick up Abby."

"Oh yeah, the new girl. Things must be going pretty well if you're introducing her to the family."

I paused. It hadn't occurred to me what kind of message I might be sending by inviting Abby to a family event. "Uh, yeah, I guess. We've only been out a few times, but we get along pretty well."

"Cool. I look forward to meeting her. We'll see you over there."

"Sounds good."

Mike set off toward the south parking lot while I turned toward my van located near the visitors' center.

Abby looked stunning when I greeted her outside of her home. I'd never had an opportunity to see her truly dressed up before, and I immediately realized that had been my loss. Her conservative yet elegant red dress highlighted her raven hair, which she was wearing down for the first time since I'd met her.

Unfortunately, her mood didn't seem to match her appearance. My repeated attempts at conversation were met with little more than silence as we drove to a reception center in Mesa that Maureen felt would be more in keeping with a Landry gathering than a regular church building.

The closer we got to the reception, the more Abby's brooding silence was causing me to panic. She was meeting my kids for the first time, and I was anxious about first impressions on both sides. Pulling into the parking lot, I decided to deal with this now rather than risk the unknown later. I parked in a shady spot separated from the other vehicles and turned to face her.

"Is everything all right?"

After several awkward seconds, she lifted her eyes to mine and asked the question that had obviously been troubling her from the start. "What am I doing here?"

I was pretty sure what she meant, but I played stupid anyway, in the hopes I was wrong. "You're providing me with a date for my father's wedding reception?"

Closing her eyes, she placed her index finger just above the bridge of her nose and began rubbing as if she were trying to massage a headache. "No, what I'm asking is—why did you invite me to such a personal family function?"

"I don't know. My new stepmother informed me I should get a date, if possible, and since you're the only woman I'm currently seeing, you seemed the logical choice."

Her eyes opened, infused with a grave look of concern. "Is that how you see us? As a couple—exclusive?"

"Well, I don't really date around so . . . I guess I'd have to say yes—I'm dating you exclusively."

Abby tugged at her dress nervously and looked out the passenger window. "Wow, hearing you say it out loud makes it . . ." She trailed off and sat silently staring toward some flowers in the distance.

"Abby, I'm not sure—" Before I could finish, she cut me off.

"See, the thing is, I'm not dating anyone else either, and that's what scares me."

"Why does that scare you?"

"Because I'm perfectly happy not dating anyone."

Her disclosure seemed to confirm what I'd been dreading. This conversation did not feel destined to end well for me.

"What does that mean? If you didn't want to date me, why'd you agree to go out with me in the first place? I thought I gave you every opportunity to decline."

"You did. That's not what I mean." Balling her hands into fists, she put them to her forehead in frustration. After several calming breaths, she faced me and tried again. "I've enjoyed going out with you. I've had a great time with you, but I need to know—where do you see this going?"

"You mean us?"

"Yeah."

"I don't know. I honestly hadn't thought about it."

"Exactly. Me either. And that's where it gets dangerous." Again, she turned and focused her attention outside the vehicle.

Slightly confused, I replied, "I'm not following you."

"I've been having fun, but we've never talked about expectations. Now, I'm a hundred feet away from meeting your entire family, and . . . all day I've been realizing I'm not ready to do that."

My heart pounded faster against my chest. "So, what are you saying?"

As she looked my way again, I saw a sadness in her eyes that caused my stomach to tighten. "I'm saying that I'm happy in my life right now and I'm not really interested in getting married again."

"Whoa! Who said anything about marriage?"

"You did. By inviting me here tonight."

I started to object but stopped. As much as I hated to admit it, I could see where she could get that impression.

"You're right. I apologize. I can take you home and . . . and we can forget this ever happened. I'm sure Maureen will give me all kinds of grief, but . . ."

"Todd, you're not listening. If it's not tonight, then when?"

I shrugged. "I don't know. It can be weeks from now—months from now. Whenever you want."

"That's just it. If I'm being honest about *when* I truly want . . . then when I want is never."

I felt like an anvil had landed on my head. "I don't understand. If you enjoy being with me and we're having a good time together, then what's the problem?"

She smiled sadly and shook her head. "I'm beginning to like you too much, and this is starting to move beyond just having a good time. The problem is—I'm not eighteen anymore. I have a seventeen-year-old son I'm responsible for, and I have to consider what's best for him. On top of that, I'm sure your children are wonderful, but at this point in my life, I don't want to be a mom again. I know that sounds selfish, but . . ."

My lungs were having trouble finding air. "Are you saying you don't want to see me anymore?"

Abby sighed. "No, I'm saying the opposite. When I agreed to go out with you, I never thought I'd end up liking you. I mean, be honest. Did you?"

With a noncommittal shrug, I implied she might have a point.

"But you caught me on a lonely day . . . and a person will do crazy things on a lonely day. So I went out with you to remind myself what it feels like to be alive.

"It's too bad that decision came back to bite me. Come to find out, you weren't the cocky jerk I'd expected after all. Too late I discovered you were the kind of guy I could fall for. And that's why I have to end this."

Looking helplessly into her eyes, I saw a mixture of regret and relief staring back at me. I wanted to argue, but in my heart, I knew nothing was left to say.

"I assume you'd be more comfortable if I took you home."

"I think so."

I nodded and started the van.

Neither of us spoke the entire way back to her house, but when we arrived, she leaned over and kissed me on the cheek.

"I'm really sorry, Todd. For what it's worth, I think you're a really great guy."

"If you could add something about still wanting to be friends, I think that would cap our relationship off nicely."

She smiled sadly and looked as if she wanted to

say something more but then thought better of it. "Good-bye, Todd."

"Good-bye, Abby."

As she walked away, I felt an enveloping sense of hopelessness. It wasn't that all of my hopes and dreams were tied to this woman, but right then her departure symbolized everything in my life that had deserted me.

The rest of my evening was spent in a blur. I vaguely recall Maureen fretting over the empty space I'd created in her seating chart, but, beyond that, I don't remember who I spoke to or what excuses I gave for being Todd Landry, party of one.

By eight o'clock I was done. I wasn't sure how much longer everyone intended to stay, but the invitation had specified six to eight, and that meant my duty had been fulfilled.

Through the course of the evening, I'd had plenty of time to think. I'm not certain that was a positive. What had started off as a small case of despair soon grew to include anger and frustration. By the time I was driving home, I was a mess.

Alex, bless her heart, could tell I was not in a good place and took the lead on getting the other two ready for bed. I made a halfhearted attempt to help, but after putting both of Drake's legs in the same hole of his pajama pants for the third time, I gave up and retreated to my room.

I've always believed that all stupid ideas originate early enough to allow their host a chance to change their mind. In my case, what I was about to do had first occurred to me some time around the cutting of the cake. Almost immediately I recognized it for the horrible idea that it was.

But then, when someone asked me where my date was for the fourteenth time, the idea returned—and this time it refused to leave. I told myself over and over that no good could possibly come from this, but as I sat on the edge of my bed, Abby's statement from earlier became prophetic. Lonely people will do crazy things.

I picked up the phone and dialed the number from memory. Right about the second ring, my senses returned and I tensed in anticipation of hanging up, but I was too late.

"Hello?"

The sound of her voice was even sweeter than I remembered. Up until that moment, I'd never known it was possible to relive so much regret in such a short amount of time.

"Uh . . . Emily? It's Todd."

My words were met with silence.

"Umm . . . I'm sorry to call so late, I just—I needed to tell you something, and I felt it was best not to wait."

Again, no response from the other end of the line.

"Look, I need to apologize for the way things ended between us. I was just trying to do what was best for my daughter, but I've recently learned how things must have felt from your perspective. At the time, I really thought I was doing the right thing. Now—I'm not sure. I just want you to know—"

Midsentence, I stopped. Everything I'd planned on saying had sounded so much better in my head. This was a disaster.

"Emily, I'm sorry. I'm sorry I hurt you. I'm sorry I screwed up the really good thing we had. And if I could somehow fix it, I would in a heartbeat."

I was out of breath and out of things to say. I wanted to continue pleading, but my closing argument was complete. All that remained now was her verdict.

"Todd, I'm engaged."

I'm not sure how I managed to hold on to the phone. My entire body went numb, and for just one instant, I lost my desire to live.

Failing miserably to mask the anguish in my voice, I replied, "Well, congratulations. I'm happy for you."

My mind drew a blank on what to say next. Emily took advantage of my hesitation.

"I appreciate you calling, and please know I accept your apology—but I really should go." A slight pause preceded her final words. "Good-bye, Todd."

"Good-bye, Emily," I whispered.

I replaced the phone and slipped to my knees. An abyss of darkness was opening up in front of me, and I became frightened. The reality of what was happening was all too familiar. Grabbing hold of the one anchor available to me, I began to pray.

"Heavenly Father, please help me. I can't take any more."

I knew there was so much more to say, but I couldn't. The dam holding my sanity together was crumbling. So I allowed the events of the last year and a half to play out in front of my mind's eye and let the mounting recollections of all I'd lost serve as my petition.

Minutes later, as the last wisps of memory faded, I regained a consciousness of my surroundings. My fatherly instincts said I should get up and check on my kids, but I remained beside my bed. I needed to know I'd been heard. I needed some sort of answer.

But nothing came.

I clenched my eyes shut, willing some form of communication to come, but eventually I had to accept that my worst fears were true. God wasn't listening to me anymore.

I'd barely gotten back to my feet when it came. My answer wasn't delivered by a voice, but rather a page of scripture flashed in my mind. I can't remember the reference, but the words of a verse were as clear as if they'd been written on my wall.

My son, peace be unto thy soul; thine adversity and thine afflictions shall be but a small moment. . . . Thou art not yet as Job.

I was stunned. Never in my life had I actually felt like I'd been given an answer so clearly, and yet . . . what kind of lousy answer was that?

Anger erupted through me like lava. What was I supposed to do with an answer like that? It solved nothing!

Hot tears of resentment stung my eyes. Filled with bitterness, I was desperate for a way to vent how unacceptable I found His response.

Jerking its cord from the outlet, I grabbed a lamp from my bedside table and hurled it across the room. It smashed against the wall, sending hundreds of glass shards in every direction.

I dropped back to my knees and began to weep.

The tears simply poured out of me with no end in sight.

Through all of this, I never heard the door to my bedroom open, but somehow, through my pain, I heard a soft voice call out to me.

"Daddy?"

Peering at me from the hallway, her face filled with alarm, was my sweet, beautiful Alex. Though my vision was hazy, I could see her cheeks were wet with tears of her own.

"Daddy, are you okay?"

As she spoke, two more sets of eyes cautiously appeared from behind my doorframe. My voice had abandoned me, so I smiled as best I could and waved them in.

Within seconds, I was enveloped in the arms of my three wonderful children, and together we sat on my bedroom floor, embracing each other and crying.

Peace began to work its way into my heart. I love my kids. I would do anything for them. And right then I realized, regardless of where my life was going, I had them—and that was enough.

My mind flashed again to the words I'd seen earlier:

My son, peace be unto thy soul. . . . Thou art not yet as Job.

Humbled, I squeezed my kids. And thanked God for the best answer He could ever have given me.

Friendship Means Always Having to Say You're Sorry

Sunday, November 2

AT 6:58 THIS morning, the sun's first ray eased through my window, settling directly on my eyelid. I shifted my blanket and tried to pretend nothing had happened, but it was too late. I was awake.

Turning onto my back, I stared at the ceiling as the morning shadows crept along the wall, advancing daylight farther and farther into my room. The stillness of the morning allowed my thoughts to roam. Before long, I found myself rifling through enough emotional baggage to fill a dozen of Dr. Schenk's binders.

I thought about Abby and took a few moments to mourn the passing of an enjoyable but short-lived relationship. That led to thoughts of Emily, but I didn't dwell there long. I'd messed up. But what was done was done, and there was little I could do to change it.

As I tried to think of anything but Emily, I began to reflect on my mother, which caused an overwhelming sense of emptiness to fill my chest. It's possible she may not have been the best mother of all time, but she was perfect for me, and I missed her. Even though it had been four months since her passing, I suddenly felt her loss more than ever.

Finally, I thought of Marci. Smiling wistfully, I relived a thousand mornings just like this one. Of the two of us, I'd always been the earlier riser, so when I'd wake up to a quiet house like today, it wouldn't be long before I was tormenting her out of her slumber.

If she'd been here this morning, we'd have laughed and talked and snuggled—oblivious to the world around us. Moments like this were our one chance to be *us* without any outside influence.

Thinking of Marci brought my loneliness full circle. If only she wasn't gone, how different would my life be?

Eventually, my pity party was interrupted by the sound of a bathroom door down the hall. My leisurely time of reflection was almost over. I thought about getting up and preempting the room invasion sure to come, but decided I was perfectly comfortable right where I was. If one or two kids ended up crawling into bed next to me—well, I could think of worse things.

Nestling further under my covers, I allowed my mind to resume its travels. But this time, my thoughts steered clear of romances lost and ventured instead to friendships ignored.

I sighed.

Since my talk with Grant, I'd wanted to reach out to Kevin. But while anger may have been my reason for avoiding him initially, now it was strictly embarrassment. I had no way of explaining why I had left him alone so long.

But as I lay there, a thought occurred to me. Was I really willing to further damage one of the most important relationships in my life over pride? I shuddered at the thought. I knew in my heart making contact with Kevin was never going to get easier. I needed to treat the situation like getting a shot of antibiotics for strep throat—take the nastiness up front in exchange for immense relief later on.

With a grim smile playing on my lips, I resolved today would be the day.

Once church was over, I returned to my house to drop my kids off before heading off to Kevin's. I explained that I needed to run an errand, and Alex would be in charge until I got home. Unfortunately, as a single parent, this occurs far too frequently, so my announcement was greeted with relative uninterest. But as she stepped from the car, Alex turned back.

"By the way, where are you going?"

"To Kevin's."

Her face filled with excitement. "Does that mean whatever you two are fighting about is over?"

Her reaction made me feel small. "I hope so, babe."

"Me too. Tell him I miss him and he still owes me a Blizzard. He'll know what I'm talking about."

"Okay, sweetie, I will."

She slammed the door and waved before running into the house.

The drive to Kevin's apartment was amazingly short. I was hoping it would last longer as my opening line remained sketchy at best.

Standing at his threshold, I breathed in sharply,

held it, closed my eyes, and knocked. I heard rustling inside and suddenly the door flew open. For the first time in a month and a half, I was standing face-to-face with the one person who knew me better than any one else alive.

Kevin's appearance was startling. He'd lost weight, and heavy dark circles had formed under his eyes.

Desperately, I searched for something witty to say—something that would take the sting out of my prolonged absence. Nothing came. Finally, I said the only thing that seemed appropriate.

"I'm sorry."

The effect of my apology was immediate. Kevin's lower lip trembled and tears filled his eyes as he stepped forward and pulled me into a massive bear hug. His weight loss, which had been noticeable when he'd opened the door, shocked me as I returned his embrace.

We separated, but he left his arm around my shoulder as he guided me into his apartment. He seemed almost worried that I might turn and bolt if he let go of me.

It wasn't until we were well inside that he removed his arm to gesture toward a chair. "Thanks for coming. Can I get you anything?" he asked nervously.

The carefree, easy-going Kevin I'd known my whole life was not the man now standing in front of me. This replacement looked beaten down and defeated.

As I stared into my friend's sunken eyes, a thought struck me. Was this how I had looked just one year earlier? The realization hit me hard. I should've been here much sooner.

Kevin continued to watch me anxiously, eager to meet my needs. Placing my hand on his shoulder, I assured him, "I'm fine. Let's sit down and get everything worked out so I can get my golfing partner back."

His entire body relaxed, and when he grinned, I saw a glimmer of the friend I was used to. But as we sat down opposite each other, his smile was replaced by a hardened expression of hurt and anger.

"Why didn't you call?"

"I was scared."

Though the pain remained, the anger in his eyes was replaced by confusion. I needed to explain.

"When you said you were gay, I had no idea what that meant. To be honest, I still don't. I reacted out of fear. Fear of the unknown, fear for my family . . . fear of you."

His confusion deepened. "Why on earth would you be afraid of me?"

I really wanted to say I didn't know or give some trite answer that carried no weight. I wanted to say anything other than the truth.

"Because I was raised to be homophobic . . . just like you."

We stared at each other as the implications of what I'd said hung between us.

Finally, Kevin looked away as he asked, "So what exactly does that mean?"

"Well . . . I suppose it means a lot of things. It means I've been a bad friend. It means I can't change anything I've done over the last six weeks, but I can tell you how sorry I am. Your friendship means more to me than any earthly possession I have, and I feel like dirt for having placed that relationship in danger. You're my best friend, and I'm so sorry I haven't been here when you needed me."

Kevin dropped his head into his hands and began to sob. I sat there awkwardly for quite a while, unsure of what to do. Then, almost as if someone else were controlling my movements, I stood and walked over to sit beside him. Clumsily, I reached my arm around his shaking body and pulled him toward me.

"It's okay, Kev . . . it's okay."

Through his tears, he replied, "No, it's not. And I don't know if it ever will be again."

The despair in his voice caused my heart to break. Without thinking, I offered the standard words of comfort.

"Come on. It can't be that bad."

Kevin shrugged off my arm and wiped his eyes. "Really? How does it get worse?"

My silence only validated his point.

"Exactly!" He stood and walked toward his kitchen. "I need something to drink. Are you sure you don't want anything?"

I sat unmoving, trying to craft a rebuttal to his fatalistic view. When I didn't answer his question, Kevin turned back to face me, waiting. Finally, I rose to follow. "Let's see what you got."

Within minutes, his kitchen table was covered with crackers, cheese, ice cream, and leftover Chinese takeout—all the staples from our Sun Devil days.

Seeing Kevin leaned back in his chair, sipping on a Pepsi, brought back memories of countless times we'd shared a similar spread in college. We were so wise in those days. We could single-handedly solve the world's problems. The mood felt so much heavier now that we were in our late thirties and seemingly incapable of solving our own.

After a few minutes of small talk about Kevin's lousy taste in ice cream and whether it would be breaking the Sabbath for me to buy a Dr Pepper from his apartment complex's vending machine, we retreated into silence. Both of us knew what needed to happen, but neither of us knew where to begin.

Finally, I asked the question I'd been wondering about from the beginning. "When did you know?"

"Know, or suspect?"

"Both, I guess."

His brow furrowed as he struggled to produce an answer. "You remember how much I dated in high school? I remember thinking at the time how odd it was that I could kiss a girl for the first time but then turn it off and walk away without a second thought. I didn't spend days obsessing over when my next chance to make out again would come. It was more of a . . . 'eh, whatever.'"

Remembering my own experiences, I knew exactly what he was referring to. My first kiss monopolized my thoughts for three days after. It even drove basketball from my mind in the middle of the season. To learn Kevin hadn't felt the same seemed almost bizarre.

He continued, "I think I finally admitted to

myself what was going on about two years ago. Now admitting doesn't mean accepting. I tried everything I knew to suppress what I was feeling. But after a year of things not getting better, I decided to visit with my bishop.

"What's interesting is that he was the one who finally convinced me to stop banging my head against a wall trying to change something that wasn't going to change. He counseled me to try to find out if I could live with who I am within the framework of the Church. I took his counsel to mean finding a woman and getting married. However, that wasn't what he meant at all."

My face registered a look of surprise. "It wasn't? I thought that's what bishops were supposed to say."

"I did too, but when I told him I was engaged, he was concerned. He shared the statistics with me for failed marriages when the man is experiencing homosexual tendencies. They're incredibly high. He suggested that I should pray long and hard about my decision. I left that visit with a lot to think about. I didn't want to hurt Caralee, but . . . what if hurting her eventually was inevitable? I should've pulled the plug earlier. I know that. But I was scared. If I'm honest, I'm just grateful I had the courage to do it in time."

"Have you talked to her?"

"Yeah, several times. It's kinda funny. She's probably been the most supportive person of anyone I know."

"Really?"

"Yeah. I mean, she was pretty devastated at first

and refused to talk to me. But once she allowed me to explain everything, I think it dawned on her what could've happened. She still ripped into me pretty good, but since then—she's been a good friend."

Stuffing two saltines in my mouth gave me some time to process everything he'd said. Finally, I swallowed and asked, "So what do you do now?"

Kevin chuckled grimly. "Well, that's the question, isn't it? In some ways, nothing's changed, but at the same time, everything has. Right now, I just wake up each morning and hope like crazy I make it to the end of the day."

For the first time, a black fear gripped me. What he'd said sounded all too familiar. "Kevin, tell me the truth. Are you really okay?"

"What do you mean?"

I could feel the blood rushing to my cheeks out of embarrassment. I hesitated to answer because of the shame associated with what I was about to confess, but I knew I had no choice.

"I never told you this, but do you know why I ended up going to the bishop and . . . I guess eventually to Dr. Schenk?"

Kevin narrowed his eyes. "No. I just assumed it was the natural thing to do."

"Natural," I snorted. "Sure. As natural as people who dress up their dogs and put them on Christmas cards. Coming clean about problems to my bishop was never part of my 'natural' makeup."

"Then why?"

I clasped my hands together in hopes it would help me avoid choking up. "Several months had passed since Marci died, and things weren't getting better. Climbing out of bed every morning, let alone functioning as a father, was becoming almost more than I could bear. Then one day, my dad came over about eleven o'clock in the morning and found me in my pajamas. My house was a wreck. For him, that was the last straw.

"He told me he was done holding his tongue. From his point of view, I was wasting my life and ruining my children, and if I didn't start pulling myself together, he was going to insist my mom stop helping me so much. I think he was trying to provide a little tough love. But there was no way he could've known he'd just chosen the worst possible things to say to me. Without realizing it, he'd confirmed my greatest fears about myself. I was useless and I was a detriment to my kids."

Kevin's eyes remained transfixed on me as I shifted uncomfortably under his gaze. Knowing I couldn't turn back now, I continued, "That night, I asked my mom to babysit, using some excuse about needing to get a project done for work. Once they were gone, I sat at my kitchen table for over an hour. The one thought that kept repeating itself over and over involved the shotgun in my closet.

"I never actually went and got it, and I choose to believe I never would have. But I have no idea how long I would've sat there or what ultimately would've happened because my spiraling meditation into blackness was interrupted by a phone call. It was you."

Instantly, tears sprang to Kevin's eyes. Nodding, he recalled, "I know the night you're talking about. I came over, and we watched a *Quantum Leap* marathon on the SyFy channel."

I nodded, "That's the one. I'm still not sure why I answered the phone. But every day since, I've been grateful I did. Since I was embarrassed to tell you what I was thinking about when you called, I never got the chance to tell you thank you. *Now* I need you to tell me you're not in the same place I was."

Kevin's eyes fell. "Not always."

In an instant, I jumped from my chair and was around the table. Grabbing him by the shirt, I picked him up and hugged him as tightly as I've ever hugged another human being.

"Don't you dare! *Don't . . . you . . . dare!!!*" With each word I pounded his back for emphasis. "I need you. You're my best friend, and I don't know what I would do without you."

By this time, Kevin was sobbing. In a voice filled with anguish, he implored, "But what am I supposed to do?"

I wanted to lie. I wanted to tell him something that would make everything better. But I couldn't.

"I don't know . . . I really don't know. But you better understand, whatever you do, you're not doing it alone. I'm sorry I wasn't here before, but I'm here now—and I'm not going anywhere. We'll figure this out together, and no matter where your life leads, I will be there to support you. You got that?"

Kevin's head nodded against my shoulder, and I could feel the relief coursing through his muscles. Closing my eyes, I whispered once more, "I'm not going anywhere, no matter what." And I meant every word of it.

Angling for Escape
Saturday, November 15

LIVING IN ARIZONA can create a warped sense of reality. For instance: in my world, year-round golf qualifies as a basic necessity; not being able to wear my dress shorts to Thanksgiving dinner borders on sacrilege; and having easy access to a relaxing day of fishing, regardless of the season, should be included as part of our inalienable rights.

In actuality, I don't really fish that often. But once the idea strikes me, I've learned there will be no relief until I'm casting my line and waiting for my bobber to drop beneath the surface of a nearby lake. I inherited this from my father. He may only fish two or three times a year, but if he's decided the time is right, few things on earth will stop him. This leads me to the phone call I received last night at 9:45 p.m.

Anytime my phone rings after nine, my initial reaction is concern. When I was a teenager, my mother insisted that all phone calls were to take place between the hours of 9:00 a.m. and 9:00 p.m. The irony of my father being the most common transgressor of this rule isn't lost on me. However, his innumerable offenses tend to be sins of the a.m. rather than the p.m.

Last night, Alex and I were watching college football highlights when the harsh ring of my landline suddenly echoed through the house. I shot Alex a questioning look, which she answered with a confused shrug of her shoulders.

A stream of minor-league swear words raced through my mind as I slowly shuffled toward the kitchen to retrieve the phone. I knew it wasn't Kevin or Grant. They would've called my cell.

Reaching for the handset, I was completely prepared to verbally assault the person on the other end of the line should they be a telemarketer. I despise telemarketers, especially ones who call after eight o'clock or on Sunday.

To my surprise, the number flashing on the caller ID was my father's. My anger was quickly replaced by panic. A phone call from him at such a late hour was unheard of. Snatching up the receiver, I anxiously answered, "Dad?"

"Todd, this is your father."

I exhaled grumpily. The fact that his baritone voice had been free of alarm spoke volumes, and I was annoyed instantly. "Yes, Dad, I know. That would explain why I referred to you as 'Dad' when I picked up the phone."

"I was . . . what? What are you talking about?"

Shaking my head, I replied, "Nothing. Forget it. It's awfully late. What's up?"

"What're you doing tomorrow?"

Despite knowing my day was completely free,

I still strained to see the calendar posted across the room. "As far as I can tell, I'm open."

"How about your kids?"

"They're free as well."

"Good. Let's head up to Canyon Lake tomorrow morning and go fishing."

I closed my eyes and grabbed the bridge of my nose with my thumb and forefinger. It was true I didn't have any plans for the next day, but all I could focus on was how much effort it would take to pull off an excursion like this. Suddenly I had a headache.

On the other hand, I knew if my dad was dead set on going, I could argue with him until midnight and tomorrow's sunrise would still find us traveling to Canyon Lake.

"What time do you want to leave?"

"I was thinking around six."

"Then you must have been thinking of going alone. Make it seven thirty and you've got a deal."

Mentally, I began counting off seconds as I waited for the inevitable bargaining. I'd reached five when he said. "Do you think we could try for seven?" He's nothing if not predictable.

"Fine, but don't you dare knock on my door a minute earlier."

"Agreed." We both hung up knowing he'd be sitting in my living room at 6:45.

Despite my initial misgivings, the trip itself turned out to be a great idea. November can be a fickle month in the desert, but today was beautiful with an occasional breeze and high temperatures in the low seventies.

When we arrived at the lake, Samantha and Alex decided their first priority was a hike. My first hour was spent teaching Drake to cast with his new Scooby Doo fishing pole. I'm not sure how great of a teacher I am, but by the time we were done, he was no longer getting his line tangled every thirty seconds.

Once Drake was settled, I joined my father in the perfect spot, twenty feet down from my son. I cast my line near a partially submerged boulder and then sat down next to a fallen tree several feet from the bank. Neither my father nor I spoke for some time as we took in the fresh air and sounds of nature so often lost within the roar of the city.

A slight breeze blew in off the lake, forcing both of us to pull our jackets a little tighter. Giving in to my tendencies as an overprotective parent, I called out to Drake and asked if he was getting cold. His response was to ignore me completely.

With the silence broken, I decided it was time to press my father on a question he'd ducked earlier.

"So, Dad, you never really said why Maureen didn't come with us today."

Dad never moved a muscle as he continued gazing out over the lake. "Nope, I didn't."

After a prolonged silence, I realized he had no intention of expanding on his answer. "Fine, if you're gonna make me ask—then I'll ask. Why'd you leave your wife at home?"

"She had things to do," he shot back tersely.

"All right then." I knew his answer had been designed to end the conversation, but it had only served to pique my curiosity.

"What's going on with you?"

My father turned with one eyebrow raised in surprise. "Nothing. Why do you ask?"

"Well, for one, I can't recall a single event that mom wasn't a part of. Now you've been remarried for all of two weeks, and I'm sitting here with you at the lake while your wife is doing who knows what back home in Gilbert."

Dad shifted uncomfortably. "You're trying to read way too much—"

Cutting him off, I continued, "Second, for a newlywed, you've seemed awfully distracted. And not in a good way. You've been irritable, distant— just not yourself. I'm starting to get a little worried about you."

My father carefully laid his pole down and removed his baseball cap. He closed his eyes as he ran his fingers through his hair in a gesture of frustration.

"Your mother used to get on me all the time about how stubborn I could be."

I chuckled. "Gee, I wonder why."

He turned and glared at me defensively. "I wouldn't get too mouthy if I were you. She used to say the same thing about you. In fact, she used to lecture me all the time about how similar you and I can be when it comes to digging in our heels."

Properly chastened, I raised my free hand in surrender.

Returning his gaze to the variety of pebbles at the lake's edge, he waited a moment before continuing, "I've never found it easy to admit when I'm wrong."

"Well, I don't think that comes easy for any of us."

"Yeah, well, that may be, but . . ."

I sat motionless, waiting for his explanation. The air around us seemed to crackle in anticipation.

"I think I made a mistake."

At first I thought I'd heard wrong. "A mistake? What do you mean a mistake?"

Out of obvious embarrassment, my dad shifted his position again in an effort to avoid looking at me. "I think I got married too quick."

In a hundred and one different ways, my siblings and I had tried to broach this subject with him in the weeks leading up to his wedding. The fact that he had refused to listen made this the perfect opportunity to deliver a well-timed "I told you so." But knowing how hard this must have been to say out loud removed all desire to kick him while he was down.

"Oh, Dad, I'm sorry. I shouldn't have forced the subject."

"No, son, it's fine. It gives me the chance to apologize . . . and explain."

His blunt yet tender response caught me off guard. Not knowing what else to do, I joined him in surveying the lake, waiting until he felt comfortable to continue.

"When your mom died, I thought I knew exactly what to do. When I was a bishop, I'd counseled several people through similar situations, and each time my advice was always the same. 'Man is not meant to be alone,' I would always say. I missed your mother terribly, but the path to follow when losing a spouse seemed so clear."

He coughed nervously and then continued, "Looking back, it pains me to realize how prideful I was. All I wanted to do was prove to you, and every other person who'd rejected my counsel, how simple everything could be with the Lord's help. Unfortunately, I was wrong. It's not simple at all."

In a much more quiet and sincere manner than before, I repeated my question. "What's going on with you, Dad?"

"She drives me crazy. I hate to say it, but I'm not sure I like her very much."

Without thinking, I sat back and let out a low whistle. His statement was more than I'd been expecting. Seeing his hunched shoulders and defeated expression, I wondered for the first time if there were worse things in life than being alone.

"I never appreciated just how special your mother was. She was an angel. Maureen is a fine lady, but . . . I think I understand a little better why you were so hesitant to let Marci go. I miss your mom. And every minute I spend with Maureen, I'm reminded of who she's not."

"Oh, Dad, I'm so sorry."

"No, Todd, I'm the one who's sorry. Don't you see? I was wrong, and you were right."

"Come on, I hope you know that isn't important to me. I don't want you to be miserable just so I can claim victory." Hesitating, I added, "What are you going to do?"

"What do you mean?"

"With Maureen?"

His head whirled in my direction, his expression

one of shock and horror. "Are you asking if I'm planning on divorcing her?"

I shrugged my shoulders. "Yeah—I guess so."

His chest puffed out with indignation. "Heavens no! I will do what any respectable man would. I'll honor my commitment to her and find a way to make it work." With much less bravado, he included, "And if that means a lot more outings like today, then so be it."

I couldn't suppress my grin. "So the reason we're out here is so you could get away from your wife?"

"No! No, of course not . . . well, yeah . . . probably."

Before I could stop myself, I laughed. At first, Dad looked hurt, but then he too smiled and chuckled. "I can't imagine what this says about me."

Struggling to subdue my laughter, I replied, "I can. It says even the great Adrian Landry isn't perfect all the time."

"I've never said I was perfect."

Reflectively, I leaned back against the tree. "I know, but you've always been so close. Sometimes, it's hard to remember that you're not. But, hey, if getting to spend a day out on the lake is the price I have to pay to help you through this, then I'll take one for the family any time you need me to."

My father gruffly reached down and picked up his pole. "I'm glad this is a joke to you. This is my life we're talking about here."

"Oh, Dad, I know that. I'm not trying to laugh at you—I'm trying to laugh with you. If the last year and a half has taught me anything, it's that sometimes laughter sure beats the alternative."

He didn't answer. I could tell his ego was still smarting a bit, but I could also see he was thinking about what I'd said. To ease his suffering, I decided to inject one more thought.

"Look, I really am sorry things have worked out this way, but I hope you know I still love and respect you a great deal. So do the rest of your children. As far as divorce goes, I knew that was never an option before I asked. You are the most stand-up, committed person I know, and while it can be extremely difficult to live up to your standards, I'm proud to be your son. I will always be proud to be your son. And whatever you need from me to make your life easier, I will be happy to do it."

My dad has never been one to show his emotions, and today was no different. He held my gaze for a long moment before saying, "I appreciate that, son. I really do."

I smiled back at him, and then we both returned our focus to the line of clouds just visible on the horizon.

Eventually I glanced over and noticed Drake had given up on fishing and had moved on to throwing rocks into the water. I certainly didn't understand the fascination, but I knew his new activity would keep him busy for hours. Alex and Sam weren't likely to return anytime soon, so I closed my eyes and relaxed.

My newfound tranquility was fleeting as my dad's voice cut through my meditation. "Son, since we're speaking so candidly, can I ask you a question that's been on my mind for a while?"

Sitting up a little straighter, I answered cautiously, "Sure. We got nothin' but time."

"Why did you choose to go to a shrink?"

"Boy, we're hitting all the good topics today, aren't we?"

Acknowledging my point with a slight nod of his head, he conceded, "I suppose so." Then he quickly added, "We don't have a history of talking much. I feel as if I should bring it up now since I'm not sure another opportunity will present itself."

"Fair enough." I leaned my head back and contemplated how best to answer him. For his part, Dad made a show of testing his line, which had no need of testing, simply to take any additional pressure off me until I was ready.

"Let me ask you this—what would you have told me if I'd come to you and said I was suffering from depression?"

"I'd have prayed with you. I'd have gone to the scriptures and talked about the miracles possible through reaching out to our Heavenly Father through prayer and temple attendance."

"You did tell me all of those things. Is there anything else you would've added?"

"I don't know." His voice took on an agitated undercurrent. "I just know that helping people through life's challenges is exactly what the gospel is all about. From my perspective, you never gave it a fair chance."

"And there's your answer."

He stared at me, clearly baffled. "What do you mean 'there's my answer'?"

"I mean, it sounds like you believe I wasn't doing any of those things, but I was. Maybe not as well as I could have, but I was. Yet my life wasn't getting any better. I didn't want to go see my bishop. Believe me—I fought the idea as long as I could. Mainly because I knew it would disappoint you."

He started to protest that he'd never been disappointed, but thought better of it. Probably because we both knew it wasn't true.

"However, I reached a point where something had to change. I didn't know where else to turn, so I went ahead and made the appointment. Ten minutes into our first visit, Bishop Lincoln placed a call to Dr. Schenk's answering service, and the rest is history."

Dad sat silently reeling in his line. My confession was undoubtedly hard to hear, but to be fair, he was the one who asked.

"Dad, I never wanted to hurt you, and I truly am sorry if you feel like I let you down."

Quietly, my dad asked, "Do you believe he's helped you?"

"I do."

He nodded his head slowly without turning away from the lake. In one last effort to provide understanding, I tried again.

"Look, I know you view Dr. Schenk as an alternative to prayer. But I see him as my answer."

A smile crept across my father's lips at my last statement. "You know, there's a good chance we'll never completely agree on this, but there's one thing I can't deny. Whatever he's been telling you, it seems to be working. I may not have liked the prescription, but I'm more than satisfied with the cure."

"Thanks, Dad."

For the second time, a contented silence settled between us. The fish weren't biting today, but neither one of us seemed to notice.

After countless minutes watching our bobbers float on the waves, I finally asked, "You wanna try a different spot?"

Dad shook his head. "No, this is fine. Unless you want to move."

"No, I'm good."

"Todd, there's one more thing I need to tell you."

I braced myself in anticipation. What else could he possibly have to say? We'd covered more ground in the last hour than in all the years of my life preceding it.

"Okay, shoot."

His eyes remained fixed toward some random point on the distant shore. "I'm sorry we never went to San Diego."

For an instant, my heart stopped. I couldn't believe he even remembered, let alone regretted his decision made over twenty years ago. Gently, I set my pole down and walked to his side. Together, shoulder to shoulder, we watched the small gentle waves of the lake wash toward us.

In the distance, the gleeful voices of my daughters warned of their imminent return. Our special moment was ending. I wanted to say something to communicate just how much his last confession meant to me, but no words felt adequate. So instead,

I placed my arm around his shoulders and said, "It's still there, you know."

With an intrigued smile playing at the corners of his mouth, my father chuckled.

"You're right, son. I suppose it is." A second passed before he added, "What should we do with Maureen while we're gone?"

TODD'S LANDRY LIST

'Twas the Night before Thanksgiving
Wednesday, November 26

BEING PART OF a large, tight-knit family can be tough. Your privacy is rarely respected and your business is never just your own. On the other hand, few things are as rewarding as a long-held family tradition. And if that tradition happens to be associated with a holiday, then it's doubly satisfying.

Since every member of my clan happens to live within a few miles of each other, I'm sure we have more traditions than most, but my favorite has to be the annual Landry Family Pie-Making Festival. This "festival" is held each year on the night before Thanksgiving, and it's more popular among my family than Thanksgiving Day itself. Knowing this treasured event was born out of an argument between my parents only makes it better.

I was nine years old, and my dad had been bishop for a little less than a year when the holiday season seemed to arrive unexpectedly. Pressure had been building around our home for months as we struggled with the new stresses associated with his calling. And a pressure cooker with no outlet is really just another name for a bomb. The night before Thanksgiving, that bomb exploded.

Mom started cooking Wednesday morning, preparing for the next day's feast. Dad, on the other hand, had left our house before dawn despite his business being closed for the entire week. Several ward projects were taking place that day, and he felt obligated to be a part of each one.

My mother's audible grumbling started sometime after lunch. By the time darkness rolled around, the grumbling had grown to include pot banging and cupboard slamming.

In retrospect, I feel a little bad for my dad. When he finally walked through the door sometime after seven, he had no idea what he was walking into. Every ounce of frustration and resentment my mother had been storing up for months flew at him like shrapnel from an exploding hand grenade. I can't even begin to recount all of the threats and ultimatums she issued, but I distinctly remember the last one. "You get your hindquarters in that kitchen and help me or your Thanksgiving dinner will consist of a new dish I've created called dog food surprise."

Completely humbled, my father timidly asked what items were left to help with. The poison-laced answer was delivered with a single word, "Pies." Mom had not had a chance to start even one.

Ever the survivalist, Dad ushered my mother out of the kitchen and into a relaxing bubble bath before rallying the troops. My brothers and I were enlisted to help make an apple, a pumpkin, and a cherry pie.

Dad looked long and hard at a lemon meringue recipe but wisely decided three pies was plenty—especially considering his new kitchen staff's combined age didn't crack twenty.

The next day, our Thanksgiving meal was one of the most exquisite we'd ever eaten. Mom had more than outdone herself. However, all three of us boys could hardly contain ourselves wishing dinner would end so we could move to dessert. We were beaming with pride over the amazing creations we'd had a chance to help with.

They were the worst pies I've ever tasted.

To this day I don't know what we did wrong, but there was not a salvageable one in the group. My parents tried hard to pretend nothing was wrong, but it didn't matter. We were eating the same pies they were.

The memory of the horrified silence around our table remains as vivid as if it happened yesterday. I can also perfectly recall the look of disgust mixed with feigned excitement on mother's face. Nobody knew what to do. That is until Mike blurted out in perfect five-year-old bluntness, "This tastes like garbage."

His pronouncement caused my parents and me to break out in unrestrained laughter. Mike and Brock didn't have a clue what was so funny, but quickly joined in anyway. Mom stood, picked up all three pies, and headed to the kitchen, promising a properly baked apple pie in three hours. Waiting would be tough, but the alternative was not really an alternative at all.

That night, as we ate her delicious pastry topped

with vanilla ice cream, Mom promised never again to delegate the pie making. Imagine her surprise when all three of her sons protested. We'd loved being a part of Thanksgiving dinner, and it had been the first time in months we'd had our father all to ourselves. We begged her to reconsider.

Every year since, the night before Thanksgiving has been set aside for the making of pies, and every Landry's presence is required.

Sadly, tonight would mark the second year in a row we would be celebrating minus one. Last Thanksgiving had been tough for me with Marci gone, but this year would be harder for everyone with the passing of our matriarch. It didn't seem right to invade her kitchen without her there.

After consulting with my kids, we all agreed to volunteer our house instead. The offer was greeted with reserved appreciation. No one wanted to change venues, but our mother's kitchen now belonged to Maureen, not our family.

Fortunately, once the decision was final, acceptance soon followed and excitement for tonight began to build. At five thirty, the festivities started with a hamburger fry. My job was to cook the burgers, and Mike's job was to keep Brock from trying to cook the burgers. We both filled our assignments admirably, and by seven, everyone was full and ready for the main event.

My responsibility was among the most important and the most treasured. I was tasked with making the pumpkin pies.

Mom's recipe for pumpkin pie was legendary

throughout Gilbert. For years she'd refused to let anyone help her with them. However, when I'd returned home from my mission, she informed me that I had been selected as her one and only apprentice for pumpkin pie preparation. And that had been my coveted position ever since.

With Mom gone, it seemed appropriate to take on an apprentice of my own. I thought long and hard about my decision for at least, oh, two seconds before offering the job to Alex.

It had been years since my kitchen had seen so much activity. My sisters-in-law had cordoned off the kitchen table and declared it the lemon meringue zone. Mike and Katie were huddled around a hastily erected card table trying to determine whether to attempt a new key lime pie recipe, while Brock was cracking pecans on a stool in the corner. Everyone else was on the back porch for the all-important fruit preparation under the direction of my dad.

I snuck a glimpse at Alex and smiled. We'd been allowed the place of honor right next to the oven. Currently, we were scraping the pumpkin out of its skin and already, unbeknownst to her, Alex had a pumpkin seed dangling from her hair. I took that omen as confirmation. Tonight was going to be special.

A short time later, the doorbell rang. Alex and I looked at each other in confusion. We were preparing to mix the first round of ingredients, and I could see my thoughts reflected back at me in my daughter's eyes. Who would dare interrupt us at this critical juncture?

Alex had already washed her hands while mine

remained covered with pumpkin residue. Holding them up, I asked, "Can you get the door, sweetie? I'm kinda . . ." I let my slimy hands speak for themselves.

"No problem," she said, but her voice betrayed concern over missing even the smallest step.

"I'll wait."

"Thanks, Dad." And with that, she scampered out of the kitchen.

I stepped over to the sink and began washing the slimy pumpkin entrails from my hands. Before I could even get the soap rinsed off, Alex's voice drifted in from the front door.

"Umm . . . Dad? It's for you."

My head snapped up in concern at the hesitation in her voice. I looked over at Katie and Mike only to see I was not alone. Quickly grabbing a dish towel, I dodged my way through the crowded kitchen and into my living room heading toward the entryway. Probably out of sheer curiosity, my two siblings followed closely behind.

Alex was standing next to the door, holding it open, while another figure waited at the edge of my porch, partially obscured in shadow. The parent in me was horrified—my daughter knew better than to leave someone standing outside in darkness.

I opened my mouth to chastise her when suddenly my heart stopped. From the glow of the street-light, I saw that our visitor's hair was an unmistakable shade of red.

"Emily?"

Emily turned and immediately gasped when she caught sight of my brother and sister behind me. "Oh, my gosh, you're having a party." Clearly flustered, she backed away as she muttered to no one in particular, "I'm so stupid. I knew I shouldn't have come." When she reached my steps, she whirled around and walked quickly down my front path.

I glanced back at my family in bewilderment. But if I was expecting some helpful advice from my family, I was destined to be disappointed. Mike and Katie looked as baffled as me.

I turned to Alex. With a tilt of her head combined with a major eye-roll, she conveyed the clearest of messages. "What are you waiting for, stupid? Go after her before she gets away."

Staring into my daughter's eyes with an unwavering intensity, I asked, "Are you sure?"

Alex's expression was unprecedented. I can only describe it as a fusion of resignation and wary excitement. How I love the world of teenage communication.

"Go. But make it quick. We still have pies to bake."

"Deal." I wanted to hug her and tell her how much I appreciated the obvious sacrifice, but I let a quick kiss on the forehead suffice.

As I ran down my driveway, I spotted Emily approaching her car several yards away and moving fast. I sprinted after her.

"Emily!" I called out. "Wait up."

Her pace slowed but not much.

"Emily, come on."

She took a few more steps before stopping. I was closing the distance between us rapidly, but I could see her decision to wait was tenuous at best. I picked up my pace even more.

Seconds later, I came to a stop a few feet behind her and bent over to catch my breath.

"Man, you move fast. Are you some kind of secret track star or something?" My weak attempt at humor died quickly in the chilled night air as Emily remained motionless, facing away from me.

I tried again, this time leaving the wit aside. "Emily, what's going on?"

Without turning around, she replied, "Todd, look—I'm sorry. I shouldn't have come, I shouldn't have interrupted your family time, and . . . I just shouldn't be here. Forget I came, and let's pretend this never happened."

"But I don't want to. I'd rather know why you came."

My insistence deflated her. Her shoulders slumped and her head dropped even farther. "I don't know why I'm here."

Carefully, I inched closer. "I don't believe you."

As Emily spun around to face me, I saw pained defiance in her eyes. "Why would you say that?"

"Because you came to my house. You wouldn't do that without a reason. I just want to know why."

Defiance turned to rage, and before I knew it, she advanced. In a voice filled with accusation, she demanded, "Why did you call me?"

Her aggression shocked me into retreating a couple of steps. "I'm sorry. I . . . I don't . . ."

My ridiculous excuse for an answer was cut short as Emily launched into the message she'd originally come to deliver.

"Who do you think you are? You come into my

life, make me fall in love with you, and then you leave. I get why, but do you have any idea how devastating that was to me? *Do you?*"

"I—"

"Of course you don't! Because if you did, you'd know the honorable thing to do would be to never, ever contact me again."

Her attacks had caught me off guard completely. But shock was swiftly giving way to irritation as I snapped back, "What's your problem? You're the one who's engaged again already. Sounds to me like you're doing just fine."

"SHUT YOUR MOUTH!" she yelled, pointing her finger directly into my face. "You have no idea what you're talking about."

Her outburst made it clear I was dealing with something I didn't fully understand.

"You're right," I said, taking an additional step backward while raising my hands in surrender. "I shouldn't have said that. I . . . I just don't understand what's happening here. I mean, you're engaged and . . ."

"I lied."

My jaw stopped mid-sentence before falling open. "What?"

"I lied. I'm not engaged. I never was." With those words, her strong exterior crumbled and she began to cry.

I wasn't sure what to do. My instincts said to reach out and hold her, but her communication toward me so far suggested that might not be well received.

"I don't get it. Why would you lie?"

Through a voice choked with emotion, she admitted, "Because I was mad at you. I was just barely feeling that, maybe, I was ready to move on, and then out of the blue, you're calling me again. I panicked."

My head was reeling. "So you made up a fiancé?"

Emily shook her head slightly. "I didn't make him up. It's the guy I told you about at the singles conference. We've been dating for almost three months. He started asking me to marry him after one."

Emily stopped talking and wiped her eyes. I stood breathless, waiting for her to continue.

"Every time he'd ask, part of me would beg to say yes—but I couldn't. I wasn't ready.

"That is, until three weeks ago. In his patient yet aggressive way, he took me out for a romantic dinner and asked again. For the first time, I didn't say no. I told him I'd have to think about it." The longer she spoke, the more the anger animating her features dissolved into sadness.

Then quite suddenly, her ire reignited. She lifted her gaze to mine and glared at me, eyes narrowed and jaw tightened.

"That was the same night you called," she seethed. "I was getting there. I thought I was through with you. Then suddenly you show up out of nowhere and ruin everything. For three weeks I've tried to pretend it didn't matter, but . . ." She closed her eyes and turned away.

"But what?" I whispered.

Emily remained quiet as she breathed in deeply. I placed my hand on her shoulder and gently turned her back toward me. "But what?" I repeated.

"But tonight he asked again, and I . . ." She shuddered as if recalling a horrible memory. "I just couldn't. I had to tell him I couldn't see him anymore." One last burst of fury distorted her features as she cried out, "I walked away from a good man because of one stupid phone call that probably meant nothing to you!"

Feeling my heartbeat quicken, I asked, "Why would you do that?"

Emily sighed as her head tilted pleadingly to one side. "Are you really gonna make me say it?"

I decided to take a chance and closed the space between us. "Would it help if I confessed that I'm as deeply in love with you right now as the night I asked you to marry me?"

Deep within Emily's tear-filled eyes, I saw the last of her fragile defenses slipping away. With one final effort to protect herself, she challenged, "No, it doesn't help at all if nothing's changed."

Taking her hand, and with my own tears spilling onto my cheeks, I said, "Emily Stewart, I never should've let you go. Yeah, things *are* different now, but it wouldn't matter if they weren't. I'd still beg you to take me back. I love you, and everything about my life is better when you're a part of it. So I'm asking sincerely—could you find it in your heart to give me another try?"

No longer able to speak, Emily stared at me for what felt like an eternity. Finally, she nodded as she reached up, grabbed the back of my neck, and pulled me closer. Our lips brushed together, igniting a flame of passion and a fountain of cleansing.

In an instant, our time apart never existed. I

placed both arms around her and drew her in even closer. As our lips met a second time, a deeper desire rushed through me, and I lost myself in a wave of affection.

In hindsight, I hope no children were peeking out of windows as we stood wrapped in each other's embrace on the street just down from my house. I'm not certain what my reputation is among my neighbors, but our rather extended public display of affection would not likely improve it.

After some time, I leaned away to take in the sight of this beautiful woman I cared so deeply about. Even with tear-stained cheeks and bit of smeared mascara, she looked gorgeous.

Grinning broadly, I teased, "Well, I hope you're satisfied. You've officially thrown my entire night's schedule off-kilter."

Emily brushed aside a stray lock of hair as she playfully slapped my shoulder and scolded, "You're such an idiot."

"That's true." I grabbed her hand and directed her gently back toward my house. "Come on. If we're really going to do this, you might as well be thrown into the fire feet first."

Emily stopped cold, her expression filled with horror. "I can't go in there. I look like death."

"You do not look like death."

"Yeah, I'm pretty sure I do."

"I have multiple bathrooms and a sister who majored in makeup repair." With a grin, I added, "My entire family is waiting for me. I have no choice but to go back. However, you're insane if you think there's any chance I'm letting you out of my sight tonight. So, you might as well accept what you cannot change."

Fresh tears filled her eyes as she continued to resist my efforts. Hesitantly, she asked, "Are you really sure?"

I bent down and kissed her gently once more. "Positive."

Sighing heavily, she said, "Fine. Let's see what kind of miracle worker Katie really is."

As we entered through the front door, we were greeted by the raucous chorus of family. My father completely ignored Emily's protests and hugged her as if she were the prodigal daughter returning. He was about to follow that up with some grand pronouncement when an ear-splitting shriek cut him off.

"EMILYYYY!!!"

Samantha appeared around the corner, running at full speed, followed closely by Drake. Emily bent down just in time to absorb the impact as both of them enveloped her in two giant bear hugs.

"Oh, it's good to see you two," Emily murmured as she stroked their hair affectionately. Sam began to cry, and Drake pulled Emily's face closer and kissed her incessantly on the cheek. The whole scene felt surreal. Seeing my kids so happy caused a lump to form in my throat. It was then that I realized only one thing was missing.

Behind the crowd, I saw Alex hanging back, doing her best to appear invisible. I eased around the mass of humanity congregated in my entryway and silently moved to her side.

"You okay?"

Without looking at me, she shrugged in response.

"Well, I hope you know I love you. And I hope you'll give this a chance."

Alex turned and looked at me with a smirk. "Dad, I wouldn't have told you to go get her if I wasn't gonna give it a chance."

I couldn't help smiling at her answer. Shoulder to shoulder, we continued to survey the scene in front of us. Despite Katie's best efforts at a rescue, Emily was still being hugged and welcomed by every member of my family. For the first time in a long time, my world felt perfect.

Placing my arm around Alex's shoulder, I leaned down and whispered in her ear. "Then I guess I should be saying thank you. Sweetheart, this means more to me than you will ever know."

Alex did her best to hide the tears forming in her eyes as she shot back, "Just remember this when I'm sixteen. I'll be expecting a car."

Epilogue

DR. MELVIN SCHENK sighed with satisfaction as he turned the final page of the binder titled "Todd Landry." His sigh turned to a smile at the sight of the wedding announcement nestled in the plastic sleeve of the back panel. It was hard to believe that three years had passed since Todd had last sat in his office—a mere week after the events described in the binder's final entry.

"I'm getting old," Dr. Schenk muttered to himself as he stood and replaced the binder on the shelf directly behind his desk. Taking a step back, he smiled with pride at the cherry wood bookcase filled with case studies of successfully treated patients. If this was a reflection of his life's work, it was certainly one he could live with.

However, as the seconds passed, his satisfied smile faded and a look of apprehension slowly took its place. The reason for pulling out Todd's file was still troubling him. One week earlier, Todd had called his office and scheduled an appointment for today.

He had failed to give a reason why.

Dr. Schenk pulled his attention from the bookcase and returned to his desk. Once again he consulted the notes he'd taken over the past week while reviewing Todd's file, but just as before, nothing he could see raised any specific concerns. Reclining in his chair, he eventually accepted he could do nothing more than wait.

Three minutes later, at precisely 10:00 a.m., Dr. Schenk's receptionist announced Todd's arrival. The doctor stood and prepared to greet his former patient. He was surprised to discover a small knot of nerves had formed in his stomach.

This was ridiculous. He was a highly regarded psychiatrist well into the twilight of his career—not some giddy schoolgirl preparing to greet her prom date.

"Grow up, Schenk," he chided. "If he has fallen off the wagon, it is through no fault of yours."

His stern self-lecture returned him to his senses. If Todd needed additional help, he would be the consummate professional and oblige. There was simply nothing to be gained by allowing silly emotional connections from years gone by to cloud his judgment. He straightened his shoulders and stepped forward as the door to his office opened.

A thousand recollections followed Todd Landry through the door. This was definitely not the same man who had initially dragged himself into this office carrying the burdens of a depressed widower. No, this was the same strong, confident person from their final visit. Nevertheless, there was no denying the troubled aura that surrounded him.

They shook hands, but as they took their seats, the younger man seemed hesitant to begin. So the doctor initiated his well-rehearsed ruse of small talk. The exercise was designed to make Todd feel as if they were simply catching up on old times. In actuality, the seasoned psychiatrist was probing into the purpose of Todd's visit.

"So, my friend, how is your family?"

As if being drawn from a different world of thought, Todd stared at Dr. Schenk for a moment while comprehension caught up with him.

"Good. They're doing really good."

"How is Emily?"

Todd smiled, and the knot in Dr. Schenk's stomach eased considerably. "She's fantastic. If it's possible, life with her is even better than I could've imagined."

"That's wonderful. Do your children share your assessment?"

The smile on Todd's face broadened. "I suppose it depends on the day and which child you ask."

"So I take it your children are relatively typical."

"Pretty much. Alex is sixteen now and very independent."

The word *independent* caused Dr. Schenk to take notice. "Describe independent."

Todd shrugged. "Maybe independent isn't the right word. She's just loyal to her mother's memory and isn't afraid to remind us exactly who her mother is not. But to be fair, I'm generally the one she spouts off to.

If she heard me say this, I'm sure she'd deny it, but she and Emily have become remarkably close. I think she sees Emily as the older sister she never had and looks to her as an ally when she thinks I'm being unreasonable."

"If anything, she sounds like your standard teenager."

Todd tilted his head thoughtfully. "Yeah, that would probably be a fair statement, except she's mature beyond her years. I don't worry about her—or the decisions she'll make. She's a really good kid, and as a father, I couldn't ask for a better daughter. Of course, I think having a new little brother to dote on has been a good thing for her as well."

"You and Emily had a child?"

"We did. Daniel Jay Landry. The cutest little red-headed boy for miles around."

Dr. Schenk leaned forward and extended his hand. "Well, that's wonderful. Congratulations."

"Thanks," Todd replied, accepting the gesture.

"And how are your other children?"

The younger man dropped all pretenses of humility as he said, "Doc, I really have the best kids in the world. We have our good days and bad days, like any family, but I'm blessed with far more good ones than I deserve."

"I'm pleased to hear that."

Shifting in his chair, Dr. Schenk moved on. "And how is your father these days?"

Todd lifted his gaze over Dr. Schenk's shoulder. "For someone I once thought of as stubbornly rigid, it's unbelievable how different he is from the man I knew growing up."

Dr. Schenk leaned forward in anticipation. "Interesting. In what ways has he changed?"

"He's way more laid back. He's content to let life come to him now as opposed to seeking it out. He no longer considers a day spent idly with family a waste. The change is quite stark."

"Do you think his new wife plays a significant role in this transformation?"

"I think she has everything to do with it. It's an odd dynamic. Maureen is close with her kids, but Dad can barely tolerate them. Yet it seems as though she's changed his understanding of how families are supposed to work. He's even started planning separate vacations every year with each one of his children and their families."

Dr. Schenk's eyebrows lifted in amazement. "How utterly fascinating. I thought you said he hated to travel."

"He did. But not long after Emily and I were married, he and my family went to San Diego, and he had a blast. He played Frisbee on the beach, made sand castles for hours with Drake and Sam, and even agreed to a hot dog roast around a sandy campfire. In those five days, I think he discovered a lot of things about himself."

Dr. Schenk collapsed to the back of his chair. "Astounding! Does Maureen accompany you on these yearly retreats?"

"No, just Dad. To be honest, I'm not even sure she's invited. Like I said, she's pretty close with her own kids. I don't think either one of them had any desire to take on new family relationships when they got married. So, by and large, they don't."

"At one point, a mission was important to your father. Is that still a priority?"

Todd couldn't repress a smirk. "Not that I'm aware of. I think they'd kill each other."

Dr. Schenk laughed, and Todd chuckled appreciatively at his own joke. Calming himself, Dr. Schenk mentally checked Adrian Landry off his list and moved on.

"I must admit, I've long wondered what became of your friend Kevin."

Todd sat quietly for a moment. "Actually, not much has changed for him. He did move to a new apartment because he no longer felt welcome in his ward. I know that was really hard for him. But the new ward he's found has a bishop and a core group of members that are supportive and have welcomed him in like family."

"So he's choosing celibacy?"

"For the time being, but I can't guarantee that'll last. He has a strong testimony, but loneliness is a brutal companion. He won't talk about it much, but at times I can tell he's struggling."

"And what if he chooses to end that struggle and adopt an alternative lifestyle? What happens to your friendship under those circumstances?"

Todd stared directly into Dr. Schenk's eyes as he answered, "I made my decision regarding Kevin a long time ago. No matter what choices he makes, Kevin is, for all intents and purposes, my brother, and I will continue to love him and support him."

"Even if his decisions make him a sinner?"

Todd never blinked as he held Dr. Schenk's gaze.

"I've gone back and read my job description—and, lo and behold, labeling sinners isn't included. On the other hand, it's specific about loving my fellow man. I don't know what Kevin's future holds, but I've made it clear to him I expect to be a part of it."

As their eyes remained fixed on each other, Dr. Schenk smiled and nodded appreciatively. "From my admittedly Jewish point-of-view, that sounds very Christian of you, Todd."

His visitor didn't answer, but instead, he allowed his focus to shift upward to the ceiling. Dr. Schenk decided it was time to proceed further with his ever-shrinking pool of possibilities.

"Have you been in contact with Jason?"

The younger man's attention snapped quickly back to the doctor. "Wow . . . that's a name I haven't heard in a while. But no—I haven't heard from him since he left. I talked to his parents about a year ago, and they said he's still in Texas. Beyond that, it sounded like not much else has changed."

"That's unfortunate," Dr. Schenk observed regretfully.

Todd nodded in agreement but remained silent.

"How is your friend Grant? I still get referrals from him every once in a while, so I assume all is well."

Todd's smile returned. "Grant and Stacy are great. It can be tough with our busy schedules, but we try to get our families together as often as we can."

It looked as if Todd had more to say, but his voice caught in his throat. Eventually, he continued, "It's crazy. When Marci died, all I could see was the void it had left in my life. I never stopped to consider how her passing might affect others."

Dr. Schenk gazed at his visitor quizzically. "I'm afraid I don't follow."

"Stacy was Marci's best friend. They did everything together. It was only after Emily and I were married that Grant felt comfortable telling me about Stacy's depression following Marci's death. I was so caught up in myself, I never saw it."

"Well, all things considered, I think your lack of sensitivity would be somewhat expected."

"I know. But I still feel bad. Thankfully, Emily is a blessing to others besides me. She and Stacy are now inseparable.

"The other night, Stacy pulled me aside and thanked me for finding her new best friend. It was an emotional moment for us. I don't know why I'm telling you this except to say—things are really good. Not just for me, but all around. Things really are good."

Dr. Schenk stroked his goatee with an expression of perplexed bewilderment. "Then, Todd, I have to admit that I'm mystified as to why you wanted to see me."

Todd laughed. "Is that why you've been asking me all these questions? Oh, Doc, it's nothing like that."

Defensively, Dr. Schenk responded, "Well then, why don't you tell me the reason you're here?"

"I need your help."

"Really? How so?"

"I assume with all you know about the LDS community, you understand what it means to have your ward split."

"Is that the process where one of your larger congregations is split into two smaller ones?"

"It is."

"Then yes, I'm familiar with the process."

"Well, they split my ward . . . and called me as bishop."

Dr. Schenk grinned widely. "Congratulations. That's wonderful."

Todd stared back with a healthy look of skepticism. "No, it's not. It's horrible. I had no idea the problems that exist all around me. And I don't know what to do to handle most of them. The reason I came today was to see if I could refer someone to you."

Dr. Schenk chuckled. "Todd, I would be honored. But you didn't have to come in person. A simple phone call would have sufficed."

Sheepishly, Todd dropped his eyes to the floor. "Not for me."

Not wanting to blur the patient/client relationship, Dr. Schenk avoided the obvious emotional trap by moving on with business as usual. "All you would need to do is provide the individual's information to Janice on your way out and we will take care of it from there."

The two men stood and Dr. Schenk once again extended his hand. Todd brushed it aside and fully embraced the stiff form of the psychiatrist. "I've missed you, Doc."

Accepting that the damage was done, Dr. Schenk relaxed and disclosed, "I shouldn't admit this, but I've missed you as well."

Together, they walked to the door of the office. Before turning to go, Todd looked back and asked,

THE RELUCTANT BLOGGER

"Out of curiosity, what made you get rid of those chairs you liked so much and go back to a couch?"

With a blank expression, Dr. Schenk replied, "Someone, whose opinion I value greatly, convinced me that a sofa was the better option."

Todd nodded appreciatively in response—oblivious to the compliment.

Then, slowly, the former patient allowed his gaze to make one final sweep of the room. Dr. Schenk made no effort to rush him. Finally, Todd's focus returned to the therapist.

"Thanks, Doc. For everything."

Dr. Schenk smiled. "It was my pleasure, Todd. It was my pleasure."

Acknowledgments

IT WOULD BE unfair to allow my solitary name on the front of this book imply that I accomplished this alone. So many people deserve my thanks and recognition, and if I tried to name them all, I would certainly leave someone out. But there are a few who went above and beyond and deserve my utmost thanks. First, Heath and Timilee Brown. Their input and support from the very beginning was invaluable. I will forever remember and appreciate "the argument" and the role it played in making this book, and its characters, better. I appreciate my fellow author, Jennifer Griffith, for her encouraging and always spot-on advice during the editing process. I want to thank all of the people behind the scenes at Cedar Fort who have given this book a chance. Without you, it would still be sitting in my office, on a shelf, in a binder.

I am thankful to my brother, Jerry Rapier, for his support and, more important, his friendship. I value having him, Kirt, and Oscar in my life more than he will ever know. Finally, there are not enough words to express my gratitude to my wife, Shannon. She deserves her own tropical island for all of the hours she invested in editing and improving this story. Without her, Todd Landry would never have completed his journey. I love you, sweetheart. You're the best.

Discussion Questions

1. ARE TODD'S INITIAL reservations toward psychiatric counseling common among Latter-day Saints? And if so, why?

2. WAS TODD'S CONCERN for Marci's feelings about plural marriage legitimate when placed in the context of his relationship with Emily?

3. DID TODD DO the best thing for his family by giving in to Alex and ending his relationship with Emily?

4. STATE YOUR REACTION to Grant's question of Todd, "How differently would we act if the 'Golden Rule' was the only rule?"

5. WHAT IS THE purpose of someone like Todd keeping someone like Jason as a part of his life?

6. WAS ADRIAN'S CHARACTER arc more about actual growth on his part or a reflection of Todd's growth being projected onto the character?

7. WAS DR. SCHENK always correct in his assessments?

8. HOW DID KEVIN'S revelation make you feel toward this character specifically and toward the book in general?

9. IN A SCENARIO where both are available and interested, who is a better fit for Todd—Emily or Abby?

About the Author

RYAN RAPIER is an Arizona native and through the course of his life has come face to face with a rattlesnake more than once. For that reason alone, he would likely have left the desert behind years ago were it not for one thing—the luxury of year-round golf. When  Ryan isn't on the course or in front of a computer screen, he can usually be found chasing behind his four children or doing errands for his amazing wife in the isolated beautiful valley they have both called home forever. Ryan's further thoughts and opinions that concern nobody but himself can be found at his website, RyansRapierWit.com.